P9-CRH-529

THE TUNNEL

Books by A. B. Yehoshua

The Lover

A Late Divorce

Five Seasons

Mr. Mani

Open Heart

A Journey to the End of the Millennium

The Liberated Bride

A Woman in Jerusalem

Friendly Fire

The Retrospective

The Extra

The Tunnel

THE TUNNEL

A. B. YEHOSHUA

Translated from the Hebrew
by Stuart Schoffman

Houghton Mifflin Harcourt
Boston New York 2020

First US edition

First published under the Hebrew title *Haminhara* by Hakibbutz Hameuchad, Tel Aviv, 2018

hmhbooks.com

Library of Congress Cataloging-in-Publication Data
Names: Yehoshua, Abraham B., author. | Schoffman, Stuart, translator.
Title: The tunnel / A. B. Yehoshua ; translated from Hebrew by Stuart Schoffman.
Other titles: Haminhara. English
Description: First U.S. edition. | Boston ; New York : Houghton Mifflin Harcourt, 2020.
Identifiers: LCCN 2019039795 (print) | LCCN 2019039796 (ebook) | ISBN 9781328622631 (hardcover) | ISBN 9781328622556 (ebook)
Classification: LCC PJ5054.Y42 H3613 2020 (print) | LCC PJ5054.Y42 (ebook) | DDC 892.4/36—dc23
LC record available at https://lccn.loc.gov/2019039795
LC ebook record available at https://lccn.loc.gov/2019039796

Book design by Greta D. Sibley

Printed in the United States of America
DOC 10 9 8 7 6 5 4 3 2 1

For my Ika (1940–2016)

Eternal Beloved

THE TUNNEL

AT THE NEUROLOGIST

"So, let's summarize," says the neurologist.

"Yes, summarize," echo the two, quietly.

"The complaints aren't imaginary. There is atrophy in the frontal lobe that indicates mild degeneration."

"Where exactly?"

"Here, in the cerebral cortex."

"I'm sorry, but I don't see anything."

His wife leans toward the scan.

"Yes, there's a dark spot here," she acknowledges, "but tiny."

"Yes, tiny," confirms the neurologist, "but it could grow larger."

"Could," asks the husband, voice trembling, "or likely will?"

"Could, and likely will."

"How fast?"

"There are no firm rules for pathological development, certainly not in this part of the brain. The pace also depends on you."

"On me? How?"

"On your attitude. In other words, how you fight back."

"Fight against my brain? How?"

"The spirit versus the brain."

"I always thought they were one and the same."

"Not at all, not at all," declares the neurologist. "How old are you, sir?"

"Seventy-three."

"Not yet," his wife corrects him, "he's always pushing it . . . closer to the end . . ."

"That's not good," mutters the neurologist.

Only now does the patient notice that tucked among the doctor's curls is a small knitted kippah, which he apparently removed when Luria lay on the examination table, lest it fall on his face.

"So take, for example, the names that escape you."

"Mostly first names," the patient is quick to specify, "last names come easier, but first names fade away when I reach out to touch them."

"So here's a little battleground. Don't settle for last names, don't give up on first names."

"I'm not giving up, but when I try hard to remember them, she always jumps in and beats me to it."

"That's not good," the neurologist scolds his wife, "you're not helping."

"True," she says, accepting blame, "but sometimes it takes him so long to remember a first name that he forgets why he wanted to know."

"Still, you have to let him fight for his memory on his own, that's the only way you can help him."

"You're right, Doctor, I promise."

"Tell me, are you still working?"

"Not anymore," says the patient. "I retired five years ago."

"Retired from what, may I ask?"

"The Israel Roads Authority."

"What is that exactly?"

"It used to be called the Public Works Department of the Ministry of Transportation. I worked there forty years, planning roads and highways."

"Roads and highways." The neurologist finds this vaguely amusing. "Where? In the North or the South?"

As he considers the proper answer, his wife intervenes:

"In the North. Sitting before you, Doctor, is the engineer who planned the two tunnels in the Trans-Israel Highway, Route Six."

Why the tunnels? wonders the husband, these are not his most important achievements. But the neurologist is intrigued. And why not? He's in no hurry. It's his last patient of the day, the receptionist has collected the doctor's fee and gone home, and his apartment is located above the clinic.

"I haven't noticed tunnels on Route Six."

"Because they're not so long, maybe a couple of hundred meters each."

"Still, I should pay attention, not daydream on the road," the doctor reprimands himself. "You never know, other road engineers might come to see me."

"They'll only come if they can't hide their dementia under the overpass," says the patient, attempting a joke.

The neurologist objects: "Please, why dementia? We're not there yet. Don't rush to claim something you don't understand, and don't raise unnecessary fears, and above all, don't get addicted to passivity and fatalism. Retirement is not the end of the road, and so you need to find work in your field, even part-time, private work."

"There is no private work, Doctor. Private individuals don't build highways or plan roads. Highways are a public affair, and there are others out there now, younger people."

"So how do you spend your time?"

"Officially I sit at home. But I also take walks, all over the place. And we go out a lot, theater, music, opera, sometimes lectures. And of course, helping my children, mostly with the grandchildren, I take them around, pick them up, bring them back. And I also do some housework, errands, shopping at the supermarket, the produce market, and sometimes—"

"He loves going to the produce market," says his wife, eager to end the recitation.

"The market?" The neurologist is taken aback.

"Why not?"

"By all means, if you know your way around, it's fine."

"Because I cook."

"Aha, you also cook!"

"Actually I mostly chop, mix, reheat leftovers. I'm in charge of making lunch before she gets back from her clinic."

"Clinic?"

"I'm a pediatrician," his wife says softly.

"Great," says the doctor, relieved. "In that case, I have a partner."

Although she is twenty years older than the neurologist, he interrogates her about her medical experience as if she were not a senior physician at a major hospital, but a young candidate for his own department, about to join him in the fight against her husband's suspicious atrophy, which will most likely grow.

"Which sleeping pill do you give him?"

She lays a gentle hand on her husband's shoulder. "I don't

give him sleeping pills, because in general he can sleep without them, but on rare occasions, when he has trouble falling asleep, he takes . . . what is it you take?"

The patient does not remember the name, only the shape: "Those little triangles . . ."

"He means Xanax."

"If it's only Xanax, no problem," says the neurologist, "but be sure not to give him anything stronger, because the region in the brain that differentiates between day and night will be sensitive for him from now on, and it's unwise to disturb it with pills like, say—"

Whipping out a notepad, the doctor jots down names of forbidden pills. She examines the list, folds it, and sticks it in her purse. The doctor presses on:

"Have there been similar symptoms in his family?"

She looks quizzically at her husband, but he keeps silent, preferring that she speak for him. "No sign of it . . . not his parents, or his sister."

"And previous generations?"

Now he has no choice. "I didn't know my father's parents," the patient explains. "They were younger than I am today when they were murdered in Europe, so who knows whether what you say I have was hidden in them too. My mother's family, all born in this country, were outstandingly sane and lucid till the end, so far as I know, except . . . wait, maybe, just maybe, a distant relative of my mother's, who came from North Africa in the late '60s, and here, in Israel, sank into deep, silent depression . . . maybe out of anger . . . or who knows, maybe in her case, only maybe, also this dementia?"

Amazingly enough, the neurologist does not dismiss the ineffable word that the patient has again uttered, but takes another look at the scan before carefully sliding it into an envelope, labeling it ZVI LURIA in big letters, and to avoid any error, adding the patient's ID number. But as he turns to hand the envelope to the wife, his newly appointed collaborator, Luria snatches it from him and clutches it to his chest. For a moment it seems that the doctor wants to say something more, but the sound of footsteps from his apartment above the clinic silences him, and he stands to see them out. The patient also stands, ready to go, but his wife hesitates, as if afraid to be left to face the illness alone.

"The main thing is to be active," the doctor says firmly. "Not to avoid people even if it's hard to recognize them. You must not run away from life, but on the contrary seek it out, bring it on."

As he speaks, the doctor begins turning out lights, but doesn't hurry upstairs to his apartment. He escorts them to the front door, switching on the little lights in his spacious garden to help them find the path to the street. Before parting he adds final words, in a new and gentler voice:

"You are intellectual, open-minded people, and I can speak to you frankly, without holding back. When I said you must not run away from life, I meant every aspect of it, including the most intimate. Between the two of you, of course. In other words, do not give up on passion, don't be afraid of it. Despite your age and condition. Because passion is very important for mental activity. You understand what I'm saying, Dr. Luria? In other words, not only not give up, but intensify. It works, believe me, from my personal experience." Suddenly he pauses, as if he's gone too far. But the patient nods his agreement and gratitude, while his frightened wife whispers, "Yes, Doctor, absolutely, I understand, and I'll try, I mean, both of us will . . ."

BUT WHAT EXACTLY DID THE DOCTOR SAY?

As the neurologist withdraws to his flat, the two feel raindrops, tiny but persistent, so he suggests that his wife wait at the bus shelter while he retrieves the car. She refuses.

"Just don't tell me," he sneers, "that you're afraid I won't find the car."

"I didn't say that or think it, but I don't want to wait anywhere alone."

"And the rain? You just had your hair done yesterday."

"If you give me the envelope I'll put it over my head."

"You want what's left of my brain to wash away in the rain?"

She laughs. "Don't be silly, the rain won't ruin anything. Let's run." With desperate enthusiasm she grabs his arm and pulls him forward.

"Why did you tell him about the tunnels on Route Six, why them?"

"Because I had a feeling he wouldn't respect you when you said you didn't work but only went to the market. I wanted to defend your honor."

"Not respect me? Why not? Why the tunnels, they weren't my greatest projects."

"Because you talked about them a lot."

"About the tunnels on Route Six?"

"Yes."

"Then why just two and not three? It was *davka* the southernmost tunnel, near the exit for Route One to Jerusalem, that was the most complicated."

"There were three? I didn't remember, next time I'll say three."

"Next time you won't say anything," he scolds her, "I don't care about these tunnels. And I don't need anybody to honor me. Here, we parked in this alley."

"You're wrong, the car is on the next street."

"No, it's here. You're the one confused."

And the car faithfully winks at its owner from the end of the street.

He tosses the wet envelope onto the back seat and hurries to start the car and turn on the heat. As he buckles his seat belt he is overcome by despair: will he depend on her mercies from now on, and will she be a captive of his delusions?

"In any case, thank you for not telling the doctor what happened at the kindergarten."

"Thank me why?"

"Because he would have had me committed."

"That's ridiculous."

"Why not? A grandpa who comes to a kindergarten to pick up his grandson, and without noticing takes a different kid instead, shouldn't he be in a hospital?"

"No, because what happened wasn't entirely your fault. The boy, what's his name?"

"Nevo."

"Yes, this Nevo, according to his teacher, tried once before to latch onto another grandfather. Maybe he's embarrassed by the Filipino woman who picks him up, or maybe he's scared of her."

But in the darkened car Luria decides to incriminate himself.

"He tried or he didn't try, that's not the question. The question is, how did I not realize I was trading my grandson for some other kid, and if the Filipino woman hadn't started screaming, and running to grab him away from me, I might have taken him home and fed him."

"No way, you would have caught yourself long before that. And anyway, even Avigail admits this kid looks a little like our Noam, who was asleep in the sandbox when you got to the school. Please, Zvi, don't make a big thing of it, you were slightly confused, but not that much."

"Not that much?"

"Not that much. Believe me. As the doctor warned you, don't start scaring yourself and running away from life for fear you'll do something stupid. Listen to me. I trust you."

She shivers all of a sudden. Before they drive off, he unbuckles the seat belt, giving her an old-fashioned hug as she grimly faces his decline.

Later, at home, well aware of his wife's distress, he starts to make dinner while she thaws out in a hot shower. Of late he has preferred the stovetop to the microwave and the oven, the blue whoosh of the flames lifts his spirits, so he lets them burn after the cooking is done. While the two of them, after a long medical day, satisfy their hunger with eggs scrambled with fried potatoes, a tasty dish he prepares with confidence, his mobile phone abruptly comes to life, and their daughter Avigail wants to know if her father's brain scan has turned up something real. It's clear to Luria that he himself cannot restore the trust that was wrecked at the kindergarten, so he hands over the phone to the neurologist's new partner, who can testify as a physician that the atrophy is still minimal, and there's no reason not to reinstate the grandfatherly privilege of the Tuesday pickup.

But he can't resist dealing on his own with the concern phoned in from the North by his son, deluding himself that he can amuse Yoav with his early dementia. With feigned cheerfulness he says, "No worries, I still recognize you, my son, but who knows how long it will last, so if you want something from me, you should hurry up." But flippancy is no match for a medical scan. Over the past year the son has tried, for the sake of his father's dignity and also his own, to discount the signs of confusion and other odd behavior that his keen-eyed wife Osnat has noticed. But now his denial has turned into panic, and rather than console his father and pledge love and devotion, he insists on speaking to his mother for an authoritative answer, because Luria's mischievous remark is not only meaningless, but could be interpreted as the first sign of dementia.

Luria hands the phone to his wife and moves out of earshot, to spare himself the medical details that the pediatrician delicately recites to their son. It's not just his fear of the little thing that "might likely" get bigger, but also it's hard to witness the anguish of his son, who certainly understands that his parents' lives will soon be ruined, as well as his own. From up north in the Galilee, where he is both the owner and slave of a successful computer-chip business, Yoav asks, over and over, what the doctor said exactly, and when he hears that the spirit might block the degeneration of the brain or at least slow it down, he seizes on this remark and demands that his mother make an effort to stimulate his father's spirit, which he believes has shriveled since his retirement.

And so, instead of being pensive and melancholy, the mother's phone conversation with her son turns emotional and angry. And when it's over, Luria's wife turns to him furiously:

"How could you tell him that we fired the housekeeper?"

"Who said fired? I said we reduced her hours."

"But he accused me: 'You cannot turn Abba into your servant.'"

"Your servant?" gasps Luria. "What's wrong with him? He's apparently so scared of my dementia that he's looking high and low for someone to blame."

"No, no," she fumes, "don't keep saying dementia. The doctor warned you not to."

"So what should I say?"

"Say fogginess, fuzziness, confusion . . . we'll find better words."

He looks fondly at his wife. She is still in her bathrobe, a towel wrapped around her head like a turban, and despite her age she resembles an Indian or Turkish dancer. Can she endure his dementia if it's called by other names?

THE CAR

Sleep snatches her from his arms before she can find those "better words." Drained by the day that began at her pediatric clinic, and terrified by the second clinic, where she was recruited to help treat an incurable condition, she pulls away from her husband and mercifully dozes off. He covers her dangling feet with the blanket, but before drifting into sleep himself he needs a closer look at his cerebral cortex, to decide if the atrophy that escaped his gaze was real or merely possible. The scan is still in the car, now parked in the garage of their apartment building. He goes down in old clothes and slippers to the car, still speckled with raindrops.

It's a midsize car, as opposed to the big, comfortable one that sped along highways and barreled down dirt roads, provided to him as a senior engineer at the Roads Authority. Even after retirement the old car remained his, in return for a nominal fee, but when it proved cumbersome in downtown parking lots, and its drab gray color made it harder to find in underground garages, it was replaced by a new one, smaller but taller, easy to get in and out of, bright red in color, quickly identifiable even with failing eyesight. Lately, once in a while, Luria has been secretly exchanging a few words with it.

Truth to tell, it was the car that talked to him first. After he'd figured out its devices and controls, he thought he heard, when he started the engine, a brief, soft murmur amid the gargle of gears and pistons, the voice of a Japanese or Korean girl, possibly planted in the electrical system to wish the discriminating driver a safe trip in his new car. Obviously he has never told his wife about this female voice, so as not to compound her anxieties, but when he is alone in the car he sometimes hums to the girl: *Yes, my dear, I hear you, but I don't understand.*

Yet now, at night, there's no reason to start the car and break the silence of the garage. He turns on the interior lights, retrieves the envelope, his name and ID number smudged by the rain, and carefully removes the scan to determine if the atrophy, so speedily confirmed by his wife, is indeed real, and if so, where it's going. But where is it? What does it look like? Many dark spaces are scattered on the image, most of them presumably good and even necessary, disregarded by the neurologist. How to distinguish between good dark and bad dark?

He leans his head back and closes his eyes. If it's first names that go missing in the new atrophy, there's a risk that the names of his wife and children and grandchildren could also vanish into the black hole. Was the disgrace in the kindergarten simply a moment of mental weakness? Or was there something stamped in his mind that drew him to this child? Yes, from now on it will be easy to blame every mistake or failure on mental frailty. Will the spirit, as the neurologist defined it, be able to battle his deluded brain, or get swept up inside it?

He decides to test his memory of the ignition code of the car. He remembers it well, but is disappointed that the growl of the engine now lacks the manufacturer's young womanly voice. *That's good,* whispers Luria, the fewer the delusions, the easier for the spirit to reinforce the shrinking brain. The main thing is to be careful behind the wheel. For if his license is revoked because of an error or accident, his life will lose its purpose. And so, to test his control of the car, he carefully advances a few inches, till it is nearly touching the wall. Then he shifts into reverse, honking rhythmically, and backs toward a car parked on the opposite side. Suddenly a beam of light floods his face, and a car rapidly entering the garage brakes with a screech to allow the red car to complete its turn toward the exit, but Luria doesn't want to exit, merely to check his competence, so he tries to return the car to its original spot, and the waiting driver gets nervous about Luria's pointless moves, and as a good neighbor feels obliged to ask if the elderly driver needs help. "No, everything's fine," says Luria to the young man knocking on his window, "I forgot something in the car and also checked the engine." The young man observes the brain scan on the seat, and the feet in old bedroom slippers. "Good night," says Luria, to get rid of the busybody. "Good night," mumbles the neighbor, but again asks Luria if he's sure he doesn't need help.

You have to be careful in public, even in the garage of a private building. Medical scans, shabby clothes, and slippers raise suspicion of mental infirmity. Even if the neurologist refuses to call it dementia, and his wife seeks more pleasant words, one must appear presentable. He returns the scan to its envelope, and before other neighbors show up he hurries back to his apartment, where his wife has cast off the blanket in uneasy sleep. He turns on a reading light to put things back in order. Dina opens her eyes.

"Where'd you disappear to?"

"I went down to the parking. I was worried that I left the scan in the car."

"Why worry, there's a copy in the computer, and anyway they'll do another one soon, to see if anything has changed."

"But how will I know what changed if I don't understand what it is now."

"There's not much to understand; what they found barely exists."

"What's the name of the neurologist, it suddenly escapes me."

"Doctor Laufer."

"No, his first name."

"Why do you need it?"

"He told me not to give up on first names."

"I think it's Nadav, or Gad, but why is that important?"

"Because you surely remember what he said about desire."

"Of course."

"That it's also important for the struggle."

"Important or unimportant, we won't give it up in any case."

"Now?"

"No. Now would be difficult not only for me but for you too. What's the rush, you know I'll always be with you."

TOMATOES

The next morning he says to his wife: "Today the car is yours. We're short on many staples, food and soap and detergent, so I have to send a big delivery from the supermarket. Here's my list, see if anything's missing or unnecessary."

"You won't go to the *shuk*?"

"If I do, just for a special vegetable or fruit."

"On condition they are nice and fresh. Don't worry about price, just quality. And when you see the flowers, ask Iris for a bunch of poppies."

"Iris?"

"The older woman, not the young one. She'll recognize you and make sure the flowers are fresh."

"But the house is already full of flowers."

"Wilting flowers, we need fresh ones. So remember, only poppies, they're in season. Don't let them sell you a different flower."

"Understood."

"I'll be back by two, the latest. Don't eat without me, control yourself."

"I can hold out till two. But wouldn't it be good to show my scan to someone in your department, without saying whose it is, of course."

"There's nothing to show. Everything is clear. And you should get your head out of your head. What showed up was so tiny and blurry that anyone not an expert in reading such scans won't see a thing."

"Excuse me, excuse me, how come you, who are not an expert in reading such scans of adults, were so quick to confirm the diagnosis?"

"Because I'm an expert in *you*."

"Come on, be serious."

"Wait a second, I'm not an expert in you?"

"Part of me . . . only part. And when the dementia arrives in all its glory, you'll be lost."

"That word again."

"So suggest another word and we'll see if it fits."

The shopping mall is not far away, and in the morning not crowded. Since the walk there is short, Luria decides to extend it and take a stroll in the municipal park, where he comes upon a motley group of dogs at play, some dancing around their owners and others running free. Luria watches wistfully, trying to find one resembling the gray Alsatian, the loyal family dog who three years ago moved to the North, to live out his life in freedom and comfort offered by his son and grandchildren in their new home in the countryside. But the country air emboldened the homesick dog to return to Tel Aviv, and on his journey back he disappeared, doubtless killed on a road. Removal of animals —dogs, foxes, wolves, sheep, and cows, trampled to death or only wounded on interurban roads—is the responsibility of the Israel Roads Authority, and Luria knew the old veterinarian in charge of such work; but on Highway 6, a toll road, the responsibility for animals rests with the private operator, who reaps the profits. And because the North is full of wild animals, whose living space was suddenly divided by a broad highway flanked by fences, the Nature and Parks Authority demanded that a tunnel be dug through a hill, to preserve some species of plants and primarily to enable deer and wild boar, foxes and jackals, porcupines and rabbits, to walk above the noisy highway safely, especially at night. Yes, this was one of Luria's three tunnels, and he needs to remind Dina, who was oddly proud of them, of its initial ethical objective.

He confidently steers his cart through the huge supermarket, but since he is following his shopping list and not the order of the shelves, lest he load the cart with superfluous items, he visits various aisles, often retracing his steps, encountering other customers, mostly women, who know him to be a reliable source of advice and directions. The fruits and vegetables look fresh, so he decides to skip the *shuk* and add these to his home delivery. He circles the piles of produce several times, examining items and generously filling his cart. He thought he had stated his wishes clearly at the meat counter, but at the checkout he discovers, just in time, that instead of chicken thighs, they somehow gave him goose, and before the cashier rings it up, he grabs the package and tosses it into the rack of candy meant for restless children in the queue.

The address is legibly written down, and the order will arrive within two hours, and he can send items that require refrigeration, but not frozen food. Luria thus leaves the supermarket unburdened, except for a package of ice-cream bars. Again he walks through the pretty park, and the rows of flowers gracing the lawns remind him that he needs to bring his wife poppies, which make her happy, even if he thinks that the flowers at home are still serviceable. The *shuk* beckons, but the ice-cream bars will melt, and rather than toss them, he eats one, then another, and offers a few to passersby, not to children, nor to adults who might suspect his intentions, but rather to a serious-looking Filipino woman and a tall Sudanese, and to an elderly couple who stop and stare. He finally arrives at the flower stall with hands free, but to his dismay the poppies bunched by the vendor, who knows him by name, seem strangely limp, and despite her indignation he refuses to buy them, but to avoid coming home from the market empty-handed, he heads for the stalls of fruits and vegetables.

The supermarket delivery arrived home before him, blocking the doorway. He steps gingerly so as not to squash the groceries, which enter the flat one by one and assume their proper places. Luria loves the unpacking and arranging, and hopes it strengthens the mind no less than the effort to find first names. He is shocked to discover that between the supermarket and produce market, he has unwittingly purchased more tomatoes than his household could possibly consume in the days or weeks to come.

Should he quickly throw some tomatoes in the garbage to diminish the disgrace of confusion? That's feasible, but painful, since the tomatoes, handpicked from several varieties, are of rare quality and beauty. In need of a bold, creative solution, he phones his sister, the legendary cook. "How did you two manage to accumulate so many tomatoes?" "It wasn't us, it was me," he explains. "I was at the supermarket and bought tomatoes, and then I went to the *shuk* to buy poppies for Dina, but I didn't like how they looked, and the tomatoes, on the other hand, were beautiful."

Silence. For many months his sister, younger by two years, has sensed the decline in her brother's memory, but avoids saying anything that would pain him and herself as well. Finally she asks: "How many tomatoes did you buy?"

"In the *shuk,* two or three kilos."

"Why so many?"

"I thought—"

"You thought what?" Her tone is not so much of sorrow as of mild rebuke.

"I guess I didn't really think," he admits, "maybe because the poppies were wilted and the tomatoes looked so nice, I forgot I already bought tomatoes at the supermarket. I guess I thought that was a week ago."

"How many did you buy at the supermarket?"

"Also something like that, two, three kilos. But why be so uptight? I can throw them all out, how much did it cost? Pennies . . . If you have a better idea, tell me, otherwise, no big tragedy."

"Wait, don't throw anything out, let's see what you can do."

"That's what I'm asking. Instead of the third degree, give me an idea. Like soup or sauce."

"Just a minute, Zvika, you don't want to understand what went on in your head?"

Why hide the truth from her? She overshares her myriad maladies with them. "That's the point, not much to explain. There's a little space in my mind, a sort of black hole, that's been swallowing up first names, acquaintances of mine, and when they're swallowed, there's free space left behind."

"Space for what?"

"Let's say these tomatoes."

"Now you're talking nonsense."

"No, seriously, totally seriously, because I haven't had a chance to tell you that yesterday we went to a specialist, a neurologist, Doctor Laufer, a serious man who examined the scan of my cerebral cortex, and so listen carefully, be ready, because your brother will soon disappear, ha ha, not in body but in spirit . . . won't know he has a sister . . . Dina will explain to you how this will happen. But in the meantime give me some culinary advice, before I throw out the tomatoes."

"Wait," she shouts, "stop with the tomatoes, first tell me exactly what the doctor thought."

"Exactly what the doctor thought, Dina will explain to you.

I'm obviously exaggerating, just to scare you and have a little fun. But don't worry, it's not contagious, although this neurologist also looked for a genetic connection, asked if something like this ran in the family, but much as we tried to accommodate him and find a few feeble-minded relatives, we were unsuccessful, because we didn't want to tell him about you, ha ha . . . but seriously, you do know that all in all, we are a lucid family. On the morning of her dying day, Mama and I got into an argument and she insisted there'll never be peace here. That afternoon she was gone, and now we're stuck with all the wars."

"Sounds just like her."

"So you, personally, have nothing to worry about. For now. And our descendants, if the need arises, should make an effort to invent new cures. Anyway, genetics is an iffy business. And only because the neurologist insisted on finding some family clue, I remembered that relative of Mama's who arrived after the Six-Day War, what was her name? Mimi?"

"Phoebe, why mangle the name?"

"Yes, Phoebe, who after one year in Israel sank into depression and moved to an institution in Kfar Saba . . ."

"A nursing home."

"Exactly. And every month or two, you and I took turns driving Mama to visit her. But I never quite understood the family connection."

"She was a second or third cousin, but Mama felt a responsibility."

"If only a second or third cousin, there's no great danger. I have only a vague memory of her, because on those visits I preferred to wait outside. When did she die? Before or after Mama?"

"Who told you she died?"

"Just a minute, if Mama died more than fifteen years ago, why should that one still be alive? Anyway, why be hung up on her? Only because the neurologist insisted on finding a thread, I came up with her. But don't worry, sister, I have lots of lucidity left in me, you all won't be rid of me so easily. And forget the tomatoes. I'll handle them on my own."

"Wait, don't throw them out yet. With me, there's no need to feel ashamed of your confusion. Give me a second to look in a cookbook, and maybe I'll find something for you that's not too complicated."

A good bit of time passes before his sister phones back and dictates a complex recipe for roasted tomatoes that Luria quickly realizes is beyond his powers, but as he tries to end the call, his sister has surprising news: the distant relative, who sank into depression after moving to Israel, whose name is, in fact, Mimi and not Phoebe, still survives, at the same institution. She is now ninety-five, alone and peaceful. And whoever wants to visit her may do so with no problem, since she doesn't recognize anyone anyway. "If she's important to you, brother, so you can plan your future," says his sister, "just hop over and see her."

"So I can what?" says Luria, fearfully.

LET ME ALSO LOOK AT THE SCAN

For now, the tininess of Luria's atrophy is reassuring only to his daughter, who hadn't managed to find anyone else to pick up the grandson from kindergarten on Tuesdays. But his son Yoav is alarmed. Despite his faith in his mother, an experienced physician, this rational man of forty-seven thinks that the spirit, and not the brain, is the source of the confusion, and announces on a rainy morning that he is driving down from the North, to prod the spirit to do its job.

"But Imma is at the hospital this morning, and she'll be sorry to miss you."

"On the contrary, it's best she not be involved. I'm coming to see you, only you."

And Luria, who knows his son well and can imagine his distress, is glad for the panicky visit, despite the inevitable reprimand, and tidies up the already tidy flat as a model for his son, whose home in the country is forever chaotic. And because the son always comes to his parents' home hungry, no matter where he's been and where he's going, and upon arrival goes straight to the fridge and opens its doors like a holy ark, standing rapt before it, seeking food he cherished in childhood, his father preemptively sets a table of cheeses and spreads, bread and nuts and cookies, and heats the big pot of shakshuka, the inexhaustible vestige of the tomato invasion, hoping for an active ally in demolishing the memento of his confusion.

And here he is at the door, wet and caffeinated, in his old army raincoat, and he hugs his father so hard it hurts, as if to revive him. After a few words about the grandchildren, and the expanding business that enslaves its owner, the guest says to his father: "Just a minute, before we talk about the future, let me see your brain scan."

Luria laughs. "And if you look, you'll understand? I can't see anything."

"And Imma understood?"

"So she claims."

"But she could also be wrong."

"Don't forget she's a doctor."

"So what? One time in eighth grade she made me go to school when I was coming down with the measles."

"Because we always suspected you of faking. But in my case, *habibi,* we're not just talking about interpreting a scan, but also evidence from real life."

"Meaning?"

"I already told you. Not just the first names of friends, or famous people, that suddenly vanish, but I'm also getting confused about time."

"Not from darkness in the mind, Abba, but dullness of the spirit."

"You came prepared with that line? Very clever."

"Which is why it's good that Imma's not here, she would dominate the conversation and steer it her way."

"But you know I have no secrets from her."

"Tell her later whatever you want, but now hear me out patiently."

"Not only patiently, but with love and gratitude. As you said, you came only for me, on such a stormy day."

"And despite Osnat's warning me not to provoke you. You know me, I don't give up. But first, please give me the brain scan."

"First you have to taste the shakshuka, before it gets cold."

"Shakshuka, in such a huge pot?"

"Another example. You'll soon see how shakshuka in a big pot is connected with why you came running down here. But don't worry, the shakshuka is delicious, and every day when I reheat it, it just gets better."

The father ladles the thick red tomato sauce with floating yellow egg yolks into two deep, white dishes, and makes room on the table, next to the cheeses, for the brain scan. And as the storm rages outside, and daylight grows dim, he turns on a reading lamp so the son can study the convolutions of his father's brain like the innards of a computer. Yoav is careful not to touch the image with his fingers, as if it were a living organ. He peers at it with a sigh and finally says: "I'm sorry, but in my humble opinion this brain of ours, I mean yours, as I read the image, is perfectly normal. It's no accident that even you didn't see anything wrong with it."

Luria nods with a smile. "Thanks, your generous opinion means a lot to me, but nonetheless, what can I say, the doctor, and Imma—"

"Okay, sure, but even if we accept that some tiny atrophy is lurking in here, what does this neurologist suggest you do?"

Luria is tempted to raise the subject of sexual desire, but instead returns the scan to the envelope and removes it from the table.

"The neurologist's advice is simple, to fight for my memory. For example, not to give up on first names."

"Very nice. But how?"

"With the help of spirit and will. What a surprise, *habibi,* the opinion of the neurologist you think so little of is mighty close to yours."

"The spirit, yes, exactly," Yoav says, "and that's why I'm here. People with dementia are not feeble-minded. Their spirit is exhausted. Don't be offended by what I have to say. You are a senior engineer with broad technical experience, you built roads for many years with great expertise. I therefore reject the idea that all that skill, some of which you've handed down to me, will go to waste, dribbled away in housework and shopping and needless chores, and cooking enormous shakshukas."

"We'll get to the shakshuka in a minute. Keep talking, I'm listening."

"It seems that after you fired the housekeeper, you decided to take her place and be Imma's servant. And that's how the spirit starts to shrink."

"Again that nonsense that we fired the housekeeper."

"But you did."

"No, we did not, drop it, we just reduced her hours."

"To how many?"

"What is this?" objects Luria. "I'm under investigation?"

"Exactly. Investigation by a son who cares about your future and all of ours. So please, the truth, tell the truth, you cut her back to how many times a month?"

"It's not fixed. Say, once a week."

"That's not enough. That's nothing." Yoav raises his voice. "Imma keeps working at the hospital, and even when she's home she hates housework, and the whole burden is on you."

"First of all, it's not a great burden, there's only the two of us, and besides, it's a nice burden."

"Sure, very nice . . . especially to justify your escape from reality, which makes you start—"

"Why did you stop?"

"No reason."

"Start what?"

"Nothing. The escape from reality."

"Which reality?"

"The reality of what you did your whole life with great success."

"How very odd, my dear boy. You're talking just like my neurologist. In any case, he knows nothing about my line of work, so he can crank out absurd suggestions, but you know very well that private individuals don't plan roads. Roads are official national projects. At the Roads Authority there's a new generation of talented young people, who have no need or reason to employ an old fogy like me, even part-time."

"Even so," objects his son, "there are private firms that provide engineering services for the State, or for local governments, and they could use highly experienced engineers. On a part-time basis, with a modest salary and no benefits. Just so you won't sit at home making shakshuka."

"Wait, I'll explain the shakshuka, which has everything to do with what's bothering you. But the possibility of my finding work at a private firm is pure fantasy. Those firms are filled with pensioners who will block any new old man, for fear he would replace them. Not to mention the children and grandchildren, destined to inherit the company. Be honest, you think it would be dignified for me to sit next to some pisher and take orders from him?"

"And all those friends who worked with you? They're in the same situation, so why not stay in touch? With guys like that, you could come up with something original."

"All those friends, Yoavi? The people I worked with were usually not my friends, and if there were friends from other places, where would I find them now? Sometimes there are events or lectures at the office and they invite the retired people too, to prove we are not forgotten. And of course, there are also the dead, and we go to their funerals, and pay condolence calls to their widows, but then, when I realized I had a problem with the first names of engineers I worked closely with for years, it made me anxious. I'd rather go to a movie, or concert, or restaurant, where I can relax. And if I have to meet friends, I prefer doctors, in other words Imma's colleagues, whose names I don't need to remember."

"Only names of diseases."

"Not diseases, mainly rivals who messed up diagnoses and treatments. But I owe these people nothing, so I can sit by the side and hear stories about healthy people who died or half-dead ones who came back to life, without having to know their names."

"But wait," his son insists, "why do you need the first name, the last name is enough, or better yet, no name at all."

"I often get away with that, but it's not always possible, there are situations where the first name is essential, it's obligatory, and when you get it wrong, you get no mercy, only hostility. Why should you forget the name of a person you've worked with for years, not just in the office but out in the field? Why on earth, dammit, does this Zvi Luria want to erase me, a person demands to know. There are a few old-timers whose last name became their only name, swallowing their first name. Everyone, sometimes even their wives, called them only by their last names. But such people are rare, and if I happen to run into them, I have no problem, because I'm still doing fine with last names. But there are people in my generation whose last names I never knew, only their first names, and if I run into them at a party, I get very tense and I'm afraid I'll make a mistake."

"In which case," counters the son, "you've decided never to go to any reception or lecture at the office? Not even the farewell party for Tzahi Divon, your deputy for so many years?"

"How do you know about that party? From Imma, eh?"

"Yes, from Imma. So what?"

"And maybe Imma asked you to come down from the Galilee to speak with me?"

"Let's say she did. She's not allowed? You said you have no secrets from her."

"But apparently she has secrets from me."

"What's the big secret? That she asked me to convince you not to avoid people? Avoid your friends?"

"Divon has not been a friend for a long time."

"He was your close assistant, your partner in the tunnels you dug on Highway Six."

"Oy, Yoavi, you're still so excited about those pathetic tunnels, like Imma? Tunnels we were forced to dig not because of topographic requirements, but to enable animals who were confused by the highway to cross safely from one side to the other."

Yoav smiles. "Why shouldn't I be excited? Every time I drive through one of those tunnels I remember how you once asked me to go with you, under a full moon, to check if there were actual deer or wild boar who understood the tunnel was dug for them."

"I seriously doubt that the animals up north have any idea what the Society for the Protection of Nature wants them to understand."

"In any case, on that night, while you dozed off, I saw a deer, or a huge wild boar, who climbed over the tunnel and crossed from east to west, and after a few minutes, for some reason, went back the other way."

"Yes, I remember your telling me, but even now I'm not sure you weren't just imagining it."

"Excuse me, you think I'm also delusional?"

"We have no choice, *habibi,* listen to the neurologist, there's a genetic thread."

"Eventually we'll see how long and strong a thread, but now explain to me why you're skipping the farewell party for a guy who was your right-hand man for so many years?"

"Yeah, he was a loyal and dependable worker, but when I retired five years ago, instead of taking my place and running projects we both worked on, he bailed out to manage a project in Kenya that paid a big salary. And now that the job in Kenya is finished, or maybe he got kicked out, he's throwing himself a goodbye party here, not in Africa where he got rich."

"What do you care? There'll be other friends there, retirees like you. Maybe some ideas will come up. Go. It's an opportunity to renew your contacts. You were popular, people loved you, nobody's going to be crushed if you forget their name."

"Finish your shakshuka, it's getting cold."

"I ate enough."

"Listen, Yoavi, you're a good son and I respect and appreciate your concern. But both you and Imma refuse to understand that if this is early dementia, it's not just about forgetting names. The big pot of shakshuka is connected to what's happening inside of me."

Luria returns to the shopping day. First the big order at the supermarket, then the flower stall at the *shuk,* and finally the six kilos of tomatoes, which turned into shakshuka, for lack of an alternative.

"But why?" Yoav protests. "You could have dumped the surplus before Imma got home from the hospital."

"No, no, no!" cries the father. "I deliberately did not throw away even one tomato. The shakshuka that lasted for many days is evidence. It is here to warn me about myself, and warn all of you."

"Warn us?"

"Yes, about my gaffes and blunders, and the disasters I might bring down upon this house, upon myself and you."

Yoav says nothing, crestfallen. When he finally looks up, his father sees the same fear he saw in his eyes while changing his diaper.

"Don't be sad," Luria says brightly, "you haven't come in vain. For you, I'll go to Kobi Divon's party."

"Tzahi," his son says gently.

"Right, Tzahi." Luria smiles.

"And Imma promised me she'd go with you."

"I don't need her there. No reason that after a workday at the hospital she should stand around with a plastic cup of fruit juice, listening to boring road engineers. I'll deal alone with the change in my brain, and maintain my dignity. I might even make a little farewell speech. You corrected me and said Tzahi, not Kobi, before the party I'll jot his name down on the palm of my hand, not to embarrass anyone."

THE GENETIC THREAD

Since the death of their mother more than fifteen years ago, Luria and his sister have not gone to visit the distant cousin their mother persuaded not to emigrate from North Africa to France, but to make aliyah, ascend to the ancient Jewish homeland of Israel, where she promptly withdrew into deep depression.

Luria's mother, who felt guilty over the aliyah that failed, took upon herself the duty to visit the ailing immigrant every few weeks and try to lift her spirits, speaking in French, the cousin's native tongue. At first Luria would accompany his mother to the ward, and not knowing French, he would attempt to make conversation in Hebrew with other elderly depressives who seemed amenable. But he soon tired of chatting up people who had lost one identity and were incapable of creating another, and so preferred to wait for his mother in the lobby, or in the car, where he would listen to good music interrupted by news bulletins. When he was curious afterward if any improvement or decline was expected in the cousin's condition, a glimmer of hope, his mother would hem and haw, then deliver a favorite line: "If you or your sister feels that I'm beginning to lose my mind, please put some poison in my coffee." To which Luria would respond: "What kind? Sweet or bitter? You have to decide, so we can get it ready now."

And here he is, en route to the institution, this time not as a chaperone but on a personal mission: to investigate the existence and nature of the thin genetic thread his neurologist insists on unveiling. After fifteen years, the roads to the institution are wider, with new interchanges and fewer traffic lights, but Luria has no need for any app on his phone. His instinctive grasp of roads and highways guides him precisely to his destination.

Not only has traffic flow improved, the nursing home has grown two stories higher, its entrance redone in marble. The furnishings and equipment, originally standard government issue, have been upgraded thanks to a philanthropist whose wife was a patient here. Although Luria remains dubious about his sister's claim that their distant relative is still alive, he has brought her, as their mother always did, a modest gift, a handsome box of plump Medjool dates, in hopes they will sweeten her dementia. And if it turns out that she has passed away, at least the devoted staff, who cared for her till the end, can enjoy them. But where is that staff? In which department, on what floor? This time it's the first name he's sure of, but has no inkling of the family name. So he walks up one floor at a time and looks around, hoping to remember someone who took care of her in the past. He is spared the arduous climb to the top, for on the third floor he recognizes a pretty nurse who caught his eye in the past, her braid gone white with age.

She warmly greets the surprise guest, and of course remembers his mother, and also his sister, who unlike him was not afraid to circulate among the patients.

"I wasn't afraid," says Luria, miffed by the insinuation. "I just didn't want to bother anyone. And because I didn't know French, there was no point in staying in the room with my mother."

"Even without French you could have stayed."

"True," admits the visitor, "and by the way, what's her last name?"

Now he learns that in the late 1960s something strange happened. Last names generally dominate, but in her case the first name absorbed the last without leaving a trace.

"Mimi is all we have," admits the nurse, now chief of her department. "We can't explain how her family name disappeared. When your mother brought her here, she was registered under her first name only, alongside her ID number, and that was sufficient. Now too, she's quiet and stable, with only a first name. I see you remembered to bring her some dates, as your mother used to do, yes, she'll be happy to eat them, but there's no chance they will help her recognize you."

"I don't need her to recognize me," counters Luria. "I just happened to remember her lately, I was sure she had passed away long ago, but my sister for some reason insisted she was still alive, and I decided to come and see why my sister insisted, and if her condition is still stable. Our mother saw herself as her guardian of sorts."

"There hasn't been any significant decline in her condition, or improvement," says the nurse with a radiant smile. "You're welcome to visit her and give her the dates." Luria is surprised that the whiteness of her elegant braid only enhances her beauty.

"Medjool dates," says Luria, tapping the box label with his finger.

Luria conceals the true reason for his visit, lest he tempt fate. The last thing he needs is for the thin genetic thread to turn out to be a steel wire, which will soon render him a candidate for this place. Still, he's eager to see her.

"I'll give her the dates," he says cheerfully, "and maybe she'll at least remember my mother, who never abandoned her."

The head nurse leads him to a room, not large but clean and bright, with two wide beds, separated by a curtain. As he enters, two stout elderly women sit down quickly, and he wonders which one carries his genetic thread. One is wearing a red apron, and next to her is a strange-looking flute, long and black, open at both ends, and he thinks this woman dimly recognizes him, maybe because he resembles his mother, or because of the dates in his hand. "Here, please," he says, offering the dates with compassion.

She accepts the gift, but seems not to know she is supposed to open the box, so the nurse takes it from her and shows her the gleaming rows of mouth-watering dates. Before returning the box to her, the nurse selects three dates: the first for the roommate, who smiles as if she's met an old acquaintance, the second one for the bearer of the gift, and the third she eats herself, daintily removing the pit from her mouth and extending her hand to collect the two others.

"How old is she?" whispers Luria.

"Ninety-five."

"She looks marvelous for her age and condition. Apparently you have to lose your mind to survive this long."

"Not always," says the nurse, a touch of annoyance in her pretty eyes.

But Luria doesn't quit. "Does she know she's still in the State of Israel, or does she think she's in the World to Come?"

"That's hard to know," says the nurse, "but if she thinks she's in the World to Come, she should be happy, since you brought proof of a nice life in the World to Come."

"Life . . ." Luria chuckles.

"Don't belittle it. Apart from the devoted care we give her, she also enjoys her music."

"Music?"

"Yes, a year after your mother died, a relative of yours arrived from France to take care of Mimi's financial affairs. Before he went back to France, he bought her this big flute, called a *kaval.* At first she ignored it, we begged her to try, she refused to even touch it. It's not an easy instrument. I can't get one note out of it. You have to hold your lips just so and blow. But one day she suddenly picked it up, and we were amazed to hear her playing, and now she plays it sometimes, usually before a meal, when she's hungry. Maybe she'll agree to play for you, to thank you for the dates."

And the head nurse picks up the flute and puts it in the old woman's hands, placing the tip against her lips, and a simple melody floats through the room, possibly North African in origin, but its sadness is Israeli.

A RETIREMENT PARTY

Most floors in the Roads Authority building are dark, but the lobby of the meeting hall on the ground floor is brightly lit and packed with guests at the retirement party thrown by Divon for himself. Before shutting off the engine in the red car, Luria undoes his seat belt and puts a loving hand on his wife's shoulder.

"There is really, really no reason for you to be here with me.

Better you should be with the grandchildren at their bedtime. You haven't seen them for five days, and they'll be happy to hear a true story about a sick child cured at your clinic. You got Yoavi to convince me not to skip this party, I should navigate it on my own steam."

"But—"

"But what? If you're not concerned about my embarrassing blunders when I'm wandering alone at the *shuk* or the mall, you certainly don't need to worry about me at a place where I worked for many years among friends. And you certainly mustn't distract me."

"Distract you how?"

"By your very presence, your being, because with you at my side I'm stuck, aware of you looking at me, and anxious. And when friends and acquaintances approach us, alone or with their spouses, they're drawn to you and not to me. And because you're afraid that if I speak I'll make a mess of names and forget things, you grab hold of the conversation and steer it toward our children and theirs, so we can brag about the grandchildren, and then come the medical stories people drag you into—there'll be old friends here who remember you are a physician, and won't miss a chance to milk you for advice or the name of a drug. You and Yoavi didn't send me here tonight for that. Oh, look, blacks, real blacks, I mean distinguished Africans from Divon's staff in Kenya, and maybe from their embassy here, invited to upgrade the importance of the party. If one of them makes a speech about Divon, maybe I'll also say a few words, talk a bit about his exploits. After all, he was my close assistant and deputy for almost seven years. Don't worry, I have his first name on my palm, here, look . . ."

"Just watch your tongue," says his wife with a laugh, "his family will be there. And from all the people and the music I can tell the food will be something special."

"But you wouldn't enjoy the food, because when there's a crowd you don't like shoving your way to the buffet."

"And instead of bringing me food," she says, "you only look out for yourself and leave me hungry . . . Fine, fine, this time eat for me too, but in moderation, and remember to tell me what was most delicious. If you don't find a road-building project, at least get some ideas to diversify your cooking."

"That's not fair, you know how hard I try."

"You try but don't always succeed, not that I am complaining, there's really no need to attach such importance to food. Let's just decide what time I should pick you up."

"Why pick me up? There'll be plenty of friends happy to give me a lift. Stay at Avigail's house, I'll come there. Just be careful, don't daydream on the road and don't speed, because the rain that you think is harmless makes the asphalt as slick as butter."

The large hall is decorated in a manner unfamiliar to Luria from all his years at the Roads Authority. Flute and drums emanate from an unknown source, and he can see that his wife was right, the food is lavish and plentiful, with young and old gathering to partake. Instead of the lonely table commonly found at retirement parties with a few platters of bourekas and mini-pizzas, this evening there are three tables, with food arranged for easy access without crowding and pushing, and a stack of dinner plates augurs a full meal and not merely hors d'oeuvres. At the front of the hall, near a small stage, stands the honoree in suit and tie, who introduces his two African guests, attired in colorful robes, to the directors of the government institution he left more than a few years before. Amid the tumult he notices Luria, his old patron, and waves hello from a distance, and his wife, in an embroidered, figure-hugging pants suit, does the same.

Luria waves back, careful not to come closer before testing his memory. He tightly balls his fist and mumbles to himself the name of the celebrant, then opens his hand to confirm that the whispered name is the same name he wrote down.

But Divon's wife? He is suddenly seized by the question: what is her name? He closes his eyes and bows his head to pluck the name from his mind, but no name emerges through the fog. Has his atrophy swallowed the name of that "tragic" woman, or is the spirit to blame? He decides not to run possible names through his memory, hoping the right one will shine through. No, this time he must be careful. If some sneaky name impersonates the real one, which happens sometimes, this woman in particular would be very hurt.

He secretly studies her from afar, hoping her face will give rise to her name. But even a first letter refuses to crop up. He'll have no choice but to retrieve her name from an old friend. Here are his colleagues, some bald and slow-moving but loud and laughing, some sad and withered, some with wives and others alone, all crowding the food, plates in hand. A few wave hello to Luria, who was well liked as a talented and effective engineer, open to the ideas of others—but Luria keeps his distance, not taking a plate, first inspecting what's available at a nearby table, making plans to sample what looks best. To his surprise he discovers little dishes of gourmet shakshuka, each with a tiny yolk, perhaps a quail egg, floating like a setting sun in a red sea. Suddenly he misses his gigantic shakshuka at home, which was finished off just a few days ago, and the little dishes seem like its newborn offspring, so he picks one up lovingly and tastes it, and to his delight, its flavor and aroma could have come from the womb of the big mother pot. Ah, what a shame that he can't bring home one little dish to prove to his wife that his cooking, despite its monotony, is of professional caliber.

A waiter carrying a big tray urges Luria to try the canapés, which artfully combine clashing flavors, sweet and spicy, and competing textures, crispy and soft. Luria tries one canapé while already reaching for another, and the smiling waiter suggests a third one, a pity not to try that too, and Luria complies, and as it crumbles in his mouth he moans with pleasure and wipes his lips with a napkin and says, "Yes, they are marvelous, don't tempt me any further, because others are hungry too," but the waiter doesn't relent and points to an hors d'oeuvre of red meat he must sample, and Luria sighs and eats it, protesting, "How come you're spoiling me like this?" And only now does the waiter in a black vest and bow tie reveal his identity—it's Havilio, veteran driver of the big earth-mover, a vehicle that was retired along with its operator. In honor of the good old days, Havilio recommends another treat, and Luria is happy to see the worker who years ago, under his guidance, bull-dozed an entire hill of basalt between Route 85 and Route 866, and in the joy of running into the power-shovel operator turned waiter, he can even remember his first name, but resists the additional canapé, there's a limit to snacks, more delicacies await at the table, to miss them would pain him greatly. True, agrees Havilio, and you have to leave room for the wonderful desserts with the burning sparklers.

"Dessert with sparklers?" Luria marvels. "I see Divon wants his party to be unforgettable."

He makes his way to the table, hoping that amid the food and the diners a snippet of an engineering project may materialize, to help his spirit do battle with his dwindling brain, but he is intercepted by the incoming director general of the Roads Authority. The young man, promoted following a purge of corrupt managers, asks Luria to honor the retiree with a few words.

"A speech?"

But keep it short, as there will be many speeches. The two African engineers who worked with him in Nairobi will deliver a firsthand report, illustrated with slides, about the ideas and plans that the Israeli brought to their country. A representative of the Foreign Ministry is coming from Jerusalem to speak about the importance of Israeli aid for countries in distress. And he, the incoming director general, will also say a few words. And Divon will respond to his well-wishers. But he dropped a hint that it's very important to him for someone from the inside, namely, the former director of the Northern Division, to reminisce about major initiatives that were realized before he left for Africa. After all, Divon insisted that his party be held here, at the institution where he spent most of his career.

But Luria, who already figured he'd be asked to speak, remains hesitant.

"True, the two of us worked as a team, and we had a few successful projects in the North where Tzahi Divon was the prime mover, and therefore I was not only disappointed but angry that after I retired he refused to take my place, and quit instead."

"Disappointed, okay, but why angry?"

"Why?" Luria laughs and peeks at his palm, in case the new director's name is miraculously inscribed there too. "I trained him to be my successor, and trusted him to take the lead after I retired, and then, for a fat salary, he defected to Africa and left the department in confusion, as if, I don't know, some dullness or even dementia had come over it."

But since this young man is the one who approved Divon's request to hold a farewell party at the institution he left five years ago, he tries to defend him. The departure for Africa was not a matter of greed, he explains, but because of his mentally disabled son, to provide him with a secure future after his parents' death.

"Wait a second," interjects Luria, "do you by any chance know the mother's first name?" He suddenly can't recall it.

Her first name? The new director met her this evening for the first time, but if Luria wants to include first names of family members in his remarks, he'll find out for him.

"No, no, no, don't ask anybody. If I need her name or other names, they'll surface on their own, provided I drench my atrophy with black coffee, so it won't trip me up."

"Your what?"

"Forget it, just a word that came to me."

Meanwhile, the honoree and his entourage approach. And as Tzahi Divon hugs his former boss, his wife also walks over, and pulls Luria away, facing him silently, unsmiling, studying him sternly as if to determine if he notices any change in her. Yes, she is thinner, the "tragic woman," her wild hair is stylishly short now, with a splash of red, her facial wrinkles are smoothed, and the embroidered blue suit flatters her figure. Her husband's ample salary, and the servants surrounding her in Africa, apparently have dispelled her gloom. Luria wonders if her first name will spring from her tiny, reptilian eyes, as the two adult sons introduce themselves to the engineer who mentored their father many years ago at the Roads Authority. And following his brothers, in a wheelchair, attended by an elderly, bearded African, is the third son, tall and bent, with the face of a fallen angel, and the young man suddenly seizes Luria's hand and lifts it, as if intending to kiss or bite it, and as Luria nervously withdraws his hand, the lights go down and a bluish darkness envelops the hall.

A SHORT FILM

The Africans did not bring slides from Kenya, but rather a film, twenty-five minutes long. Highways, bridges, and tunnels appear on the screen, also a small interchange, isolated and inexplicable, that pops up in a barren desert, and Luria's professional eye notices similarities to an interchange he and Divon designed for the Upper Galilee, but whose budget was not approved. It's a film clearly made in haste, lacking sound or subtitles, and even Divon himself, enthusiastically posing beside a bridge or tunnel, is struck dumb in mid-enthusiasm. To fill in the blanks, one of the African engineers stands beside the screen, and in precise English provides explanations and expresses appreciation for the chief planner and leader, who invited him and his friends to his farewell party in Israel.

At the end of the screening the lights stay off in the hall, as the guests are invited to gorge discreetly on scrumptious desserts that arrive from all sides, adorned with colorful sparklers. Luria, sitting nervously next to the new director general, not far from the honored family, skips the desserts and listens intently for a chance mention of the first name of the "tragic woman"—a nickname her husband once mentioned, inadvertently.

The man from the Foreign Ministry is asked to say a few words. He is young, thin, and balding, an intellectual type, unafraid to read out a page of bold reflections to an audience of strangers.

"To my shame and sorrow as an Israeli citizen, and especially as an official of the Foreign Ministry, most Israeli aid and exports in recent years to developing and failed countries in Africa and Asia involve weapons systems and military know-how. Senior officers, retiring from the army at a relatively young age, are not satisfied with the handsome pension they receive from the Defense Ministry and are driven by the desire to make a lot of money quickly. They take advantage of the vast knowledge they acquired during their army service, typically not on the battlefield but by calmly operating computers and secret electronic equipment in fortified bunkers, to hook up with shady international arms dealers, who enable corrupt dictators to tighten control of their regimes and fight ruthlessly against their enemies via the expert experience of the Israeli army.

"And so, dear friends, employees, and pensioners of the Israel Roads Authority, you know better than anyone else that in the 1950s and '60s, a different tune was heard in our little country, and the State of Israel, poor but ethical, extended a different helping hand, civilian and not military, to young African countries, newly liberated from the yoke of colonialism. During those glorious years, it was not the art of warfare that came from Israel, but guidance in fields such as agriculture, transportation, water planning, and education, and people from the Water Authority and Public Works built roads and factories in Africa, and the Solel Boneh construction company founded an entire university in Ethiopia for the benefit of all its inhabitants.

"And so, ladies and gentlemen, I've come down here from Jerusalem on this rainy day not on a mission from the Center for International Cooperation, but on a mission of my own, to take part in the retirement party of Mr. Yitzhak Divon and express appreciation for this accomplished engineer, who willingly left a top position at the Roads Authority to benefit the people of Kenya with his creative knowledge of engineering. He even brought along his whole family on this important mission, in the hope that they would ease his loneliness in a difficult country and provide vital moral support to ensure the best results of his work.

"You see with your own eyes, ladies and gentlemen, that it is not only I who have come from afar to salute him, but also people from Kenya and its embassy in Tel Aviv are here to celebrate his retirement. Here is my wish: may it come to pass that young engineers and planners, serving at the Roads Authority or other agencies, will follow in the footsteps of Yitzhak. And although I am still a minor official at the Foreign Ministry, I promise that I will afford them all the practical and moral support I can."

"If this boychick keeps talking this way, he'll be a minor player at the Foreign Ministry for a long time," whispers the young new director general to Luria as the audience applauds. Luria gets up and approaches the minor official, to congratulate him on his candor and to ask if he can have the text, faintly hoping that the first names of Divon's family are included there, but it turns out that what's written is only what he read.

Luria's last resort is the new director, who in his remarks will surely mention the name of the woman who keeps staring at him. But the new director realizes that he knows little about the former employee, who left five years ago, never to return, and rather than stumble into vapid words of praise or inaccurate details, he now decides not to speak at all, and instead invites Luria to congratulate the heir apparent who declined his legacy.

Meanwhile, the host has instructed the waiters to bring in another round of sparklers with the coffee and tea, and in order to maintain the dazzling ambience, the lights remain low in the hall, where Luria's elderly friends sit half asleep, and these dim silhouettes of forgotten colleagues inspire him not to deliver a banal and superficial speech, but to dare to say something personal about a talented engineer who defected to a distant continent before reaching retirement age.

First Luria looks at the palm of his hand to make sure that the first name, faded by now, is correct, and, maintaining the hope that the wife's name will bubble up from the well of forgetfulness, he begins speaking to his friends.

THE SPEECH

Luria has delivered many a speech in this hall, or more precisely, routine salutations, usually at the launch of joint projects with government ministries, the Jewish National Fund, the settlement department of the World Zionist Organization, the traffic police, the road safety organization Or Yarok, and of course municipalities, mainly Arab and Druze towns in the North that benefited, if only rarely, from new roads, or at least repairs. But sometimes Luria had been asked to say a few words of farewell upon the retirement of subordinates, either lower-level or senior employees. He would draft these in advance, to be polished by his wife, who would add, often without knowing the retiree, a few elegant turns of phrase to inject warmth and feeling into her husband's dry prose. Once, to mark the expansion of a complex highway junction, in partnership with the traffic police, she embellished her husband's remarks with a few lines from the renowned poet Avraham Shlonsky, whom Luria had never heard of.

But this evening Luria has nothing on paper, no heartwarming poetry. He had a hunch that if he came to the party he'd have to speak, but it didn't occur to him to come equipped with the name of Divon's wife.

And now, for the first time, he will speak knowing that the dementia diagnosed by the neurologist is a permanent component of his personality. He must navigate carefully between the new reality he's stuck with and his original, sane existence. In the darkened room, with dessert sparklers flickering and coffee cups softly clinking, Luria decides to position himself someplace between the family and the audience:

"Dear Tzahi, my loyal and able deputy for ten years in the Northern Division, the natural candidate to replace me as director, I wish to congratulate you, and also your wife, a devoted and loyal partner, and your three children, whose names I have not forgotten, because I never knew them to begin with. And you, dear friends, may be asking yourselves: how can it be that a manager didn't know or want to know the names of the children of a person he worked so closely with for many years, not any person, but his close deputy, destined to take his place when the time came? And my explanation may seem strange or repellent to the young people among you, but it is a valid reason, and I believe a basis for good working relations everywhere, especially in public institutions such as ours. Dear friends, I, today, am seventy-plus, but from the time I began working here as a young road engineer, I decided to draw clear boundaries in my relationships with other employees, those I worked for and especially those who worked for me. I decided to do all I could to avoid mixing personal, family, or political matters with work. And to do so, of course, while preserving openness and transparency in all things professional. Let's be honest

—there's always a risk that intimate relationships among employees, or political opinions both left and right, or disputes between religious and secular, will interfere with clearheaded professional thinking, and lead to failures on the job, and even encourage corruption, such as fixed bids and nepotism. Millions of shekels, if not billions, flow through the Roads Authority, in numerous projects. So despite the close working connection between me and Tzahi Divon, in the office or during field trips, we did not discuss personal or family matters, but only highways and interchanges, and the best angles for entering and exiting intersections, and the proper placement of road lighting, and the precise location of traffic signals. And we consulted with each other about how to get around budgetary restrictions, in a legal and ethical manner of course, to improve roads in remote places. And because my relationship with Tzahi Divon was purely professional, never involving personal matters, good or bad, do not be surprised, ladies and gentlemen, that it never occurred to me to invite him to the *brit* of my first grandson, nor did he invite me to his second son's bar mitzvah, and we scrupulously avoided talking about family problems, or the illnesses of spouses, children, or relatives that sometimes kept us away from the office. Between me and him, and all my other subordinates, there was an atmosphere of trust, an assumption that whoever didn't come to work was absent for a good reason, and there was no need to justify it with a doctor's note. In all the years we worked together, Tzahi never visited my home, not even for a brief conversation about work. Whereas I was in his house but once, after he went off to Africa, when he asked me to bring his wife, dear Mrs. Divon, who had remained for a while in Israel, a few obsolete plans and photographs from the archive."

Meanwhile, all the sparklers have fizzled out, but the person in charge of the lights refrains from turning them on, startling the speaker and his attentive audience, thus leaving the remainder of the speech in darkness.

Yet Luria feels that the heart of his speech is yet to come. He peers at the Divon family, a murky block in the dusky hall, and walks a few steps toward them, hoping that Divon's wife's name will flare like a final sparkler. The sound of rain, the soothing darkness, inspire Luria to address the man directly:

"Yes, Tzahi Divon, despite the personal freedom we gave each other, and absolute nonintervention in personal matters, I must admit I was angry when you announced, upon my retirement, that you had undertaken a mission to Africa instead of taking over my position. I was angry because I knew that after my retirement and your departure, a number of bold and beautiful plans we had prepared together for Route 754 would go down the drain, and there would be no one to insist on repairs and an additional lane for Route 879. I also knew that whoever was appointed to replace me would be unable to understand the ideas you and I shared regarding the interchange of 96 and 989, where so many accidents had taken place. It was obvious to me that both of us leaving would bring about confusion and paralysis, and although I said nothing to you, my anger did not subside during the many years you were absent from Israel, so much so, I confess, that I hesitated to come to this impressive party you organized in your own honor.

"But, but, but—when I heard just now this young man, a brave representative of our Foreign Ministry, praising the human contribution, civilian and not military, that you and other Israelis have bestowed on poor, confused countries, and when I saw that engineers who worked with you in Kenya came from far away to demonstrate to us concrete examples of how important your work was to them, and when I understood it was not easy for your family, especially your wife, dear lady, to leave Israel and live in a distant African land, the anger I brought with me into this hall abated, even disappeared. And I am pleased, Kobi—excuse me, Tzahi-Tzahi-Tzahi—that not only did I come, but I agreed to the request of the young, dynamic new director general, whose name I haven't yet learned or written down, to congratulate you in my name and in the name of all the pensioners whose ranks you join today. And because I am sure that with your talent, and with the increased experience you bring from the Dark Continent, you will not remain unemployed in our little homeland, I permit myself to reach out and inform you that if you invite me, a veteran pensioner, to be your assistant or adviser in a new project, private or public, I think I would not refuse."

And he considers stopping here, or improvising another idea, for he feels that the darkness in the hall corresponds nicely with the darkness that grips his mind. But applause and a quick hug from Tzahi Divon dictate that he yield the floor.

TELL ME MY NAME AND I'LL LEAVE YOU ALONE

The lights have yet to come back on, as the master of ceremonies continues to surprise his guests. Instead of one more tedious speech, he screens another video for the well-wishers, not further evidence of his engineering feats but rather a nature film, replete with breathtaking landscapes and exotic animals, documenting a family trip to neighboring Uganda, which at the dawn of the twentieth century, unbeknownst to the Ugandans, was proposed by bold if naïve Jews as a contender for the ancestral homeland. It is obvious to the assembled that the newly minted pensioner is doing all he can to upgrade the party he threw for himself, to ensure it will be remembered not only as a worthy farewell, but also as atonement for his premature desertion. Accordingly, he shows the Israelis what they lost, but also what they gained, by dismissing the notion of an alternative homeland.

But Zvi Luria has no interest in assessing delusional profit and loss, and quietly slips away from the family to try to find among the pensioners a friend or acquaintance to drive him home to his wife. But a female hand, soft but strong, grabs the nape of his neck and pulls him to the drinks table. "Thank you for agreeing to speak," the woman intimately whispers, "and thanks too for letting go of your anger, because Tzahi was sorry you weren't there with us in Africa to see the scope of his important work and understand why he turned down the chance to replace you."

"Yes," he says, slightly aroused. "I decided to let go of stubborn and superfluous anger."

"But the anger you abandoned landed on me."

"On you? How so?"

"Because instead of mentioning not just his name in your speech but mine too, you got all tangled up in formality. What's with the 'devoted partner,' 'Mrs. Divon,' 'dear lady,' instead of simply my name?"

She fixes a serious look at him. And Luria asks himself whether in her remodeled appearance, the result of the good life in Africa, she still qualifies as a "tragic woman."

With a cautious smile he tries to defend himself. Why would he need to add the first name of a woman unknown to most of the audience, having stressed in his speech that the professional success of his long partnership with her husband was based on avoidance of private and family matters?

But she is adamant: he didn't just happen to omit her name, he did so on purpose.

"On purpose? Why?"

"To prove you had erased me from inside you."

"Why would I erase you?"

"If you have no reason, then let's have it, Zvi Luria, say my name."

"Say it to whom?"

"To me!"

He looks at her with fearful curiosity, hoping that the lost name will miraculously float to the surface from within her pain.

"Why tell you something you know so well?" he jokes.

"Because it's the only way you can prove you haven't erased my name, because, let's say—"

"Because what?"

"Because you lusted after me."

Luria is shaken. "If there was lust, it was nipped in the bud. I immediately blocked it."

"But who asked you to?" she whispers in a strange tone. "Who wanted you to block it?"

Luria's glance wanders to the family: will her husband notice that they are engaged in conversation and come and join it? He takes her arm gently and steers her toward the exit. "Not block the lust? In what sense?" he whispers.

Now she is angry. "What is sense and what is nonsense, Luria, we'll postpone for another time. Give me back my name and I'll leave you alone."

Give her back her name? He is shocked. What's going on? Did

Africa add madness to the "tragedy" of the Israeli woman? How to give her back a name that vanished? In order to appease her, he may be forced to confess that the tiny atrophy is eating away at first names, but if he confesses, will she believe him? And if she believes him, she'll end up taking revenge for the unrequited lust and warn her husband and the others not to get mixed up with an old fool looking for work.

He looks around to find someone or something to distract her, but everyone is watching the family journey to Uganda, and wow, it's magic, she herself is on the screen at this very moment, attractive in a safari suit and pith helmet, feeding a corncob to an animal, maybe a deer or an antelope or some new sort of camel with a crown of golden horns.

"Look, look," he points at the screen, "it's you! Look! But what is that amazing animal called? You weren't afraid to feed it?"

Before she can answer, he gently touches her hair and mumbles, "Wait, wait here a second, I'll bring you back your name right away." He turns around, hurries down the corridor, escapes up the stairs, and goes to the second floor. From his working years he remembers a magnificent men's room, intended for foreign visitors or members of the board of directors. And though the second floor is dark, he needs no light to find the door, which alas is locked from the inside, probably by an elderly pensioner who also knows his way around. But he can't wait for the door to open, so he rushes to the elevator, which takes him to the top floor, to the offices of the Northern Division, where everybody worked for him. Here too it is dark, but not dark enough to deter a person who, thanks to many years on the job, can identify every door he passes. From far off he sees a thin ribbon of light licking the last doorway, his old office. What's this?

SHELVED PLANS

A few years prior to his retirement from the Roads Authority, Luria was asked by the Ministry of Defense to plan a bypass road in northern Samaria, to buttress the security and peace of mind of a small West Bank settlement that was accessible only by a road adjacent to a Palestinian village. He assigned the planning to Divon, and it soon became clear that owing to topographical conditions, the cost of the bypass road would exceed the cost of moving the whole settlement to a different place. So Divon went out into the field to find a way to "bypass the bypass"—in other words, not to build a new road, but to upgrade an old dirt road that, according to the archaeologist of the Roads Authority, dated from the Second Temple period. This road was also not far from the Palestinian village, but its hillside location made it less vulnerable to rock throwing or Molotov cocktails. Divon worked hard, took photographs, drew maps, calculated costs, and submitted an inventive, inexpensive plan to the Defense Ministry. But then it turned out that this old road ran over an ancient graveyard, possibly from the First Temple period, and rather than fight with the ultra-Orthodox burial authorities over every bone, it was decided to shelve the plan, and instead build a stone wall alongside the Arab homes nearest the access road, thereby hiding the Palestinians from the Jews, and the Jews from the Palestinians, and each side could indulge its own identity without fearing the gaze of the other. Divon's creative plan, with its photographs, maps, and diagrams, was buried in the archive, but Divon himself did not forget it, and a few weeks after he went to Africa, he surprised Luria, then preparing for retirement, by asking him to locate the abandoned plan and send it to him, for reasons unknown. And since Divon's wife had been delayed in Israel to deal with renting out their home, Divon decided the safest and quickest way would be for the Roads Authority to deliver the plan to her by messenger.

In fact, as the settlement expanded and the stone wall grew so high as to erase the name of the Palestinian village from Jewish memory, there was no need to preserve, even in the archive, an audacious plan to resurrect an ancient dirt road. But to forestall gossip about a public plan falling into private hands, Luria decided that he, and not some blabbermouth messenger, should personally fulfill the final request of a man he worked with for so many years. "Just confirm your home address for me," he had asked. "And if possible, remind me of your wife's first name."

And so, a few months before his retirement, Luria removed the shelved plan from the archive, stuck it in a big envelope, and on a cloudy morning, as prearranged, he parked in front of a house he had never visited before—a large home in a rural area, older than he'd expected and, on the eve of its rental, also a bit sad and neglected. On the yellowing lawn, amid trees of withered fruit, were scattered cardboard boxes and, in a corner, a pile of old kitchen utensils and some dilapidated furniture. But near the gate with the FOR RENT sign stood a beautiful young woman, clearly of Asian origin. Her dainty hand rested on the shoulder of a boy with the face of a tormented angel, staring from his wheelchair into the distance. This was Divon's mentally disabled son, whom Luria had heard of. He wore a leather helmet, to cushion his head-banging on walls, but now, with no wall nearby, he intermittently clapped his hands two or three times, to fortify himself. Before Luria could say anything, the young woman surprisingly addressed him by his full name, informing him in a pleasant voice that the door was open and he was welcome to enter.

"She had a long, rough night," the young woman explained, "and now she's finally sleeping, but in any case, don't leave that envelope anywhere around here. The house is so chaotic that even a big envelope can easily vanish. So please don't be afraid to wake her up and hand it to her, that's what she said you should do."

The sweetness and beauty of the East Asian woman, and her precise Hebrew, with no trace of a foreign accent, stole the messenger's heart. And since he was not eager to enter a strange and chaotic house and wake up a woman he had always taken pains to avoid, he suggested to the caregiver that he leave the envelope with her, to ensure it would reach its destination. "After all," he added with a hint of regret, "I gather they are also taking you with them to Africa."

"To Africa? Why? I'm not leaving Israel," said the young woman. "There will be plenty of affordable servants there to deal with everything necessary and unnecessary. No, I'm already out of the picture," she repeated emphatically. "Today's my last day. His grandparents are coming to pick him up, and he'll stay with them till next week's journey. So you have no choice, Mr. Luria, you must deliver the envelope to her personally, that is what she requested, along with permission that you wake her up."

Despite the personal invitation to invade the privacy of the sleeping wife of a colleague who worked beside him for years, he was in no hurry to enter. Impressed by the young caregiver's fluent, unaccented Hebrew, he asked when she had arrived in Israel. And it turned out that the beautiful woman had not arrived, but was born here, and proudly explained that her parents were Vietnamese boat people, refugees who were rescued at sea by an Israeli ship. No other country would take them in, and a generous Israeli prime minister offered them citizenship. But her parents, who could never stop longing for their old identity, returned years later to their country. "And you," asked Luria kindly, "you didn't want to join them?" "I tried it out, if only to understand why there had been such a horrible war there." "And did you understand?" He could not take his eyes off her. "No, I understood nothing," she laughed, her pupils glittering like pearls, "and believe me, Mr. Luria, the Vietnamese, North and South, also don't understand why they killed each other with such cruelty. But it wasn't because I didn't understand that I returned to Israel, which is crazy in itself, but because my parents planned to marry me off to a relative. You tell me, Mr. Luria, why should an Israeli citizen like me get married in a poor and distant country to some dubious relative if I have many suitors here?"

Such a candid revelation prompted Luria to pry out more details about the house he was soon to enter. Before the grandparents could arrive and cut off conversation, he wanted to know who these many suitors were, and giddily jested that if he weren't an old grandpa on the verge of retirement, he might be tempted to join the crowd. The Vietnamese sabra half seriously bowed her head in thanks, but the boy in the wheelchair, running out of patience, interrupted their chat with a loud sigh. With her small, shapely foot the caregiver released the brake on the chair, but Luria grabbed a wheel: wait, one small question before parting. The young beauty wisely felt that the boy should not hear the question, or the answer, even if he understood none of it, and freed the chair from Luria and gave it a nudge, to encourage the boy to wheel himself, and as the chair inched forward, Luria quietly asked if she happened to know, or had herself heard, that Divon sometimes called his wife a "tragic woman." "Yes," answered the attendant, "that's what he calls her sometimes, even in front of strangers, but not in a mean way, only because that is how she has defined herself ever since she was forced, against her will, to give birth to this child, her third."

"Forced?"

"That's what she told me, more than once."

"But who forced her?" Luria is alarmed. "And why?"

"That," she said impatiently, "is something that you, Mr. Luria, need to find out for yourself. As I told you, the door is open and you are welcome to enter, and even if she's still in bed, don't give up, she really is waiting for you."

THE CHAOTIC HOUSE

He rings the doorbell repeatedly, even though the door is unlocked, hoping the ringing will free him of the duty to rouse a strange woman from her bed. But no human sound responds to the bell. So he must push open the heavy door and enter the house, whose chaos exceeds all expectation. Pieces of furniture, evicted from their regular places, huddle in the center of a large living room, presumably to expose walls that need plastering. In a corner, a stack of cartons full of books and other items, apparently destined for the trash. A pile of obsolete Israeli road maps sits on an armchair, as if hoping Luria will return them to the archive. The new tenants seem impatient: some of their belongings, stashed in a corner, have moved in before them. Divon left Israel in a big hurry, so as not to lose the cushy job in Kenya, and took his two healthy sons with him to begin the new school year, so the long-term rental of this house was placed in the hands of a woman saddled with a sickly child born against her will.

But where is she now? This is an old, spacious house in the country, apparently enlarged several times, and quite dark, because stacked cartons are blocking the windows. Yes, Luria could shout her first name, to wake her and ask her to come out, but wouldn't it be ridiculous to stand amid this chaos and call out the first name of a woman he had avoided meeting till now? That morning, his wife was surprised and even resentful to learn that he wanted to deliver the envelope in person, yet now, on the eve of his retirement, he yearns to know more about the private life of a talented coworker who evaded the job Luria intended for him. And in fact, he's not sorry he came.

But when he enters a huge kitchen, the disarray disappears and a painful barrenness prevails. The cupboards, their doors open, have been emptied of all cookware and dishes, and only a carton of milk remains in the open, dark refrigerator. This means they will be leaving soon. He goes into a corridor leading to the living quarters, passes two vacant rooms, possibly of the two older boys, and the doorway of the youngest son, where a spare wheelchair stands by an unmade bed, and continues down another corridor, which brings him back to chaos, a dark bedroom, a heap of blankets and clothes. Three suitcases lie open, and, curled up in the big bed, a woman.

Did she really not hear the doorbell or his footsteps, or did she pretend to be asleep as he entered the room? Because the hour of his visit was agreed upon in advance, this was probably a performance intended to prove the extent of the "tragedy" she attaches to herself. Luria is no random messenger who would address her as "Mrs." or "Madam," yet it seems too intimate to call her by her first name, which he learned only two days before, and since he has no idea where the light switch is, he decides, as someone on the verge of retirement, to gently touch the warm blanket and say, "I'm sorry, but the caregiver asked that I hand this envelope to you personally."

From her quick awakening and easy smile, it seems very likely that she indeed heard his ringing and footsteps, and not only stayed cozily in bed, but neglects even now to turn on a light, merely extending a long white hand to receive the envelope and place it on the pillow beside her, where her husband's head should be, and in a hoarse, dreamy voice she says, "Thank you, Zvi Luria, but explain to me what's so special about these old plans that he's making you crazy over them too."

It is odd for Luria to converse with a complete stranger who defies her husband from her bed in the dark. Yet he leans a little forward and tells her about the old request to build a bypass road to ensure the serenity of a small settlement, and says that although the plan was scrapped long ago, maybe it can spark her husband's imagination for an African project. A spark? Yet another spark? Divon's wife sighs with despair. Of course, she knows her man well, always looking for sparks, usually in his former projects, this house is filled with such old plans. "But tell me," she says slyly, "are they planning to build settlements in Africa too?" "I hope not," Luria smiles, and begins to wonder with mild anxiety whether she intends to get out of bed, or even can, or if by staying there she is telling him to say goodbye and leave. But instead she commands him with womanly authority to clear her clothes off the armchair so he can sit down and not stand over her. "Spark or no spark," she sneers, "thank you anyway, Zvi Luria, for not sending a messenger, but coming yourself, this way I finally get to meet the man Tzahi cannot stop praising, not only for his superb professionalism but also his patience and generosity. And although you are famously afraid of mixing personal matters and professional relationships, now that Tzahi has left Israel Roads for good, and you are about to retire, why don't you let yourself sit a few minutes with me, since most likely we'll never meet again."

Apparently her "tragic" self-image has inflated her self-confidence. He studies her in the dark bedroom, trying to decipher her face, a cold, hard mask crowned by wild, dry hair. With a quiver of sudden compassion, he indulges her, but only, he warns her, for a few minutes, because the caregiver told him about the sleepless night, and cautiously carves himself a small space among the clothes flung on the armchair, while she, at the same time, takes the envelope from her husband's pillow and stuffs it under her own, lifting her eyes toward the guest who faces her.

"I gather," she says, "that our caregiver managed to brief you before you came in."

"Yes, she was very sweet."

"I wouldn't call her sweet," she sniffs. "She can attract men with her good looks, but she won't go far in life because she doesn't want to study, she just wants a husband who will study for her."

"But I think your son is very attached to her," persists Luria, in defense of the Vietnamese sabra.

"No, you're wrong, the boy isn't attached to anyone, maybe a little to Grandpa and Grandma, and now his heartless father wants to cut him off from them too."

Luria nods his head in a show of empathy and concern. He is startled, a man wary of personal relations with coworkers, thrust into intimate dialogue with a close colleague's wife, who lies on a bed before him in a dark, disheveled room, her naked white shoulders softly gleaming at the blanket's edge.

"Still," he says, defending the boy, "to me he seems connected to the world. I saw his face, as pure as the face of an angel, maybe a tormented angel staring into the distance, but an angel nonetheless."

"You're wrong, he's no angel, and not at all tormented, he is so unaware of his condition that I sometimes suspect he enjoys his disability. No, Zvi—may I call you by your first name?—it's not the child who is tormented, only I, his mother, because even before he was born I had a sense of impending doom. I didn't want to have him. Given my age and living situation I was content with two healthy, talented sons, and I wanted to end the pregnancy. But your friend, who worked with you for many years, insisted on another child, because he dreamed of a cute little girl, but instead we were stuck with tragedy. I made a mistake. I didn't fight hard enough to stand up for myself."

His wife was right, muses Luria, archived plans should be sent with an office messenger and not a senior engineer about to retire. He needs to cut this short. To smooth his exit, he takes on a warm, fatherly tone: "Don't get up, no need, and don't worry, I'll tell Tzahi that you have the old plans in hand, and you go back to sleep so you'll be strong enough to control the chaos around you."

But she objects to a hasty goodbye. "No, wait, don't go, I have to give you something to eat, but would you believe the refrigerator is empty?" "I would," he laughs, "I already saw there's nothing in it, no problem, go back to sleep." She wriggles in her bed. "If not food, maybe a gift, something nice. Tzahi said you needed to find out, after all the years you worked together, what our address is and what my name is." "Yes," he shrugs, "that's how it goes." "In which case," she purrs, "since you had no choice but to come here and learn my name, I now have the right to escort you to the door, and maybe give you a little something for your trouble."

She throws off the blanket and gets up and stands there naked, shining in the darkness, more shapely than his wife and younger, radiating heat. Flustered, he bows his head. Can this really be how she seeks revenge on her husband, who forced her to bear a child she didn't want, or is she naïvely incapable of imagining the powerful lust of a man on the verge of retirement? Despite his embarrassment he stares at her, trying to appear indifferent. She pleads with him: "If I can't feed you, at least take a souvenir for yourself or for your wife, I'm throwing out so many things." He remains calm: "No, no, I don't need a souvenir, I just need to know you'll take care of yourself till you return safely to the one who is waiting for you." She rips the sheet from her bed and covers her nakedness, and like a barefoot mummy she leads him through the messy house to the front door. And he is careful not to touch her with even a finger, merely making a deep bow of farewell, in the manner he had just learned from her son's caregiver, and, to assure her that he'll remember her name, he says it once and says it again.

THE FORMER OFFICE

He is drawn to the strip of light that seeps from his old doorway, and now, all at once, the atrophy presents him with the woman's first name, the same plain and simple name he was given before he went to her on a mission from her husband. So he's got her name, but warns himself: even if her old "tragedy" has dissolved in Kenya into annoying idiosyncrasy, it's still dangerous in his atrophied condition to rub shoulders with her again. Only recently, as his memory burrowed into that country house where he was led from chaos to emptiness by a barefoot mummy, has it occurred to him that maybe then, on that cloudy morning, the seed of atrophy took root in his brain.

But now, despite the pounding rain, why pass up a chance to peek into his old office, if only to know if someone forgot to turn off the light, or whether at this late hour an industrious worker is poring over maps. To his surprise the door opens with a mere touch, and a young man sits behind his old desk, a huge computer screen illuminating his handsome face and stubble beard. A quick glance tells the former occupant that not much has changed in the office. Even the photo of Israel's second president, from the 1950s, Yitzhak Ben-Zvi, still hangs on the wall.

"Zvi Luria?" The young man sits up, astonished. "To what do I owe this honor?"

"It's not intentional, not at all," says Luria, delighted to be recognized. "I was asked to say a few words at an old friend's retirement party, and I couldn't resist taking a peek at the place where I spent many good and productive years. Lucky for me, the door opened so easily, and at my desk sits a nice young man who even knows who I am. The only question is, can I identify him too?"

"Him, no, but his father, yes." The young man grins. "Namely, the legal adviser who worked with you for many years."

"Maimoni? You're the son of Yosef?"

"Yohanan."

"Of course, Yohanan, Yohanan Maimoni. But before you explain what you're doing at night in my old office, tell me how your father is."

"My father is ill, Mr. Luria, in and out of hospitals. But I'm sure he already told you himself, because his illness is his whole life now."

"Told me? When? I haven't heard a thing."

"But just a few weeks ago you met in the street, and it can't be that he didn't tell you, the illness scares him so much. Is it possible you simply didn't recognize him?"

"Maimoni? How could that be?"

"For some reason he thought—he complained—that you really didn't know who he was."

"Impossible."

"Maybe because of the illness?"

"Whose illness?" Luria is taken aback.

"Abba lost a lot of weight, his hair fell out . . ."

"Even so, I couldn't possibly not recognize him. For years his office was here on the seventh floor, and sometimes he would come with us on our surveys, to see for himself the fields and homes we asked him to expropriate for the good of the State."

"Yes," says the young man, "he liked those trips very much, to get away from the paperwork and go out in the field to confront people who may have been difficult but were at least real. Do you remember, Mr. Luria, that I as a boy sometimes went with you?"

"You? How come?"

"Because after my mother left Abba and me, he would sometimes take me along, so I wouldn't hang out in the streets."

"Maimoni's wife left him? Strange, he never even hinted that to me."

"Because Abba knew, like everyone else, that you really didn't want to know about the personal lives of the people who worked for you."

"Or the people I worked for," Luria is quick to add, "because only that way, as the director of the division, could I avoid getting entangled in problems I couldn't influence or control."

"But now," says the son, "when neither of us works for the other, am I getting you in trouble by telling you that Abba is extremely ill?"

"No. Now, as a free man devoid of control or authority, I take an interest in what's going on with friends I worked with for years, so by all means, tell me how to find your father."

"The best way to find him is at the hospital. He will soon be readmitted for a long stay, and if someone he respected and loved in the past would sit by his bed in the present, even for a short time, it would cheer him up."

"Good, let's do that, please don't forget me."

"Forget you? It's impossible to forget you. This room is filled with certificates of appreciation from localities where you built and expanded roads, also from the electric company, the traffic police. At the Society for the Protection of Nature they remember you fondly and every year send you a calendar with a photo of a pretty nature lover. No, how could anyone forget you when the president who was in office in your day is still hanging on the wall."

"Now you are mistaken, young man. President Ben-Zvi was no longer alive when I moved into this room, but because I knew he had lost a son in war, and was also an honest and humble man, whose presidential home in Jerusalem was merely an expansion of his simple bungalow, I left this picture as a role model for me, mainly as a warning against the creeping corruption I sensed all around me."

"And I, too, following in your footsteps, have left him on the wall and not replaced him with any other president, mainly because I learned that when he was young, in the early days of Zionism, he and his good friend Ben-Gurion regarded the Arab farmers and Bedouins as descendants of Jews who stayed loyal to this land, even if they were forced over the generations to convert to another religion."

Luria chuckles. "I never heard that one, but I remember that your father was also fond of such strange and implausible stories."

"Maybe strange and implausible, but at least they provide hope."

"Hope for what?"

"If all those around us are merely Jews whose identity was forgotten, then we, with no effort required, are a solid majority in this scrambled country."

Luria looks hard at the young man to be sure he's not mocking him, and as he studies the handsome face he has a flash of recognition that the ragged figure who stopped him in the street a few weeks ago, and expected to be greeted warmly, was not, as he'd thought, a forgotten project manager or old steamroller driver, but his legal adviser, whom he couldn't place, regardless of all their years together.

Despite the rain pelting the windows, urging him to hurry and find a pensioner to take him back to his wife, he tries to make up for the insult to the father by reaching out in friendship to the son, who unlike his father is not a lawyer but an energetic road engineer, newly assigned to plan a secret road for military use.

"Secret road? Such things exist?"

"At this early stage, yes."

"Where? I know the road system in the North by heart, you can't hide any road there."

But it's not in the North, but the South—the far South. The young engineer invites the pensioner to look at the Ramon Crater and environs on his computer screen, the expanse between Route 40 and Route 171, in a desert with no trace of settlement, no ranches or outposts, just desolate hills and craters and barren wadis, bearing ancient names—Saharonim and Harerim, Ardon and Harut, Nekarot and Mahmal, Mish'hor and Ra'af and Geled. Dirt roads and dry riverbeds snake through the simulated terrain, and among them, like an uninvited guest, is a short, orphaned stretch of paved road dating from the British Mandate, with no destination. The only sign of life in the glaring white landscape is the tiny icon of a traveler briskly hiking on a winding stretch of the Israel National Trail. And as the elderly engineer wonders where and whither the secret road might lead, the young man steers the cursor, which wobbles like a drugged mosquito, stops in the middle of nowhere, and emits from its tail a strong, thick blue line, a possible route for the future road.

Never in his life has Luria seen so barren a map, but the young man, more intense than his father, seems agitated over the assigned project.

"I haven't been down in the Negev for years," admits Luria, "and it never appealed to me professionally. Also your father had nothing to expropriate there, it all belonged to the State anyhow."

"That needs to be checked out," mutters the young man to himself. Gripping the mouse in his fist, he plays around with the map, widening and narrowing the desert as he wishes.

Luria finally tires of computer tricks, and before taking leave of his old office, he asks the new tenant for his first name.

"Asael." Maimoni smiles. "Made by God."

Luria is pleased. This name won't be easy for his mind to

swallow up. And he reminds Asael that when his father goes back in the hospital, please not to forget to let him know.

But when he returns downstairs to find a friend or acquaintance to take him back to his wife, he is met with deep silence, as if he had slept for seventy years since the day he escaped from the woman who demanded he say her name. Darkness in the hall, the movie screen rolled up, plates and bowls cleared, tablecloths removed, chairs stacked at the side, and not a crumb left of all the marvelous dishes. Even the front door is locked, the security guard gone. But the pensioner still remembers the exit to the parking lot, which is empty except for a solitary car, crouched in the evening fog like a strange gray animal. Does the dementia chew up not only first names but also the sands of time? He is wary of phoning his wife to come pick him up. She's a careful driver, but needs him to navigate, and in the fog and rain she's likely to get lost. Anyway, it's surprising she hasn't called. Is she that indifferent to his condition? Or is it a comfort to be free of him for a while? He now understands that barring her attendance was a mistake. Not only did being alone at the party not lead to any offers of projects, but had she been present, the mummy would not have dared to demand that he speak her name.

Yes, lust that he shoved aside: he seizes the fervid memory while rushing to the elevator to return him to his old office. Without knocking, he enters in a tizzy, and remembering the proper name, he says, "Listen, Asael, I ran into trouble, can you get me out of here?" And the young engineer, who had left his desk, removed his shoes, and begun to doze off in the discarded armchair Luria had found near the town hall of Hurfeish, throws off his blanket and stands at attention like a soldier. "Get you out, Mr. Luria, of course. Where to?"

AN UNPAID ASSISTANT

The rain has tapered off, and the cloudless moon darts among the exits and intersections, and Luria is glad he didn't summon his wife. He sits, relaxed and comfortable, in a big, old, and quiet American car, much like the one that served him well in the past, enjoying the ride as the young engineer, a smart and nimble driver, takes him to his red car and to his waiting wife and daughter, as well as a little boy eager to kiss Grandpa good night.

"Guess who rescued me from the party that suddenly ended without my noticing," he says to his wife as he hugs and kisses his half-sleeping grandchild, sniffing his unmistakable scent. Dina smiles at the rescuer, who instead of a mere wave, turns off his car and gets out to shake hands. "If you remember Yaakov Maimoni, this is his son, Asael, but the son isn't a lawyer, he is a road engineer I found working at night in my old office, planning a secret road for the army near the Ramon Crater."

"Yohanan Maimoni," Dina corrects him and cordially extends her hand to the handsome young man, asking why he hadn't also driven his father from the party.

"My father is ill, Dr. Luria, he can't go to parties."

"Ill? What is ailing him?"

"Cancer," says the son, simply stating the ineffable name.

"What kind of cancer?" she persists.

"Pancreatic."

"Ah," she sighs. "I imagine his doctors are gently hinting that he give up hope."

"Exactly," replies the son, who is obviously close to his father. "But Abba insists on fighting, as always."

"He must," says the pediatrician, backing the battle of a sick old man. "There's sometimes a bit of hope even with pancreatic cancer, and please tell your father I said so."

"Of course, I will. Abba always spoke highly of you, though he didn't dare approach you."

"Approach her?" asks Luria, but the young man keeps talking to his wife:

"For example, after my mother left us, I broke out in a rash and the itching made me crazy, and Abba, who knew you were a senior pediatrician, wanted to ask your opinion, but it was well known at the office that your husband disapproved of mixing personal matters and work."

"Yes, I was well aware of that," scowls Luria's wife, "and I must tell you, Zvi went overboard with that separation."

"Overboard?" Luria protests. The sleeping child grows heavier in his arms. "What if you made a wrong diagnosis, or prescribed a harmful medicine, why should a road engineer like me take responsibility, even indirectly, in matters he knows nothing about."

"Nobody is asking you to take responsibility for diagnosis or medications," his wife chides him. "Your caution and fears sometimes made you deaf to the troubles of other people."

Energized, she turns back to the young man: "Wait, before you go—a secret road? Is that possible?"

"It's in the desert."

"Ah, in the desert, I see." She continues to investigate, as she does with her patients, probing and prodding: "It's because it's a secret that you're working at night?"

Maimoni laughs. "No, it's because I have too much to do."

"You're planning this secret road by yourself?"

Luria wants to end the conversation, but the grandson in his arms has rested his heavy head on Grandpa's heart, in search of a lost pillow.

"For now, by myself."

"You wouldn't want someone to help you?"

"Help me? How?"

"Very simple: another certified engineer, to work by your side on your road."

"Who wouldn't want an assistant?" says the young man. "But only on condition that somebody else pays him."

Now she shoots a smile at her husband: "I mean someone who doesn't ask or need to be paid, someone who only wants to help."

"Is there such a person?"

"Here he is," she says, gesturing grandly at her husband, "a senior engineer, the former head of his division, ready and able to take on any new project, a road, an interchange, a bridge, a tunnel, whatever, secret or not secret, in the desert or not in the desert, to help with maps, diagrams, budgets, even going out in the field if necessary. An unpaid assistant, but with tremendous experience. How can you turn down such an offer?"

Maimoni turns wide-eyed toward Luria, who avoids his look and very carefully returns the sleeping child to its mother. Once he is sure that the handover has gone smoothly, he smiles at his future employer, a handsome young man with a mysterious beard.

"You?" whispers Maimoni with amazement.

"Yes," says the pensioner softly. "But part-time. No pay, only part-time."

WHAT DID YOU EAT AT THE PARTY?

He adjusts the driver's seat, buckles himself in, and without waiting for his wife to finish her goodbyes to her daughter and grandson, he enters the digits of the security code and presses the ignition, to no avail. He tries again, but the car takes offense at the repeated mistake and indicator lights flash their protest. He turns on the overhead light to see the numbers better and tries again, slowly, in the familiar sequence, but ignition still eludes him. His wife, who has meanwhile sat beside him and buckled up, watches with concern. "Don't say a word," he warns her, "I have to figure it out myself." The rebellious dashboard not only flashes now, it beeps angrily. "I hope you didn't switch the code on me while I was at the party." He laughs sourly, and even as his wife is astounded by the absurd accusation, the vehicle responds suddenly to his random stabs at the keypad, with a rumble of the engine and the faint murmur of the Japanese manufacturer's girl.

He drives with self-assurance, encouraged by the smile of a beloved woman. An evening with her grandson has infused her with the true meaning of life. Before saying a word about the military road, someplace in the desert, that might conceivably help her husband's spirit overcome his weakened brain, she asks him to describe the food at the party. "Why is that important?" He tries to dismiss the question, but she persists, if only to test his memory. And besides, since he preferred that she not join him, he should at least allow her imagination to share his pleasure. But the pleasure was minimal, Luria insists: he was so worked up about the speech, he made do with just the hors d'oeuvres, which were wonderfully textured but minuscule in size.

"Why so worked up? You knew from the start that you couldn't avoid the duty of saying a few words. You even made sure to write his first name on your hand."

"I still hoped to get out of it. But as I walked in, the new director general came over to inform me that Divon had insisted I speak. It was important for him that despite my anger and disappointment, I praise his accomplishments over our many years of partnership. And from the minute I knew he wouldn't take no for an answer, I focused on one thought, how to navigate honestly between praise and disappointment."

"And that's why you only ate hors d'oeuvres and didn't touch the main courses."

"Dishes that looked fabulous, to judge by the mobs of people around them."

"So at least tell me about the desserts, which I'm sure came after your speech."

"Wait, you don't want to hear about the speech?"

"Yes, but first the desserts."

"Elaborate desserts. They were decorated with sparklers. They even turned off the lights."

"But what were they? Try harder. Working on your memory is important."

"I didn't touch them."

"Why?"

"I don't know, I passed. They were also served before my speech, and more came during the speech, which I delivered in semi-darkness. You don't want to know what I said?"

"And after the speech there were no desserts left?"

"Maybe there were, but then Divon's wife began harassing me because in my speech I called her Mrs. Divon, not by her first name."

"You didn't remember her name is Rachel?"

"Yes, Rachel, how did you know? That's odd, you never met her. Apparently your memory steals names from mine."

"So protect it better," she jokes. "Bottom line, we sent you to a fancy party and you came home hungry."

"Not to worry, the hors d'oeuvres were enough for me."

"You said they were tiny."

"But wonderful, and I gobbled seven or eight of them in one fell swoop. And also two shakshukas."

"What? Shakshukas?" she nearly shrieks. "I don't believe it . . ."

"Believe it, why don't you believe it," he laughs, "shakshukas in tiny dishes, with a cute little sun in the middle, apparently a quail egg."

"Now you're scaring me."

"Why?"

"To pass up wonderful food for two little shakshukas!"

"What can I do, my love, my mind seems to be drawn now to things that resemble what's inside it."

"Don't talk like that, don't talk like that, don't talk like that."

"Why not? You saw yourself that I punched in the wrong ignition code three times. And still you want to send me to the desert. And there, if I forget the code, I'll die of dehydration."

"Nobody is sending you to the desert, and definitely not in this car. And I'll never let you go there alone. I also forget the car code sometimes, and if you keep forgetting it, write it down on a slip of paper."

"A slip of paper?" he says with disdain. "If I forget the code, I'll also forget where I put a slip of paper."

"So write it on your palm, like—"

"It won't last on my palm."

"So tattoo it."

"Tattoo it?"

"Why not? It's just four digits, and you love to drive, and won't have to give it up."

"Not that, and not giving up on you either, but for the time being you are easier, because the code of desire is in the spirit and not the brain."

They're in the parking lot, the hour is late. In the elevator she finally takes an interest in his speech, but he hugs and kisses her and says, "Drop it, I don't remember it. As I expected, when I saw his youngest son in the wheelchair, all my anger and disappointment melted into praise and compliments."

THE CODE OF DESIRE

As she reaches to switch on the hall light, he blocks her path. No, he won't let the light dampen the desire that he owes to himself and his neurologist. If with her quick intelligence she has found him a project in the desert to stimulate his mind, why not spice the project with dormant lust? He pulls his wife close and hugs her gently, and by the rainy light of distant high-rises and cranes, he slides her hair aside and kisses the nape of her neck in a spot where a man's kiss may still be considered merely friendly.

She's in no hurry to push him away, and leans her head so his warm lips can brush her shoulders too, and only when it seems that he hopes to satisfy his hunger, she delicately attempts to get free of his grip. "I'm sorry," she whispers, "I'm wiped out, and it's late, and I haven't even managed to shower today." But from many years of marital experience he knows that if she goes to shower first, and lingers as usual in the gushing water, she'll emerge so cocooned in cleanliness that it will be impossible to try to touch her. He therefore refuses to let her escape, and as one hand holds her tight, the other quickly peels off the raincoat lent her by their daughter and deftly unbuttons her jacket and blouse in the dark.

"No, darling, no, my love," she whispers, struggling to rebutton, "not now, it won't work, better tomorrow, I promise."

Luria is not fighting for personal desire but for medical desire, which the neurologist prescribed for them both. And with unaccustomed insistence he doesn't let go of her, and still standing in the living room, he surprises himself and exposes her breasts, which appear more wondrous and pristine than by the light of day, and to lessen the shock of their sudden nudity, he leans over to calm them with the tip of his tongue and says: "Tomorrow? Who knows if tomorrow I'll even remember who you are." And sighs.

Instead of dismissing his devious words, she drops her resistance and freezes, as if the sigh had validated the absurd remark. And as in the early days, forty years ago, when she was still a third-year medical student, now too, despite all their years of love, he is afraid of doing something that might hurt or startle her. In those days, when she would sometimes arrive directly from the pathology lab after dealing with cadavers that had been left to science, he would interpret her reluctance not as rejection of his spirit but fear of his body, and would try to tame his passion before each sexual encounter. But today, now that the body has learned how to express and fulfill its longings, he knows it's not the body that gives her pause, but the brain, and with well-chosen words, rational and realistic, couched in longstanding love, he pulls her carefully into the bedroom, and to assure her that medical lust will be no more aggressive than ordinary lust, he carefully removes her clothes and turns on her little bedside lamp, so that darkness does not mask his sincerity. And his wife, who at her age has retained her alluring shape, lies naked before him, and it seems that his hopes will be fulfilled more quickly and easily than expected, but he has yet to muster sufficient passion, and in despair, to vanquish his sudden incapacity, he hurries back to the party that he left hungry, and to the mummy who demanded he give her back her name, and as his hands and kisses gratify his wife's body, he also walks amid chaos and emptiness in the rooms of an abandoned country home, and a naked woman leaps at him from her bed, and her limbs glow in the dark, and he combines the lust that was nipped in the bud with the passion ignited now with soaring sighs and the cry that delights his heart. And as he reaches his own climax he is thinking, On top of it all I am an obedient patient, and he turns out the light and covers his wife and cuddles up for a long night of sleep.

An hour later, he is awakened by the light. And by his side is his wife, clean and fragrant, holding a novel she has been reading very slowly for weeks.

"Why torture yourself with a boring novel?"

"Sometimes boredom is worthwhile."

"I wonder what'll happen when I can no longer read."

"I'll read to you."

"And if I don't understand what you're reading?"

"I'll explain."

"And if I don't understand what you explain?"

"Then we'll make love, because that you always understand."

He feels for her hand under the covers, takes it and plants a kiss on it, and she strokes his head and says, "And regarding the desert, don't worry, I'll never let you go there alone."

"Nonsense. There's no way that young man will need me. Why does he need someone senior hovering over him? I myself would hesitate to take on an assistant like that. He has a computer program to do the job, he doesn't need me."

"But you could expedite matters. Your signature on his map would spare him a debate at the first meeting of the planning committee."

"What? How do you know about the first planning meeting?"

"From you, only from you. I always listen to you, so I'm a great authority on the subject of you."

TWO CHILDREN

On Tuesday afternoon, when Luria arrives as usual to pick up his grandson from kindergarten, the teacher says to him: "Today, grandpa of Noam, take two children with you and not one."

"What's going on? It's not bad enough I got in trouble here two weeks ago, you want to mess me up some more?"

"No, this time without any trouble, the opposite, with thanks. Perhaps you remember the boy you took by mistake two weeks ago?"

"Who basically latched onto me."

"That's possible."

"Nevo."

"Right. You even remember his name."

"Because I have a special corner in my mind for strange names."

"Nice. So Nevo's mother asked that today you take him with Noam to your house, and in an hour, two hours max, she'll come pick him up. She arranged this with Avigail, who gave her your address."

"But why me?"

"Because Nevo and Noam are good friends and play nicely together. I think they had sleepovers a couple of times at each other's house."

"And what about the Filipino woman who ran after me screaming?"

"She's at the Interior Ministry now, arguing about her visa, and Nevo's mother has a rehearsal."

"Rehearsal of what?"

"Orchestra rehearsal."

"In which case, Nevo will need to eat lunch at my house."

"Definitely. But without meat."

"Why?"

"Because he is a vegetarian."

"What are you saying, so little and already a vegetarian?"

"Today, the new generation is tough," explains the kindergarten teacher, "you have to get used to it. Even little ones have principles that must be respected."

"He also has principles against an egg?"

"Egg? No problem."

"So maybe I'll give him a nice shakshuka. What do you think?"

"Ask him. He's a smart, easygoing kid."

Meanwhile, the teacher's aide has brought over the two boys, spruced and combed, colorful baseball caps on their heads and little knapsacks on their backs.

"Hold hands," orders the teacher, "and go quietly and politely with Noam's grandpa."

So, thinks Luria, two weeks ago they suspected me of kidnapping, now they blithely hand over two little boys. He affectionately watches the two friends, still holding hands as they enter the elevator.

After he removes their backpacks and insists they wash hands and faces, he seats them at the kitchen table and announces: "Children, welcome to the Luria Restaurant. May I take your order?" He is happy to discover that the little guest not only knows what shakshuka is, but is willing to taste it. While he reheats the shakshuka, he brings the boys paper and pencils and urges them to draw. And when the shakshuka is ready, and Nevo eats it slowly and warily, Luria gets a good look at the boy who had misled him two weeks before. Could it be that this kid clung to him because he just wanted to avoid his Filipino nanny?

"What's the name of the lady who picks you up from *gan*?"

"Yolanda."

"And you like her?"

The child drops his fork and looks around anxiously, expecting a trap. Rather than lie, he keeps silent. But Luria insists. He grows more certain by the minute that he wasn't mistakenly drawn to this child by chance. Something in his face, those dimples, reminds him of someone who fascinated him long ago. "What's your father's name?" he asks quietly.

The child freezes.

"Sabba," Noam jumps in, "Nevo has no father." So Grandpa doesn't get himself in trouble, Noam pulls him aside and whispers: "Nevo is a single-parent boy."

But the single-parent boy overhears the whisper and winces in pain, his eyes glistening with tears of humiliation. "Not right, not right," he insists, defying the slander. "I'm not single-parent, I have a father."

"So where is he, your father?" challenges Noam, with a mean, ugly grin that shocks his grandpa. The unanswerable question is met by the cry of a wounded animal, and the fork flies in the air, the shakshuka spills all over the table, and the boy, as if pushed, suddenly falls, pounding the floor with his fists: "Not right, not right, I have an abba."

Luria clamps his hand on his grandson's mouth to prevent further provocation, kneels down, and tries to lift the little guest from the floor. The child resists, seizing the table leg with both hands, then for some reason abruptly lets go, thrusts his two skinny arms at the old man, grabs him tightly by the neck, and buries his shame in the chest of the man who once took him for his grandson. Luria will remedy the humiliation no matter what. Yes, he scolds Noam, he is right and you are wrong, he has a father. He gets carried away: "Yes, he has a father, I know it, I even know him. Except that his father traveled to a faraway country, but I'm sure that he'll come back."

Cautiously, slowly, Nevo lifts up his head to look at the old man who found him a father. His thin shoulders tremble but his big teary eyes shine with hope. "Yes," Luria continues, uplifting the boy's status for his astonished, embarrassed grandson, "yes, my dear Noam, your friend has a father, just as you do, only maybe he went all the way to Africa, and in a few years he'll come back."

He carefully sets the boy in his chair, turns over the plate, gathers a few scraps of the shakshuka smeared on the table, and tries to locate the fork flung in the air. Noam regrets his nastiness and says, by way of reconciliation, "Nevo has a harp in his house."

"A harp?"

"A real one."

Nevo, who has found the fork, confirms that Noam is right this time. He has a big harp in his house, with forty-seven blue and red strings.

"And who plays it?"

"Imma, only Imma," says Nevo, "but she has another harp at the orchestra."

Now that a father, as yet anonymous, has been found for him, Luria feels free to ask the harpist's name.

"Noga," both kids shout at once.

"A beautiful name," says Luria, "the Hebrew name of planet Venus in the sky."

"Like Ma'adim and Shabbetai," adds Noam.

"Yes, Mars and Saturn," the grandfather confirms. And before you go watch television, and I go for a little nap in the bedroom, finish up the shakshuka, Nevo, so your mother Noga won't be mad at me for not feeding you."

"Imma won't be mad at you," declares the child, by now back to normal, "because Imma wants me to eat only what I like."

The man of the house has no choice but to clear the table and dump the leftovers, and make his two guests wash their hands again and sit close to the television, because the volume must be kept down. All agree on a children's channel that specializes in puppet monsters, and after they promise to wake him when Nevo's mom arrives, he takes the luxury of disconnecting the telephone.

But before he dozes off, he wonders if he was too quick to

affirm the existence of a father who never was. Nevertheless, he rationalizes, if the boy himself insisted he is not single-parented, maybe he knows something others don't. As the host of an unfamiliar child, he is obligated not only to feed, but to calm and console. Lively laughter drifts from the living room to the bedroom, as the boys enjoy the pranks of adorable monsters. If so, the promised father is already doing a good job. Darkness descends on him slowly. Is the dementia dozing along with him, or is it sneaking into his sleep to scramble his dreams? Here he is, walking on sunlit soil, clearly not in Israel, perhaps an African country, where a road is being paved. Are the workers African, or is the tar they pour turning them black? The ancient green steamroller, the big, dumb old steamroller from a children's song, moves back and forth to smooth the road, but who's that driver in the wide colonial hat that hides his face? Isn't that Divon, who declined to head a division at Israel Roads in favor of driving an antique steamroller in Africa? No, no, this is someone else, with a hard, sad face, and Luria, fearful of dementia, recognizes the father he himself had sent to a faraway land. I promised your son you would come back, screams the dreamer bitterly, but the driver just speeds up the noisy steamroller, while the two boys shake Luria hard. Sabba, Sabba, shouts Noam. Sabba, yells Nevo, who by virtue of the father he got from Luria over lunch considers himself a new grandson. Get up, Sabba, Imma's here, she's here.

And in the fog of his dream, in the rectangle of light from the living room that fills the bedroom doorway, stands the image of his wife, though much younger, in a pair of high heels not worn in years, and the ponytail she chopped down over time. With the same bright, happy smile in her eyes, but of a different color. Yes, now he understands why her son captured his heart at the kindergarten. I asked, she apologizes softly, that they let you rest, but they both insisted you wanted us to wake you. Luria casts off his light blanket and sits up with a pang of guilt, facing the wondrous figure who appeared at his bedroom door. Yes, he says, a mischievous glint in his eye, I wanted to be woken up so I could be sure that you would take the right child. And yes, her sparkling laughter is just like his wife's. Has the dementia blended the two women, or are they actually similar?

"Don't be upset about what happened two weeks ago," Noga reassures the old man, "it's not the first time Nevo tried to cling to a stranger, especially if he's like you, I mean, a bit on the older side. My father died before I even thought I wanted to be a mother, and a grandpa from the other side is only theoretical. So he's a child in search of not only a father but a grandfather too."

Luria quickly changes the subject, lest the child mention the father newly discovered over the shakshuka. "Yes," he mumbles, "I understand, I liked it that he tagged along with me. But tell me, what's with the vegetarian thing? Does it come from you?"

"The vegetarian thing?" She appreciates the change of subject. "I have no idea how he got into it. He's not a child who's attracted to animals, the opposite, he's frightened of them."

"So maybe, who knows," says Luria, offering a new hypothesis, "maybe he imagines the animals will take revenge if he eats them."

"Take revenge?" She recoils from the sleepy pensioner's wild speculation and sends her son to fetch his cap and backpack. But Luria refuses to part from his wife's youthful self.

"Wait, one more little question, if I may. I never came across Nevo as a first name, only a family name."

"Yes, it's rare as a first name, but since I had him without a partner, I had a monopoly on picking a name."

"You were thinking of the mountain?"

"Har Nevo?"

"Exactly."

"Do you know where it is?"

"In the Sinai Desert, no?"

"No, many make that mistake. Mount Nevo is in Jordan, a few kilometers east of Jericho. When he gets older, for his bar mitzvah, the two of us will go up to the top, where there is a little church, and look out at this land, to establish if this is the right land or if we made a mistake."

"Like Joshua," whispers Luria with admiration.

"Joshua?" says the harpist. "Why Joshua? It's Moses. I gave birth to this child at the very last moment I could, so he will need to look at the world independently when I'm no longer with him. Maybe the symbolism of his name will enable him to see from afar."

"To see from afar," merrily repeats Nevo, ready to travel, pack on his back and cap on his head.

INSOMNIA

Much to his surprise, the mother takes his grandson with her too, as requested by Avigail, who apparently still doubts her father's ability to control his dementia. True, he is now free to float back into his afternoon nap, but he knows that now that he's met the harpist, not only will the imaginary father soon pop up in his dream, but the harpist too, who will berate him. Thus it's best not to sleep, so he moves to the living room and sits in front of the television, which still airs the cuddly monsters tormenting one another. Since he has no way of knowing which ones are good and which are bad, the suspense of watching them subsides and he dozes off again, until a gentle hand strokes his hand and shuts off the TV.

"You sleep too much in the afternoon," scolds his wife, "so no wonder you suffer from insomnia at night."

"It's the reverse—because I can't sleep at night, I'm wasted during the day."

"You need to break that vicious circle. Besides, it's unhealthy for anyone, especially you, to fall asleep in front of a TV crawling with surrealistic characters."

"They're immoral, too."

"So try to stay awake till I get home from the clinic, and after we eat you can nap with me like any normal person."

"If that's the definition of a normal person—"

"Enough," she interrupts, "do what you want. But why did Avigail hurry to pick up Noam?"

"It wasn't Avigail who came to get him, it was the mother of the kid who had latched onto me two weeks ago, and today they gave him to me officially."

"So today you had two boys?"

"The second one was a vegetarian."

"Don't tell me you tried to feed him one of your shakshukas."

"Why should I tell you what you already know?"

Now she gets serious: "Don't be such a wise guy all the time. Speak, talk, tell me, not just what I don't know, also what I do know. Be careful, Zvi," she warns, "don't avoid the issue. I need to know and understand everything that happens to you before you fall into the abyss."

He turns pale, bites his lip, as though "abyss," a new word in this house, came out of his mouth and not hers. She also understands that she went too far, but her pride won't let her retract it, so she stands before him in anguished silence, and all he can do is hold her close to his chest, inhaling the smells of her pediatric clinic. "Yes, you're right, you are, there's no avoiding it. So you stay on guard and don't let go, because I have no one else by my side. And now you must admit that some dubious project in the desert doesn't need me."

"Wait . . . wait . . ."

"Wait for what? It's obvious that this handsome young man has guessed by now that there's something fishy about the old pensioner you offered him for free, because he's backing off from his promise to invite me to visit his father. Maybe he's afraid that a man on the verge of the abyss will only harm his father, who faces an abyss of his own."

"Don't be ridiculous, he'll call you. And don't get stuck on a word that's just a word. Wait."

"Okay, I stand and wait."

And as she watches her husband enjoy his stroll around the abyss that slipped from her lips, she shifts to the woman who picked up Noam along with her own son.

"Her son is called Nevo," says Luria.

"No, the woman, what's her name?"

"Something like Noa or Yona, a single mother, not so young. Avigail didn't mention her?"

"Never."

"She's a musician, she plays the harp. She seems like a strong person, reminds me a little of . . . never mind . . . I asked her the meaning of the odd name she stuck her son with, and if it's connected with the mountain in the Bible, and it turned out I was right, it is connected, and she intends, get this, before his bar mitzvah, to take the boy to his mountaintop, Har Nevo, in Jordan, not far from Jericho, to look out on this land like . . . Josh—"

"Moses—"

"Exactly, to see if the land where he lived until his bar mitzvah will also suit him after his bar mitzvah, or whether he should hurry up and move to Berlin."

"She told you all that?"

"Berlin is my little addendum. Anyway, what a presumptuous thought, to double-check this land from across the Jordan, from the beginning of time, as it were. So after she took Noam too, I panicked that she took him without asking, maybe to take him, too, up some mountain. But who knows what the truth is, because Avigail is in a meeting and her phone is turned off."

"Right."

"Then what?"

"Nothing. She wouldn't have taken Noam without coordinating with Avigail. So why worry?"

"I don't know. I felt a little like worrying . . ."

"So, what's her first name?"

"Noa or Yona, something like that. Seems like the strong type."

"A pretty woman?"

"Not really . . . maybe nice-looking . . . and a bit, just a bit, she reminds me of you when you were young."

"If she reminds you of me, what are you worried about?"

That evening, watching the news on the bedroom TV, she is half asleep as the broadcast nears its end. But because she is convinced she can follow the day's events while sleeping, and even analyze them in her dreams, she won't let him turn off the television, just lower the sound. So he waits for her to lose consciousness before turning off the set completely and drifting off slowly beside her. Awarding a father to his afternoon guest still bothers him. Sooner or later the little boy will demand that his mother produce the promised father, and when his daughter learns of this, it will further diminish her trust in him. Thinking of the reprimand that awaits him, he gets out of bed and continues to churn his obsession in the dark apartment. Should he defend himself with the help of his incipient dementia, or rely on the human kindness aroused in him by the suffering child? He pours himself a cognac to dull his distress. Beyond the glass door of his big balcony the city dims its lights. A thin crescent from the east flirts with a flock of stars in the clear, open sky. The rain was welcome, but it's good to have a respite. The stars provide Luria enough light to start the dishwasher. Also to switch on the computer, to check his paltry crop of emails. Before leaving the screen, he prowls the internet for landscapes and animals of Uganda, where Divon toured with his family. Why did he have to burden Nevo's mother with a man she didn't need? For a moment he thinks he ought to call her and explain his foolish act of kindness before the boy demands what she can't give him. But he doesn't know her family name, and what's her first name again? If he asks Avigail, he'll have to explain why. He goes back to bed and tries to fall asleep, unsuccessfully. So take a pill, mumbles Dina in her sleep, it will help relax you. He gets up and swallows the pill, certified as kosher by the neurologist, and lies immobile in bed, paving the way for the drug to do its work, but the distress of the imaginary father only gets stronger and won't let go.

It's past midnight now. No big deal, as a pensioner he can handle two sleepless nights. He wraps himself in a blanket and goes out on the balcony to enjoy the stars. The neurologist did mention the possibility that the difference between day and night would get fuzzy as the dementia progressed, but that's a problem for those who still work and not for demented pensioners. In the park surrounding his apartment tower walks a solitary man with a little dog running around him. Before he takes on a cheerless Filipino to prevent him from getting lost, he'll try to train a clever dog who will sense when he wants to go home and lead him there. Luria smiles: There's no doubt that a dog would be not only less expensive than a Filipino but less humiliating. But until that time comes, better to lift his eyes to the sky, to the swarm of stars that grows brighter as the darkness of the city deepens. Before his son Yoav immersed himself in his successful business, he was an avid amateur astronomer. In his youth he belonged to a science club at Tel Aviv University, and visited the observatory near the Ramon Crater in the desert. His parents gave him an expensive telescope as a bar mitzvah present, and he would report to them and his friends the latest news from the solar system. If this were a more reasonable hour, he would no doubt be happy to guide his father through the mob of stars in the sky. But at this hour he will not bother his son, who sometimes lingers at his factory past midnight. All the same, says Luria to himself, so he'll know I'm thinking of him and his stars even at this hour, I'll send him a text message: *Yoav dear, if you happen to be awake, I have a question about the stars I happen to be looking at now.*

The ringtone of a quick reply. Yoav, driving home from the plant, is eager to guide his father. Are the skies this bright in the North? I didn't notice, answers the son, but I'll pull over and look. What do you want to know, Abba?

"First, remind me of the names of the planets." Yoav recites them one by one, and Luria remembers the name he is looking for.

"So I could, for example, see Mars?"

Yoav explains how to locate Mars, east of the moon.

"And Jupiter?"

Yoav doesn't think his father can find Jupiter right now.

"And what about Noga," says Luria, "where do I find her now?"

"You can only see Venus close to sunrise or sunset, because that planet is very close to the sun."

"Okay, *habibi,* that's enough. I'm sorry I'm delaying you, drive home safely, it's late."

"And how are you, Abba?"

"Fine for now."

"Hard to fall asleep?"

"So what? I can sleep as much as I want during the day."

"Imma told me you gave a very nice speech at Divon's party."

"'Very nice' is her embellishment."

"What did you say?"

"Not now, *habibi,*" says Luria, his mind already fogged by Xanax. "You're overdoing your diligence. The time has come to make less money and use the time to sleep more, because when you get to my age, you won't always persuade sleep to get into bed with you."

As the sunlight strikes his eyes and a radio plays in the distance, his wife stands over him, dressed and ready to leave. Why so early? It turns out that the doctor is not hurrying to her clinic today, but to the operating room, to attend a long and complicated operation on a girl of five, in order to bolster her parents' faith in the necessity of the surgery. Good for you, her husband lovingly says.

"And you? What's with you? You dropped off like a dead man. Next time, please take half a pill and not a whole."

Half would not be enough for his anxiety.

"Anxiety over what?"

Nothing. He'll explain this evening, not when she's in a hurry.

Tell it quickly anyway.

"I got carried away yesterday with that single-parent boy, after Noam quite maliciously started teasing him that he had no father, and this Nevo, apparently a black belt in hysteria, threw himself on the floor and started having spasms, like an epileptic fit. To calm him down I invented a father for him, who for the time being is far away, in Africa, for example."

"You invented him a father?"

"Only out of pity, not from dementia. I couldn't do nothing after I saw the evil erupt from a child who seems sweet and innocent. Who knows if the source of the evil is only his parents and not the previous generation, meaning you and me. By the way, his mother's name is Noga, like the planet Venus, not Noa or Yona. In the middle of the night I remembered the right name."

"So what?"

"What do you mean, so what?"

"What do you want with her?"

"I thought of asking Avigail for her phone number so I could explain—"

"No, no, don't call and don't explain. Your explanations will only make it worse. Drop it, your imaginary father will be forgotten if you don't dwell on him. In the future, in your condition, try to invent a simpler solution."

GUARDING HIS FATHER'S BED

Even if this young man is afraid to include me in his desert project, even without pay—Luria grumbles—he can't prevent me from visiting his father. It's precisely now, when I myself am beginning to decline, that I need to encourage others, but also be encouraged by their illnesses.

He doesn't have to go through any switchboard to get through directly to his old office phone, whose number, Luria is convinced, no atrophy could ever erase. But it seems that in the daytime the young man is out in the field, or running from office to office, so Luria catches him late at night.

Of course, Maimoni exclaims, of course he remembers, and his father was excited to hear that his old division chief was concerned for his welfare. Especially since it seemed, when they met by chance on the street, that Luria barely recognized him because of his worsening condition.

"Whose condition?"

"My father's, of course."

But because the former legal adviser is reluctant to invite an important man to a house reduced to disorder by illness and isolation, he recommends that the visit be at the hospital, on a day when Maimoni goes for his monthly treatment. As toxic medicines drip into his body in a quiet, private room, the two can reminisce about the days when they did more important things.

The suggestion that he get together with Maimoni during his chemo treatment seems right to Dina, who considers joining her husband, but Luria vetoes the idea: "If you're with us, we'll only talk about illness and medicines, and I'm planning to entertain him with memories of the houses and fields he expropriated when we built roads and interchanges in the North." After a date is set for the visit, Luria takes out a tiny pad, easily hidden among paper money in his wallet, marked "Anti-Dementia" on the cover. Here he has listed the ignition code for his car, his home phone number, the cell phone numbers of his wife and children, and also that of Asael Maimoni, a temporary addition to the family. Just prior to the visit Luria adds to the notepad the name of the philanthropist who endowed the oncology clinic, along with the floor and department and number of the room where chemicals would be poured into Yohanan Maimoni. And when Luria parks in the underground lot, he adds the floor and zone where the red car will be waiting for its master.

The "anti-dementia" proves effective as Luria strides through the wings of the hospital, goes to the designated floor, and arrives at the outpatient clinic in late afternoon, exiting the elevator as waning sunlight floods the windowpanes. He buys a bar of Merci chocolate, imported from Germany, and heads with mild anxiety down a quiet, darkened corridor. He doesn't see a nurse who might give him directions, so he goes from room to room, some of them not numbered, till he arrives at the one where, as recorded on the "anti-dementia" pad, he will fulfill the mitzvah of visiting the sick.

It's not a large room, and the patient lies in bed, his head slightly elevated, with a carousel of IV bags dangling above him, some already empty and others still filled with a clear fluid, except for one that is conspicuously yellow. The patient's eyes are closed, with a white silk scarf across his forehead that extends down to his shoulders, its hem embroidered in red. One pathetically thin arm is exposed on the bed, with the IV tube stuck in an invisible vein.

Luria momentarily thinks he's with the wrong patient, goes out into the hall to double-check the room number, which is indeed the number he was given that morning, and there's no one in the empty corridor to tell him otherwise. Is his legal adviser really in such dreadful condition? Or has the original person disappeared into one of the black holes of his memory? Maimoni is a few years older than Luria, and retired before he did, and apart from that chance encounter on the street a few weeks ago, they had not seen each other for many years, and if even a healthy person looks different in old age, wrinkled and shrunken, or else fatter, all the more so a person with an aggressive illness that reshapes him altogether. So fear and shock are inappropriate at a time like this, which calls for heightened attention and understanding, and Luria reenters the room, determined to be at his best, and whispers, "Maimoni," and glances at his notepad to be sure of the first name, and says, "Yohanan, Yohanan Maimoni, it's me, Zvi Luria, I've come to tell you not to worry, there's hope."

But there is no movement in the bed, and the name floats past the sick man like a cloud of dust, not like the greeting of a longtime colleague. Maimoni doesn't open his eyes, and it would seem that his deep sleep is blessed with drugs that battle his disease and color his dreams. If so, I'll wait till he wakes up, I have time, there are more IV bags waiting their turn. On the little nightstand by the bed is a copy of *Israel Today,* by now the Israel of two days ago, and Luria tosses it in the trash, confident that yesterday's lies won't become today's truth, and in place of the newspaper he sets down the Merci chocolate in its golden wrapper, folds his hands, closes his eyes, and imbibes the deep silence. But little by little he realizes the silence is incomplete, for a reedy Middle Eastern tune trills from the radio beside the chocolate. Is Maimoni trying, at life's end, to reassert his roots?

Does visiting a sleeping sick man count as visiting the sick? He stares at the drug dripping from the intravenous tube. The rate is slow as each drop hesitates before taking the plunge, and for a moment seems to want to return to the bag it came from. Many years ago, when his father was a similar outpatient, Luria would go to the hospital on the days of his father's treatments and drive him home, to spare him the stress of public transportation. And because he was pressed for time between meetings, Luria would secretly speed up the drip just a bit, so the treatment would be over sooner. He feels a sudden urge to do the same today, but since the bag on the carousel is shriveling, and the nurse will soon arrive to replace it with another, he is wary, and rightly so, as the door flies open and into the room walks an officer wearing the uniform of the Border Police, solidly built and ruddy-faced and bearing a submachine gun, and under his arm a small watermelon. Without delay he wakes his father: "*Baba . . . Baba!*" The sick man opens his eyes and answers in Arabic with a heavy sigh: "*Aywah, ibni, aywah.*"

In that case, this isn't Maimoni, concedes Luria. But why hurry to apologize to an armed Druze officer, who seems unperturbed by the stranger beside his father, and sets the submachine gun on the bed, and moves the Merci chocolate to a lower shelf, and begins cutting up the small watermelon quickly and efficiently to feed its juicy flesh to his father. Before he, too, is invited to eat, Luria begins his silent retreat, as if he were a paramedic assigned to check the IV drip. Smiling sadly at the ailing man, he walks out without a word, closing the door behind him, and continues down the hall toward the window at the end, toward the sun reflected in the glass, and there is a nurses' station here after all, and a nurse fiddling with her cell phone. He asks for Maimoni, and the nurse, without a word, points a delicate finger at the lounge where the father and son are impatiently waiting. With the father sunk in an armchair, bald and depleted, wizened and pale, a walking stick wobbling between his legs, the son irritably wants to know the reason for the delay. "Abba's treatment was over half an hour ago," he says coldly, "and we had given up on you."

"Yes, give up on me," Luria concurs, frightened by the father's deathly demeanor. "Yes, give up on me, because I not only got the wrong room, but also the wrong patient."

"Also the patient?"

"Yes, yes, even the patient."

He calmly decides to confess his illness. Yes, this is the hidden truth. Not everyone who looks healthy is healthy. He too is sick, not in his body, or in his spirit, but in his brain. He has been diagnosed with atrophy in the frontal lobe, and first names are escaping him, and lately people get switched too. He arrived at the right hour, and imagined he was going to the right room, but discovered that he was sitting at the bedside of the wrong patient.

A little smile brightens Yohanan Maimoni's tormented face. The confusion described by his former division chief clearly amuses him. There are many versions of the human tragedy. Would he be willing to trade pancreatic cancer for mental atrophy? Yes, his immediate suffering would be relieved, but what if his beloved son turns into a stranger?

"Anyway, how are you?" says Luria with a feeling of relief after blurting out his confession without error or embarrassment. He leans toward the true patient and peers into his eyes. Maimoni strokes his hand. "What can I say, Zvi? You can see for yourself. I'm dying."

"No, no." Luria smoothly segues from impending death to the story of the ribbon of light that leaked from under his office door on the seventh floor, and revealed a young engineer sitting at his former desk, working at night on a project in the desert. "This is the world, Yohanan, generations come and go." And the father, who knows the story, nods his head and turns toward his son, who looks hard at Luria as if discovering something new.

"Just imagine, my friend," Luria continues cheerfully, "that my wife, with the arrogance or innocence of a pediatrician, dared to propose me, a demented pensioner, as an assistant to your Asael on his project. In other words, to suggest a man who easily sits down beside a Druze stranger as if he were an old friend, to help him plan a secret road in the desert."

The father nods. He is surely worn out not only from the treatment, but also from waiting for the disoriented visitor who oddly imagines himself a cancer patient. And his son, instead of sending the visitor away and readying his father for the ride home, jumps into their conversation.

"No, Luria, your wife is not arrogant, and certainly not naïve. If, as a doctor aware of your condition, she proposes you as a partner or assistant in my project, it means she trusts both you and me."

"Meaning what?"

"Meaning that despite the confusion, some of us more confused and some less, we still build roads in this country, and if we make mistakes, we can always correct them."

"In other words?"

"In other words, I am not afraid of you, Zvi Luria. For a senior engineer with wide experience, dementia can be a liberating and creative factor. And your wife said you would do it without pay—"

"Of course, without pay." Luria is energized. "My pension is just fine, and my wife earns a good living in her children's clinic."

The father closes his eyes as if stabbed by pain. The condition of the Druze, currently reviving his spirit with watermelon cut for him by his son, is vastly better than the condition of the legal adviser. Smooth words of encouragement can never compare with the consolation of a juicy red slice.

"So?"

"So?" Luria snaps out of his reverie. "So yes. Without pay, but a part-time assistant, only part-time."

THE BEIT KAMA INTERCHANGE

"Just a minute, before you two get going, listen to me for a moment, young man. You may not realize it yet, but you'll soon learn that you've been blessed with a top-notch assistant, an experienced senior engineer who designed many interchanges and bridges, dug tunnels and built roads, all with wisdom and calm professionalism. He is easygoing by nature, with a reputation for finding simple and inexpensive solutions for engineering problems that seemed complicated. That way he saved the State a great deal of money, which became available for myriad corrupt purposes."

"Dina, what are you saying?"

But his wife is swept up in her monologue, enjoying the moment.

"You're getting a strong man, in good shape for his age, seventy-two, and these days men like him can be good friends with intelligent women. He has no problem climbing up a hill, or down into a wadi, even a small crater, but as he himself confessed to you, he has lately manifested a few failures of memory and spatial orientation. He will need supervision, so that his enthusiasm will not get him lost in the desert. Therefore do not rely on the mobile phone or shouting out loud, but make sure to maintain eye contact, because if he disappears in some wadi, or crater, or behind a hill, I will have neither the strength nor the hope to find someone to console me for his loss."

"Enough, Dina," interrupts her husband, "he gets the idea."

"Do you get it? Are you sure?" She shoots a motherly look at the handsome young man wearing an old army windbreaker, his eyes dancing in awe of the old folks' enduring chemistry.

"It'll be fine, Doctor Luria, I'll look after him like a second father. Zvi should take a warm coat, because out there in the desert, in the evening and at night, it can get very cold."

"Evening? Night?" Dina is uneasy. "When are you planning to bring him back? We agreed he is only a part-time assistant."

"Of course, only part-time. But if we go down into the Ramon Crater to determine the exit point of the new road, it could take a while."

"In which case," says Zvi, "I'll go get my old windbreaker."

"You won't find it, because Yoavi took it a year ago, but what about the old blue sweater?"

"Just a minute," says Maimoni, "why a blue sweater, or any sweater, my father's old windbreaker is in the trunk of the car. It will fit your husband too."

"You sure it will fit?"

Luria finds the conversation between his wife and Maimoni excessive and humiliating, and he interrupts: "*Yalla*, man, take out the jacket and let's hit the road." He plants a kiss on his wife to signal her to let him go, and gets in the car with a jaunty *yalla, yalla, yalla:* no more wasting time, the desert awaits.

After many years devoted to the roads of the North, he is keen to see the overpasses and exits his colleagues have added to the roads of the South, but Maimoni is in a hurry and takes the quicker, more monotonous Trans-Israel Highway. At first Luria is unnerved by the speed of the old American car, but its size and suspension absorb the shocks of the road. He soon gets used to the velocity, and quietly notes when it exceeds legal limits.

"Your father breaks my heart," he says softly.

"Yes, others feel the same way. It's a pity you got him mixed up with another patient, because Abba waited a long time for you, and was proud that after so many years you still took an interest. But when you finally showed up, he was out of it and couldn't derive any happiness from you."

"In which case I'll come again, and next time I'll be more careful."

"I doubt there will be a next time, Luria, the doctors are giving him at most another few months, but I think it's just weeks, which is better for him. He's determined to wrestle the angel of death, but physical suffering purifies the soul only in philosophy books and second-rate novels. It's unnecessary and degrading in real life."

Luria nods his agreement, and the driver glances approvingly at his part-time assistant.

"You do know, Luria, that you've been blessed with a sweet wife."

"Sweet?" Luria is astounded. "What do you mean, sweet? Why sweet? She's a smart and devoted woman. At sixty-four, a woman's sweetness is only in her love and caring."

"And that's exactly what my father lacked after my mother abandoned us. That was when he began to decline."

"As I told you, I knew nothing about his wife. Nor did I want to know."

"Just as well," says the son with a smile. "You were wise not to know and not to pry, because otherwise you'd have discovered that your serious and devoted legal adviser was not an innocent victim. He was a man not looking for love and care, but sweetness, and because I lived with him in the same house, he looked for it in all sorts of places hidden from me, including his office at night or on weekends. Just imagine, Luria, that with his master key he had access to the whole seventh floor of the Northern Division, and each time he'd pick a different room to partake of the sweetness."

"I never suspected," Luria mutters uneasily.

"That's just as well," Maimoni repeats, "you were wise, very wise."

Luria attempts to adjust the sun visor to ward off the strong rays. The dubious compliment "you were wise" is also beginning to annoy him. So he shouldn't wander in the mall, seeking inspiration for new recipes, his wife and the neurologist have conspired with a junior engineer to dispatch him to the desert, the cradle of the sun. The Trans-Israel Highway ended an hour ago, and they are now on Route 40. "Maybe you want to move to the back seat," suggests Maimoni, noticing his pensioner's battle with the sun. "There's a blanket in the trunk if you want to get cozy."

Best to postpone coziness till the drive back in the evening, Luria tells him. Meanwhile, he will shield himself from the sun with a map found in the glove compartment. After consulting it briefly, he asks Maimoni to take a quick detour to the interchange under construction near Beit Kama. A few months ago he caught a glimpse on the nightly news, now he's curious to see it up close. And despite the delay—a four-kilometer detour from Route 40—and though their destination is still far away, Maimoni agrees, and on a bumpy dirt road they approach a spidery structure that will straddle the extension of the Trans-Israel Highway. Luria's desire to inspect the quality of the work is so intense that he rushes from the car and heads off on foot toward a huge steamroller crawling beyond the big overpass. The young man watches the pensioner with wonder as he hops between boards and poles atop an overpass with no guardrail, the inveterate professional who still wants to learn from the work of others. And as Maimoni folds the map and stuffs old papers and empty bottles into a bag, he recalls the pediatrician's warning not to let her irreplaceable husband out of his sight, and jumps out of the car for a closer look. But with no sign or warning the pensioner has vanished. Is he out there somewhere, navigating his way back, or did he get confused and go off in the wrong direction? Suddenly panicked that he hadn't noticed the uninsured part-time helper sailing in the air beyond the nonexistent guardrail, Maimoni scrambles onto the overpass, not daring to look down at what's underneath, just running to the other end, where, in the shade of an elderly eucalyptus, amid a group of project managers and Jewish and Arab workers, Luria sits, wearing a helmet, a cup of coffee in his hand.

Maimoni can't find the right words. He stands in stony silence before the pensioner, who serenely sips his coffee and stares at him, apparently without recognition. "I thought you didn't notice there's no railing and you fell down on the Trans-Israel Highway," Maimoni says at last, forcing a smile. "There was no railing?" says Luria and turns to his friends. Now Maimoni cannot contain his anger. "How could you disappear on me like that, and forget the promise I made to your wife?" And the husband quickly mumbles his apologies, gets up, removes the helmet, and gestures at the group watching the scene with amusement: "Sorry, Maimoni, sorry, Asael, I found some old friends here. This is Yosef Barazani, the chief engineer of the entire interchange."

"Yaakov," whispers Barazani.

"Yes, excuse me, Yaakov, and would you believe we were connected in the past."

"Just connected? I was Luria's student, I learned everything I know from him. I sat at his feet, as they say."

"So here you go, Yaakov, here's another highway engineer, a young go-getter planning a secret road in the desert. And he's no student, he's a manager, and I'm his volunteer assistant. Except he worries too much. Yes, *habibi*"—he turns to Maimoni—"you overdo your anxiety. And why do you believe that my wife will be angry if you lose me? How do you know? Maybe she'll thank you."

BEN-GURION'S GRAVE

Before they continue on Route 40, Maimoni asks if Luria would like to go into Beersheba for a late breakfast, or wait till they arrive at the Genesis Hotel in Mitzpe Ramon, where Maimoni has arranged fine dining at minimal cost. And Luria, buzzing from black coffee and uplifted by the words of Barazani, is happy to endure another eighty kilometers of desolate road, then sit like an honored guest at a table with a view of an ancient landscape.

On the way, he tells the young man about his first encounter with Barazani. Together, after the Six-Day War, they had rehabilitated the old road to Jerusalem near Latrun. But despite his fond feelings for Barazani, he cannot help but criticize the man. When he stood on the new overpass he noticed that the eastbound exit was too sharp a curve. Two warning signs should be installed, and maybe a speed bump as well, so that drivers do not run off the road. What can I say, that's how I am, even in my atrophied state I try to stay professional, and if you thought I would help you cut corners on safety, we may as well go home.

Maimoni smiles. No, Luria will have no reason to turn back. And after heading south at the Halukim Junction, they come upon large signs beckoning travelers to bear left and visit the grave of David Ben-Gurion.

"Why don't we?" Luria is enthusiastic. "We visited there, Dina and I, many years ago and were deeply moved by the words inscribed on his gravestone. Not 'first prime minister,' not 'founder of the State,' not 'the great leader of his generation,' but simply: David Ben-Gurion, the dates of his life, and the year he immigrated to Palestine. That's all. I didn't notice what it says on the grave of his wife, who died before him. But she's the one, as it happens, I remember personally from my childhood. In the 1950s the prime minister's house wasn't on Balfour Street like today, but on Ben Maimon, and on my way to school I would pass the simple old house and say hello to the policeman—can you imagine, back then one policeman was enough, and that one was sometimes dozing off or reading a newspaper, apparently it never occurred to anyone to assassinate Ben-Gurion, they only wanted to come and pester him with all kinds of suggestions, and to keep them away one policeman was enough, and Paula, his wife, would sometimes come out in her bathrobe and send the policeman to buy milk or bread at the corner grocer, and she would stand guard on the house till the policeman came back, and I would say good morning to her. Yes, those were the days, would you believe it?"

"If you remember Ben-Gurion's wife, who am I not to believe you?"

"So what do you say, Asael, do we have time for a quick visit?"

"Very quick."

Maimoni turns off toward the Midreshet Ben-Gurion boarding school, where a dirt road flanked by desert plants leads to the gravesite. The two get out of the car and walk on a path with a spectacular view of the deep canyon of Nahal Tzin and the Ein Avdat spring. In the far distance is a long line of soldiers hiking toward the crevice of the spring. The air is clear and dry, perfect weather for a desert hike, declares Maimoni. Here are the graves, the large, plain tombstones surrounded by a black iron chain. Silently they read the names and numbers engraved on the stones. Two births for Ben-Gurion: the first in the Diaspora; the second, the real one, the date of his aliyah to the Land of Israel. He stipulated the same style for his wife Paula, two dates of birth and one of death, and vetoed any additional words about her loyalty and love. The pebbles that visitors had placed on the grave, to assure the first prime minister that he had not been forgotten, are gathered at the bottom of the tombstone, so as not to conceal the inscription, but Maimoni decides nevertheless to place a pebble next to the first name—David—and Luria, following suit, sets one next to Paula. Afterward they fall silent and watch the ibexes, gazelles, and fawns munching grass near the gravesite. These animals have lived here since time immemorial, and their bond to the desert is stronger than Ben-Gurion's and his wife's, and when visitors try to befriend them, they mistrust them, and shy away gracefully.

Maimoni finally breaks the silence: "I've heard that this Paula was not an easy woman." And Luria answers him firmly: "There are no easy women. Why should a woman be easy if she always has to protect her husband?"

"But you lived not far from their home in Jerusalem," says Maimoni. "How is it that you only saw her and not him?"

"Him, only one time. The office of the prime minister was then in the middle of the Rehavia neighborhood, at the corner of Keren Kayemet and Ibn Gabirol. And Ben-Gurion used to go on foot from his office to his house, not far away, barely a kilometer—a distance that didn't satisfy his urge to walk, so he moved down here to the wilderness, where he could walk indefinitely. Once, late on a Friday night, I went home via Alharizi Street and suddenly felt a firm tap on my shoulder, that I should get out of the way. I turned my head and there was Ben-Gurion with a smile on his face, as if he were slightly embarrassed by his greatness. I made way immediately because he walked faster than I did. He didn't say excuse me or thank you, just passed by quickly, creating a little breeze with his mane of white hair, and vanished in the darkness."

GENESIS

The Genesis Hotel is not far away, facing the Ramon Crater, and Maimoni intends to arrive while breakfast is still available. Since he began coming to the area, he noticed that around noon, when the lavish buffet is removed, there's a brief window of opportunity when someone, not an actual guest but familiar to the hotel staff, is able, on the pretext of getting a quick cup of coffee, to snatch some perishable food that would otherwise be discarded. Maimoni aims for that window: the last of the guests are leaving the dining room, the waiters are removing the leftovers, the woman who checks names has gone away, and he slips quietly into the hall like a guest who has forgotten something, takes a big plate, and fills it with fine food. Then he pours himself a cup of coffee and goes out with his prize into the garden, to peer into the depths of the crater.

A hotel employee, a woman no longer young, struck by the young engineer's good looks, gives tacit approval to his incursions, which occasionally include a nap in a room whose guests have left but has yet to be remade for new ones. The fact that Maimoni is involved in developing the desert provides this woman with a rationale for breaking the rules, in the belief that even a secret military road will attract new customers to the hotel.

Maimoni receives a per diem from Israel Roads for his trips to the desert, and has no financial motive for sneaking into the dining room of the Genesis Hotel to make a meal of food destined for the garbage bin. The real reason for his visits here is to cultivate the insider status that enables him to rest in unmade rooms, and maybe spend a night there in the future. But today, since he is accompanied by an unpaid assistant with no per diem, the stolen breakfast is economically justifiable. And since it's impossible to ask a senior retiree to impersonate an authentic guest returning to the dining room for a cup of coffee, Maimoni decides to introduce Luria to the woman, his patron at the hotel, as one of the amazing road engineers the State of Israel is blessed with, an engineer who volunteered to serve without pay in planning the new secret road. This is an engineer who worked his whole life in the North, and hasn't been to the South for many years, and needs to be shown a panoramic view of the crater, and no better lookout point exists than the patio of the hotel dining hall. From there, over coffee and a cookie, he'll get the full picture.

Clearly, a cookie is a metaphor for something more substantial and tasty. The two engineers sit on the patio as a Sudanese waiter, still in his bow tie, offers them not a choice of leftovers, but enough to sustain them till the next day's breakfast. As Maimoni indulges ravenously, Luria eats with moderation. A bluish cloud trapped in the huge, dark crater captures his gaze. Has he ever in his long life, on a youth-group hike or army exercise, gone down into this crater, or is his information based entirely on a passing glance at a map? He lowers his head and closes his eyes and tries to concentrate. Will the dementia that shreds names and events make an exception for the memory of a hike or the army? He fixes on the cloud as it struggles to break free of the crater and float to the sky, but the big, deep crater won't let go and grabs hold, trying to hitch a ride to outer space. What time is it? Luria asks fearfully, rubbing his eyes to shake off the delusion. It's nearly twelve, says the young man. Twelve what? Twelve noon, Maimoni smiles, asking whether the croissant on Luria's plate is available. Take it, it's yours, says Luria, I ate too much. He looks kindly at the young man, who wolfs down the croissant lest Luria change his mind. *What do I really know about this guy whom Dina hooked me up with to challenge my brain?* When he sees that the cloud is gone and the crater is back in place, he turns to the young engineer with a brief announcement:

"Listen, Maimoni, listen, Asael, as opposed to what I had with your father, or other people who worked with me at Israel Roads, between you and me there's no hierarchy, nor will there be. I'm not your subordinate and you're not mine, I'm not responsible for your actions and you're not responsible for mine. We are two engineers, free agents, cooperating as we see fit. Today I'm here with you, but tomorrow I might refuse to come. Today you need my help, but tomorrow you'll tell me I'm useless. Therefore, this time, unlike in the past, I don't want to ignore your private life. I'm interested in knowing all about it, to avoid surprises, like the story of your mother leaving your father. So please, before we begin the actual work, clarify a few basic details. Are you married, with children?"

It turns out Maimoni has a wife two years older than he is, an economist in a government office, and they have twins, boy and girl, in second grade, but in separate classes. "Nice," says Luria, "I can rest easy."

"Easy about what?" asks Maimoni.

"That you have a stable family life, so you won't go looking for adventures that will involve me too."

"You're really so sure that marriage is an institution that precludes adventures?"

"There are no absolute rules anywhere," Luria says, qualifying his remark, "but having a wife and kids involves basic responsibilities that rein a man in."

"You say that because you imagine my marriage is like yours, like the connection between you and your wife."

"Between me and my wife?" Luria bursts out laughing. "What can you possibly know about that connection?"

"I can't know," admits Maimoni, "but I can feel it."

"Feel what?"

"The love, the dependency, the worry. Tell the truth, Luria, is there ever a moment when your wife is not in the back of your mind?"

"What?" Luria sits up straight. "Where do you get that idea?"

"Am I wrong?"

"Wrong or not wrong is not the point," says Luria, avoiding the question. "The issue now is your superior attitude. You're so confident about your feeling. Tell me, are you going to plan the army road based on a gut feeling?"

"Why not? Why reject feelings that reinforce my knowledge? Especially now," he adds, "that I've added your knowledge to it."

The cloud that dissolved in the sky has returned to the crater. The midday light grows murkier. The dining hall is desolate. The waiters have disappeared, and the buffet is empty except for a few loaves of bread covered with a red cloth. Silence in the desert world. The swimming pool is far away, and most of the guests have gone for an afternoon nap in their luxurious stone cabins. The old man watches closely as the young man puts a cigarette between his lips and hesitates to light it, though no one is around.

"And the dementia?" Luria whispers in pain.

"It will be your feeling," says Maimoni, striking a match.

SHIBBOLET

Before they leave the Genesis Hotel, they need to inform the local supervisor of the Nature and Parks Authority of their presence in the area.

"The Nature Authority?" Luria is stupefied. "Can a little army road in this enormous crater really harm plant or animal life?"

"Always and everywhere," says Maimoni, "there are animals, big ones or little ones, to arouse overblown sympathy. But there's something else here, something human, that is dear to the heart of this local supervisor, which is why he is afraid of my road, which from now on is your road too. By the way, I don't even know if he is an official supervisor or just a volunteer at the Nature Authority. He is a former army officer, a complicated person who lives in the center of the country, but rents an apartment here in Mitzpe Ramon, where his wife can come when her asthma acts up."

"What's his name?"

"Shibbolet."

"Shibbolet? Shibbolet what?"

"Shibbolet. That's it. A last name and first name merged into one."

"There are in fact cases like that," confirms Luria, feeling slightly anxious.

"A very complicated man," continues Maimoni with strange enthusiasm, "a man who in the past knew how to scare people, me in particular."

"Scared you? How so?"

"Would you believe it, he was my commander in basic training. And from the minute I first saw him, I was inexplicably afraid of him."

"In my basic training," recalls Luria, "you couldn't be afraid of your company commander, because you barely knew who he was. In those days a company was huge, and therefore neither a company commander nor a platoon commander, but some corporal, usually a new immigrant, could jerk you around to his heart's content, mainly to warn you not to make fun of his ridiculous Hebrew."

"No, Zvi, Shibbolet is a native, going back generations, and his Hebrew, as you will hear, is clear and precise. In any case, I'm talking about personal, irrational fear, not collective fear. Friends in the unit were amazed, even took pity on me: 'What's with you? Why do you go pale when he walks in the tent or asks you a question? He's no worse than any of the others.' And I couldn't explain the terror, which gripped me till the end of basic training. Yes, terror. My father, in a desperate attempt to calm me down, said it wasn't fear but metaphysical terror."

"Metaphysical?" Luria laughs. "That's what he said? Metaphysical from a company commander?"

"Just an elegant word he picked up from a newspaper, to let me know my fear was stupid and childish."

"Yes, your father had a way with words, which is why his expropriations went so smoothly."

"But because of this childish fear, I made sure to be a motivated and disciplined soldier, beyond reproach, but nevertheless, before every group discussion or trip, or just a Friday lineup, I sank into depression."

"And he could see this? How did he respond?"

"Gradually my fear was justified. Though I was one soldier among many, he noticed my reaction and it made him angry. Would you believe that even my name, Asael, began to irritate him, and he would twist it around, mocking it, and he told my platoon commander to give me extra chores."

"Disgraceful."

"Very disgraceful. And then one night I'll never forget, a rainy night of guard duty, cold and foggy, and Shibbolet is prowling around silently, to check the alertness of the guards. I was posted at the edge of the camp, and apparently dozed off and didn't notice as he came near, and he grabbed me by the neck and in one quick move threw me to the ground. I made not a sound and immediately fainted and refused to wake up, and he freaked out until I regained consciousness."

"They didn't send you to a neurologist?"

"Neurologist?" Maimoni is shocked. "Why a neurologist? You mean the mental health officer, a psychologist."

"Yes, maybe the psychologist."

"But what good would a psychologist have done me? By the time we finished rummaging through my childhood to find the root of my weird fear, basic training would be over, and the fear would remain only as memory."

"But memory is also important," Luria says softly.

"Of course, which is why I kept track of him in later life. I learned that he'd been promoted from captain to major, that he was transferred to an intelligence unit in the North. After a few years I saw him for a moment on television, and noticed he was then a lieutenant colonel, which is as high as he got. They bumped him over to the civilian administration of the Central Command. That part he told me himself."

"How did you happen to meet?"

"It was three months ago, here on Route Forty, past Independence Road. As I began to look for the place where the new road would branch off, he suddenly popped out from some hill, and looked exactly the same as twenty years before, quick and nimble, but his hair had turned white. I hoped he wouldn't recognize me after all that time, if only because of my new beard. But he clearly suspected, and was not satisfied with my last name and insisted I tell him my first one, and he immediately flashed his sarcastic smile, ah, you're the soldier who fainted in basic training when I only touched him. But he didn't say a word."

"Obviously, Asael is an uncommon name, and even my atrophy, which has demolished many names, holds yours in great respect, because it knows it will not easily be crushed."

Asael studies the old man kindly. "Good to know that your memory won't torpedo my name. It's precious to me because my mother named me that, against Abba's wishes. Maybe that was the first sign of their breakup. She told my father, 'God made this baby, not you.'"

"She actually believed in God?"

"Only when it suited her needs. She was one of those people who take God out like a handkerchief, to wipe away tears or sweat. Not a cloth hankie but a tissue, which afterward blows away in the wind."

THE TURNOFF

Midday is long gone, and the young engineer is still deliberating whether to get in touch with Shibbolet before descending into the crater. What authority does this guy have? Luria, deprived of his afternoon nap, is grouchy and impatient. Is this a relapse of the raw recruit's old fear? Maimoni is unperturbed by his assistant's mockery. His psychologist has taught him that in matters of the mind, every interpretation, no matter how far-fetched, is worth a second look. But beyond the old fear, real or imagined, there is now an actual human problem that involves him and Shibbolet.

Human? Luria has had many run-ins with environmentalists, and despite their concerns about endangered animal species and protected plant life, he was able to maintain a clear line between nature and humans.

Yes, humans, Maimoni is dealing with Shibbolet only regarding humans. It's doubtful whether there are animals indigenous to the crater, and the plants are sparse and pathetic. But not far from the proposed turnoff are people whom Shibbolet has taken under his wing. Unfortunately, these people are sort of secret nomads, they come and go, and it's impossible to know if they're here at the moment.

"Secret nomads?" says the pensioner. "Listen, young man, I came here for an engineering project, to plan a road, not to search for missing nomads. So make up your mind now—are we moving ahead, or am I going home? The sun will go down in this desert, and it's a long way home. So let's move on, please, save the explanations for later."

"Of course, we're moving on. But down there at the designated spot, there's an electronic black hole, and when you think you've made phone contact, you can't make out what they're saying, and when you talk, it turns out you're talking to yourself. So it would be a good idea to call your wife now, so if she looks for you when there's no reception, she won't think you are lost."

The pensioner shakes his head. He appreciates the young man's concern for his wife, but the doctor is still at her clinic, where presumably her mobile phone is turned off. But no worries, since she's the one who made the match, she surely trusts Maimoni to navigate her husband's dementia.

They drive on, finally descending into the crater. The car handles the switchbacks of Independence Road gracefully and quietly and within minutes finds itself trailing behind a massive cement mixer. The driver readies himself to pass.

No, please don't overtake this monster, Luria begs him. Don't pass, because when I study a winding road like this behind an enormous truck, I can better understand the methods of excavation and the quality of the asphalt. I worked in the North, haven't been in a wilderness like this for ages, so let me slowly feel the temperament of this road, where soon we'll need to find the right place for the new turnoff. And if it takes a few more minutes, that's okay.

A small caravan forms behind them, testy, honking, wondering why the American car won't pass the truck. How come they're so angry? If they're in such a hurry, they can overtake us, leave them some room, Luria says. But the curves are sharp, visibility is limited, no way to know how many vehicles are headed toward them or how fast they're going, so the caravan waits, until a small, irate red car darts out recklessly, honking like mad as it passes them and the huge truck, and barrels toward longed-for freedom at the bottom of the big crater, as Luria whets his appetite with traces of bulldozing on Independence Road. White rocks turn gray, greenish, pink, the cliffs block the sunlight, and little sand devils begin their whirling dance.

"This is the place," announces Maimoni, who veers onto a patch of earth at the side of the road and waves to the caravan that the way is clear, and with much honking the caravan rushes past the truck, which suddenly drives faster too, while Maimoni turns off the engine, gets out of the car, and lovingly surveys the site he has chosen. He takes out a large map, drawn at a scale of 1:10,000, a mosaic of red and blue lines, and spreads it on the hood so Luria can confirm he made the right choice.

But Luria doesn't want to pick the turnoff point according to a map. He wants to look at the area itself, and after a glance at the map he silently heads back to Route 40, crosses it, and keeps on walking, to check out the chosen place from a proper perspective. Now and then a faraway horn blares a warning at the lone walker, but Maimoni, not looking up from the map, believes that the veteran engineer, who survived the teeming highways of the North, will take the same precautions on a desolate desert road. Only after he adds another red line to the map and looks into the distance does he discover that the old man has disappeared on him again.

He does not panic as he did at the Beit Kama overpass, because the barren landscape makes it easy to locate the figure who walks resolutely toward a hill resembling a flattened cone, which rises not far from the road.

Maimoni shouts, but the sound is lost amid the mighty cliffs of the crater. He breaks into a run and sees the pensioner standing still, trying to send a text message. No, Zvi, an SMS won't work here either, says Maimoni as he reaches Luria. I warned you, this is a dead zone, no call and no response, but if you suddenly remember something urgent or serious, I can drive another half kilometer, to a place where there's coverage. Not urgent, not serious, says Luria, just something technical I remembered. But if your wife's cell phone is back on, insists the young man, go for it, you left her ten hours ago and should send her a sign of life.

"I already told you, she doesn't worry, because she relies on you, the text isn't about me, but something to do with her."

"Like what?"

"Something small, not important."

"Tell me anyway," the young man insists. "I'm your partner. You told me we're at the same level, and you asked about my personal situation, my wife and kids, so now I need to know more about you. If you talk about yourself, I'll open up too."

Luria looks straight at the man who is younger than his son, taking hold of his arm. "It's a simple matter," he says, "simple and trivial, you won't believe how trivial. Almost embarrassing to talk about."

"Tell me anyway."

"Because Dina knew I wouldn't be making her lunch, she decided to bake herself a quiche from a recipe she got from someone at the clinic, and she left this quiche on the kitchen table, and went to bed knowing that I, being a light sleeper, would put it in the fridge after it cooled down. But I put it in the freezer, not the fridge, which is bad. Because if I know my wife, she won't think to look in the freezer, and might think I took the quiche with me down south, or that she never baked it."

"That she didn't bake it? You can't be serious."

"The dementia of a close loved one can be contagious . . . You too, *habibi,* be careful you don't catch my dementia, especially now that we're alone in this wasteland."

"You're joking."

"Yes, a little."

"So what'll happen to the quiche?"

"Forget it, maybe she'll find it after all. Meanwhile, let's talk about the place you picked for the turnoff, and this time listen to me, young man, I'm talking from years of experience and not from dementia."

"I'm listening carefully."

"The place you chose is wrong for safety reasons, and the Ministry of Transportation would probably not approve it. First of all, the communications blackout disturbs me. Most accidents occur at intersections and exits, so how could people get help, since there's so little traffic here?"

"We could request an additional antenna."

"You can request, but till you get it is another story, especially if there's some inherent thing blocking the signal. Nobody is going to move a hill or cliff so your antenna will get reception."

"But—"

"But that's not all. The turnoff you chose is too close to the last curve of Independence Road. It's where cars pick up speed that a turnoff sign could go unnoticed. Don't forget, there are no traffic cops here, very few cars, fast drivers. And the ones coming from the South won't be able to see from afar the traffic coming in from your road. Their field of vision is limited. And those who exit from your road onto Route Forty, whether they go south or north, will have the same problem. That way, Asael, you are unintentionally courting disaster, not least because it's an army road, and army drivers are inexperienced, or wild and crazy. Listen to me—move your turnoff three hundred meters farther south, and everyone will have a good field of vision."

"Just a minute, Luria. You saw on the map the old Nabatean road I discovered farther down, a road that will make the work easier and cheaper. If you want me to move the entrance to our new road three hundred meters south, we'll have to go around the hill in front of us, which would add another four hundred meters of road—"

"No," Luria interrupts, "no need to go around the hill, just get rid of it. In the North, I bulldozed hills bigger and more complex than this one, hills of basalt. I had this Kurdish guy, Havilio, who drove a huge excavator, and the night I first met you in my old office, I met him at the reception downstairs, where he was working as a waiter. A serious person who could level a hill, alone, in a month or two. He was an expert in finding the weak spot of a hill and penetrating it with his giant shovel, sometimes with a little help from explosives, till it cracked and crumbled, and then the small earthmovers came in to collect and remove the dirt."

"You're saying we should level this hill?"

"What's the problem?" Luria picks up two stones from the

ground and smacks them together to demonstrate that desert rock crumbles easily.

"Are you serious?'

"Of course. Theory and practice I have not forgotten. Do you doubt that?"

"I have no doubt this hill could be pulverized. Unfortunately, people live there."

"People? So what? So they'll move to a different hill. Plenty of hills in the desert."

"If we move them from here, they'll disappear."

"Disappear?"

"Disappear from someone they are connected to. These are Shibbolet's people. His secret people."

"Secret in what way?"

"Let's go up there. Maybe they're around, and you'll understand."

"Listen, Maimoni, I didn't come here to deal with people, but with roads, detours, turnoffs."

"Obviously."

"So what do you say we get rid of the hill?"

"You're right, Luria, it's possible if necessary to level the hill. Don't think I haven't thought of it."

"I'm glad you've arrived independently at the right idea. The proper location for a turnoff depends on safety, not topography. So don't take pity on the hill."

"But there is also a compromise solution."

"Which is?"

"Not to destroy the hill, but to dig a tunnel through it. I've already calculated it, a tunnel of one hundred fifty meters, not more."

"They will not approve a tunnel here, Maimoni. Why dig when you can pulverize? Think of the cost, the supports, the inside walls, not to mention lighting and ventilation. There are clear standards for tunnels."

"If you recommend it, maybe they'll approve it."

"Me?"

"Your expertise and experience will convince them."

"And the dementia?"

"On the contrary. It will give your position added oomph. Like the dementia of a prime minister, which strengthens his authority."

Luria looks closely at the handsome engineer. Now he understands why he jumped at the offer of the unpaid assistant.

"Tell me, Asael." He reaches out and touches the young man's face. "Your little beard is actually very nice, how long have you had it? I have a son older than you, he also tried to grow one like that, but the beard refused to grow and stuck to his cheeks like clumps of tar, till his wife threatened to throw him out of the house unless he shaved. But you, your beard is nice, and most of all, aesthetically pleasing."

"It's a young beard. I started growing it a few months ago, when I got this project in the desert."

"And your wife likes it?"

"My wife is oblivious unless it actually touches her."

THE HILL

The hill is not tall, but looking up from its foot, Luria can't quite make out the summit. Did that heavy cloud that tricked him over breakfast leave a trace up there, or maybe this is a hilltop with two humps, like the reluctant Mongolian camel in that movie *The Story of the Weeping Camel,* who at first refuses to nurse her newborn white calf, but weeps at a musical ceremony and then offers her breast. What's the height? Luria asks, and quickly offers his own estimate: Eighty meters, ninety at most. Good eye, the young man tells the old man, eighty-five meters by electronic measurement, thirty, thirty-five minutes on foot. But if the climb would be hard on you, Zvi, we'll force my old car to take us to the last place it can make a U-turn. Luria feels sorry for the ancient government car, which can surmount its defects on the open highway, but on a bumpy dirt road leaves a trail of screws and springs not replaceable at any repair shop.

"So let's walk," says Maimoni, and the two engineers head for a dirt road showing no signs of life—no thorn or thistle, no grasshopper or lizard—except for the occasional tracks of an all-terrain vehicle. And Luria, quickly finding the climb to be steeper than expected, questions why they should exert themselves if "Maimoni's people" have an ATV to make this easier. But Maimoni explains that the four-wheeler belongs not to them but to Shibbolet—actually, to the Society for the Protection of Nature, which lets him use it to locate and take care of wildlife.

But Luria, growing shorter of breath as the road gets more precipitous and the refreshing desert wind disappears, is annoyed with the people whose identity Maimoni keeps murky. Will they even be there, at the summit? Why the secrecy? Does Maimoni think his dementia is unable to absorb a slightly complicated story? Why are you talking in riddles?

"What do riddles have to do with your dementia?" says Maimoni in self-defense. "Maybe it's the other way around."

"The other way around?"

"Maybe your dementia allows me greater liberty."

Maimoni senses that he went too far with the word "liberty."

Wait a second, Zvi, before you go on complaining, let's clarify the dementia that you, and only you, bring up over and over. Is it real, or are you pulling my leg? Because from the minute we hit the road, I haven't noticed any sign of confusion in you. You are as clear and sharp in your thinking and professional analysis as you were back in the days when my father would sing your praises. So it seems to me that this dementia you've adopted is just a word, maybe a wish, or in fact a joke that I, with good humor, try to find amusing.

"A joke?"

"A joke you or your wife cooked up, who the hell knows, in order to confuse me, make me laugh, or tempt me."

"Tempt you? How so?"

"Say, to include you in the project as an unpaid assistant."

"Excuse me, Maimoni, don't try to deny reality. My dementia is very real, my neurologist found it in my brain scan and showed us where it is."

"In a scan?" Maimoni is alarmed. "What does it look like?"

"It doesn't look like anything, just a tiny dark spot in the cerebral cortex, atrophy that swallows first names."

"We all get first names mixed up."

"But I get mixed up about many other things—time, for example, even days of the week."

"You mean to tell me that you don't know what day it is today?"

"Today?" Luria hesitates.

"For example."

"Today is Saturday."

"Saturday?" Maimoni laughs. "Why Saturday? Where'd you get that?"

"Because if yesterday was Tuesday, today is Shabbat, no?"

"No, not really . . ."

"Because it's so quiet and peaceful all around."

"But we're in the desert."

"Ah." Luria furrows his brow with a mischievous smile. "Right . . . it's only the desert. In that case, what day is it really?"

"Today? An ordinary day, Wednesday."

"Right," agrees Luria. "Now I recognize it too. Simply Wednesday. How good of you to check and correct me, which is what my wife intended. I would make sure you wouldn't make engineering or safety errors, and you, for your part, would grill me about names and times, to make it harder for my brain to pulverize reality."

The young man studies the old man sadly, silently, wanting to explain himself, but then says in a whisper: Come, Zvi, let's keep going on this boring road, but don't worry, there are stairs as we approach the top. They're broken and crooked, but easy enough.

PEOPLE WITHOUT IDENTITY

As they leave the dirt road and climb the stairs carved in the rock, which are in fact broken and crooked but easy enough, the sunlight becomes less oppressive, and the wind returns to life, bearing human voices and a whiff of smoke. And Maimoni, making sure that the dementia won't trip up Luria on the stairs, suddenly exclaims: "Yes, they're here, they're here! And now you'll understand why this hill needs a tunnel and not removal."

Luria's professional eye had not failed him in imagining a double hump, for he can now see two high places on the hilltop, combinations of rock and earth, maybe man-made, maybe a whim of nature, impossible to tell. Between the two, thirty meters apart, hangs an old military camouflage net, sheltering an archaeological structure, a house, or a bathhouse, or perhaps the remnant of a temple, in whose small courtyard, sitting around a stone table, are the "people," three in all: a young man, a young woman, and, between them, a bearded man of about fifty.

"Oh, no!" cries the young woman when she sees a stranger has come with Maimoni. And her cry is like a burst of gunfire for the two men, who dive under the table and disappear, perhaps through a makeshift tunnel. Maimoni sees that the woman, likewise panicked, is about to do the same, and he grabs her by the arm: "No, no, don't run away, he's only an engineer like me, another engineer, who knows nothing about you and doesn't want to know, so tell them to come back."

Luria approaches the young woman, who has calmed down, Maimoni holding on to her nonetheless. And really, why should he let go of such an attractive, agile woman, with the allure of a lost civilization in her Pharaonic eyes. Luria extends her an elderly hand, enabling her to get free of the young man's grip, and from within the smile that lights up her face peeks a dimple, like the dimple that long ago sparked his love for his wife before they had exchanged a single word.

"Zvi Luria," he graciously provides his full name. "Ayala," she replies, stress on the last syllable, her first name only. The gentle precision of her accent arouses the memory of a gray morning and an attendant with slanted eyes, positioned behind a wheelchair holding a youth in a leather helmet, who in accurate Hebrew with a proper accent encouraged him to enter the chaotic house where his dementia took root.

The two men hesitantly emerge from behind one of the high places, shaking the dust of their escape from their clothes. The younger one is Ayala's brother, a tall man currently called Ofer, but who will soon have a different, better name. *Inshallah,* the brother whispers, with God's help, not just a new name, but an identity card and number. And this is their father, says Maimoni, placing a friendly hand on the shoulder of the bearded man, who needs to practice saying his own name. With a sad smile, flashing a gold tooth, the father mumbles his name, and his daughter insists that he repeat it, properly accented on the last syllable. With a dismissive wave of the hand, the father glances around. Yeru*ham,* Yeru*ham,* he growls with eyes closed, bowing his head. As his daughter smiles her approval, an impish spark appears in his wide-open eyes and he adds a family name. Yasour, he formally announces, Yeruham Yasour. The name is unfamiliar to his son and daughter: Yasour? Where did that come from?

"It came. Yasour," he firmly declares. "That's how it came and how it will stay."

The Hebrew names, properly pronounced, and the unique surname newly added, befuddle the unpaid assistant, who feels suddenly dizzy and sits down at the stone table, where three abandoned glasses of tea are surrounded by scraps of brown pita bread. He supports his heavy head with his hand and quietly, cautiously tries to get a fix on reality: "Excuse me, what are you? Jews or not?"

"Jews?" The young woman is surprised. "What for?"

"So you're Palestinians?" concludes Luria.

"We were," she answers sadly, "we once were, but no longer."

"So now, what are you? Just Israelis?"

"Not yet, but maybe we will be, maybe . . ."

"Anyway," he gently persists, "meanwhile, what about meanwhile?"

The young woman shrugs her shoulders: "Meanwhile . . ." Her eyes wander, her voice fails.

The father, however, likes the inquisitiveness of the guest. He sits down beside him at the stone table, takes a pack of cigarettes from his shirt pocket, and offers one. Luria, who did not abstain in the past from the pleasures of tobacco, is wary of further clouding his weakened mind, and the rejected cigarette is back with its owner, who lights it and hungrily consumes its smoke. With a little cough he revives his daughter's faltering word: "Meanwhile? Meanwhile, sir, we are Nabateans, we have gone back to being Nabateans," and with a broad wave of his hand, he shows off the power of the ancient identity, since not only the remnants of the house, but also the hill and even the crater, are proof of its grandeur and vitality.

But Maimoni hastens to set a limit: "Meanwhile, my dear Luria, they are not Nabateans but *shabazim,* simply *shabazim.*"

"You mean *shabahim,*" says Luria, "living here without permission."

"No, wrong acronym, these are *shabazim—shohim b'li zehut,* living without identity. Which is why they need a tunnel."

THE PICTURE

"Yes, he's right," the son chides the father. "We have nothing to gain from your Nabateans. Even if they really were here, they'll never come back. So we really are *shabazim,* and the officer has to find us a solution."

"The officer is no longer an officer," mutters the father.

"But he's the one who started this whole story."

"It doesn't matter what he was in the past," interrupts Maimoni, "or even what he is now, the question is, where is he? Five days ago we agreed to have a business meeting here at the hilltop, and I've brought along another road engineer."

"Apparently his wife is not over her *katzeret,*" says the young woman, in defense of the absentee.

"*Katzeret?*" Her father is puzzled. "Like shortness?"

"Yes, Abba, that's the Hebrew word for asthma, it makes a person short of breath. Two days ago he phoned me at the college to tell me his wife was choking in Tel Aviv from the air pollution, so he rushed down to the apartment in Mitzpe Ramon and the clean air of the crater, so she wouldn't—"

"So she wouldn't what?"

The young woman is silent.

"So she wouldn't what?" insists the father.

"So she wouldn't die on him."

They all fall coldly silent. From far away, at the crater's edge, the wind wails as if announcing the death of Shibbolet's wife. Luria's eyelids flutter with fatigue. Desert light dances in his bloodshot eyes. A huge truck angrily groans on Independence Road as the driver refuses to shift its gears. On such afternoons, in their bedroom in Tel Aviv, a dark curtain blocks the sun, the telephone is unplugged, and the doctor, back from the clinic, enjoys her nap.

"Even so, with all respect," protests Maimoni, "why does Shibbolet inform you and not me about his wife's illness, and drive you up here to be with your father, even though he knows there's no way to communicate from here to the outside."

"That's deliberate," the brother chimes in, "someone in hiding needs a place with no communication."

"Hiding from what?" Luria opens his eyes.

"No, no," Maimoni quickly interrupts, "please, don't start telling the story that even I haven't fully understood. Mr. Luria is with me only as a professional, he is a respected road engineer, and he was my father's department head and his friend, which is why he volunteered to help me find a solution that would not compel your father to move from here. I brought him up here, a difficult climb for him, not to hear your complicated story, but so he could see from the hilltop where my road needs to go. And since Shibbolet decided not to come, we can say goodbye now and leave."

"Wait," the father says, "if the engineer made the effort to come up here, he should at least see the picture."

"The picture of what?" Maimoni asks uneasily.

"The picture of my mother," explains the young woman, "the picture you liked."

"Why should he see the picture? What would he get from it?"

"Nothing at the moment. But in the future it might give him an idea."

"What idea could your mother's picture give him?" sputters Maimoni. "No, no, I know you, you want to show him the picture so you can also tell him the story. But I insist that Mr. Luria has no interest or need to hear your story, and in my opinion he would not understand it."

"Why wouldn't he?"

"He wouldn't. It's been hard for me to understand, it'll be even harder for him."

"Okay, no story, just the picture," says the daughter, "Abba knows how to show it without the story."

"But why?" seethes Maimoni. "So your father will cry in front of him too? Why must you make your father cry now, in front of a stranger?"

"I won't cry," the father promises.

"If you cry, that's all right," his daughter reassures him, "you cry not only because you miss Imma, but to win sympathy from the Jews over a death that this time they're not to blame for. So please, Asael, let it go, Mr. Luria will not be coming back here, so he should at least look at the picture and take pity because of what happened to us. Who knows, maybe the anguish of an engineer, even without the story, could bring the solution for this hill."

And with no further ado, she slides under the table like a gazelle and disappears down wooden stairs into an underground room, a cellar or ancient granary. When she returns, she appears to be clutching not a picture but an infant swaddled in cloth, which her father takes carefully and places on the table, removing the cloth, brushing away imaginary dust with his hand, and sheds his first tear. "Here," he turns to the old engineer, "the picture, with no story."

It is a black-and-white photo of a woman of fifty or so, serious and pale, her face unblemished and angular. The vestige of an ancient civilization is visible in her enormous Pharaonic eyes, bequeathed to her daughter. Luria nods somberly, to confirm his sorrow and pity for the beauty that is gone forever. But in the mist of his mind he begins to think of the beautiful stranger as a distant relative confined to an institution.

"How long ago?" he asks.

"Three years have passed."

"And you still cry over her."

"For another hundred years . . ."

"What did she die of?"

"No," Maimoni says. "No way. You promised."

"Right," says the father, "not the story, just the short version. So, sir, the army knew, from the Israeli hospital, that her heart would not last long, so they sent us the officer, this lieutenant colonel, to offer to replace it in Israel with a new heart, but only on condition—"

"A heart transplant," his daughter says.

"Yes, a transplant, but on condition—"

"No condition," Maimoni interrupts.

"Wait, just the condition—"

But Maimoni is determined to stop the condition: "This isn't the short version, it's the whole story. What's going on? When you saw him, you were scared and ran away to hide, and now you want to tell him everything? It's bad enough that I got dragged into this story, leave him out of it. He has no need or interest in complications that are impossible to untangle." He covers the picture with the cloth, to indicate that the conversation is over. "Let's go," he nudges Luria, who seems frozen in place. "And you all tell Shibbolet that I was here, and if he forgot me, he can forget everything I promised him."

Frantically, he turns to the daughter: "And you, young lady, what are you waiting for? You understand, don't you, that nobody is coming today to take you out of here. So if you still want to make it back to school tonight, get ready."

"What?" The father is fearful. "Again she'll ride alone with you?"

"Alone? As you see, this time she'll have a distinguished escort."

SHIBBOLET OR SHIBBOLETH

But the distinguished escort, a pensioner of seventy-two, walks slowly and fearfully down the ancient broken steps, whose owners turned out to be easygoing and pleasant. The steps are trickier on the way down, so the young man doesn't let him out of his sight, and at times extends a helping hand, since an unpaid assistant is also uninsured, and if he falls, no institution will reimburse him for the injury. And as they cautiously descend, the young daughter Ayala, expert in the secrets of the hill, doesn't plod alongside them, but skips, knapsack on her back, taking shortcuts that only she knows. And while she waits now and then for the engineers to catch up, she climbs on a rock or mound to capture with her sophisticated digital camera, from various angles, the two men who may or may not be aware of the lens immortalizing them.

Here's Route 40, Independence Road, black and solid as ever, and Ayala is waiting by the car parked at the roadside, but when she reaches for the rear door handle, Maimoni suggests that Luria stretch out on the back seat for the ride home. If he wants, he can ignore the seat belt and get cozy under a blanket.

It's 3:30 p.m., and though sunset is still far off, a darkness is settling into the crater, and the surrounding cliffs begin to change from pale yellow to bright red. Do you have anything for a headache? Luria asks Maimoni. Your people up there made me dizzy and confused. But Maimoni exonerates them. Don't blame them, blame the dry desert air, you're a man of the North, not used to it. And since ancient government cars don't come with painkillers or first-aid kits, but only old emergency instructions for changing a tire or putting out a fire, Maimoni promises to stop at the Genesis Hotel to get some Tylenol.

As they head up Independence Road, Luria's cell phone comes back to life, and a text message, helplessly fluttering in the ether, lands with a chirp. *What's happening? Are you okay?* Dina wrote. *If you haven't gone missing, send a sign.* And the husband quickly establishes his existence with a phone call: This is me, hale, hearty, and lucid, on the way home. You were right, even a person without dementia could get lost in this wasteland. But I didn't call before, because we just came down from a Nabatean hill boycotted by electronic communication. We're still feeling our way professionally, but Dina, get ready for big surprises from the human angle. One of them is sitting in front of me, next to the driver, and we'll soon find out why she's upset.

Big American cars like this one are graced with a wide windshield, so a careful driver can expand his field of vision. Among the approaching vehicles that appear and disappear on the winding road, Ayala glimpses a small ATV four-wheeler, and asks that Maimoni pull over at the first opportunity. Fearing that Shibbolet could drive by without noticing them, she gets out of the car, crosses the road, and stands facing the oncoming traffic, to make sure Shibbolet will not miss her. And indeed, when he comes around the bend he sees her, slows down, and stops the ATV on the side of the road, then stands imperiously in the middle of Route 40, halting the vehicles in both directions, then returns to his ATV and makes a quick U-turn, parking nose-to-nose with the old American car.

So this is Shibbolet, Luria says to himself, but he doesn't leave the car, merely lowers a window to get a fix on the man. Though Shibbolet is over sixty, his body is thin and youthful, but his hair is white and his face grooved with wrinkles. Shibbolet approaches the open window.

"Asael tells me you also think a tunnel is possible."

"Everything is possible," responds Luria, "but impossible that someone will approve such a huge expense."

"All the same, is it lawful, in order to build a military road, to destroy a hill with important archaeological ruins?"

"It depends whose ruins. If they are of other nations, we have officials who enjoy destroying them. Yes, Mr. Shibbolet, I had such cases in the past."

"You can call me Shibbolet, without the Mister."

"Thank you, but it's still not clear to me if Shibbolet is the family name or the first name."

"The word 'shibboleth' exists in other languages too, you can find its echoes all over the internet. Maybe that's how the first and last names were united."

"But the internet can't explain," says Luria, "why Maimoni was so scared of you."

Shibbolet smiles with satisfaction. "I see he managed to tell you that history. But the internet can't tell you, and neither can I, why Maimoni the new recruit was so terrified of me. And I must confess, his fear encouraged me to torment him, to give him good reason to be afraid of me."

"Bravo, Shibbolet." Maimoni welcomes the confession.

"Still," says Luria, not dropping the subject, "your name has a pleasant ring to it. What soothes the heart more than a golden stalk of grain standing alone in a field?"

"Excuse me," objects the former commander, "that is not the only meaning of my name. Look again at the internet, a *shibbolet* is not only a lovely plant, but also a whirlpool."

"Did you know that?" Luria asks Maimoni.

But the answer is drowned out by an immense, double fuel truck, which shakes the road with a deafening roar. "Watch out!" shouts Shibbolet. "It's a reckless monster." He seizes the young woman with both hands and pulls her behind the car to protect her. And when the truck emerges from the curve to reveal its full length and bulk, it really is a monster, its body festooned with dozens of colored lights, and the driver, a hairy giant bare from the waist up, and perhaps below as well, is startled by the little group undermining the elegance of his driving, and blares his three horns, yelling for good measure, "Crazy! Crazy!" and disappears.

"He's right," says Shibbolet, "it's crazy to stop in the middle of this road."

"But how else would I catch you?" says the young woman.

"What do you mean, catch me? I was on my way to you, and the envelope is ready. Have I ever forgotten you? This is where we stand, I have to hang on to your money, because no bank will take you as customers."

Luria is still in the car. The window is open, his headache is pounding. Can the empty space in his head hurt, or is this normal pain of the part that remains healthy and rational? He watches Shibbolet, who zips open a shoulder bag, takes out a brown envelope, and hands it to the young woman without identity, who thanks him with a big hug. Maimoni gets in the car and starts the engine, calling out to Ayala to join him. Shibbolet watches them blankly, not hurrying to move his four-wheeler to clear their way. "Excuse me, Shibbolet," Luria calls out, "do you happen to have something for a headache?"

"I sure do," answers the officer, "and for good reason. A man like me, who wanders in the desert, has to have a first-aid kit." He fetches a large, unlabeled tin box, rummages through it, and asks, "Which do you prefer, Acamol or Optalgin?" He holds out his palm with two identical white pills.

"Which do you recommend?"

"That depends on how severe the pain is."

"Not where it is?"

"Only if you can locate it. But why hesitate, you have a long ride ahead, so take the stronger one, the Optalgin. But I have no water for you, the water in my ATV is only suitable for rabbits or foxes."

"There are animals in this crater? Not just imaginary ones?"

"There are animals."

"Nice. I don't need water, Shibbolet. At my age you know how to swallow pills without water. On your recommendation, I'll take the stronger one."

Shibbolet chooses one pill, the twin of the other, and gives it to Luria, who puts it in his mouth and tilts his head back. As the pill slides into his throat, he again notices the murky cloud that at noon tried to lift up the whole crater, and new, unfamiliar anguish pools inside him, and he suddenly feels sorry for the former officer, who waits to be sure the pill reached its destination.

"I share your sorrow," Luria says, "even though I didn't know her."

"What sorrow are you talking about?"

"Over your wife who died in the mountains."

"My wife?" Shibbolet is shocked. "What mountains?" He turns angrily to Maimoni, who hasn't heard the conversation. "What on earth is he talking about?"

"If nobody died," says Luria, flustered, "that's great." And he rolls up the window and quickly fastens his seat belt.

TWO SUNS

With Independence Road behind them and the car cruising pleasantly along, Luria takes off his shoes, unbuckles the safety belt, and stretches out on the seat. "You can get comfortable if you want," says Maimoni, fondly observing his unpaid assistant. "If you want a blanket, let me know."

The young woman turns her head and beams a big smile at the old man, and the solitary dimple on her pretty face again reminds Luria of that first spark of love for his wife. No need yet for the blanket, he says, I first have to see if Shibbolet's pill is doing the trick. But what did you tell him, says Maimoni, that made him so angry? "Something about death," says Luria, playing dumb. "Whose death?" "Nobody's," Luria says warily. "Death in general, the idea of death."

It's 4:15, and who knows if Maimoni plans to stop en route to rest, or if the smooth drive overrides his fatigue. Through the car's dusty windshield it looks as if winter is closing in. Waves of sand are swirling. The darkness falling on Sde Boker College deepens its isolation. Again, a sign urging a stop at Ben-Gurion's grave. Good thing we already visited him and his wife, thinks the pensioner, because the pill I swallowed reduces the pain to a kind of sweet dizziness. Is it possible that this Shibbolet wanted to drug me? Instead of getting mixed up with his wife's alleged death, I should have talked to him about the certain death of Ben-Gurion. Nevertheless, I sense a sliver of hope in his furious reaction. Will I, like Maimoni, need to fear him from now on? But who says we'll ever meet again?

The eight-cylinder gas guzzler cushions the ride, the hum of the engine puts the passenger to sleep. But when the car stops and turns silent, his nap is cut short, and while the tank is filled, a Bedouin boy smiles at the passenger as he cleans the windshield with a wet rag. Could you also check the tires? Maimoni asks. Of course, sir, no problem, just tell me what pressure. Let's see, says Maimoni, moving the car to the air pump at a corner of the gas station. But the elderly American car isn't listed on the pump's chart, so Maimoni and the Bedouin discuss the likely air pressures for front and rear, and he gives the boy a nice tip and suggests to Luria that he go stretch his legs in the mini-market.

But the windblown, dusty raindrops deter the pensioner. I'll be fine if you bring me a large cappuccino, he says, and watches through the spotted window as the young man and woman, his arm around her like a father, break into a run.

True, Luria had scrupulously kept his distance from the private lives of his subordinates, all the more so from the lives of people he worked for, but now he wonders whether the distance, so very useful in the past, is still an advantage in his present condition of mild confusion. For if, as the neurologist advised, the spirit is obligated to fight the darkness crawling through his brain, maybe poking into the secret lives of others would help it get sharper. As he raises his eyes to look for the suddenly vanished sun, Ayala exits the mini-market holding the hot coffee. By the air pump, the Bedouin boy, wearily removing the spare tire from the trunk, freezes in place and, as if hypnotized, watches the young woman as the rear door opens for her. The pensioner carefully accepts the steaming coffee, filled precariously to the brim, and repays the woman for her trouble with the chocolate square accompanying the cup. The few raindrops that landed on her add a fresh scent to her soft femininity, so he invites her to sit beside him till the driver returns. At first she is embarrassed, hesitant, but when Luria inquires as to her real name, she is surprised but also responsive.

"Hanadi," she reveals in a whisper.

"Hanadi?" Luria slowly repeats the enchanting name. "What does it mean?"

"It's a flower," she says. "Which flower?" "A purple flower." "By the way, your Hebrew—" Luria is about to say. Yes, yes, she knows that her Hebrew has no foreign accent, the result of several years of effort at an Israeli school.

"With your brother?"

"No, Shibbolet put us in different schools, so we wouldn't talk Arabic to each other."

"Really, why not?"

"Why not?" A fiery look in her eyes. "Why not? This is exactly the story Maimoni didn't want us to tell you. Because we, sir, have no identity card, not this one or that one or the other one."

Luria has no time to guess which countries refuse to grant them an identity card, because Maimoni, laden with purchases, taps on the window, and Hanadi devours the chocolate and hurries back to the front seat, and Maimoni, resting the bags at her feet, wonders why a mini-market at a desert gas station charges such high prices. "Because there are so few buyers," explains Hanadi, but Maimoni thinks the opposite—if there are few buyers, prices should be lower. "But if they're overpriced, why did you buy so much?" she teases him affectionately. Why? Because he must always have something sweet for his twins, a boy and a girl, when he comes home late at night, and it goes without saying that each has to get exactly what the other gets, plus a bonus of something that is special for each. "So it's all for your kids?" she asks. "No, also something for Mr. Luria." "And something for me?" Hanadi says. "Most of it," he assures her, "is for you to eat this evening in your new room." He turns to his unpaid assistant and asks for permission to detour from the Trans-Israel Highway, so he can bring the young lady directly to her college, an extra half hour at most. "Unless," says Maimoni, "your wife is impatiently waiting for you?"

"She's always waiting for me, and I'm always waiting for her,"

Luria defines the relationship, "but this time, because she gave me to you without salary or benefits, it's not me she's waiting for but you, to bring me back safe and sound. She is a patient person, but it would be a good idea to tell her when we'll arrive."

Maimoni laughs. "In an hour and a half." He steps on the gas, and after bypassing Beersheba on the ring road, he accelerates some more, and since he knows all the roads of the South, a few of which he helped to plan, he takes the best exit and speeds toward Sapir College, near the city of Sderot.

"What are you studying?" Luria asks.

"She's going to study film, but for now she's training as a photographer," Maimoni answers for her. "Shibbolet bought her a state-of-the-art camera, and she's taking pictures of desert flora and fauna."

"And also pictures of the sun," says the girl, "because sometimes there are two suns shining in the Ramon Crater."

"Two suns? Really?"

"Really." She opens her pack and takes out a photograph showing two fiery suns at the edge of a cliff, similar in size and color.

Luria grins. "This isn't just an illusion of your fancy camera?"

"No, the illusion is in the world. It's not mine."

Luria nods. He understands.

DEATH

With no vacancies in the small dormitory lot, Maimoni parks on the street in a spot designated for the disabled, picks up the food bags, and escorts the student to her room, to help her get settled.

"If it's okay with you," he says to Luria, "wait for me in the car. The key is in the ignition, so if somebody disabled shows up and complains, you can move the car, and I'll be back in ten minutes, fifteen tops, to drive you home. I'm also leaving the car light on so you won't feel lonely."

And Luria immediately phones his wife: "Believe it or not, I'm actually on the way back to you. But you made me not only an assistant without pay, but an assistant without rights, because you didn't define the working hours with the employer, and now I'm in his hands, subject to his rhythm. Yes, he's a charming and intelligent boy, good-looking, and therefore, apart from the army road, he has other interests, mainly romantic, a story I'm trying to follow, in order to train my spirit in delicate matters, to quote the neurologist."

"Very good," agrees his wife, "as a doctor, I'm telling you that the mind or spirit can push back the illness. It's a shame your spirit didn't notice that you stuck the quiche I made yesterday in the freezer instead of the fridge." "I was thinking," he sighs, "that you would have a hard time finding it, because there are whole areas in the fridge you are not familiar with." "So why did you hide it where it can't be seen?" "You can see if you try, it wasn't me who stuck it there, but the demon running around inside me." "The demon?" She laughs. "Now it's a demon? Anyway, why would the demon put it in the freezer and not the fridge?" "Because this demon loves you, and thought that if you decided, after such a long time, to bake something, it should be preserved. Wait, Dinaleh, I hear ringing, must be Maimoni's mobile he forgot in the car. So I'll hang up, and we'll see each other at home in an hour."

Finding the phone on the floor of the car is no simple matter. He has to get out and lean inside, as the ringing persists, and then he hears the strong voice of an older woman, looking for Asael.

"He's not here now," says Luria, "he'll be back in a few minutes." "And who are you?" "I'm a road engineer who's helping him." "What is your name?" "Zvi Luria is my name." "Ah," she says, "many years ago I heard that name. Listen, Zvi Luria, tell Asael that his father died, and he should hurry home." "I am sorry to hear that, but who are you? Hello? Are you still there?" "No, I don't belong there anymore, I didn't see him, but a neighbor who went in found him dead, and called me. Asael will know which neighbor, and he can call her for the details. He shouldn't call me back, I'm going to a concert and my phone will be turned off. He should just go fast to his father, he's there alone, dead. That's all."

Luria, agonized and upset, runs to look for Maimoni. So, he says to himself, the imaginary death of Shibbolet's wife has turned into a real one. But where to find Maimoni? How will he summon the strength to tell him? Students pass by, but apart from the name Ayala he has nothing to offer. Good, there's no point in looking, and no reason to hurry, the dead man is dead, when Maimoni gets back I'll tell him, very gently, little by little. And he gets in the car and thinks, If his father has died, the tunnel will have to wait, and might not be built in any case.

A parking inspector taps on the window. Sir, if you are not disabled, move the car from here. Given no choice, Luria moves to the driver's seat, feels the key in the ignition. But how to turn on the headlights? And how do the gears work? The car is not only outmoded, it's not automatic. Luria dives into his past. Many years ago they gave him a similar car. He slides the seat closer to the wheel, turns the key, remembers there's also a clutch, sticks out his left foot to feel for it, and the car staggers forward, without lights. Very carefully, as if on its own, it drifts into a crosswalk and stops in front of large garbage dumpsters. The responsibility to get out of here is no longer his. Luria rests his head on the steering wheel and closes his eyes.

Maimoni returns more than half an hour later, and when he locates the car and the elderly assistant, he seems cheerful and satisfied, pleased with himself for remembering to leave the key, and with a friendly wink suggests that the pensioner drive the rest of the way home.

But Luria does not reply, just hands him the mobile phone without a word and gets out of the driver's seat. "When you were away, someone tried to call you, someone was looking for you." "It wasn't my father?" "No, I would have recognized his voice." "Of course," says Maimoni, "and he would have recognized yours, because I told him you were coming with me, and he was very happy about that." "Sure, why wouldn't he be happy?" says Luria. "But wait, I think it was actually a woman." "A woman?" Maimoni is surprised. "Which woman?" "I don't know." "What did she say?" "She said not to call her back, she was going into a concert and turning off her cell phone. So maybe she'll call you after the concert." "If she went to a concert, it wasn't my wife, it had to be somebody else." "Yes, somebody else," agrees Luria. "So she'll certainly call again soon," reasons Maimoni. "Yes, for sure," confirms Luria, agonized that he cannot bring himself to give Maimoni the bitter news that flops in his brain like a black fish, banging against walls, unable to escape, but not swallowed up entirely by the atrophy.

He watches Maimoni driving rather recklessly, and says to himself: Until I can set the black fish free, I have a chance to learn something about this Ayala. Maimoni tells him he helped her move to another room, smaller, but where she'll live without a roommate and be able to take better care of herself. "Yes," says Luria, "if she has no identity card, she'd better not talk in her sleep." Maimoni is shocked: "Who told you she doesn't have an ID card?" "She did," says Luria. "Amazing," says Maimoni, "how quickly you won her trust. That's not good, she should watch her tongue."

Luria says nothing. The road is wet, foggy. Yes, it's been a long day, with no afternoon nap and meager professional rewards. Luria grips his head in both hands and tries to remember the voice of the woman, but the upbeat tune that Maimoni is softly singing muffles her words.

They approach Luria's home, obviously Luria must not let the young man go until he can liberate the news trapped in his mind, and he phones his wife and says, "Can I bring a guest? He heard about the quiche and would like a taste." "He can come," says Dina, "but he should know that I take no responsibility for how it tastes." "Come up," Luria says to Maimoni, who is still in a good mood. "Come up for a minute and give my wife a report on your unpaid assistant." "You sure?" says Maimoni. "You're not tired?" "No, it's strange, I feel refreshed after today, even the dementia feels young. Come taste the quiche Dina learned to make from the mother of one of her sick kids. A quiche of noodles intertwined like the human brain." "Human brain?" Maimoni recoils. "Yes," insists Luria, "at least in the scan the neurologist showed us." "But a tasty brain, I hope," says Maimoni. "Yes, try it and you'll see."

THE QUICHE

The intriguing noodle quiche waits on the kitchen table for the master of the house and his guest, and only in the wildest imagination can it be compared to a human brain. Dina is proud of it but also apprehensive, and has therefore not yet taken a knife to it. Very warmly she greets the handsome engineer, and sends him too, not only her husband, to wash the dust of the desert from his face and hands. "How's the helper I gave you?" she asks Maimoni, his beard moist, glistening. "He's too good," answers Maimoni, "he wants to know everything, even things nobody wanted him to know." "In that case," Dina grins, "you might have to pay him a salary." Maimoni laughs, but Luria remains gloomy. The news imprisoned inside pains him. "Why aren't you eating, Zvi?" asks his wife. "Asael will finish it all." Indeed, Maimoni shamelessly holds out his plate for more. But the name Asael, pronounced now in a woman's voice, sets Luria trembling, and he says to Maimoni: "By the way, I just remembered, the older woman who called was looking for Asael, not for Maimoni, and she sounded like someone who knew you well, like a family member—'tell Asael,' she said, 'where is Asael?,' 'don't forget to tell Asael,' again and again Asael." "In which case," Maimoni says nervously, "it must have been my mother, who still takes pride in the strange biblical name she pinned on me, while everyone else, my wife included, calls me Maimoni. But what did she want? When she calls, there's always something bad on her mind. Never just to ask how I am." He looks at his phone to check the last incoming calls, but the number he finds is unfamiliar. "No, that's not her phone. She forgets to charge it, so she uses the phone of the man she's with at the moment. No big deal, I'll call Abba, maybe he knows what's bugging her. They've been apart for many years, but he somehow keeps up-to-date about her and can even sense what's going on in her head."

Luria is horrified. The black fish begins to burn deep within. He tightly grabs Maimoni's hand as it prepares to call his father, and cries out, "Wait, no, don't call, listen, I remember now, I remember that the woman said the neighbor had phoned her."

"The neighbor? Which neighbor?"

"She didn't give her name, but now I'm sure she said that the neighbor called her, a neighbor who happened to go into your house, I mean, your father's house, and found him, apparently, only apparently, that's what she said, I mean the neighbor, and she said that Asael would know which neighbor and could get the details from her."

"My father's neighbor?" Maimoni jumps from his chair.

"Yes, that was the message, I remember now. In other words, all there is for now is only what the neighbor told her, but wait, why didn't this neighbor call you directly?"

"Because she was afraid to tell me," Maimoni cries out, sobbing in anguish. "Because she knows how much I love him, how hard it will be for me without him, so she was afraid to tell me, oh, the good woman. So she called my mother, because she knew that Abba's death would just slide off of her."

"Impossible."

"Totally possible. Just like her to give such news through a stranger and go to a concert and not call again. But you, you," he turns to Luria, "why did you say nothing? How could you say nothing? How could you let me sit calmly and kid around with news like this buried inside you?"

"Don't be mad at him," says Dina, defending her husband. "He forgets things innocently, it happens to him."

"It's not me, it's the dementia," mumbles Luria. "I told you, beware of me, sometimes I erase things that were just said. For no reason."

"Okay, no big deal, never mind, I'm sorry. That's it. The end." And Maimoni paces around the room, tugging weirdly at his beard.

"You did tell me on the road," says Luria imploringly, "that you knew his death was coming soon."

"I knew, yes, I even prepared myself, but now that it's real, final, it hurts so much. How could you forget to tell me he was dead, how could you possibly forget something like that? And I'm making small talk with the two of you, and he's lying there dead, all alone . . ."

"Alone? Why alone?"

"Yes, alone. I'm leaving, excuse me, we'll talk, we'll talk."

"Be careful," says Dina, taking his hand, "maybe you'd like us to drive you."

"No need, I'll drive there alone."

"At least be in touch when you set a time for the funeral."

"No funeral, no funeral," Maimoni interrupts angrily. "He donated his body to science, naïvely thinking science would save him. No funeral. Maybe a shiva. Why not? There'll be a shiva." Flooded with tears, he hugs Dina tightly and touches Luria gently. "Yes, we'll do a shiva, and the two of you will come to console me." And he opens the door and disappears down the stairs.

The remains of the quiche sit forlornly on the table, and Dina looks at her husband, his eyes downcast. Finally she asks: "Anyway, Zvi, how and why did you suddenly remember?"

"Your quiche."

"The quiche?"

"Yesterday, when I got up in the middle of the night and the quiche was cooling on the kitchen table, it looked to me in the moonlight like a brain, a human brain, so apparently I put it in the freezer to preserve it."

"What are you talking about? The quiche?"

"Never mind, craziness, because I remembered something similar in the scan the neurologist showed us. And this evening, when you started to slice it, I said to myself, That's what I need too, to slice my brain to find what's forgotten there inside, something that I knew was really important and I didn't remember what."

THE SHIVA

Maimoni managed to place a death notice in the next morning's newspapers, and since there would be no funeral, he had hastily decided to begin the shiva immediately, and listed the address without specifying visiting hours, so Luria could only hope the science people would collect the body at the crack of dawn, otherwise the son's promptest consolers would have to part from the dearly departed in person. Luria has not shared this anxiety with his wife. She may be a doctor, but she also denies death and refuses to talk or even think about it, which is why she chose pediatrics and not gerontology.

The next evening they have tickets for Gounod's opera *Romeo and Juliet,* and decide to pay their shiva call beforehand, in case friends and relatives were slow to arrive and Maimoni was left sitting alone in his father's house. And because it was at their home that Maimoni first learned, however awkwardly, of the death, they should be the first ones at the shiva.

They are not mistaken. When they arrive at the one-story house in Hod HaSharon, they find a home empty of guests and even of the mourner himself, who has left the front door open. They hesitantly enter the living room and then part ways, Dina heading to the patio to look for Maimoni in the garden, while

Luria is drawn to the dead man's bedroom. I worked with this legal adviser for many years, he says to himself, I spent hours with him in endless, exhausting meetings, and sometimes we took field trips to plan land confiscations, but never once did I visit his home, and I refused to take any interest in his private life. And now, when he is no longer among the living, here I am at his bedroom door, staring at his unmade bed, his pajama bottoms flung on the floor, witnesses to his final fight for life. I connect with his final intimate moments and try to think new human thoughts. Through the window, as he may have seen in his last days, the sun inflames a distant horizon, doubling and tripling itself in farewell, a tribute to the deceased.

He is startled as his wife touches his shoulder. "No, Zvi, it's not nice to peek into his bedroom this way, let's wait in the living room. I found the housekeeper, who said Maimoni went to the store and would be back soon." With a firm hand she shuts the bedroom door and steers her husband to the living room. The housekeeper emerges from the kitchen, a young, barefoot woman, her hair wrapped in a black scarf, carrying a tray with two cups of tea surrounded by sesame cookies. Luria nods his thanks and takes a cup and a cookie, and when he lifts his eyes he feels dizzy. Is the dementia again conflating his worlds? Is this religious housekeeper the double of the photography student, the young woman with no identity? There is a glimmer of friendship in those Pharaonic eyes. Yes, it is her, he shudders, Maimoni whisked her here to help him with the shiva and maybe other things. And as he considers how to explain her existence to his wife, Maimoni flies into the house, laden with groceries that the woman quickly takes off his hands. "It's good that you came," he says, hugging the couple, his voice shaky with emotion. "I'm worried that very few people will notice the death announcement I placed today, but in any case I bought groceries and got someone to help me. My wife is in marathon meetings, and she's no good for cooking anyway, but she's sending over the twins with her mother, so at least you can meet them."

"Why bother with cooking?" wonders Luria. "Why not?" retorts Maimoni. "Aren't people who take the trouble to come and comfort me entitled to hot food to comfort them?" "Why hot?" says Luria. "Something symbolic is enough, cookies, pretzels, nuts, soft drinks, no need for real food or to bring in the girl from the college." "Excuse me, Zvi," Dina scolds her husband, "you forgot that this is his shiva, not yours." "Precisely, Zvi," says Maimoni, "listen to your wife," and his eyes caress the woman who could be his mother. "This is the first time, and I hope the last, I am organizing a shiva, because my mother's shiva will be organized by her last man, whoever that may be." And he hurries to the kitchen, to see what fell and broke.

"In any event," Luria remarks with vague hostility, "he grew his mourning beard even before his father died."

The visitors trickle in, gradually increasing in number. Among them are avid readers of death notices who knew the end was near, and maybe a few who rushed to come for fear that science, which had robbed them of a funeral, would shortchange the shiva too. Divon and his wife also arrive, and before consoling Maimoni, they go straight to Luria and his wife, who are leafing through photo albums. "How could you disappear on me, Zvi, after your speech?" Divon reproaches his former boss. "You didn't give me a chance to thank you and marvel." "Marvel about what?" "That you didn't show a shadow of your anger and grudge against me. If you're not angry at me anymore, it means I'm no longer important to you."

"I'm done with anger," replies Luria, "but not with disappointment. So many beautiful roads that we planned together went down the drain because of your Africa. But at the party, when for the first time I saw your youngest son in the wheelchair, I realized you needed a higher salary than they would pay you as a division manager, and so, without relinquishing my disappointment, I gave up and forgave you."

All the while, as Luria speaks, Divon's wife watches him severely, and lashes out when he's done: "Excuse me, why did you say 'for the first time'? Before we went to Kenya, when the house was nearly empty, for some reason you decided to personally deliver the plans Tzahi asked for, and you got me out of bed to hand them to me, and you saw the child in the wheelchair in the garden, and you touched him, and looked at him closely, and questioned his attendant about his condition. Even so, after you saw him, we heard in Africa about your anger at Tzahi." She turns to Dina: "What's going on with your husband, is this his usual method, to fudge and then forget, with a kind of indifferent contempt? He blotted out my name in his speech, spoke with unfriendly formality about 'Mrs. Divon,' as if I have no name, and then ran away when I asked that he give me back my name. Is this his new style? Sort of a game of make-believe? Or is it maybe, God forbid, something in his head?"

"Both," Dina replies with a smile.

"Both?"

Luria nods. "Yes, something in the head, what can I do?" And Dina, sensing his discomfort, gently drops the vanished name: "Yes, Rachel, don't be angry with him, even I can't always tell when his forgetfulness is real and when he's pretending."

"All the same," says Divon, "none of this prevents Maimoni from seeking his help with his new military project."

"But without pay," adds Maimoni, who joins them, carrying piggyback a sweet little girl, brought to the shiva with her twin brother by the mother-in-law, a woman of advanced age who sits down on the sofa beside a bowl of nuts, picking at them one by one like a weary bird.

The living room is filling up. Apparently people waited for the father to die so they could rush to console his son. "Who are they all? You know them?" Luria asks his former deputy. "They would seem to be the landowners Maimoni compensated well for his confiscations," says Divon with a wink. "Really, or are you kidding?" "Both." Divon smiles and steals a fistful of nuts from the grandma's bowl.

The sun is nearly gone, ushered out by light rain. There's heavy traffic from Hod HaSharon to Tel Aviv, and Luria doesn't want to be relegated with other latecomers to a remote balcony in the opera house. But since they were the first to arrive at the shiva, they are entitled to be the first to leave. "Anyway, it's too bad we didn't meet your wife," says Dina to Maimoni. "That's okay," he says with the wave of a hand. "You met old friends instead."

On their way out they pass the kitchen, where Ayala is feeding the twins. They sit up straight at the table with napkins tucked at their necks. The young woman's black headscarf is gone, her long hair is down, but she's still walking barefoot. She looks like the young mother of well-mannered twins. When they ask for something they raise their hands, as if this weren't their late grandpa's kitchen but a classroom. Dina, in typical fashion, wants to enter the kitchen and get a good look at the babysitter, but Luria is reluctant to introduce her to a young woman with no clear identity.

PHANTOM OF THE OPERA

The Golda Meir underground garage is full. There's no choice but to occupy a disabled spot, decides Luria, "and you will testify as a doctor that I'm allowed, because I'm a little disabled." "Disabled," she says without emotion, "and soon to be banned from driving."

As they enter the lobby, the gong is rung for the third time, and in the dimmed hall they manage to slip into their regular seats alongside their longtime neighbors, who rise to let them through. They didn't have time to buy a program, and Dina is upset. "It's not so bad," says her husband, "opera programs often detract from the beautiful music with summaries of absurd plots, but this time, Dinaleh, it's *Romeo and Juliet,* familiar, and though we'll have no problem understanding why they kill themselves at the end, we'll try to get a program at intermission."

The seats are comfortable and they are sweetly drowsy. Gounod's music flows along pleasantly, albeit lacking melodies suitable for singing in the shower. Luria watches the thrilling duels of feuding Venetian families, swords clashing on a circular stage slanted toward the audience. What are opera swords made of? From afar they look thin but strong, and it's surprising that in the heat of battle no singer has lost a nose or an eye. Do the music and singing accompanying the fights protect the singers from mishaps? He likes the idea and wants to whisper it to his wife, but now, as the music picks up pace, Dina dozes off, her head nodding in tempo. He strokes her hand, and getting no response he shakes her. "What a shame," he pleads for the opera's sake. "But I hear it," she whispers without opening her eyes. "Not enough, you also need to see it." "Yes," she admits, and her eyes open as Romeo is impaling his rival with a sword.

The shiva had robbed the doctor of her afternoon nap, but she perks up with food and drink at intermission, her loving eyes twinkling at Luria. The program she was after is forgotten, but he wants to prove that his memory can sometimes be better than hers, so he reminds her. Oh, you're right, at least I can read about what I had missed in the first half. The first gong has sounded, and they agree to meet inside the hall.

The unsold programs have been returned to the office, but the salesman, an art history student, is still at the counter. He is determined not to leave the tardy buyer without a program, lest he miss an original article about the evolution of the theme of love between a man and a woman who belong to opposing camps. Romeo and Juliet are one small example, declares the student. Shakespeare did not invent anything new, including the short-term poison the friar persuades Juliet to swallow. He insists that Luria wait until he brings him a program. But there's no time, says Luria, the gong already rang for the second half. "Don't worry, we have plenty of time, they threaten the audience for no reason. By the way, sir, what is your profession?" "I am an engineer," answers Luria, "but the program is for my wife." "And what does she do?" "She's a doctor." "That's fine," says the student, oddly patronizing. "The two of you will be able to follow the article and appreciate the many citations."

A few minutes go by and the gong issues a clear warning—three minutes to curtain time. Little by little the lobby lingerers head for their seats. An usher is in the process of dismantling the empty counter. Enough, thinks Luria, I've waited too long for the program, but the wish to win his wife's grateful smile holds him back.

Not three minutes elapse before the final announcement that the opera is about to begin. The silence grows deeper. There is a limit. Probably the student himself wrote the piece, if he's so eager to supply it. And even if a one-minute warning is only a false alarm, Luria will have to dislodge many music lovers to reach his wife, who no doubt suspects by now that the dementia has led him to sit for the second half next to another woman. And as he runs toward the entrance that swallows the last of the audience, the student catches up to him, waving the program, already opened to the page of the article. Thanks, *habibi,* says Luria, snatching the program, we'll read it tonight and remember you. By the way, what's your name? Here, says the student, proudly pointing to his byline, if you suspected, you were right, it's my piece, and everything in it is checked and reliable. And before Luria manages to get free of him, he is delicately asked to pay twenty shekels for the program, and then finds that his way in is blocked.

A zealous usher, determined to put an end to anarchy, decides to send the latecomers to the designated balcony in the far reaches of the topmost level. Luria is the first and only candidate. As he ponders whether to accept his fate or beg for his life, he sees an overdressed woman, tottering on high heels, who ignores him and knocks loudly, three times, on the wood-paneled wall. This is not a woman with dementia worse than his, for a buzzer sounds beyond the wall, and a narrow hidden door slowly opens, and the woman quickly slips inside, and Luria, deftly sticking the program between the door and its frame, enters in her wake.

The student who authored the article was correct. Judging by the noise in the hall, the management had recalled the audience too soon. The performance is far from imminent, with musicians still tuning their instruments. At first Luria imagines that he can sneak into the main hall through the orchestra pit, quietly tagging along with the conductor, but it turns out the orchestra is at a lower level that leads only to the street. It's too late to escape outdoors, because the conductor has made his grand entrance to a round of applause. Luria needs to find a different way to prove to his wife that he hasn't gone missing.

Here, backstage, the sound is muffled, as though the music and singing come alive only for the audience in the hall. The circular, modern space from the earlier part of the opera is hidden by black screens, intended to block the audience's view of the changing scenery and the singers and supernumeraries getting ready to enter the plot. Here is the chorus, swords on their belts, looking self-conscious in blue uniforms. Here's your chance to handle an opera sword, to see if it's actually hard and sharp, says Luria to himself, inching toward the chorus. The swordsmen, amid a hive of technicians and stagehands, are unperturbed by the elderly citizen joining them, as a plump woman walks around with a makeup cart, mopping sweat and refreshing makeup. The choral conductor, a young redheaded guy in jeans, gets up on a chair and signals to the chorus to start singing and slowly flow onstage. Here's Juliet in all her bridal glory, dressed in white, making small talk with the friar about to dose her with short-term poison that her lover will think has killed her. Luria feels for the young woman, doomed by naïveté, and before the music forces her to sing of her disaster, the makeup lady rushes to wipe the sweat from her face and neck, touch her up with eyebrow pencil, and add blood-red color to her lips.

One of the stage managers carefully raises the black screen and waves Juliet onstage. Luria marvels at the simple set. The floor is made of rough wooden boards painted a fading gray, and the splendid altar seems to be made of cardboard. Are all the grandeur and magic that move the audience just a function of the lighting?

Juliet vanishes from his view, but her tormented singing about Romeo, who in a flurry of revenge doomed their love, makes his heart tremble. Because the Hebrew supertitles, visible in the hall, are unavailable to him, Luria has an urge to follow the singer to better understand her lament. He picks up a reddish sponge from the makeup cart, wipes sweat from his face or perhaps powders it, and his white hair glints for a second through a slit in the black curtain, but a powerful hand violently yanks him backward. "Where are you going? Are you insane? Who are you, anyway?"

"Who am I?" Luria bellows indignantly. He is a longtime season ticket holder at the New Israel Opera, who went looking for a program at intermission, and meanwhile they blocked his entry to the hall. "So why did you go onstage?" "I had no other way to see the end of the opera." "You won't see anything from here, sir, and you're not allowed to be here. Leave now and go to the upper balcony, and you'll find an usher to seat you. The stage is no place for you." But Luria won't budge. No, he pleads, he'll get mixed up in the empty corridors searching for the latecomers' balcony, and will meanwhile miss most of the performance. He has an expensive seat in the hall, right next to his wife, but they blocked his entry, and if there's no way to see the end of the opera from the hall, at least give him permission to watch from up high, in the huge space where they raise and lower the scenery, there must be some little balcony up there, so he can see how this tragedy ends. He is a veteran engineer able to find his way in complicated structures.

The stage manager looks at the veteran ticket holder with a mischievous grin, then looks at his watch. No problem, the opera will be over anyway in half an hour. "Anything you say, sir," he says, pointing to an iron stairway. "Climb up to the first level, no more than ten steps, and from there you'll see what you can, but when the applause begins at the end, come down and hurry off the stage, otherwise you could end up as the Phantom of the Israel Opera."

"Phantom?" Luria laughs. "Why should I? My wife, who has surely figured out by now that I got lost because of the damned program, will be waiting for me outside."

AND AGAIN AT THE NEUROLOGIST

"Before we understand what the new scan tells us," begins the affable neurologist, his hand resting on the unopened envelope, "please tell me what has happened since the last visit. And maybe," he continues, motioning Luria to be silent, "we'll start with you, Doctor Luria, although, why not, it'll be interesting first to hear what the son, whose name I've forgotten, has to say."

"Me? Yoav."

"Yoav, I'm sure you didn't come here with your parents just to listen, but also to be heard."

"To inquire."

"Of course, to ask questions and receive answers. In any case, you start. How would you describe your father's behavior in recent months?"

"I worry."

"Too much," shouts Luria, "which is why he asked to come along."

"Just a minute, Abba."

"Yes, a minute, of course, *habibi,* a minute, but first I have to explain to the doctor that Yoav does not live near us in Tel Aviv, but up North, where he has a very successful factory for computer chips."

"But—"

"In other words," Luria continues, "his perspective is limited. Yes, he calls his mother or me almost every day to gauge the progress of my deterioration, but from afar, only from afar."

"Not deterioration, Abba, I'm sorry—"

But Luria is carried away. What's happening in his son's imagination is much worse than what is actually happening, so much so that he thinks, Doctor, yes, he remembers the name well, Doctor Laufer, that maybe we should, ha ha, scan my son's brain too.

"You exaggerate, Zvi. Let him explain."

"Yes, Abba exaggerates. It's not for me to say if there's deterioration, but I want to understand how you, as a neurologist, see the process, I want to know the future so I can face it. I am a rational man, a tech person. I always want to look ahead with open eyes and no illusions. And most of all I want to be sure that we're doing all we can to slow down the process."

"Doing?"

"In a simple medical sense. I want to know, which is why I came along with my parents, whether you really intend, as my parents told me, to focus your treatment only on my father's spirit, or do you have a plan for actual treatment?"

"Actual treatment?" The neurologist adjusts the kippah on his head and leans in slightly. "What do you mean?"

"Treatment with drugs, or physiotherapy, or maybe, if it exists, electroshock. I'm told there are protocols for patients like him." From the beginning, he too has been studying the illness, to understand its inner core. The web is packed with information. As if dementia, or dullness, same difference, have taken over the internet. "But one thing is clear, you can't leave it all to the spirit."

Yoav stops for a moment, confused, even suffering, but still riding the wave of worry that carried him down from the North, determined that the doctor show him in the new scan any change in his father's brain since the last time.

Dina grabs her son's shoulder to silence him. But Luria hangs his head, wearing a blank expression. His stormy son's devotion and concern touch him deeply and give him comfort.

Clearly, the neurologist sympathizes with the son who came from the North to take part in his parents' anxiety, but his hand has not moved from the envelope. He himself has not yet opened it. "Before looking at the scan, we need to hear the stories of the patient and those around him, because beyond the scan, every head, what it contains and what it lacks, is unique, one and only." Now he asks the patient's wife to report what's new in her husband's behavior.

"All in all his behavior is stable. No troubling symptoms have presented themselves."

"Good. And yet?"

"In the car he gets the ignition code mixed up more often, but otherwise his driving is stable and confident."

The doctor smiles. "I sometimes get mine mixed up too."

"So it wouldn't hurt you either, Doctor Laufer," she makes a little joke, "to scan your own brain every few months."

"It wouldn't hurt anybody, but do go on."

"Two days ago he had a serious memory lapse, brief, strange, and even outrageous, in a matter of life and death, but he corrected it himself. And also here and there, confusion regarding doors, as at the opera house. But all these setbacks are dwarfed, Doctor Laufer, by the good news that Zvi has returned, as you recommended, to work in his field, although part-time and short-term."

"Bravo!" says the doctor joyfully, "and you both said it couldn't be done."

"As it turned out, we found a way."

"Wonderful. And so, Mr. Luria, are you digging another tunnel?"

"Maybe there'll be a tunnel," says Luria, impressed by the doctor's memory, "but for now I'm only helping to plan a new road in the desert."

"In the desert?" asks the neurologist anxiously. "I hope you're not walking around there by yourself."

"No, not by myself, I'm attached to a young engineer who watches over me as if I was his father."

"Good, because Zvi must not roam around in the desert alone," the neurologist warns them all.

"Of course."

"Because getting lost in the desert for a man in his condition is not the wrong door at the opera."

"And more dangerous than wandering in the wings and trying to go onstage," Yoav mumbles irritably.

"What?" The neurologist is amused. "You went onstage?"

"Yes, the dementia you pinned on me pushed me to go onstage, but I understand why."

"At least you understand . . ."

"In my dementia, Doctor, I think I am not only confused but sad, a tendency to deep sadness, and I knew that Juliet was about to go onstage and make a fatal mistake, and I took pity on her, and I tried to follow the singer and warn her."

The neurologist is clearly enjoying this. "To warn Juliet, or the opera singer?"

"Both of them."

But Yoav is not pleased with the neurologist's amusement, and adds, in his testy mumble: "Would you believe it, Doctor, Abba put on makeup before trying to invade the stage."

Dina shoots her son a furious look, but Luria is unfazed.

"Correct," he cheerfully confirms. It still amazes him that he put on makeup. It means there is rationality in dementia after all. And the stagehand who pulled him away at the last moment did so gently and without anger, and let him watch the opera from up above. There, in the darkness, he watched the death of Romeo and Juliet from a balcony, like the Phantom of the Opera.

"Phantom of the Opera?" The doctor is excited. "That was an old black-and-white film I saw in my childhood, and I would toss in bed for entire nights afraid that the Phantom, who had acid thrown in his face, would come to visit me."

And in a slightly upbeat mood, he gets up, pulls the new scan from the envelope, and slips it into the light box on the wall, and since his broad back conceals the image, the others do not see it. Even if they did, it's doubtful they would understand its meaning.

The doctor then takes out the scan from several months ago and inserts it into the light box as well, to compare the two. Finally he asks the pediatrician to join him, to see the developments in her husband's brain.

"There's a mild change in the very same place," he points and explains. "The atrophy in the frontal lobe has grown slightly, and it seems that one or more fibers that connect the right and left lobes have been damaged. Nothing much can be done, except maybe give him Seroquel, thirty milligrams once a day in the morning, before he goes to the desert. Some prefer to cut the pill in two and take it in the morning and evening, but I'm for once a day, in the morning. Apart from that, nothing. Seeing and hearing him, I'm encouraged. The process is slow, we have a long road ahead."

Luria gets up and comes closer, to try to see for himself the new developments in his brain. Yoav hesitates at first, but then joins his parents. Side by side, the four look silently at the illuminated scans. Had they not brought their son, the neurologist would again speak in praise of desire, but because their son is standing beside him, the neurologist places a hand on his shoulder and says, "Don't be so worried, my friend, it won't be anytime soon," and turns off the light. Then he removes the new scan and the old one and hands them in one envelope to Luria and, as last time, gently steers him to the exit and turns on the garden lights.

In the street, between the two cars, they consider where to discuss the new results, at home or at a café. No, says Luria, neither, it's late and Yoav has a long drive home. "We'll talk on the phone, if there's anything to talk about." Dina says nothing, but her husband and son can sense her pent-up anger. "What's the matter?" asks Luria, giving her a hug. "Not important," she whispers, but then, without looking at her son, she directs her complaint at her husband. "I don't understand why this son of yours feels the urge to spill everything he's been told." Yoav protests: "What did I spill, Imma? I know you're angry that I said Abba put on makeup before trying to get onstage. But whom did I tell? His neurologist. You want to tell me that a neurologist who's taking care of Abba doesn't need to know everything?" "No," parries his mother. "No. Even Abba's neurologist doesn't need to know everything. I'm a doctor, and I'm telling you, Yoavi, that I explicitly do not want to know everything about my patients, it's enough that they tell me the main thing. You saw I reported to the doctor everything he needed to know, and kept back what wasn't necessary that he know, so why did you have to embarrass your father like that?"

"He didn't embarrass me," says Luria, "but I was amazed you told him that foolishness."

"I told him," says Dina defensively, "because he calls me incessantly, secretly, at the clinic too, and insists on knowing everything that happens to you. That way he manages to milk details from me that I don't want to give him."

"But Dinaleh, he only does it out of love and concern."

"Exactly," says Yoav.

"I know, only from love and concern, and that's the trouble with him," says Dina. "He worries too much, he's too frightened. Panic will get us nowhere."

ARRANGEMENTS

Luria felt it would be good to visit Maimoni again at the end of the shiva, if only to get to know other mourners, especially Maimoni's wife and possibly his mother, and thereby deepen his relationship with him. But Dina saw no need for a second visit. Yes, the neurologist is pleased that Luria has found a job, but it's a job that so far has amounted to a single day, and who knows how the future will play out in light of the new prognosis. So why get any deeper? "But what was the prognosis? The neurologist didn't seem especially worried," says Luria. "No, not especially," says Dina. "In any case, it's your head and not his, and maybe because the mild growth of the dark spot could also be a product of age. Anyway, don't forget, Zvi, you are a temporary assistant to this young man, so why be a burden on him?" "A burden? How? True, I'm not a partner, but even so, I feel he will need me more than you imagine, and besides, after his father's death his feelings toward me will get stronger."

"Feelings?" She is surprised. "Suddenly you also need his feelings?"

"I don't need any extra feelings, the love I have here is enough, but if I started something, something you yourself initiated to help me in my condition, why cut it short just because the desert now worries you?"

"Why the desert?"

"The neurologist scared you that I would get lost in the desert."

"Why should you get lost if Maimoni is with you?"

"Exactly, but so he won't take his eyes off me I want to strengthen the connection between us, because I also have no desire to get lost in the desert. And I also don't want him to start doubting my professional ability because I forgot or neglected to inform him about his father's death. I feel lucid and stable. And I know the way to his father's house, and I don't want some other pensioner, an old friend of mine or his father's, to offer his services in place of me."

"In place of you?" she says with a trace of mockery. "As an unpaid assistant?"

"Could be. Every pensioner seeks meaning in life."

"All right, drive over, but please, let him know in advance so you will not go there for nothing."

But Luria refrains from announcing his visit, lest Maimoni try to avoid him. And on the last day of the shiva, on a clear winter morning, he sets off for Hod HaSharon, and although he knows and remembers the roads, he does get a little lost. And again, on arrival he finds an open door to a silent house. There is no one in the kitchen, no sign of cooking or baking. But cardboard boxes are strewn in the big living room, and a big blanket on the floor is piled with pictures removed from the walls. Luria feels shaky, as if he were suddenly thrust back to the chaotic house where, five years ago, his dementia had germinated. For a moment he considers an about-face, but then goes into the garden, which, as he had noticed on his last visit, is truncated and fenced off from the much larger garden of the loyal neighbor. He realizes now that half of Maimoni's house had been sold off to finance his divorce.

Returning indoors, he is jolted by the sight of the son asleep in his father's bed amid old government folders, the reading light burning from the night before. Did he at least change the linens? Or does his love for his father extend to his sheets?

"Asael." Luria whispers the name his mother gave him, and Maimoni snaps awake in confusion, but seeing it is only his unpaid assistant, he stretches and curls up in bed, a bright smile on his face: "How good of you to come again, because yesterday nobody came, so I started getting ready for the sale. You'd be amazed at the anarchy of this house. Sure, I could have thrown stuff away randomly and no one would know or care, but the mess left by my beloved father deserves some mercy too."

"Mercy?"

"Yes, mercy."

"What does the estate consist of?" Luria cautiously inquires.

Maimoni had never imagined that his father was a compulsive scribbler who kept records of all his legal procedures, describing the interested parties and the courtroom arguments, possibly for fear of accusations that he overpaid those entitled to compensation.

"Interesting."

"Even you, Luria, are mentioned in his writing, because it covers the years he served as your legal adviser. And just so you know, he complains that you overdid the expropriations you told him to carry out. 'The chief engineer, Luria, wants to flatten the whole country into one straight, safe road'—that's what he wrote in one of the files."

"No kidding, the whole country . . ." Luria comes near the bed. "But don't be angry at him, there are such comments about other engineers and managers too."

"Why should I be angry? I liked him very much. And it's very good that you're not throwing stuff out without knowing what you're throwing out. You are truly a good and devoted son. I too, by the way, have a son like you, but he lives in the North, and he runs a successful company he's totally enslaved to. Still, I know he loves me, though he's gone slightly crazy lately because of his excessive fear of the black mark in my brain."

"To tell the truth," says Maimoni, "after you forgot to give me the message about my father, I too am a little worried about you."

"But I did remember after a while."

"Yes, but you might have gone on forgetting for a long time, and Abba would have been here by himself all night."

"He was not by himself, he was dead. Also, if you didn't show up, there's no way the neighbor wouldn't have tried to find you. But really, Maimoni, you must know that I greatly admire your love for your father. And I see you are not squeamish about sleeping in the bed in which he died and curling up in his blanket. But I hope you at least changed the sheets."

"The sheets?" says Maimoni, rising lazily from the bed and checking the sheets. "I told Ayala to change the linens, but I don't know if she did, because she left on the second day. But even if they're the same sheets, what could happen to me? Cancer is not contagious."

"True. And why did Ayala leave so early?"

"Shibbolet came on the second day and ordered her to leave, took her with him."

"Ordered? Took her with him? What is this? On what authority?"

"His authority over that family. He got them into trouble, so he has to take care of them."

"How did he get them in trouble?"

Maimoni looks at the pensioner suspiciously. "Listen, Zvi Luria, you're asking too many questions, and I don't know where you store the answers, and what you do with them."

"What could I do with them? Forget them."

"I'm not so sure."

"And if I happen not to forget, it's only to help you get approval for a tunnel in a road that so far, maybe I know where it begins, but have no idea where it will end."

"Correct."

"So what's going to be?"

"Eventually you'll know everything. First let me handle the mess in the house."

"But don't forget, my ability to think is living on borrowed time."

"You have a doctor on hand to look after you."

"She's only a pediatrician."

"You'll also become a child in the end."

WINTER

From the midst of a friendly, hesitant winter, a sort of second autumn whose gentle winds and tender drizzles dim the memory of a long hot summer, there erupts a cold, shivery winter, complete with heavy rain and hail, sending young and old to emergency rooms. The pediatrician has to extend her working hours, sometimes till evening, and the sandwich and salad provided by the hospital kitchen are her only lunch. Luria is not only left alone in the morning but is forced to eat lunch by himself, and feels no urge to surprise his wife with delicacies from gourmet shops or meals he cooked from recipes. He hasn't yet been barred from picking up his grandson on Tuesdays, but the kindergarten teacher is careful not to burden him with any other child, single-parent or otherwise. Is the pretty harpist done with orchestra rehearsals? Or maybe she heard that a scrambled grandpa created an imaginary father for her son, and fears he may try to prove his existence.

Ever since the last visit to the neurologist, Luria has become more suspect in the eyes of his family, who have stepped up their surveillance. Despite the frenzy of her work at the hospital, Dina calls him periodically to find out where he is and where his thoughts are taking him. Yoav calls from the North and talks politics with his father, to check whether the dementia has derailed him from his old opinions. And Avigail escapes for a moment from her sacrosanct seminars to confirm delicately that her father picked up the right child and brought him to the right house. "Yes," sighs Luria over the phone, "everything is in order, you also have warm greetings from the right schnitzel on a plate in front of the boy you gave birth to."

It is thus no wonder that amid the storms that imprison him at home and the mounting concerns over his actions and thoughts, Luria's delusions sail into the azure desert skies, to the gazelles nibbling the grass around the grave of Ben-Gurion. His heart flutters as he recalls the grand view of the Ramon Crater from the dining room of the Genesis Hotel, and wistfully unfolds a road map and wanders to an unmarked hill from which the new road will make its way. And as the huge howling trucks in the reddish-brown crater rumble through his soul, he pencils the approximate route of the future road, though he still has no idea why it is necessary, or where it is meant to go. It's inconceivable that Maimoni will go on hiding the endpoint from him, even if he conceals its purpose.

In a protest against the gnawing uncertainty, he makes himself a thick sandwich of bread and yellow cheese, inserts a sour pickle, takes it into the bedroom, closes the window shades, gets into bed, hides with the sandwich under the blanket, and there, in the dark, he munches slowly, to tide him over till his wife returns. He hovers half asleep as a picture flickers between pillow and blanket, of a woman who did not find a new heart in Israel, and her husband, still grieving her loss, peeks at him from the ruins of an ancient Nabatean village.

But where is Maimoni? Ever since Luria left him burrowing through his father's papers, he has fallen silent. Has he been so caught up with the estate that he's forgotten about the road? Or has the young engineer begun to rethink his heavy responsibility for a pensioner likely to turn into a child—and in the desert, no less.

Dina, newly terrified of the next trip to the desert, implores her husband to drop the subject. "Keep your distance and preserve your dignity," she cautions him. "If this young man needs you, he'll call you. Don't run after him. You've done your share by explaining to him where this road should intersect Route Forty, this is your main contribution. The end of the road is the responsibility of the army that commissioned it."

"And the tunnel?"

"The tunnel is Maimoni's fantasy, and nobody will approve it. You said so yourself. You don't think it's ridiculous to believe that you, in your condition, can convince anyone to go along with this fantasy, which is going to cost a fortune?"

"What is my condition?"

"I was only saying."

"If I were to speak with such confidence about your medical matters, you would not be happy."

"Who says? Go ahead, talk."

"I won't talk about your medical matters, but I'll talk about you. You're pale, you look totally exhausted. Instead of poking around in my mind and worrying what will happen to me, try slowing down. At your age, toward the end of your career, it's not worth picking up some aggressive germ from one of your sick kids. In my condition, how could I take care of you?"

"You could take care of me in any condition, I'm counting on you."

"Good. So count on me even if I wander in the desert."

"Wander, but only if an actual person is with you. Let him set the pace and don't pressure him. Most of all, preserve your dignity, because your dignity is mine too."

"Good."

"You promise?"

"Yes, I said yes. Don't nag me."

For a moment Luria wants to add a few words about the people on the hill, but he fears this would only increase his wife's anxiety. Their lack of identity, in her view, might encourage the dwindling of his. And what can he tell her about them when he himself is in the dark?

And so Luria, to preserve his dignity and hers, and increasingly afraid of himself, holds back and does not contact Maimoni, much as he is tempted to do so. As the rains taper off, Luria embarks alone on invigorating walks, in Ramat Gan National Park or Yarkon Park in Tel Aviv, sometimes on the Mediterranean promenade between the Tel Aviv and Jaffa ports. He thereby proves to his wife and children that he is not doomed to get lost when on his own. He makes sure to charge his phone and take it with him, but since he uses it to listen to classical music as he walks, the calls from his wife and son are occasionally lost in a tempest of trumpets and percussion, and panic ensues.

"Why the panic?" he protests. "I'm walking among sane Hebrew-speaking Israelis, in a safe familiar area, and if I happen not to answer, no need to imagine I've been kidnapped. Just send me short text messages, and I'll answer them all." And so, when one morning a message that says *Dear unpaid assistant, where are you?* appears on his phone, he shows it to his wife before he replies, and says, "Here, Dinaleh, your dignity is intact, but what can I do if despite your professional opinion, the idea of the tunnel is still on the table?"

A month has gone by since the two engineers last met, and though the younger man is not obliged to account for himself, he holds forth on the phone, explaining his silence. It turns out that his feverish poring through papers and documents was not just about the history of confiscations at Israel Roads, but to unearth his parents' divorce agreement, to confirm definitively his full ownership of his father's house and block any attempt by his mother to take a bite of his inheritance.

"Did she even come to the shiva?"

"Yes, a few times, to see old acquaintances and renew connections."

"I never asked if you have brothers or sisters."

"That's because on principle, Luria, you do not pry into the personal matters of people who work for you, or for whom you work."

"But what if they don't pay a salary?"

"Then you can demand an answer. No, Zvi, I have no brother or sister, and therefore my father's house is all mine."

"Yours already?"

"Legally and officially in every respect. I got rid of junk, threw away furniture, gave my mother a chair she claimed she forgot to take, plus a few lamps and three tablecloths, and that's her portion."

"And what now? Sell it? Rent it out?"

"Not for now. It will be a second home until it becomes clearer for what and for whom it is destined. But you see how fast and efficiently I got it done? That's why you didn't hear from me all month."

"And I thought you gave up on me, or more correctly, on the tunnel."

"Why give up on you?"

"Because you understood that my dementia is real."

"Yes, it's real, befitting someone who has to believe that the tunnel is necessary."

"But how can I plan a tunnel if I know so little about the road?"

"So little? I thought we decided on where it starts."

"But not where it ends."

"Why should you bother with the end, which is under military authority. We have nothing to say about it."

"It's still strange to plan a road without knowing where it ends."

"The end will be at the western edge of the crater."

"If that's the case, I want to go there."

"It's not an easy trip."

"I've made harder trips in my day. It all depends on the car that takes you—just not the American car, which will conk out in the first kilometer."

"It's already gone, it left me after Abba died. At the government garage they were furious when I brought it to be tested, the radiator was cracked and rusted, the insurance expired a year ago, and we had no business driving it. They confiscated it immediately and sent it to Gaza."

"Gaza?"

"Yes, you'd be surprised, of all places, amid all that *balagan* there's a workshop for rebuilding old American cars, which end up all over the Arab world. So if you insist on going to the edge of the crater, you won't have the luxury of a big back seat, you'll suffer in an uncomfortable jeep."

JOURNEY TO THE END OF THE ROAD

It turns out to be a new model of the same Land Rover, with oversize tires and four-wheel drive, in which he would wander the winding byways of the Galilee before the Public Works Department was renamed Israel Roads. I'm not so feeble, I'm not looking for comfort, declares the pensioner, happily kicking the tires. And it is possible that all the bouncing around will plant new material in his brain to replace the disappearing portion, and he wants so much to take the wheel and drive, but he spares the young man the awkwardness of refusing him.

That morning Luria had tried to persuade his wife to stay in bed. Believe me, there's nobody in the world who knows you as I do, and you're not just on the verge of illness but deep into it, and you have no moral right not to demand of yourself what you demand of your patients. But the doctor can't miss a day of work, there are early signs of a nationwide epidemic, and two nurses and one doctor in her unit are already sick in bed. But she promises to cut her day short and come home to rest, and if Zvi would try not to prolong his excursion, he can spend sweet hours taking care of her.

Yet again, the quick and boring Route 6, and as they approach Beersheba the rain plays hide-and-seek, pouring torrentially, then vanishing. Sometimes a fine sheet of rain appears on the horizon, a gray sun fluttering behind it, but as they move on, the sun escapes and the sky is bright, yet the rain still patters on the car, as if in the South it needs no clouds to prove that it exists.

Until now, the young engineer has not researched his road in the real world, only dreamed it up on his computer screen. An actual journey along the route in the crater will likely proceed slowly, with constant cross-checking of map and terrain, so there's no time even for a quick espresso, and they bypass Beersheba, leaving the capital of the Negev blurry and pale behind them. As they come into the desert, they are met by a stiff wind and swirling raindrops, few in number but enormous.

"They say the religious people invented the shiva to dull the pain and despair of the mourners," Maimoni complains, "but my shiva did not distract me from the sorrow, it just addled my brain."

"In which case," says Luria, "from now on we are true partners."

But during the shiva Maimoni sought partnership of a different kind. After Shibbolet confiscated the young woman who was meant to help him, and his wife made herself scarce in his father's house, he was left there as a solitary mourner, and because he had not thought to limit visiting hours, from morning to late at night all sorts of people came to console him, familiar and unfamiliar, expected and unexpected, old faces and new, close and distant, real and imagined, and more than a few opportunists, such as nosy neighbors who decided to cross the open doorstep to take a peek inside the house. And since in this rural neighborhood there is plenty of parking space, and a park nearby with a pond and swans, a few visitors brought their children, to combine consolation with a nice family outing. His mother, in no apparent need of consoling, showed up several times and sat a long while by his side as a retroactive mourner, to refresh her relationship with a few childhood friends, including those unaware that she had left her husband long ago. Maimoni was amazed by the visits of unidentified single women, older and even elderly, who would arrive at odd hours, early morning or late at night, as if wanting a private meeting with the orphaned son, to tell him unimaginable secrets about his father.

Little by little he grew tired of talking about his father's life history and the stages of his illness in detail, and it was fine with him that the next-door neighbor, the one who first discovered his father dead, took over his place. When she would hear through their common wall that the house was full of mourners, she would go out to her garden, squeeze through a gap in the fence, cross the patio into the house, and act like Maimoni's relative or surrogate, talking about her old neighbor, describing the progression of his illness and how she was the one who found him dead. Sometimes she would embellish her account with bizarre stories that Maimoni doubted were true but did not try to debunk, repairing instead for a short nap in the bed of the deceased.

"And the sweet young girl from the hill, Hanadi, didn't come back again to help you?"

"Who?"

"The student photographer who fed your twins in the kitchen when we came by on the first day."

"What did you call her?"

"Hanadi, Hanadi."

"Dammit, Zvi Luria, where did you get that name?"

"She told me."

"She did? When?"

"At the gas station, when she brought me coffee, she looked upset, so I sat her beside me, and to calm her down I asked her about herself, what her real name was, before she became Ayala, and she said Hanadi, and she also told me what it means."

"What?"

"Purple flower."

"Purple flower?"

"That's what she said. I'm positive."

"Impossible, the dementia is playing tricks on you."

Luria is insulted. "You want to tell me it's a different flower?"

"It's not a flower or a color, and anyway, Luria, how do you suddenly remember a name like that when you claim that first names are the first to disappear?"

"They disappear first in Hebrew, especially simple and common names. But rare names, like yours, Asael, or names in Arabic, stick to me like glue."

"Now you amaze me."

"I amaze myself too. In any case, Maimoni, if you recruited me to convince your superiors to dig a tunnel in the hill, you can't keep hiding from me what it is you and Shibbolet are fighting for, and why I was told a purple flower instead, instead of—"

"A sword."

"A sword? Any sword?"

"A superlative sword."

"So how did the sword turn into a flower?"

"Apparently the dementia was careful not to scare you too much."

AND STILL ON THE JOURNEY TO THE END OF THE ROAD

Luria is hurt. Previously, the dementia had floated between them like a soft ball of fluff, but now a sharp nail protrudes. He says nothing, adjusts his seat for more legroom, leans back, and closes his eyes. Why the hell did he get mixed up in this? A surge of bitterness. No road in the world can stop the deterioration diagnosed by the neurologist, and instead of keeping his wife in bed and dealing with her illness, he travels far away from her. Listen, he tells the driver, see if there's any classical music in this official car, and if so, put it on, but low, I want to take a nap. Maimoni can't milk any classical music from the Land Rover, just the tender lament of a female singer who might be Israeli or, for that matter, Jordanian or Egyptian. But the soft oriental melody is good for Luria's bitterness and fatigue. It's okay, leave it, he tells the driver, but turn it down a little. With ancient expertise the old engineer works the levers to lean the seat way back, till it feels like a bed in business class, and the Bahad army base and Kibbutz Mashabei Sadeh, the Tlalim Junction and Halukim Junction, flicker before his dozing eyes, which remain closed even at Ben-Gurion's grave. Only when the vehicle stops near the stone buildings of the Genesis Hotel does he lift his head and straighten his seat and look peacefully at Maimoni, who says: "We'll make a short stop here, if you need the facilities, here's your chance, but the crater will happily absorb whatever you rain down on it."

It's too early to sneak into the hotel dining room, so Maimoni has ordered two boxed lunches for a mid-crater meal. To determine the exact route, they will follow an uncharted road entailing frequent stops and delays, and if the survey is not completed by evening, they can continue it tomorrow, to which end Maimoni has arranged a room at the Genesis.

"A room? No, dear sir, my wife is ill, I must get home by this evening."

"So why didn't you warn me earlier? This entire trip to the end of the road is at your request, and now I feel terrible, I'm making you leave your wife alone."

"She's not alone yet, this morning she didn't skip her clinic."

"In which case she's not really sick."

"She's sick, all right. Forty-eight hours I've been at her side, and maybe because I'm an engineer and not a doctor I can see better than she can every little change in her condition. This morning it was clear to me that the illness will only get worse by nighttime. So don't talk about any room at the Genesis, let's get focused and hurry up and head back north by this evening."

Maimoni rushes to the kitchen, picks up the generous box lunches, and together they make the descent on Independence Road. Without slowing down, they pass the hill whose fate teeters between a tunnel and destruction, and at the point on Route 40 that they previously agreed was unsuitable for the turnoff to the new road, they veer into the barren crater, screeching and shuddering as they circle the hill, and after half a kilometer they begin to sense from the sound of the tires that they're riding on the ancient Nabatean road, marked only by a small cross on the GPS screen, that will underlie the new road. Now is the time to get out of the car, lay out the map on the hot engine hood, and pinpoint the location.

Silence. The whispering wind. Behind them, between the two humps of the distant hill, strolls a huge deer, a buck. Luria points to it excitedly, but the young engineer shakes his head as if to say, You're just imagining.

"Your *shabazim* still up there?"

Maimoni shrugs his shoulders. His bereavement has displaced them from his mind, but he believes that the young man, having adopted the identity of a missing Druze soldier, has begun to blend in as an Israeli, and the young woman, thanks to her beauty and intelligence and a year's tuition paid in advance, will manage to persuade the college to be flexible regarding her ID card.

"Are you able to stay in touch with her?"

"When she calls me."

"And the old man?"

"Old man?" says Maimoni. "Why old? You, Zvi Luria, are a lot older than he is."

"Anyway, what's with him?"

"He's in Shibbolet's hands, or else Shibbolet is in his. Enough, Zvi, why do you have to know everything?"

"Because how will I be able to convince someone to dig a tunnel through a godforsaken hill without knowing the story of the old man who's hiding there?"

"Again, old man."

"So not so old, a man like me. But give me something to hold on to. Give me the story straight, from the start, don't talk in riddles. My brain is shrinking, before long I won't be able to understand even if you want me to."

The young engineer looks kindly at the pensioner. "You're right. The time has come to tell you the strange story. In a little while, after we heat up the food they made for us at the Genesis, we'll get into it. Meanwhile, Zvi, get behind the wheel and go slowly, and I'll walk alongside, to get a feel of the ground, and now and then we'll try to smash a stone to see what it's made of and how sturdy it is. Let's go."

Luria eagerly takes the wheel, but the engine chokes and dies, and when he revives it, the car staggers and lurches, and it's not clear if the four-wheel drive is engaged. But Maimoni treats him with respect, doesn't kibitz or criticize, just keeps walking and lets the pensioner relive his glory days. Side by side they proceed for two or three kilometers, and occasionally the young man shows the veteran a dislodged rock, asking his opinion, and Luria, relishing his control of the tall, heavy vehicle, sometimes leaves Maimoni behind, then stops and turns off the engine, bathing his spirit in the silence.

So they continue slowly, consulting the map and each other. Maimoni gets tired at times, sits beside the driver and surveys the possible route through the open window. To their amazement they come upon a paved area, which Luria assumes is a vestige of a British attempt during World War II to build an airstrip in the crater for small planes.

Here and there they need to mark on the map the route for a water pipeline, where the ground is sunken or else cracked open by the small, red clay quarries that pocked the crater years ago, before it officially became a nature reserve. What looks flat from the dining room of the Genesis Hotel turns out to be full of twisted folds of earth and odd little mounds, and the vehicle is saved from flipping over by its tenacious tires, each with a mind of its own.

In the North it's undoubtedly raining, whereas here the air is chilly and the clouds are soft, and red hairy animals, all of which Maimoni insists are foxes, peek between the rocks.

After five slow, arduous hours, as they approach the western edge of the crater, lower than its eastern edge, Maimoni announces the end of the road. "Fine, but what will they build here?" the pensioner asks, "a military base or just an installation?" "In my opinion, a listening post." The engineer smiles through his beard, which has thickened since the shiva. "A highly secret installation that will be hidden underground. The next war," says the young engineer, "will be all about listening to the enemy, only to find that he is listening to you. But all this, Zvi, is beyond what concerns us. We have mapped the route, its purpose is the responsibility of others. All that remains is to heat up our lunch."

And from the back seat he retrieves a little microwave oven, plugs it into the car socket, removes the plastic wrap from the meals, and starts heating them. He spreads two paper tablecloths over a big rock, sets out knives and forks, and produces a corkscrew and a bottle of red wine. "Here, Zvi, so you don't complain the State is neglecting you."

A young fox sprints from behind a rock, her tail longer than most, warily watching the two engineers invading her turf. Luria tries talking to her, beckoning her near, but finds that talk cannot dispel suspicion, and tosses her bits of bread. "Just so you know," Maimoni remarks, "it's against Nature Authority rules to feed the animals in the crater." "Why?" says Luria indignantly. "Look how this little one loves it." "What do you know about her?" Maimoni says. "Maybe she'll get a bellyache from your bread." "No living creature ever got a bellyache from bread," asserts Luria. "If you say so," nods Maimoni. "Apart from the army road, I'm not in charge of anything."

THE PALESTINIAN ILLNESS

"Have you ever heard of an Israeli organization called Road to Recovery?" asks Maimoni, pouring coffee from his thermos. "I bet not. In this country you only hear about disgraceful or cruel things we do to the Palestinians, not about saving lives and bringing people together. I'm sure you don't know, Zvi, about the Israeli volunteers who go to roadblocks and checkpoints to drive Palestinian patients, mostly children, to hospitals and clinics in Israel. Cancer patients, kidney dialysis patients, others with serious illnesses who need special care. Dozens of cars go out at dawn to pick up the Palestinian patients, and in the evening other Israeli volunteers come to take them back to the crossings. It's a complicated system, in operation for several years, requiring coordination between Israeli volunteers and Palestinians and the medical teams. In other words, holy work."

"I didn't know," mumbles Luria, "or maybe didn't remember. Many things go on secretly in this country."

"Secretly, that's the right word. Because Palestinian illness touches not only good-hearted Israelis, who want to atone in some way for the sins of the settlers and soldiers. Palestinian illness is also of interest to the security forces, because when you know about the distress of a Palestinian, it's easier to get useful information and activity from him and his family."

"That's how it is," says Luria, "it's logical. But still, there is such a thing as medical confidentiality."

"Confidentiality? You're naïve. There's no need to send agents to pry into medical records, the Palestinians talk about their illnesses, and there are always security people to encourage them.

And this man, the one you call 'the old man,' even though he's more than fifteen years younger than you—"

"Nahman," whispers Luria.

"No, not Nahman. Yeruham, who took a family name too."

"Yasour," remembers Luria.

"Exactly. This man, whose real name only Shibbolet knows, lived years ago in the Jenin area of the West Bank, in a village that not even Ayala, or Hanadi, will identify by name. This man, a teacher in an elementary school, teaching Arabic to children, and Hebrew as best he could, mainly to adults who work in Israel, was the husband of the woman who died, the one whose picture he showed you."

"A beautiful woman. In the picture, I mean."

"Yes, apparently a special woman, whose husband loved her very much, suffering from heart disease, treated for several years at a major Israeli hospital, and would you believe that Shibbolet refuses to reveal which hospital. And this woman was driven many times to the cardiology department, and the authorities followed her condition, and one of the followers was Lieutenant Colonel Shibbolet, during his last years of service, after he was removed from combat duty."

"Not just him," Luria defends Shibbolet for some reason. "Many of our soldiers become policemen."

"Also secret police," says Maimoni, sticking to the main story. "Meanwhile, despite the treatments, her heart condition gets worse, till it becomes clear that a heart this broken needs a transplant, a new heart, very complex and difficult surgery. Hearts for transplant are very rare and are naturally intended for Israeli citizens. In any case, how could a Palestinian woman from Jenin afford an Israeli heart without medical insurance, or another means of covering the cost?"

As he listens, Luria is suddenly anxious about his wife, and wants to pause a moment to find out if she kept her promise to cut short her shift. It turns out that in this desolate spot, at the edge of this vast crater, not far from the Egyptian border, they are able to connect, and Dina answers, though her voice is faint and fuzzy, either because of distance or illness. Yes, she's about to leave, the nurses at the clinic are making her go home. "Good that there are people besides me who love you," says Luria. "Yes," she says, sounding distracted. "And you? When are you coming back?" Luria does not want to tell her where he is, but there's no doubt that she senses the wilderness that surrounds him. She asks about the fate of the tunnel, what was decided, yes or no? "Still thinking," her husband replies, "still checking." "What's there to check?" she retorts hoarsely. "Approve it and start digging, this is your last chance, Zvi." And she hangs up.

So as not to overhear a private conversation between lovers, Maimoni has stepped aside to urinate and read a text message that landed in his phone. But when he returns he remembers to pick up where he left off. "And so, money is needed to finance a new Jewish heart for the wife of a teacher in a Palestinian village. Which is where the officer steps in, my former commander, maybe acting on his own, maybe in line with a policy that exploits private distress for the greater national good, and maybe also—as I've lately tried to persuade myself—out of compassion for such a beautiful and elegant woman, out of empathy, given his own personal suffering."

"His own personal suffering?"

"His wife's illness. But slow down, Luria, for now this is just a wild hypothesis, which I must admit gets stronger every day."

"Meaning?"

"Meaning, be patient. First let's clear away the food and not leave any garbage behind, and we'll try to understand Shibbolet on the drive home."

He stacks the paper plates and packaging, takes a folding shovel from the car, digs a small hole, buries the trash, and cries out: "Here is the first secret installation."

In the car, after shutting off the musical lamentation, now including drum and flute, Maimoni continues to spin the tale.

"To obtain financing, Shibbolet advises the teacher to get ownership deeds for a plot of land at the edge of the village, which contains an ancient grave that Jews would like to acquire. Only the fierce love of a devoted husband could enable a simple schoolteacher to get his hands on old Ottoman documents and sell them, with Shibbolet as middleman, for a tidy sum, all cash, to replace a failing heart with a new one. But in the meantime the woman's heart gave out, and after the husband buried his wife, it turned out the documents were dubious, and the land that was allegedly sold is not private land but holy Muslim ground, and the sheikh buried there is a pure Muslim, who'll go crazy if they try to convert him after his death. And though the deal was canceled, the people in the village are furious with the teacher for what he did behind their backs, and death threats are in the air. So he has no choice but to flee with his son and daughter to Israel. And in his despair and isolation, he refuses to return the money he was paid."

"And Shibbolet?"

"That's the point. Shibbolet did not abandon him. He left the army, but he did not shirk responsibility for his actions. He held on to the money because no bank would open an account for a person hiding his identity, and out of guilt for the mess he'd made, and because his wife's asthma required that they stay from time to time in a small rented flat in Mitzpe Ramon, where the clean dry desert air is easier to breathe, he found the father and two children a temporary refuge in a forgotten Nabatean ruin on that very hill which, as you will help me persuade Israel Roads, should not be destroyed, but must have a tunnel."

"If so," declares Luria, "the man who terrorized you in basic training turns out to be a man of conscience who takes responsibility for his actions, even if that gets him in trouble."

"You're right, not just trouble, even crime. But lately another explanation for his actions has begun to nibble at my brain, a crazy explanation that won't go away."

"Which is what?"

"Be patient."

A SECOND WIFE

On their way back along the route for the army road, they have a chance to appreciate the landscape as it eases into evening. It's almost five o'clock, Dina is surely in bed, and Luria, staring thoughtfully at the sun's reddish signature on the distant cliffs, can relax. Maimoni remains silent. He doesn't yet dare confide his obsessive "crazy explanation" to an outsider, not even someone suffering from dementia. Meanwhile the temperature is dropping, and Luria enjoys watching the crater being drawn into the sky, yearning to blend with the wandering clouds. Again he fears for Dina's health, as if his wife were quivering in his heart. Tears fog his eyes and he wipes them with his hand, and the young engineer produces tissues from the glove compartment and repeats: "Never say, Zvi Luria, that the State doesn't take care of you."

From afar they can see the outline of the hill that will have to be leveled if the tunnel is not built. Maimoni drives carefully while heaping praise on Makhtesh Ramon, the world's largest crater not created by a meteor but by gradual erosion. The word *makhtesh* is used worldwide to describe this sort of crater. If you say *makhtesh* in Hebrew to a Japanese geologist, he'll know what it is.

"But even so, there's no water here," says Luria, taking the crater down a notch.

"Almost none, and the rainwater that sometimes pools inside drains quickly. Even what I peed out while you were talking to your wife is already well on its way to the Dead Sea, which is why the poor acacia tree facing you has to dig its roots a hundred fifty meters down for a stray drop of moisture."

In the fading light, as they approach the hill that phones can't reach, Luria interrupts the ode to local geology and wants to hear the end of the human story, namely, the crazy idea that might buttress the need for a tunnel. The engineer looks fondly at the elderly assistant. "Zvi, you're going to tell me your dementia is contagious." "So?" laughs Luria. "If dementia is confused emotion, be happy to have an emotional pensioner who feels for you, in place of the father who no longer can."

"You could be right. My suspicion is a gut feeling. When I look for the reason Shibbolet is sheltering this family, I feel there's a hidden motive, such as binding the young daughter to him as a second wife."

"Hanadi?" says Luria with a start.

"Ayala," Maimoni corrects him.

"Hanadi," Luria insists.

"Fine, make it Hanadi. But don't tell me this isn't a crazy idea."

"It's all crazy."

"In any case, I ask myself where I got such a strange notion."

"From a desire to take revenge on your company commander," says Luria, "or from a desire to identify with him." He sticks his hand in his pants pocket to get his cell phone, but it's not there, and the left pocket is empty too, and he nervously goes through his coat pockets, but the phone's not there either, and he bends over to look between his feet, to no avail. "Wait," he shouts, "stop now!"

The two exit the vehicle and straighten the seats in order to hunt through their gear—compass, binoculars, maps—and Maimoni phones Luria's number but is met with silence. "Maybe my phone flew out the window on a curve," Luria proposes, and desperately retraces his steps in the twilight, walking a hundred meters, two hundred, three hundred, along the tire tracks.

"How could it leave me?" moans the pensioner. "I spoke to Dina when we ate lunch. Maybe you put it with the garbage you buried in the ground? Maimoni laughs. "Why? Because I'm also a little crazy, you think? Maybe it's the opposite, Zvi," he teases the pensioner, "maybe you gave it to the little vixen you wanted to be friends with." "No," shouts Luria, "don't make fun of me. My entire brain is in there, all my contacts."

"So? They can be restored. If your son, as you said, makes computer chips, he'll know how to restore your contacts."

"But till then, till then! How do I call home to hear how she is?"

"Tell me her number and I'll connect you."

"My wife is one digit. I deleted the actual number from my memory."

"And the home number?"

"Also one digit."

"Nevertheless," says Maimoni, losing patience, "it has to be someplace in your brain. Make the effort, man, don't give up. Otherwise I'll think you want to be carried away by dementia."

"Yes, I am a bit carried away," admits Luria, "maybe even enjoying it. But you're right, I must not forget my home phone number, and anyway, she unplugs the landline before she goes to sleep and keeps the cell phone turned on beside her. Now that she's sick, she must have done that."

When Luria finally remembers the number, and Maimoni calls the house, the husband can only leave a sorrowful message that the *makhtesh* swallowed his cell phone, but not to worry, he's on his way home.

"The *makhtesh* swallowed?" Maimoni fumes. "Why blame the crater? Who doesn't sometimes lose his phone these days?"

But Luria insists. Even if he did return to the place where he lost it, he wouldn't find it, the crater has taken it. From now on he has to leash his phone to his wrist, like a dog, so it won't run away.

"Yes, on a leash, why not?" Maimoni agrees. "But no need to despair, I promise you, everything can be restored."

"It's impossible to restore *everything,*" the pensioner retorts. "Because nobody really knows what's included in everything. And since Shibbolet and you are both scheming to turn this young Palestinian into your second wife, I'll get myself a second cell phone, so I'll have two."

Maimoni, red-faced, bursts out laughing. "I'm also planning a second wife? Where'd you get that idea?" But Luria doesn't respond, he returns coldly to the car, fastens his seat belt, and mumbles to himself, Let's move on, the sun is setting and home is far away.

AN UNMADE ROOM

The characters who floated through Maimoni's story are flesh and blood, standing now at the foot of the hill. Visible in the headlights of the government car are the village schoolteacher with the former West Bank army officer at his side, tall and thin, white hair shining. The daughter Ayala stands apart, beside the four-wheeler, seeming taller and older than Luria remembers, her head and shoulders wrapped in a traditional scarf. "Are they waiting for us?" he asks. "You told them we were coming?" Maimoni stops the car and turns off the lights and engine. Yes, he had planned this meeting. Shibbolet had called him for help.

It seems the village schoolteacher, not for the first time, grew sick of his hideout and wanted to give himself up to Israeli authorities, hoping that his punishment would restore his lost identity. And the officer who protected him rushed to stop him, and brought the daughter to assist. Just now, as stars gather in the sky to grace the crater with their splendor, the Israeli has again made it clear to the Palestinian that even if the money remaining from the failed transaction, a substantial sum, were returned in full to the Orthodox Jews who sought to convert a forgotten Muslim sheikh, there would be no punishment acceptable to either the Israelis or the Palestinians that would allow the schoolteacher who tricked them all to rehabilitate himself, even with Shibbolet's help. And to support this argument, the engineer from Israel Roads has come to the meeting, to reiterate his commitment to preserve the hill.

But another engineer remains in the silent car, elderly, unpaid, still mourning his cell phone, which blinks and pulses in the wilderness, oblivious to the calls of his wife and children, maybe sniffed at this very moment by the little fox who has returned to look for a forgotten crumb, and misses the kindly old man so much that she sinks her sharp teeth into his phone. Luria is sad, and worry empties him of any other thought. If the doctors and nurses at her clinic forced the stubborn woman to go home in the middle of a workday, it must mean she is worse, and now she really needs him, because he's the only one who knows how to take care of her. So he has to leave the desert soon and get home, and why the hell is Maimoni wasting time with the second wife?

In order to break up the meeting and speed things along, he moves over to the driver's seat, turns the key with a sure hand, and the government vehicle responds immediately. But since he has no time to find the headlight switch, which seems to have been relocated in the new model, he frees the hand brake and shifts into neutral, so the car will glide downhill toward the characters, to prod them to reach the end of their sad story. But the story is unaware of the dark golem sliding silently until the moment it nearly makes contact. "Have you lost your mind?" yells Maimoni, who hangs on to the slow-rolling vehicle and yanks Luria from the driver's seat. The ejected pensioner tumbles to the ground in front of the two *shabazim,* father and daughter, who quickly lift him to his feet and check if he is hurt. "It's nothing," says Luria, brushing off dirt, "nothing happened, I just wanted you to hurry up, because my wife is ill and I need to get home. *Shalom,* Rahman Yasour, *Shalom,* Hanadi."

"Yeruham," the *shabaz* corrects him gently. "What's wrong with your wife?"

"Just a virus, maybe bacteria," answers the husband, "though she's a doctor, she doesn't know how to take care of herself. So I need to be beside her."

"Yes, you always need to be beside a sick wife," agrees the widower, "but what will happen with my tunnel?"

"The tunnel will happen. Don't worry."

"The tunnel will happen, don't worry," Maimoni confirms his assistant's promise. "Digging it will be simple and easy."

"But Shibbolet says," insists the Palestinian, "that it hasn't been approved yet."

"They'll do it, they will. That's why we brought Mr. Luria here."

"You hear that?" says Shibbolet. "Listen to the engineers. You can go back up, not to worry, the hill is still yours."

"If I go back, I'll need your little tractor, because I brought down all my things."

"Of course, we'll load it all. And you?" Shibbolet turns with a smile to the young woman. "What do you want to do? To be with your father tonight on the hill, or join us in the apartment?"

"Enough, don't pressure her," Maimoni interrupts angrily. "Why should she go up the hill now, or move to your tiny flat? Leave her alone, please, I'll take her back."

"Where to? To her college?"

"It's up to her, whatever she wants. Even to an unmade room at the Genesis, if we can get one at this hour."

THE MINIBUS

The daughter turns to her father and gracefully bows her head, and the father strokes her hair, and she kisses his hand. Maimoni gently pulls her away from her father and seats her in the front of the Land Rover, between himself and Luria, and the two engineers sense the heat of her young body. Darkness slowly descends on the crater, and scattered lights twinkle in Mitzpe Ramon. But the Genesis Hotel, built of stone at the edge of the cliff to blend with the natural scenery, remains hidden. Only as they climb the curves of Independence Road, and the sparkling hotel comes into view, the young woman without identity removes her headscarf and lets down her hair, and Luria thinks about the father stroking her, and asks her if he's not sad, sitting all alone day and night on the hill. "He's not always alone," explains the daughter, "he has a good friend, a relative of ours, a Palestinian who is an officer in the Jordanian police, and my father can sometimes reach him by cell phone and they meet south of here in the Arava Desert, each time in a different place so they won't be found out." And Luria, his heart pierced by the words "cell phone," remarks, "But talking on the cell phone isn't always safe for him, no?" "Why not safe?" says Ayala. "Abba's cell phone is Jordanian, the number is Jordanian, he pays his bill to Jordan, so how can the Israelis hear conversations with Jordan?" "You only think they can't," Maimoni says, turning the car toward the brightly lit hotel. "The State of Israel hears whatever it wants to hear, but your father is not important enough for someone to want to listen to him talk to his cousin."

The car comes to a stop near the hotel's revolving door, and without shutting off the engine Maimoni gets out, along with the young passenger. He guides her to the entrance with a gentle hand on her shoulder, revolving inside with her and giving instructions, exiting through the still-turning door while she, poised and graceful, crosses the well-lighted lobby.

Maimoni seems upset and tense as he returns. With not a word to Luria he turns the car around, but instead of driving north on Route 40, he heads into Mitzpe Ramon, and when Luria, astonished, says, "Where are you going? I was supposed to be home by now," he answers: "You'll see." He navigates back streets and enters a municipal parking lot, where various large vehicles lie dormant, among them a minibus with its interior lights on. "Here, Luria, this lovely minibus will take you to your sick wife faster than I can, and I'll pay the driver extra to bring you to your doorstep, so you can never complain that the State neglects you."

"When did I complain about the State? What complaints do you keep hinting at?" grumbles Luria, annoyed but also impressed by the young engineer's logistics. He gets into the minibus, walks past three unhappy-looking men, and sits in the cushioned back seat, intending to lie down. Through the window he sees Maimoni talking to the driver, who savors a cigarette as the engineer takes out his wallet and pays him, and when the driver gets back, he invites Luria to sit beside him, but Luria declines, he likes the back seat, are more passengers expected? Not now, not in Mitzpe Ramon, but three more in Sde Boker. If so, no reason not to stay in the back, and if the driver happens to have a little pillow, it would be greatly appreciated. Yes, there is a pillow, beat-up and not too clean, but still a pillow, and the driver can't complain about the passenger who removes his shoes and stretches out on the seat and rests his head on the pillow, remembering to fasten his seat belt.

After a whole day in a tall, rugged government Land Rover with big tires, four-wheel drive, and military shock absorbers, the ride in the minibus is gentle and smooth, with a whisper of melancholy. Lying on his back, Luria cannot see the road, only the sky, which has left its wondrous stars in the crater and offers him an insipid and distorted crescent, dragging northward out of duty alone. Home, quickly home, wishes Luria with all his soul, and hopes Dina heard the voicemail and isn't trying in vain to reach him. It's only been twelve hours since they parted in the morning, and yet he yearns for her, and wants to remember all of the day's events to tell her, so she'll understand that in her childish excitement over tunnels dug many years ago, she hooked him up with a young, energetic engineer whose intentions are not limited to engineering.

He wakes in confusion and sits up only when a folding wheelchair is noisily stowed in the baggage compartment and a slight but muscular Filipino woman gets on the minibus, leading a tiny figure whose mane of white hair surrounds a bald patch. Like a man resembling a woman resembling a man. And Luria asks himself if Ben-Gurion has come back from the dead to travel from Sde Boker to Tel Aviv, to reestablish the State of Israel. But given the stiffness of his movements and a second Filipino propping him up from behind, it appears that the former leader is deeply demented, and his blank expression a sign for Luria of the end of the road he himself has only begun to walk.

Since there's no new political insight to be gained in this minibus, he may as well stretch out again on the back seat and absorb the night clouds into a dream. Soon enough, as the van bypasses Beersheba and races down Route 6, the quiet melody of the engine grows softer, but the pensioner is less inclined to nap. Open-eyed and alert, he observes the three passengers as they exit one by one on dark streets at the approach to Tel Aviv, and the minibus hurries to the heart of the joyful, shining city, arriving at the seaside promenade, where the wheelchair is unloaded and unfolded, and the two Filipinos gently escort the figure placed in their care, sit him down carefully, and wheel him toward the old Jaffa port.

Only then, with the van nearly empty, the driver tells the last passenger to come forward and provide his street address. And

Luria freezes as a black curtain covers the address. "Give me a minute and I'll remember," he says, "but meanwhile, please, so we don't lose time, drive toward Rabin Square, I'm sure my house is not far from there. You know how to go?" "Of course," says the driver, pointing to his GPS map of Tel Aviv. "And if I still can't remember the address," continues Luria, "drop me off at the square, and when I start walking I'll know which way to go. My legs know how to get there, but to give you the address in words confuses me." But Maimoni paid for a home drop-off, and this driver is apparently accustomed to simpletons, and he says to his last passenger, "No problem, sir, I have time and patience, concentrate, don't be afraid, together we'll find the right address, and that way I can take you to your doorstep. If you tell me the name of a main street you remember from the neighborhood, we can take it from there."

"Ben-Gurion," blurts out Luria, "I mean, what used to be Keren Kayemet. But I'm sure that's not where I live."

"Then maybe you live near some other leader," suggests the driver, "and the leaders got mixed up. I'll drive, and you take a good look at this map of Tel Aviv, and follow the little green beetle crawling on the screen, that's us, you and me. So think hard, maybe you live near another great leader."

"Like who?"

"Jabotinsky, for example, he's not far away."

"Absolutely not Jabotinsky," Luria says. "I know Jabotinsky, it's a long wide street that crosses Kikar Hamedina, but I live on a short narrow street."

"If it's not Jabotinsky, maybe it's a third leader, not so famous, like Max Nordau? There's grass in the middle but it's narrow on either side. Here, look where I'm pointing."

"No, no." Luria grows anxious. "Not Nordau. I told you, I live on a narrow and quiet street. It has greenery and a few trees, but no divider."

"So look, here's Nahum Sokolow Street, one-way and simple."

"Thank you, it's not Sokolow, why do you keep insisting on Zionist leaders?"

The driver laughs. "Because I learned about them recently for my *bagrut* test."

"Matriculation exam at your age? Only now? Why'd you wait so long?"

"Because I was wild in high school and ignored my studies, but I'm tired of being just a driver."

"In any case, don't stop now, go down Ibn Gabirol, because I'm sure that's the right way, but without Zionist leaders, please. I remember now that my street is named for a great rabbi."

"A rabbi?"

"Yes, a rabbi, a great rabbi, why not?"

"Your address is suddenly a rabbi? Here, pick one. Look at the map, I think that around the medical center on Basel Street are a bunch of names that sound rabbinical. Alkalay, the Holy Shelah, Emden, Eibeschutz, Ovadia of Bartenura, they're all rabbis, no?"

"Emden, that's the one," rejoices Luria. "Rabbi Yaakov Emden, Emden number five. That's the house. That's the address."

"Who is that rabbi? Why did he deserve a street named for him?"

"Give me a break, not now. Take me home quickly. My wife is sick."

A VIRULENT MICROORGANISM

The front door is closed but unlocked, meaning she entered in a hurry. Her shoes lie on the floor on her way to the bathroom, where a light is on while the rest of the apartment is dark. The woman who loves to surround herself with light didn't have the strength to turn on the one in the kitchen. The bedroom has turned into an "unmade room." Most of the bedspread is on the floor, along with clothes hurriedly removed, and also her nightgown, which she was apparently too tired to put on. Half naked, she is curled up beneath a mound of blankets to relieve her shivering.

Luria is reluctant to rouse her with his touch, so he calls her name. But her name does not wake her, she only shakes. He reaches carefully under the covers to check the temperature of her feet, but she recoils into a fetal position. On the nightstand by the bed her cell phone awaits in the hope of hearing his voice. "Dinaleh, my love, what's happening with you?" he says plaintively. "This morning I said you were sick and you didn't listen. But I'm here now, I came back. Just tell me if you heard the voicemail about the cell phone that vanished in the desert."

Does she hear? Does she understand? Her face is buried in the pillow, but from its depths rises a muffled complaint: "So why didn't you call from a different phone?" "How, how," he pleads, "your cell number was saved in preferences, but otherwise forgotten." "My number is already forgotten?" "Yes, forgotten, my cell phone made me forget, or else the dementia." "The dementia?" she says, as if recalling a forgotten friend. "Oh yes, your dementia, how's it doing?" And Luria, impressed by the flash of humor from the depths of her fever, strokes her head and says, "Yes, Dina, yes, my love, my dementia is alive and well and worried and begs you to raise your head."

She turns toward him slowly, her face burning and distorted by her illness, her greenish eyes squinting at her husband in the dark room as if he were a stranger.

"Just tell me the last time you took your temperature."

"Why take it? I know I have fever."

"But how much?"

"Why is that important? I have fever. High fever. But I brought something good from the clinic to reduce it."

He gently places his hand on her forehead and her cheeks and feels the sweat. "I can't remember you ever burning up like this, and why are you all of a sudden afraid of the truth?"

"Not of the truth but of you, because you'll panic and raise hell and I have no strength to deal with both my illness and your confusion. I am a doctor and capable of handling my own illness."

"What did the doctors at your clinic say?"

"They didn't say anything. They escaped, not to get infected. And you should start to keep your distance, if you haven't caught it already."

"Caught what? What is it?"

"It has no name yet, but it will later on."

"Fine, but where's the thermometer?" He cautiously peels away her blankets one by one and turns the feverish body over and sees the mercury glinting in the dark. The thermometer is intact and the temperature last recorded is nearly 40 degrees Celsius. Luria takes it to the bathroom and wipes it with alcohol, shakes it. Ignoring her hostile gaze, he sticks the whitish glass tube under her tongue and holds the end so it won't fall out. And now the 40 degrees is not only indisputable but clearly heading upward.

"What's going on?" he wails. "Nothing's going on," she says, suddenly smiling, "I'm a doctor, and I've seen many times that one can live and prosper with 40 degrees. So get hold of yourself, make me herbal tea and put some butter on a slice of bread, and refill my water glass, and I'll take more of the medicines I prescribed for myself and we'll wait till the morning. But you, so you don't catch the bug, don't sleep here. Go to the children's room. And after your day in the desert, first take a shower, and try not to worry too much, because I have no intention of dying on you, not only because I love you, but because somebody has to make sure that your confusion doesn't drive the world crazy."

He brings her water and hands her pills one by one, making sure she swallows them. But when he brings a tray with the tea and slice of bread, she has already fallen back to sleep, and despite the fire inside her, she sleeps peacefully. He sets the tray on the floor, by the bed. Maybe I'm overdoing it, he thinks, and my damned dementia, instead of dulling my fears, only sharpens them. And he takes off his clothes and gets into the shower, but afterward he puts on clean clothes instead of pajamas, to be ready for any eventuality.

In the children's room he gathers his grandchildren's toys that were scattered on the bed and puts on a fresh sheet. Then he calls Avigail from his wife's cell phone, and to enlist her as an active partner in his fears, he takes on a tone of gloom and doom. But Avigail, who has already heard about the illness from her mother, and been warned not to come near her, has disparaged her father's judgment of late, and interprets his bleak forecast as more dementia-induced madness. "You relax and also go to bed," she orders her father, "you're exhausted from your crater, and you haven't recovered from the cell phone you donated to it. Imma is a great doctor, let her manage the illness by herself, don't throw everyone in a panic."

His son, by contrast, is gentler and more generous, and although he has learned of his mother's illness only now, from his father, he is ready to drive down immediately and lend a hand. "No, don't come yet, but keep in touch, yes, the crater swallowed my cell phone, but Imma's phone is like a part of my body, so you can find me at any moment."

He leafs through the morning paper, but the events of his day in the desert leave no room for the dark fantasies of journalists. Matters that were unclear in the morning were clarified during the journey to the end of the road, although new uncertainties arose on the way back. But why try to imagine the goings-on in the unmade room at the Genesis Hotel, when his own bedroom is likewise disheveled. He tucks his wife's cell phone deep in his pants pocket and turns out the light in the children's room, leaving the hall light on to keep track of the illness that remains unnamed. He gets into bed with his clothes on. Through the fog of semi-slumber flash the eyes of the vixen as she chews up the list of contacts on his cell phone. *Damn,* he whispers to himself and shoves his head in the pillow, plummeting into deep sleep, and were it not for Dina standing naked and shaking him, only sunlight could open his eyes. "Get up, Zvi, there's been a little accident, the tea spilled in my bed, luckily it was only lukewarm. It seems I really am very ill." Surrounded by the scent of herbal tea emanating from her beloved body, he rushes to the bright bedroom and wonders how a solitary cup had caused such a flood. The blankets are full of damp yellow stains and her nightgown is a dishrag. "Come here," he says, pulling her near, "before we deal with the mess, I need to wash you." And she stares at him, quietly confused. The permission to wash her private parts, which even in their passionate youth was never granted, proves that the fever has undone everything that was firm and steady since the day they met.

He strips off his clothes and joins her in the shower, soaping and rinsing, whirling between worry and desire. And he towels her and brings her a dry nightgown, and leads her to his bed in the children's room, a big doll among his grandchildren's dolls and monsters. He covers her and waits till the rhythm of her breathing confirms she is asleep. He doesn't return to the bedroom to take control of the mess but takes the cell phone from his pocket and enters the kitchen, and wakes up his son and says, "No, my son, don't move yet, but I decided to call an ambulance. So please confirm, Rabbi Emden Street five, top floor, that's the address, right?"

"Yes, Abba, that's the one and only address. But if they decide to hospitalize her, call me from there. With the roads empty at night I can zip down in no time."

TO THE EMERGENCY ROOM

"This time you have a patient who is herself a doctor," Luria informs the three young people in white uniforms who pile into his apartment with a folding gurney and emergency equipment. "Actually a pediatrician," he specifies, "but a senior physician at a large hospital. And because she believed she could handle the illness on her own, she might be shocked that I called you without her permission, but I'm completely fine with my decision, because in addition to high fever, which medicines did not alleviate, she's getting confused, kind of foggy, which has never happened before, so here, this way, friends, the tea I brought spilled all over her bed, so I moved her to the children's room. This new confusion is what scares me now more than the fever, it does happen to me too once in a while, but it's very different, without fever or aches and pains.

Before you start examining her, a quick question, are you just paramedics, or is one of you by chance a real doctor?"

"A real one?" chuckles a young woman paramedic, accepting the challenge: "Yes, by chance there is, and by chance it's me." Luria thinks he hears an accent, foreign but also familiar. And the young doctor gets down on her knees by the bed of the senior physician, strokes her arm and tries to wake her, and when Dina opens her eyes, oddly unsurprised, the young woman sits her up with a gentle, practiced hand, lifts the nightgown and moves her stethoscope between pale, ripe breasts, and then the back, and when she's done she asks the name of the hospital where her patient works. The paramedics check blood pressure, take temperature, and beam a shaft of light down her throat, and as directed by the young doctor they stick a needle in her weakly offered arm to attach an IV tube. And Dina suddenly tells them hoarsely about a child, apparently from the West Bank, infected with the meningococcal bacteria, and instructs the emergency staff to disinfect themselves and put on masks and surgical gloves. "And disinfect him too," she says, pointing to her stupefied husband, "and put a mask on him. Yes, you also need to be careful around me." Indeed, having divulged the explicit name of the bug, there is no need to elaborate: out come the masks and gloves and sterile gowns, and the folding gurney turns into a big wheelchair.

"It's good that you called us right away," says the young woman doctor. "This is an extremely virulent microorganism. We're going to take her to the place she belongs, where she caught the bug, that would be best, even though her hospital isn't on duty for our runs tonight."

"Of course," says Luria, his voice sounding strange to him behind the mask, "she not only belongs there, but she's also important and well known, so maybe they'll agree to isolate me along with her."

The patient is lifted from her bed and wrapped in a blanket, and the wheelchair that will be a bed in the ambulance is pushed toward the small elevator. Luria takes her wristwatch and puts it on next to his, and runs around the house with a plastic trash bag, gathering medicines from the bedroom, her slippers and his, as well as their two toothbrushes. Energized by his decision not to surrender to her haughty self-treatment of the illness, he rummages again through his desert jacket, on the off-chance the phone is hiding in a pocket, and looks in the mirror at the mask on his face and thinks: Let's assume that the virulent microorganism of the sick Palestinian child has been passed to me too, will it ease the dementia, or make it worse?

He turns off light after light, but before darkening the kitchen he intends to console and fortify himself with dark chocolate, the darkest of the dark, and he breaks off two squares and shoves them in his mouth, under the mask, and slips the rest of the bar into a pocket, next to his wife's phone. He locks both locks on the front door, as if going on a long journey, doesn't wait for the elevator, and rushes down the stairs to the street, where the ambulance lights flash wildly, amplifying the anxiety of curious spectators.

The husband is quickly and firmly seated next to his wife, who lies flat and wears an oxygen mask. "Why this?" His heart stops. "Don't worry," the young doctor calms him, "it's just to make it easier, your wife requested it herself. They'll get her over this." "You sure?" He is near tears. "I know. I told you, I'm a doctor too," she says with a mischievous wink, "a real doctor." In order to avoid the first, embarrassing question, he moves to the second, easier one: "What are you, Muslim or Christian?" "Both," she confirms with a little smile, adding no explanation. But Luria is not looking for an explanation, he merely sighs: "Yes, that's a possible but difficult combination," and he takes out the dark packet, tears off more gold foil, and offers her chocolate consolation, and to his surprise she breaks off not one square but two, then passes the rest to her two teammates and also to the driver, who sounds the siren sparingly, only at tricky intersections.

ISOLATION

Emergency room staff are prepared for their arrival. Awareness of the wily microorganism requires the immediate isolation of the pediatrician, and every doctor, nurse, and orderly assigned to her case wears gloves, a gown, and a mask, and makes sure to scrub their hands upon entering and leaving. But Luria's case remains unclear, so he is not isolated but sent for tests to determine whether his wife's bug has infiltrated him too. "Who are you?" inquires an older nurse, who takes a generous sample of his blood, then hands him a sterile cup for a urine test. "Do you also work at our hospital?" "No," Luria says, "one doctor in the family is enough. I'm an engineer, a road engineer to be exact, and would you believe that from this morning till the evening I was running around in the desert, in the Ramon Crater, where I maybe hiked once, or at least heard about." But this is a religious woman, who in her youth bore many children, preventing her from traveling long distances and certainly from hiking in the Ramon Crater, whose name, truth to tell, she is hearing now for the first time. "Whereas I," Luria quickly clarifies, "am not touring there but working, as a government employee. "If at your age," says the old nurse, as if to herself, "you are still working for the State, you can count yourself lucky." And when she returns a while later to pick up his urine sample, she has good news: there's nothing wrong with him, all the tests are normal, he can go home, and just take an antibiotic for two days. "And this?" He points to the yellow liquid. "This hasn't been tested." True, but it's not important, and needs to be cultured for a while, so he is free to go.

If, wonders Luria, amazed if not relieved, I touched her, took care of her, stroked her, kissed her, even washed her, and the bacteria didn't want me, does that mean our relationship is getting weak? He hurries to his wife to tell her he's been discharged. But Dina is not in the emergency room. The warning is gone from the door, and an unfamiliar man lies in her bed. While he was tied up in tests, Internal Medicine A and B were told to admit her in isolation.

"A, or B?"

"Whichever one took her first, but the two departments are on the same floor, so you'll have no trouble finding it."

Although it is night, the hallways are lit and the elevators are all working, and the staff on duty in the labs and clinics are ready for any emergency. But after midnight a huge hospital like this also reveals its sadness. The shops and cafeterias are shuttered, the patients are sleeping or tranquilized, and the visitors, even the most loyal, have been asked to go home. Here and there a patient, hovering between life and death, is swiftly wheeled on a gurney, and cries of pain, or agonized dreams, echo in the distance, but silence rules overall. In the past year Luria has been here twice for brain scans, but because his wife was with him, and the scans were processed easily and quickly, and the results went straight to the neurologist, the byways of the hospital complex are beyond his ken.

Now he walks alone. Tired and frazzled, he arrives at a gigantic structure with a vast lobby, with various banks of elevators, and has no way of knowing which would take him to his destination and which would only get him lost. And if at this late hour, in the maze of this hospital, he revisits his confusion at the opera, where is the music to save him? His head spins. He walks beneath the glittering lights of the mammoth lobby as if wandering under the stars of the crater. Luria is an engineer of roads, not buildings, but can assume that on every floor of this huge building, emanating from every elevator, is a grid of corridors, shortcuts, and junctions, which can be navigated to go anywhere. He presses the button and an elevator opens before him, inviting him to enter as a cleaning worker exits, an African refugee, who assures him that A and B are both on the seventh floor.

In Internal Medicine A the lights are dimmed amid a hum of silence. At the nurses' station sits a young nurse working a crossword puzzle on her phone. Yes, they phoned from the ER to admit Dr. Luria, but we had no isolation rooms free, so they found her one in Med B. Go there, sir, they're waiting for you. He heads there, again the hum and the dark corridors, and at the nurses' station, two nurses, male and female, busy chatting. They're waiting for Dr. Luria, the isolation room is ready, but at the moment a woman is sleeping there, a patient escaping her snoring roommate. But when his wife arrives, they'll evict her right away. Where is his wife? She's still on her way, she requested an extra test at the Imaging Institute, but don't try to look for her, you'll get lost among the corridors and doors and won't find anyone to help you. If you got this far, sit down and don't move. But will he be able to go into isolation too? Because he went through the emergency room and it turned out he's fine and will stay fine. But a nurses' station isn't authorized to answer that question, and the doctor on duty just fell asleep, best not to wake him before he sees the patient. And anyway, his wife is a physician, and she'll decide if and how her husband can be isolated with her.

Ill at ease, he asks to see the room in question, walks down a dark corridor, among oxygen tanks, walkers, shower chairs, and a big medical computer on wheels, and he quietly pushes open the door, and is greeted in the window by the same blemished crescent that floated above the drive home from the desert. Snuggled in bed is the patient who got sick of her snoring neighbor, her own breathing far from tranquil. Until his wife arrives and decides if he may share her isolation, he must fend for himself. Drained and exhausted, he pads around silently in the hall and finds an abandoned mattress in an empty sickroom. He drags it back and sets it down beside the bed, and the woman opens her eyes, puzzled, and closes them again, as if Luria and the mattress were fleeting props in her dream. If I'm just a dream for this woman, who I somehow think is newly pregnant, why shouldn't I stay beside her until my wife comes to replace her? He lies down on the mattress, bare of any sheet or pillow, and plunges into the abyss of unconsciousness. With the first rays of sunlight Yoav touches him and says, "Abba, don't be scared, it's only me, I came to take you to Imma." And Luria opens his eyes and says, "Hi, *habibi*."

THE PEDIATRIC CLINIC

Since the pensioner was not just a walk-on in the dream of a female patient, but also utterly immersed in his own dream, how could he be expected to notice the text message that blinked in the phone in his pocket, telling him his wife would not be admitted to Internal Medicine, but transferred directly from Imaging to her own pediatrics department? When her fellow doctors learned about the microorganism that had attacked one of their own, it was decided, with her agreement, to isolate her in her workplace, where supervision would be strict and friendly, and she could consult in her treatment. Luria would not be staying with her there, but since there was no way they would let him go home alone at this late hour, it was decided not to wake him, but let him commandeer the mattress with no sheet or pillow, and update him in the morning.

After Yoav gets his father on his feet, he takes him straightaway to a hospital café, where he can eat and drink, and then leads him to the children's clinic. There, in a tiny room, the walls decorated with photos of cats and dogs, balloons drifting near the ceiling, Luria sees that despite her antibiotic IV and oxygen mask, the bride of his youth recognizes him and waves hello, so he can forgo his isolation and feel free to go home.

When his son brings him in the afternoon for another visit, the department is filled with laughter and wailing and tears. Parents and grandparents try to quiet and calm and amuse children of every gender, ethnicity, and religion, Palestinians included, either Israeli citizens or West Bank children who were driven from the checkpoints by volunteers of Road to Recovery, the group Maimoni had not invented. And the sick children are blended into one apolitical state, bed by bed, oxygen beside oxygen, and intravenous tubes virtually entangled. Luria observes that the parents from the West Bank, who rise at dawn to cross borders and checkpoints, are nicely dressed, and their children even more so, in the belief that bow ties or chiffon petticoats will raise the odds for meticulous medical care.

There is slight improvement, her fever is slowly receding, report Dina's colleagues, the doctors and nurses. "This evening we'll try to get her off oxygen. But between the intensive IV and her exhaustion, we'll have to keep her another two, three days in isolation, and then, if she would like, we'll transfer her to Internal Medicine. Or maybe we'll keep her here, in her own department."

Father and son put on surgical masks and gloves and gowns, so that the bacteria, if not yet defeated, will not outsmart them. As they come near the hostess of the microbe they are warned not to touch her. The high fever lingers, her face droops, and wrinkles usually blurred by cosmetics are exposed in her neck. Her hair is wild on the pillow and her arm stretched out on the sheet, to allow the antibiotic to drip unimpeded. Luria remembers the confusion that impelled him last night, for the first time, after many years of marriage, to strip naked and join her in the shower. Is this confusion gone now, or secretly plotting to join hands with his dementia? And though they are both wearing masks, she can see his new anxiety and removes her mask to find out what he's so afraid of. I still haven't got over your confusion of yesterday, says Luria. Confusion? She ponders the absurd diagnosis and turns to her son, who tries to change the subject by remarking that of all the doctors and nurses in her clinic, the bacteria picked her to fall in love with.

Luria carefully straightens the plastic IV tube to speed up the drip, which is a bit slow in his opinion, but his wife firmly finger-waves him to stop, and to return her wristwatch, now mated with his. As he gently straps the watch to her wrist, he remembers her cell phone and pulls it from his pocket and puts it in her hand, and Yoav takes it from her and puts it on a shelf next to a toy, a cat or perhaps a lamb. "And what about *your* phone?" asks Dina. "No problem," Yoav answers for him, "we'll buy Abba two phones."

"Two?" "Yes, two," confirms Luria, "so if I lose one, I won't lose contact with you." "And I," she smiles, "which one should I call?" "First the old number, and if there's no answer, you call the other number, as if from now on you have two husbands." Two husbands? She is less than thrilled by the possibility. Yoav supports the vision of two phones. "Yes, Imma, he's right, in his condition he needs two phones, with all of his codes and contacts. And if he loses both," Yoav says, "we'll buy him a third, so he won't get lost on us again, out in the world." And he glances at his watch. Time to go. But it's hard for Dina to part from her loved ones.

"Wait, the tunnel?"

"The tunnel? You said it's Maimoni's fantasy and he and I won't be able to convince anyone to approve it."

"Yes, it's a fantasy, but that's the very reason why *davka* you, in your condition, are the one to make it happen."

"My condition?" He laughs. "What is this, the bug is changing your mind?"

"It isn't, but you are. I see that you, in your condition, knew better than I did to call for help."

"Only because *you* are too smug."

"Yes, sometimes, I admit it. But explain to me, why have a tunnel in the crater?"

Luria would have liked to explain, but holds back. Could his wife at her weakest understand such strange convolutions? After all, she's right, a tunnel in a desert hill that could easily be removed is the joint fantasy of Maimoni and Shibbolet, and only an elderly road engineer with mild dementia would dare try to persuade the Defense Ministry to fund it.

TATTOO

How right Maimoni had been when he promised Luria that a son who owns a computer-chip business could easily restore everything from the lost phone. Moreover, his son can add new treasures that were never in the old phone. Yes, after the two new ones were purchased, one with a new number and the other that inherited the old, and texted their numbers to each other, Yoav briskly began loading them with the names and numbers from the old contact list, plus others that were never listed. Phone numbers of the grandchildren, of public institutions, hospitals, clinics, and repairmen, phone numbers of acquaintances and old friends discovered in abandoned notebooks, including more than a few dead souls. Luria tried to prevent his son from entering these as contacts, but Yoav insisted, why not? They were your friends, they should at least stay in the phone's memory, some have left widows behind. Not to worry, they won't take up anyone else's space. The chips in these phones, trust me, have enormous storage. I put the most important numbers in your speed dialing, everything is in alphabetical order, which you should please try to preserve, if not in your brain at least in your heart.

And in addition to phone numbers old and new, Yoav tries to install applications his father never had, apps to tally his footsteps, how far he walks, the calories he burns, his heartbeat and blood pressure. In short, Abba, says the son, now you can know who you are and how you are at any time.

At first Luria was moved by his son's technological zeal, then began to reject it. Enough, enough, his world is shrinking and he has no desire to expand it, certainly not with dead souls and burned calories. And now, with Imma hospitalized, there's another issue: the ignition code of the car sometimes goes wrong in his memory, and the soft whisper that sometimes goes with the gargle of ignition only makes the error worse. Yes, the code could be inserted among preferred contacts on the phone, but to hunt for it at a tense moment or in an emergency would confuse him even more. Writing the code on a slip of paper, pasted to the wheel or gearshift, would arouse his fear of a thief finding it. Luria has therefore come up with a simple solution, which he had already discussed with Imma, and she wasn't shocked and didn't object.

"Imma agreed that you should have a number tattooed on your arm?" Yoav is astounded.

"But it's not a drawing or writing, not a symbol or a picture, just four innocent numbers that won't bother or mean anything to anybody. Who's even going to notice?"

Yoav still hesitates. "No," says his father, "don't try to discuss it with Imma, not while she's ill. It's not a medical matter but a human one. All I want from you is a little help." "What?" Yoav freezes. "To tattoo you?" "No, dummy, of course not you, you'd only hurt me. But you will take me to the right place, help me choose the size of the numbers, and make sure they don't talk me into tattooing something extra that I don't need."

Yoav acquiesces, given no choice. He will find out where tattooing is professionally done in sanitary conditions, and will take his father there, but not this minute, because he has to go back to his office. No, don't find out anything, no reason to wait till the next confusion, now, dear boy, before you disappear up north. Just listen, I'm only talking about four numbers, the simplest tattoo in the world, and I've already found the right person, who does it without preparation or consultation or clarification. On my walks by the sea in Jaffa I discovered a quick inexpensive place in the flea market, and now I have a simple request: take me there, stand by my side, and make sure they don't hurt me too much. Only four digits. And from there you continue to the North, and I'll take a taxi to the hospital, to Imma, and maybe I'll find a spare bed among the children, and if it turns out the bacteria have already given up on Imma, I'll find a mattress and sleep alongside her.

First they go down to the parking garage and turn on the ignition of the red Japanese car, to confirm that the remembered code is valid, and only then is it written down. It seems to Luria that the gargling engine is accompanied by the whispering geisha, who thanks him for choosing the right car, but he is wary of sharing his delusion with his son. They ride in Yoav's car along the seashore and find parking near the Clock Square in Jaffa, and Luria confidently leads his son to a kitchenware workshop and asks the salesman to get his father. Out comes a jolly Georgian Jew who recognizes Luria: So you decided after all to make a tattoo to strengthen your weak memory. Yes, but painlessly, as you promised, and I've brought my son to help me pick the size. The tattooist leads his guests to the rear of the workshop, to a table for repairing copper pots. A yellow flame dances in a heating stove, and the man opens a wooden box and takes out his tools: an electric needle, bits of plastic wrap, a jar of faintly blackish cotton, a small bottle of alcohol, and tiny tins of creams and lotions. After arranging the tools, he sets up a menu board with letters in Hebrew, English, and Arabic, and numerals in various sizes. The father and son agree at once on the right size, and the tattooist approves, good choice, that's what most people choose. When did you begin doing this kind of work? asks Luria as the man applies alcohol to the designated spot, on his right forearm. Let me try to remember, the tattooist says. And without a template, while Luria closes his eyes not to witness his pain, the needle glides confidently and tattoos four bluish numbers of the red Suzuki's code, numbers that Yoav recites one at a time from the notepaper in his hand, to be sure they are done in the right order.

An aromatic transparent cream is spread on the tattoo and a pink bandage attached. And as Luria lets down his sleeves and puts on his coat, he repeats the question: "When did you start doing this sort of work, anyway?" The tattooist smiles. "It's not work, it's a pleasure to make a tattoo for people like you who need to remember what they are starting to forget. I don't tattoo birds or flowers, only names and numbers. If I remember right, I did my first tattoo for my uncle, who forgot his name. After him came other confused people from the neighborhood. You too, sir, when you start to forget your name, remember me, and I'll tattoo your name on the other arm."

Yoav smiles, but Luria darkens, and to block the forecast of his future he takes out his wallet. "How much do I owe you?" "Nothing," says the tattooist, "for me it's not work, it's a pleasure."

ON THE ROAD TO RECOVERY

Dusk. In front of the hospital, Palestinian parents and children, bundled in coats and scarves, wait for the Road to Recovery volunteers who will take them to the checkpoints. Luria waves to them warmly, to show that he knows where they are from and where they are going, but he doesn't linger, he rushes to his wife. Doctor Luria fell asleep before dinner, a young nurse tells him, her fever is down and we took away the oxygen mask, but isolation is still mandatory until we're sure the bacteria is no longer active. Before putting on the mask and gown that license him to visit his wife, he asks the nurse whether a bed or just a mattress might be found for him in the department, so he can spend the night by her bed. Why do that? The sick children aren't quiet at night, and parents go in and out of the rooms. If you stay here tonight, you won't get any rest. What makes you think I'm looking for rest, says Luria, I am a pensioner, I have my fill of rest. Bad enough that last night I wasn't at her side. Now that she's conscious with no oxygen mask, I can try to entertain her.

The darkness in the room is so complete that for a minute the husband is unable to find his wife's face burrowed in the bed. The jolly balloons are floating near the ceiling, and the colorful pictures on the walls have turned into stains. Luria steps carefully and sits down silently by the IV drip, its rhythm obscured in the dark. On the nightstand sits her dinner, untouched. Luria waits for his wife to sense his presence. She sleeps more deeply than he can ever remember. Does this bear out the tenacity of the illness, or is it a sign of recovery? But he will not interfere. Perhaps the doctor finds a special sweetness in so deep a sleep in her workplace. He lightly touches the bandage on his tattoo. The tattooist did not specify a date for removing it and revealing the code to the world, and really, why hurry? We'll wait another two, three days, hoping my intelligent son dictated the numbers to the tattooist in the right order. A living person with a mistaken code is a broken person.

"Where'd you disappear?" A muffled voice, between sheet and pillow.

"Good morning, but why would I disappear?"

"Because you did."

"I didn't disappear. I went with Yoav to buy two phones and install everything from the one that was lost, and he convinced me to add new names and applications that will enable me to know more about myself."

"And that took so much time?"

"I guess so. Because I also asked him to go with me to the place in Jaffa where they did the tattoo that you and I agreed on, the ignition code from the car."

"I agreed you should go around with a number on your arm?"

"Of course. You also understood that my only choice is to tattoo the four digits on my arm, so I don't get them confused time and again."

"Unbelievable, Zvi, you took advantage of my illness to get yourself tattooed."

"What do you mean, took advantage? When you're incapacitated in the hospital I have to be twice as precise."

"And when we trade in the car, Zvi, you'll tattoo the new code?"

"No need, you can transfer the same code to the new car."

"The same code? It's possible? You really are a marvel."

He grins. "What else is new? You knew that forty-eight years ago."

"Not to this degree. Your dementia somehow makes you sharper, maybe to help you maneuver."

"Yes. Maneuver. Because I have no choice."

"The main thing is you always have to be reachable and not suddenly disappear. The tattoo will give you confidence, but swear to me, Zvi, that you will never, ever, drive down to the desert in this car, which also belongs to me, by the way."

"To the desert in our car? Why would I? And what am I, anyway, in Maimoni's project? A marginal unpaid assistant, at your initiative, by the way."

"I'm still warning you."

"No need, I get it."

"Don't even imagine such a thing."

"Not imagine?" He laughs. "Now you want to control my imagination?"

"Your imagination can spin out of control."

"Dina, enough, you're ill. I get it. Don't badger me."

He opens the blinds. Among the night clouds is that same crescent moon, this time paler and curvier than before. He picks up the tray and inspects his wife's uneaten dinner. Plain omelet and white cheese, two slices of bread, a gray porridge suitable only for children. "You want me to go heat it up, or try to exchange it for something more edible?"

"No. I have no strength to eat now. Let's wait a little. You can have the porridge."

"But you have to eat something. You can't not eat. Raise your head and I'll help you."

"I have no strength to raise my head."

"Then don't, just open your mouth. At least have the omelet. I'll heat it up?"

"Don't heat anything."

He sets the tray on the bed, slices the omelet and bread into little squares, spreads a bit of white cheese on them, and carefully inserts them into the opened mouth, the maw of a baby bird, not a female fox.

"You see," he says as he watches her swallow the bread and omelet, "you were hungry without realizing, so we need to try a few spoons of porridge too."

But she doesn't respond, just casts an ironic look at her husband, his eyes flashing above the mask. "I see," she says, "that tunnel makes you stronger."

Luria doesn't respond. He gently strokes her hand, bends over and kisses her, then draws the IV pole closer to the bed and stacks the dishes on the tray. Before going to forage for food and getting ready for bed himself, or at least a mattress, he wants to know if she has heard of an Israeli volunteer organization called Road to Recovery, which drives Palestinian patients to and from Israeli hospitals, and it turns out that the doctor knows of this group, they sometimes bring children to her clinic. But the organization focuses on the most urgent cases, patients treated in the oncology and urology departments.

"Is there a special department for transplants?"

"Why do you ask?"

"No reason, just curious."

"Transplants, if needed and feasible, are done at the unit for organ transplantation."

"And you, who are not a surgeon, have you ever seen a transplant—of a heart, for example?"

"No, why do you ask?"

"No reason, just curious."

He straightens out her blanket and top sheet, lowers the blinds to dim the light of the crescent moon, now free of cloud cover, and goes out to the nurses' station. He puts the tray on the food cart and says to the nurse, "I managed to get her to eat everything except for that strange porridge." He removes the mask and gloves and gown and continues, "And as far as I am concerned, I'll go find something more edible in one of the cafés. But I beg you again to find me at least a mattress and a pillow, I'm uneasy and want to be with her also at night."

He goes down to a coffee shop on the ground floor, where at this evening hour the customers are few, and tables are being cleared and chairs stacked, but it's not too late to order a fragrant omelet sandwich and a big cup of hot milk. He eagerly relieves his hunger, occasionally stroking the bandage stuck to his arm to ensure the safety of his code.

A waiter collects his tray and informs him that it's closing time. He gets up and discovers that while he wolfed down his meal the place emptied out entirely, except for a thin, gloomy young man sitting in a far corner, who protests the eviction of Luria. "What is this?" he shouts, "by the clock we have the right to stay another fifteen minutes." "No right today," snaps the cashier. "Why today?" insists the young man. "Because today is today, and we're closing right away." And the young man, apparently an Arab, picks up his espresso cup, sips the last drop, pausing so Luria can exit first, and he follows, making sure to show Luria the opening and closing hours clearly marked on the door that is quickly locked behind them.

A doctor in a green gown with OPERATING ROOM imprinted on it arrives and jiggles the locked door. "Just like them," says the young man. "They felt like closing early today. Here, read the closing time." The surgeon jiggles the door again, but inside the café they shake their heads no, forget it. "Nothing you can do," says the young man, "they won't open even for you." And without being asked, he provides the disappointed doctor with a detailed inventory of vending machines in the building, their exact locations, and which foods and drinks they offer. But the doctor mistrusts the information of a pale-faced young stranger and gives up on coffee or cake, leaving in a snit. "They're total pigs," says the young man to Luria, who for some reason lingers by the locked door. "They could tell from his gown this was not just any doctor, this was a surgeon who needed coffee." "Maybe today they had special reasons," says Luria, trying to defend the café people. He looks kindly at the young man and says, "I see that you know every corner of this hospital." "Yes, I'm almost like family, I was recently hospitalized here myself, mostly because my cousin has serious kidney trouble."

"What department is he in?"

"Urology."

"And you?"

"The same."

"What was wrong with you?"

"Nothing was wrong. I was here because I donated a kidney to this cousin, which at first grafted well, but he didn't know how to protect it and now there are complications."

"Where did you donate it?" Luria is fascinated. "The transplant department?"

"There is no such department."

"But I heard that there is such a department, where they transplant other things, more serious than kidneys, even a heart."

"A heart?" scoffs the young man. "What are you talking about? There is no such thing. Who would give their heart even to a cousin?"

"The donor is already dead, and I'm telling you, I know that in Israel they transplant hearts, if necessary, if there's no alternative, maybe not in this hospital, but in others."

"There's no such thing, sir, you're mistaken. If someone tells you they can replace your heart, don't listen to them."

"I don't need a new heart," Luria says irritably. "I'm not a patient, I'm here because my wife is hospitalized, even though she herself is a doctor."

"Okay, don't get angry. I didn't say a thing. Only that in Israel there are no replacement hearts."

"Where are you from, anyway?"

"A-Zababdeh."

"Where is that?"

"Near Qabatiya. You have heard of Qabatiya?"

"I have. I know it. I was a road engineer. Your cousin is also from there?"

"No, why? He's an Israeli from the Galilee, from Tur'an, but in '48 they split us apart."

"And you gave him a kidney just because he's a cousin?"

"Also. But also because we were well paid. But now he has complications, he didn't take good care of it, and I don't have another kidney to play with. What am I, his organist?"

"Organist." Luria laughs. "Good one."

THE HOSPITAL ROOF

Contrary to Luria's hopes, the lower fever, and willing consumption of omelet and cheese, did not mean the bug was gone. A young, dynamic doctor, Dina's heir apparent as department chief, intensified her isolation, forbidding her husband to sleep at her side. At a staff meeting, members questioned whether Pediatrics was the right place to treat its own medical director. But Dina, wielding her authority, demanded to stay in the place she knows. "If this is where the damn meningococcus attacked me," she declared in an unfamiliar tone, "this is where we'll kill it."

The blood tests were still problematic, and the antibiotic IV proved ineffective against a germ both virulent and sly. They substituted a stronger antibiotic, and the ten ensuing days of hospitalization made Luria into a fixture of not only Pediatrics, but the entire hospital. Between the ignition code emblazoned on his flesh and the barrier in the garage rising automatically, he becomes an expert at entries and exits, and able to find, day or night, parking spots reserved for senior physicians only.

From time to time, while the patient slept long and soundly, Luria would remove the mask and gloves, keeping the white gown on, so he could wander as he wished like an imaginary doctor, through departments, clinics, and laboratories, acquainting himself with hidden crannies of this vast hospital, thinking it wise to absorb the spirit of the place where he will breathe his last, when the time comes and his consciousness will finally go dark. But his wanderings are not designed merely to assure tranquility in his final days. They also enable him to check whether at this big Israeli hospital complex they transplant only kidneys, livers, lungs, and corneas, or do they do hearts too, and if so, is it feasible and what would it cost to replace a wounded heart that came here from the Palestinian Authority? In other words, he wanted to know if there was ever anything real in the promise that an officer of the Israeli Civil Administration made to a village schoolteacher from Jenin, or was the trading of a piece of land for a new heart an illusion from the start? Even as images, one after another, vanish from his memory, the picture of the beautiful dead woman, raised from a Nabatean ruin by her weeping husband, remains indelible.

But Shibbolet, who concocted the deal, has adamantly refused to identify the hospital where the hearts would have been exchanged. And despite the power and prestige of the medical complex whose halls he wanders, Luria can't be sure this was the place. When he asks in an office whether the hospital is equipped to perform this complicated transplant, he gets no answer. Who are you, anyway, sir, jokes a clerk, and who sent you? Are you looking for a new heart for yourself? Or do you wish to donate your heart?

So go the ten days in the hospital. Toward the end, Dina sporadically works in her department, studying reports about sick children and dispensing advice and instructions to doctors and nurses, until Luria complains that her illness has become her work. If so, she smiles affectionately, why do you keep hanging around? What more are you looking for? You'll end up catching something bad. But Luria refuses to be separated from his wife; his fear for her is unabated. Although he has two phones in his pockets, he insists on staying by her side, and moreover, Maimoni, who recently shipped him home in a minibus filled with mental cases, has vanished. Has the widowed father come out of hiding, and is the tunnel off the table? Has Shibbolet decided to banish the two engineers? "Why don't you call him?" asks Dina. "Why me?" fumes Luria. "He knew you were sent home sick, and saw how panicked I was when my phone disappeared and I lost contact with you. So who's supposed to worry? Me about him, or him about me? Who should pick up the phone? Who owes the other one respect? It wasn't so long ago that a dear lady warned me that my honor was her honor too."

She smiles. "Yes, I said that, but don't take me too literally. Instead of spinning like a dreidel in the hospital, you should call Maimoni, so he'll understand there's no reason to give up on you because of my illness, especially now that I'm getting better. It would be too bad if he found another pensioner to replace you, an unpaid assistant but without dementia."

"He won't find one," Luria declares, "because only dementia can prove the need for a tunnel instead of simply removing the hill. If I'm no longer needed here, I'm going home, but you should know it's insulting to say I'm spinning around like a dreidel when all I'm doing is protecting you from the germ."

"Okay, sorry, sorry, a joke. What's with you? It would be sad if your condition made you oversensitive instead of giving you a little distance from the world, a touch of alienation. Relax, my love, no bug will return, you can go home in peace. And now that you have two phones, I feel I have two husbands."

"Both equally confused."

She laughs. "So what?"

The illness is subsiding. If this were an Internal Medicine unit, she'd have been discharged to make room for a new patient, but here in Pediatrics they hold on to her, out of years of friendship. She is scheduled to retire in six months, and then she'll have to find a tunnel of her own.

Now they bring her lunch and ask if Luria would also like a meal tray. Sure, why not? And he tilts up her bed and sets his tray next to hers. The joy he felt as he fed omelet and cheese to the baby bird is a thing of the past. Most of her meal remains on her tray. Out of respect for the kitchen staff, he moves the meat from her tray to his.

It's three o'clock. He says goodbye, making sure not to kiss her, since he doesn't want to kiss a germ. He takes off the white gown, now his daily attire, hangs it on a hook by the door, and takes the elevator down. In the crowded café he sees the thin young Palestinian kidney donor, again sitting in a corner with his espresso. Luria stops to think. If this man donated a kidney in this hospital, he can learn something from him about transplants, his lack of belief in heart replacements notwithstanding. He buys a cappuccino and sits down next to the Palestinian, who recognizes him at once. "*Nu,*" says Luria, "what's with the kidney you donated to your Israeli cousin?" "Getting worse every day," the young man flatly replies. "He's a stubborn guy who doesn't know how to accept what he is given." "Be that as it may," says Luria, attempting to soften the blow, "at least they paid you, you didn't just give away your kidney." "No, excuse me," the Palestinian says bitterly, "I volunteered to do it, but they paid my father. I gave him a kidney that was a good match, and it's not my fault that this guy has rejected it, and now he's hooked up again to dialysis. You tell me, sir, what more can I do for a cousin like this? Nothing, right? He should go find himself another donor. I made my donation and have nothing left to donate. Now even if God himself asks me for a kidney, I won't give it to him." "Obviously, obviously," agrees Luria, "but why do you need to stay here in the hospital?" "Just wandering around," answers the young man, "learning about the illnesses of other people. Because of my donation I got an official residence permit for three months. So why hurry back, and who to?"

Luria regards the man sympathetically. "Yes," he agrees, "after the donation you're entitled to some rest, but where do you live or sleep?" "Tell me, sir," says the youth, slyly smiling, "are there no beds here at night?" "True," admits Luria, "especially with Hebrew as good as yours. Where did you learn it?" "Why do you ask?" "I'm interested in your Hebrew, over there in the West Bank." "Already in grade school we had a little Hebrew," says the Palestinian. "We had a good teacher in the village, and he would give us Hebrew sentences in the Arabic lessons, so we would learn how to argue with the soldiers. Also, when you work for the settlers, you pick up a lot of Hebrew from them, because they are clueless in Arabic. I worked on their air conditioners for a few years."

"Wait a second, who was that teacher?" Luria exclaims. "What's his name? Does he still teach in your village? And his wife, what happened to her, is she alive or dead?" The young man grows dizzy from the barrage of questions from the Jew. "Why do you care about him?" The young man is puzzled. "He's just a teacher who came from another village, how can I know what happened to him after so many years?" Luria persists: "Why so many? How many years could it be since you studied with him?" "How many years?" says the Palestinian. "How old do you think I am?" Luria studies him. "Nineteen? Maybe twenty-three." "Twenty-three?" The young man laughs. "What's wrong with you? Can't you see, sir, that I'm over thirty? If I look so young to you, it's because I'm sickly, which is why I agreed to sell a kidney, how much longer did I have?" But Luria doesn't lose hope. "You know all about each other, what's happening in your extended families, so at least tell me the village of your well-educated teacher." "How would I know, I already forgot him." "All right, what about you, what village are you from?" "I already told you last time, A-Zababdeh, near Qabatiya, it's a village not far from here, on a clear day like today you can see it from the roof of this hospital." "From here?" scoffs Luria. "Why not?" insists the Palestinian, we're very close to you, everything touches everything. When the sky is clear like today, if you go to the roof, you can see the Jordan River." "The Jordan?" cries Luria. "Come on, my friend. You're totally confused." "Why confused?" protests the young man. "I'm telling you, on a clear day like today, you can see a great many things from the roof of the hospital." "Not on any day," insists Luria, "neither clear nor gray. Listen, I know the North and the Center very well, I've been to every remote corner, and I planned many roads, and I'm telling you, it's impossible to see from here what you think." But the Palestinian stands his ground: "It's not what I think, it's what I *know* that I see. Tell me, sir, do you want to bet?" "Bet?" Luria laughs at the surprising offer. "Sure, why not? If we go up to the roof and see Samaria and the Jordan River, I'll buy you a big meal at this café." "Don't buy me any meal," sniffs the Palestinian, "I don't need favors like that from you, let's make it a hundred shekels, or is that too much?" "A hundred shekels is nothing to me," Luria haughtily declares. "If you prove to me that you can see even the edge of your village from here, I'll give you a hundred shekels, and if I'm right, I'll take only one symbolic shekel from you. But surely it's not legal to walk around on the roof here." "If it's possible to walk around, why should it not be legal?" says the Palestinian. "But you are not a young man, you'll need to be careful not to fall."

"Why would I fall?"

"No real reason you should fall. But you still haven't told me what *you* are doing here in the hospital, what your illness is. Or are you only here for tests?"

"I'm here because of my wife, a senior physician in Pediatrics, who caught an aggressive bug from a child who was brought here from your Palestinian Authority, so her colleagues hospitalized her, but she's improving."

"If she's a patient and also a doctor here," says the Palestinian, who stands up, licking the final drops of coffee from his lips, "then obviously you, her husband, are allowed to look at the world from the roof, to see if I'm talking nonsense."

Luria is led wide-eyed along broad corridors from the main building to another one, gigantic and unfamiliar. Pairs of elevators line the wide lobby, ignored by the Palestinian, who tugs the Israeli down a long hallway to a lavatory close to a service elevator. "You should go now," the young man urges the pensioner, "if you need to on the roof, you won't find facilities." Luria, impressed by the delicate phrasing, says, "Thank you, you're right, but first tell me your name. "Aladdin," says the youth. "And what does it mean?" "The name comes from *The Thousand and One Nights,* which you have undoubtedly heard of, where the main character of one story is Aladdin, a great hero." Luria is pleased. "A classic name. I don't remember if I read the book, but the name is familiar even to someone who's not exactly an Arab. So please, Aladdin, wait for me, my name is Zvi, till I'm done."

When Luria emerges from the lavatory he sees Aladdin wrestling with the elevator door, to keep it open. It's a crude freight elevator, with metal walls and floor, and no mirror, not even a small one. Aladdin doesn't push the top-floor button but one below, the eleventh, because from experience he knows a good safe route from there to the roof. No doubt the youth from *The Thousand and One Nights* knows the way, Luria says to himself, and who knows if he might lay me down under the open sky to extract one of my kidneys and restore what he donated in vain. Huge air-conditioning units, whirling fans clattering, greet them on arrival. But no valleys or hills can be seen, only narrow paths amid solar panels and antennas scattered on the enormous roof, surrounded by an urban landscape of streets and high-rise buildings, with only small patches of green. But Aladdin advances carefully to the edge of the roof, to a corner where the crowded urban landscape disappears all at once, and a great expanse catches the eye, sailing into the distance. Gentle hills, red roofs of settlers' homes, jumbled towns and villages bursting with minarets and domes of mosques. A pleasant winter sun casts a blue-gilded cupola over the landscape, and a fine pinkish mist envelops the pastoral vision, an indivisible picture of serenity. Luria is thrilled by the ultimate proof afforded by the view. He starts to reach for his wallet to pay what he owes, but then remembers the Jordan River.

"Look over there, sir," shouts the young man excitedly, pointing toward the far horizon, "take a good look, the Jordan is there, but it's dry because they took away the water and only left the name." Luria laughs. He's something else, this crazy Palestinian. He takes from his wallet the brownish hundred-shekel bill with its picture of President Ben-Zvi.

And then, despite the din of clattering fans, the pensioner realizes that one of the phones insists on finding him. Before Maimoni can say a word, Luria grouses, "What is this, Asael? What's with you? How could you disappear like that? You couldn't figure out that my wife got very sick and had to be hospitalized, so I'm always at her bedside? You think because you stuck me in a minibus of feeble-minded people, I became insignificant?"

Maimoni apologizes, embarrassed. He didn't realize the illness was so serious, and didn't know that Luria had bought a new phone. He's also had a rough time. The young woman, Ayala, was thrown out of Sapir College, and the father again tried to turn himself in. "But where are you, Zvi, you sound like you're in a hot-air balloon, I hear mountain winds around you." "No," Luria says, "I'm taking in the view from the roof of the hospital." "In that case," Maimoni says urgently, "we need to meet, because the army is getting antsy about the road, just tell me your wife's room number and I'll come straight there." "No, Maimoni, don't get lost in any hospital, Dina will be released tomorrow or the day after, so come to our house. You remember the address." "Of course, in old north Tel Aviv, just please remind me which street." But Luria, whose address has again evaporated, plays the wise guy: "You already forgot the name of the street?" "Yes, no," mutters Maimoni, confused. "I remember it was near Basel, the name of some rabbi. "Exactly," says Luria, "the name of some rabbi." "But which one? Eibeschutz, Emden?"

"Exactly," mumbles Luria, "guess which." "Guess?" Maimoni is taken aback. "What's happening to you? Tell me the name, Eibeschutz or Emden?" "Something like that," Luria says defensively. "It's not Emden?" says Maimoni, becoming impatient. "Exactly, Emden," Luria agrees joyfully. "What's the house number? I picked you up on the street." "Yes," confirms Luria, "you took me only from the street." "So what's the number?" shouts Maimoni, "three or five?" "Exactly," says Luria, recoiling in panic, "three or five, when you get there you'll see." Maimoni, at wits' end over the memory crash of his unpaid assistant, cries out, "What's happening to you, Zvi, three or five?" And Luria replies in despair, as the pink mist of Samaria swirls in his head: "Exactly, three or five, when you reach the street you'll see the names on the mailboxes, just remember we're on the top floor, a roof apartment."

MAIMONI

Maimoni will have to wait a full week before he is invited to visit the Lurias. Two days after the phone call from the roof, Dina discharged herself from the hospital, but when she got home she felt she still needed to rest. From the living room sofa, watching TV, she directed Luria how to rehabilitate the apartment from the disarray created in her absence and make a good impression on a first-time guest. Luria was twice sent to bring flowers, and food and cleaning materials arrived from the grocery in line with a precise shopping list. And though everything is running smoothly, and their joint struggle against the bacteria enhanced their love and mutual trust, Luria has not yet told his wife about his tour of the roof of her hospital, to confirm the claim of a young, sickly Palestinian with one kidney that this land is small and crowded.

Maimoni's visit, Luria hopes, will enable the young engineer to explain to Dina, in his own words, the human and moral rationale for the tunnel that her husband will have a hand in planning and securing approval. Until now, Luria has spared his wife the story of the hill and its inhabitants. Truth to tell, he feared his wife would forbid him, as someone infiltrated by dementia, to take part in the identity crises of others. His wife still doesn't understand the inner meaning of the tunnel and the leading role he plays, and she says contradictory things, sometimes regarding it as Maimoni's fantasy, a whim that won't get financed, and other times, especially since she got sick, applauding it as a spiritual challenge to her husband, an asset in his battle for lucidity. In her view, a tunnel in the heart of so famous a crater is occupational therapy for a dwindling mind. After all, at the first meeting with the neurologist, she mentioned the tunnels on Route 6 to boost her husband's dignity.

Although Dina wants to postpone Maimoni's visit, at least till the cleaner can come and spruce up the apartment, Luria insists on inviting him right away, we need to submit our plan, the Defense Ministry is losing patience.

Maimoni arrives in the early evening with a small bouquet of flowers. A meatless dinner is ready, and alongside the bread, rolls and pitas, cheeses and salads, on the big marble kitchen table, sit Luria's two shiny new phones, not only so the young engineer can add their two numbers to his contacts, but to hint that if a phone were again to disappear, the pensioner would restrain himself and not burden the man with his hysteria.

Luria thinks Maimoni has aged a little since last seen. He looks tense, and his worried eyes survey the lovely penthouse without a word of praise. His meticulous beard has gone to seed, patchy and graying. Luria's first question concerns the beard. "What happened to it? You said your wife loves it." "*Loves* it? No need to exaggerate. She wasn't opposed to it. But your question is valid, a few days ago I decided to shave it off, and while shaving I felt a pang of remorse, so what's left on my face is Arafat's legacy to Western civilization."

"Arafat's legacy to the Western world?" Dina is shocked.

"Yes, the unruly stubble of Arafat, the beard of an eternal refugee, became a fashion statement of European youth after he died."

"That's the first time I've heard this odd explanation for the stubble fad," laughs Dina. "Yoav, our son, also wanted to grow a beard, but his wife vetoed it. I don't think Arafat was his role model."

"Not consciously, not consciously," Maimoni is quick to add. "In my opinion this is the hidden source. The minute the raggedy beard and the pistol in the belt appeared on the podium at the UN, the young people got turned on."

"Dina, please," her husband interrupts. "Don't take his theory seriously, it must've popped into his head because our army road has a problem with strange refugees who got stuck on a hill, which is why we have to dig a tunnel there."

"So this is the tunnel?" Her voice rings with disappointment. "For a couple of refugees?"

"Not just them, not just them," the two declare as one.

But the doctor, realizing that her husband has kept hidden key elements of his work in the desert, is not satisfied with half an answer, not even in unison, and demands details. And Maimoni, to the husband's surprise, begins at the beginning—in other words, his basic training. He was bullied by a company commander called Shibbolet, and nobody knows if that's his first or last name. And this captain became a lieutenant colonel, a commander in the West Bank, whose job it was to enforce the Occupation. Meanwhile, there was a beautiful woman not far from Jenin whose heart grew so weak that a heart transplant was proposed in exchange for a desirable piece of property, but while she waited for a new heart, she died.

"That's why, Dinaleh," says Luria, interrupting the flow of the story, "I asked you if they also transplant hearts at your hospital, and even though I spun around like a dreidel, I couldn't get a clear answer from you."

"Why the roundabout approach? Maimoni must know which hospital treated her, and he can tell you."

"No," says Maimoni, "I don't know. It's still secret, along with many more secrets Shibbolet keeps to himself. He's also not prepared to reveal the name of the village the family comes from, or the original names of the father and his children. They changed their names to Hebrew names. Don't forget that this officer got tangled up in this story, and developed ulterior motives along the way."

"But who's forcing you to be a party to the escapades of this Occupation officer?" protests the logical wife. "If your job is to plan an army road, then why because of a strange refugee family that invaded a hilltop do you need to dig a tunnel, instead of, say, simply going around the hill. Zvi used to take us on trips and show us how his roads managed to bypass natural obstacles rather than fight them."

A smile shines through the remains of Maimoni's beard. The smart assistant she teamed him up with will explain better than he can. But Luria suggests postponing the engineering issues till after dinner. He gets up from his chair to turn on the flame under the pot, where six sunny yolks swim in red shakshuka. His curious wife is annoyed. "Wait a second, Zvi, what's so complicated to explain?"

And now, with a flourish, her husband turns the white marble tabletop into a model of the Ramon Crater. First he gathers all the slices of whole wheat bread into a pile, meant to represent the hill. With a toothpick, he attaches a cube of yellow cheese to the top, symbolizing a Nabatean ruin, surrounding it with three black olives, father, son, and daughter, West Bank Palestinians whose identity became confused. After building the hill, he lays out all the forks and knives as Highway 40, from the edge of the table, the Genesis Hotel, into the twists and turns of Independence Road, all the way to Ma'aleh Afor, at the southern end of the crater. Finally, the military road, a dream of the distant future, marked by a juicy tomato and paved with dark peanuts, pointing west toward the Egyptian border.

With the physical model completed, spirit and imagination take over. Luria lists for his wife the disadvantages of the tomato placement between the road of knives and forks and the peanut road. Drivers have a limited field of vision and the intersection is a recipe for disaster, especially among drivers whose minds wander as they zoom through the desert. Moreover, there's an eerie vacuum of communication at this very intersection with Route 40, a dead zone that no cellular antenna can overcome, so in case of an accident, how could someone call for help? And to overcome the drawbacks, continues Luria with the aplomb of a veteran engineer, the intersection needs to be relocated, and he picks up the tomato and gently sets it down facing the bread-slice hill, which, Dinaleh, could actually be taken down by a big strong bulldozer, nemesis of mountains and smasher of boulders, but because the three olives have found refuge on this hill, the former company commander forces his trainee, who for some reason is still terrified of him, to dig a tunnel through the hill instead of simply eliminating it. Here, look, Dinaleh, says Luria, taking a long, sharp knife and pushing it carefully into the mound of bread until it cuts through the other side.

THE KIBBUTZ SEMINAR

It's good that the Lurias provided a meal and not just refreshments. Maimoni came famished to their home and dearly hoped the hospitality would not disappoint. When the hosts realized how starved he was, each made do with one egg yolk of shakshuka, while a double sun was served on his plate, followed, without asking him, by a bonus of the last two yolks.

"Yes," he says sheepishly, "everything is delicious, and I arrived dying of hunger, straight from a meeting with the new director general. Can you imagine that for four hours this hotshot wouldn't let anybody leave the meeting till we clarified the reasons for corruption in the department, and so, to strike a first blow against corruption, he allowed only pretzels and water to be served. That's why I'm gobbling up everything you put in front of me, and I shudder to think what you'll say about me after I leave."

On the contrary, it makes us happy, his hosts assure him, it's a big compliment when a guest enjoys the food. And the pantry and fridge are thrown open to explore further options.

"The good days are gone, Luria," sighs Maimoni. "The new director general insists on being involved in the details of the army plan, and demands that it be completed fast, so he can pile new assignments on me. And so, my friend and unpaid assistant, now that your wife has recovered and come home, we need your voluntary services in the final planning of the intersection and the road, and we'll humbly submit a low-budget proposal for the tunnel, and hope that the deputy accountant of the department will take pity on it, despite the fact that he's basically a crook but knows how to slip past the cops."

"You want to take me back down to the crater?"

"No, Zvi, your crater trips are over. We'll draw up the plans in my office, formerly yours. I have a wonderful new computer program that does a quick clean job."

"I don't know how to use it."

"You'll master it easily. I've already seen," he turns to the doctor, her eyes riveted on him, "that the dementia you both talk about only kicks in when he's out in the open under a strong sun, or when the sky is dark and the stars are few, but when he's in a closed and familiar place, he's balanced and logical. Don't you agree?"

She listens with a smile to the glib diagnosis. "Duly noted," she says, "but sorry, forty-eight years of marriage aren't enough for me to form a clear opinion about the change in my husband."

The three share a laugh. "Bottom line," says Maimoni, "come to the office the day after tomorrow at six, after everyone has left, and we'll get to work."

"Why in the evening? Why at six?"

"Because it's better that the new director general not know I recruited a stranger and let him walk around freely in the office."

"A stranger?" says Dina defensively. "Zvi is a senior person, former head of a division."

"Obviously, and there are employees in the office who remember who he was, but you have to understand, this guy is a tough cookie, why get in trouble with him over nothing?"

"You're right, Maimoni," Luria mutters. "No point getting in trouble with the director general over foolishness like me. You should develop a fear of him, because soon enough, after the road is paved, Shibbolet will be out of your life, and you may as well find another Shibbolet to be afraid of."

Maimoni only smiles, takes no offense. "Enough, Zvi, don't get carried away, you really don't understand what's happening at Israel Roads. Not only was the former director general arrested, so were a few senior employees, and some of them, believe me, over nothing, so why confront a guy who needs a whipping boy? But if driving at night is hard for you, we'll find a way to pay for a taxi."

"I have no problem navigating in darkness," declares Luria, "and the tattoo of the ignition code on my arm builds my confidence."

Maimoni asks to see the tattoo, touches it, and marvels how smooth it is. He is pleased. And you also have an extra phone, so you are protected from any surprise. And before he gets up to go, he adds to his contacts the number of the second phone, under the name "Luria B."

Luria is suddenly sorry that he will not be returning to the desert, that he would sit at a computer instead, but he stays frozen in place as Maimoni asks the lady of the house for permission to go out onto the roof terrace, to check what can be seen of the sea from there.

"Not much," she says, "but a few blue stripes remain among the skyscrapers to calm the worried soul." Luria's fists are balled, his eyes closed, he's trying to remember something, and as Maimoni is about to walk out, it hits him:

"Just a minute, before you disappear, tell me, what's going on with Hanadi?"

"Hanadi?" His wife is puzzled.

"Yes, Hanadi," insists Luria, "the girl, the daughter, the young Palestinian of that unfortunate family."

"Ayala," says Maimoni, clinging to the Hebrew name. "There's been a new complication, I'll tell you later."

But Luria demands an answer now.

The guest chooses his words carefully, not least because the lady of the house is listening intently. What happened was expected. At Sapir College, although she was well liked, because it's hard not to like such a sweet young woman, who had already befriended other young women there, Jewish in fact, not Bedouin, and even though Shibbolet had paid the full tuition in advance, the registrar's office at Sapir could no longer ignore the fact that she had not provided any documentation in lieu of the identity card that supposedly, *supposedly,* got lost. The main problem was the student dormitory. The number of places is limited, and without a proper document confirming she is an Israeli citizen, they could not continue to let her stay there. True, with the large sum entrusted to Shibbolet she could easily afford to rent a room from a family in Sderot, but Shibbolet was afraid that a Jewish family would be quick to expose her if they heard her, say, talking or crying in Arabic in her dreams at night, so he and Maimoni agreed they had to look for a different arrangement.

"What's this all about?" Dina has lost her patience.

"I'll tell you everything," says Luria, "I'll explain after he leaves, now let him finish the story."

"At first Shibbolet wanted to take her to Mitzpe Ramon, so

she could shuttle between his apartment and her father's hill, but I objected, this would cut her off from the world, and I said, 'Let's move her from down south to the Center,' and I got her into the Kibbutz Seminar here in Tel Aviv. They have a drama school offering a diploma in acting, and the atmosphere is warm and open, in the spirit of the old Labor Movement. The sweet, innocent Left, which accepts a person for who he or she is and doesn't dig too deep into their roots."

"And how did you suddenly come up with the idea to sign her up for acting school?"

"Here's a little story for you." Maimoni smiles playfully. "After the army I sort of wanted to become an actor, and I started acting classes, but I soon realized this was not an easy career, and the pay was low, and I could use my acting talent in more stable and lucrative professions like law, or a job with a government agency."

But Luria is excited to hear about Hanadi, and wants to know: "Are there dormitories at the Kibbutz Seminar?"

"Maybe yes, I don't know. Shibbolet and I didn't want to deal with a dormitory for a young woman with no ID. So I simply put her in my father's house. And because I knew my father's neighbor liked to snoop around and had a rude habit of walking straight in without knocking on the front door, I decided to tell her the whole truth about the new tenant and asked her to keep her mouth shut. She ended up liking our Ayala, and she looks after her and sometimes cooks her a meal. The arrangement works for now, and the brother also came to visit, and Shibbolet looked the place over, and I go there from time to time so she won't be too lonely in the evening. And we'll see, maybe one day we'll take her to visit her father, once he starts feeling less afraid of reality."

BACK TO THE FORMER OFFICE

The doctor's recovery is slow, with ups and downs. Sometimes her temperature is up by half a degree and she goes back to bed. It's not the bug anymore, jokes Luria, but the baby bacteria it planted in you, and until you get rid of them too, you won't be yourself. The Pediatrics staff call often, to check up on her, report on patients, and ask for advice. Meanwhile, her young heir apparent is pumping up his status and authority, and Dina, for her part, is sorry to be retiring so soon.

"My tunnel is also coming to an end," says Luria, trying to console her, "and I won't get a new tunnel, so when we are both free, we can have more fun."

"Fun? How so?" She peers through her glasses with an ironic twinkle. "With your dementia?"

"Sure, how do we know what it has in store? Meanwhile, don't be ungrateful. At the moment, I'm taking care of you, not you taking care of me."

"True, but all the same, you could go missing on me."

"In such a small country?"

"It's not as small as it looks on the map. Never mind, Zvi, you're basically a stable person, and now that Maimoni is putting you in an office and not taking you back to the desert, I'm relieved."

And indeed Luria arrives at dusk at his former office, for the first work meeting. Most of the employees have gone home, and it's easy to find a spot in the parking lot close to the entrance and take the elevator unnoticed, up to the office from which for many years he managed an entire division. The light is on, the door is open, and the computer screen is lit and ready to get going, but

Maimoni has stepped out. Luria enters but doesn't sit down, taking a moment to survey what has changed and what has stayed the same.

In a new steel cabinet are new folders of a different design, and on the shelf by the window stand little replicas of late-model bulldozers and cement mixers, alongside the veteran models still in place. A large calendar hangs on the wall, and the month of Iyar peeks between the breasts of a fashion model. Pinned to a nearby corkboard are professional photographs of the twins, boy and girl, as toddlers and kindergartners. How they've grown since then! Luria recalls them from the shiva, in their grandfather's kitchen, waiting for Hanadi to bring their food, but there are no recent photographs of them, or of their mother, or their father, as if the Holy Spirit had brought them into the world.

He is pleased to see, still hanging on the office wall, the photograph of Yitzhak Ben-Zvi, the second president of Israel, a thin man in a shabby suit. Although a socialist and labor leader, he did not feel a need to be photographed with his collar open, but wore a proper tie. A humble man whose youngest son was killed at the start of the War of Independence, and amazingly enough, the son's name is stored in Luria's memory: Eli, the name of the high priest in the Book of Samuel whose sons slid into depravity after his eyes grew dim. Luria steps closer to the framed picture, the glass dusty and cracked. Eighteen years ago, when he moved into this spacious office, President Ben-Zvi had been dead and buried nearly forty years, but Luria, breaking with custom, had decided not to replace him with a picture of the incumbent. As he once said to Maimoni, he left Ben-Zvi in full view as a kind of amulet against the corruption or temptation that lay in wait for a division head, even though he had distanced himself by putting his deputy, Tzahi Divon, in full charge of financial and budgetary matters. A different temptation, not financial, arrived in the person of a very pretty engineering graduate, a close assistant and secretary, who lost no time in informing him of her impending divorce, perhaps to signal her availability. When Luria became aroused as she showed him plans of highways and bypasses, he would quickly lift his eyes to the man who was the only Israeli president to serve three terms, yet lost none of his humility.

When Maimoni returns to the room and sees that his pensioner is lost in thought in front of the dusty picture, which glows red in the sunset, he gives a cheerful whistle, not to scare Luria. "I went out to get the extra key I had made for you, I forgot it in the car. I left the office open with the lights on so you shouldn't think I forgot you."

"Why would you forget me if I still haven't forgotten myself? I see the office is the same, it'll be easy for me to get acclimated. And thanks again for not getting rid of Ben-Zvi, who over the years I began to think of as a family member, a grandfather or uncle. I remember, you told me you left him here because of his wild theory that the Palestinians were Jews who forgot their identity. Israelites who stayed faithful to this land, even though they were forced to convert to Islam."

"Precisely, and that idea wasn't only his, but Ben-Gurion's as well."

"Ben-Gurion had many fantasies."

"Don't dismiss fantasies that bring hope. I knew nothing about Ben-Zvi when I moved into this office, don't forget I'm almost two generations younger than you, so I thought that before I got rid of the picture, I should find out why a president who died long ago is hanging here, instead of a more recent president or at least a prime minister, and I learned on the internet how close Ben-Zvi was to Ben-Gurion. And I also read about their shared fantasies, or, rather, their wishes. What's bad about that fantasy?"

"Not bad, but absurd. Because they arrived at that idea not based on knowledge or research, but out of desperation, because they realized that they were isolated Zionists, with no actual nation behind them. But even if there is a grain of historical truth to this, who's going to convince the Palestinians to return to their Jewish roots?"

"Really, who?" Maimoni sighs. "When I told Ayala about the second president and his idea, she burst out laughing."

"Hanadi."

"Fine, Hanadi. And maybe so she'll understand this is not a game but a serious notion, I should take this picture and hang it on my father's bedroom wall, next to the picture of me that's hanging there. Maybe this dear innocent president can convince her there is hope. But in fact you're right, it's a lost hope, so let's at least see how we can coax the road, and the tunnel, from the computer."

Maimoni turns on more lights and goes into the new program, which is hard to operate but brings results. The pensioner, alas, cannot keep up with the young man's rapid-fire explanations. Listen, he says, maybe I'm just tired, but there's no way I'll master something so up-to-date, better I should talk and you type. First we have to mark the end of the road the army asked you to plan. And after you mark that point on the screen, if your program really is so smart, maybe it can find nearby a fox that ate a cell phone.

Maimoni is amused. The first page silently slides from the sophisticated printer, with a multicolored map of the crater and the end point of the future road marked in blue.

"And now that the objective is clear," continues Luria, "we need to go backwards, to Route Forty, to the indicated intersection, which may look fine and dandy, but we will devote a full page to its defects, as you remember: a limited field of vision for drivers coming from the north and the south, especially drivers who take the desert as a license to fly; and insufficient warning to drowsy military drivers coming down the army road to Route Forty; and that's not all, the real danger is the cellular dead zone we discovered, because most accidents occur at intersections, and if it's impossible to call for immediate help, the blood of the dead and wounded will haunt the conscience of the planners. By the way, I wonder whether your new program can comprehend a communications blackout."

"It can comprehend whatever you like," Maimoni proudly declares. "But wait," the pensioner gasps, "Asael, what happened to your beard? Where did it go?"

Maimoni relishes the pensioner's alarm. "Finally," he says. "I felt insulted that you didn't notice it was gone. Yes, my dear Luria, what could I do, one day the beard looked so pathetic that even Arafat would have been embarrassed by it, so I decided, the comedy is over, three minutes of shaving every morning is not the end of the world."

But Luria misses the beard. "Too bad," he says, "you told me your wife loved it." "My wife? What makes you say that? I already told you, she tolerated it at best. Still, I'm glad you're mourning its loss, maybe one day I'll grow it back in your honor."

As they carry on, Luria transforms all the shortcomings of the first intersection into advantages of the second, but now a hill towers before him, marked by a small triangle. Luria recommends designating its absolute altitude from sea level, not the relative height as measured from its foot. Maimoni suddenly leaps from his chair at the ringtone of the phone in his pocket and rushes to the corridor for some privacy.

It is not a short call. At the other end is obviously someone in need of advice or consolation. Maimoni keeps his voice down, but Luria can pick up the patient, gentle tone: I understand, every word is important to me, it's okay, nothing to be afraid of. Luria isn't sure he knows enough to interpret the snatches of conversation, but is almost certain that Maimoni is talking to his *shabazit,* the woman with no identity housed in the bedroom of the deceased legal adviser. Vaguely distressed, Luria opens the big double window to see if the night has swept away the sun and sprawled across the world. Maimoni returns, beaming, and seems ready to reveal whom he was talking to, and maybe even what about, when Luria says: "Listen, I think we shouldn't rush the tunnel plan. We have three pages of principles, the basis for our proposal. You should start drafting the road itself, beyond the tunnel. Calculating the cost of materials, positioning small bridges, and although you claim this crater is self-draining, you can't submit a comprehensive plan for a new road without specific drainage solutions. In short, for now you should do the mundane stuff, this isn't your first road or last. As for me, I need one more great idea, for us to convince the army to dig a tunnel. And since you made me a duplicate key, I might come here at night alone, with my laptop, because your computer is too sophisticated for me, and we'll see where inspiration takes me. I had many inspirations in this room that saved the State a lot of money. And you should know I feel deeply sorry for the Palestinians who got into trouble, and also, believe me, for the officer who got them into trouble but didn't shirk his responsibility. Because, Maimoni, I try whenever possible to feel compassion for people, and while the young son has sort of become a Druze, and the sweet daughter, this Hanadi, that even an old man like me could fall in love with, is acting at the Kibbutz Seminar in some Israeli drama or comedy, a lonely widower stays on the hill, fearful of revenge."

Maimoni listens, smiles. "Nice, Luria," he says. "You're starting to talk like the prophets."

AGAIN THE GENETIC THREAD

In the parking lot waits a watchman, demanding to know who he is and what he's doing at night in an empty building. The pensioner introduces himself in the past and present, but the gatekeeper is impressed by neither, and tells him he needs authorization from the director general to enter the building at night. And instead of nodding yes and saying *shalom,* Luria for some reason starts badmouthing the young new director general, who will no doubt also be arrested soon. "From him I need authorization?" he sputters. "He's a director general but he asked *me* to make a speech so he wouldn't have to, so please, a little common courtesy wouldn't hurt." But the night watchman remains unimpressed, holds on to the open car door, and warns him that no pensioner has the right to wander around his former workplace at night without written approval.

Perhaps the flare-up with the watchman addled Luria's mind. On leaving the parking lot he turned south instead of north, and by the time he realized his error and got home, the drowsy woman waiting up for him had fallen asleep. A lifetime of love for the bride of his youth wells up in the engineer as he enters his home. He can't understand why he said to Maimoni, even in jest, that he too could fall in love with a young nomad lost between opposing identities. And so as not to alarm his dozing wife, he kneels beside her, closes his eyes, and presses his forehead to her warm feet, so she will awaken gently, as if her blanket had fallen off.

"*Nu,* you're finally back, so how'd it go?"

"Nothing special."

"You made progress?"

"A little. But Maimoni in any case will have to do most of the work himself."

"And how does it feel to work in your old office?"

"Both natural and strange. But I was happy that Yitzhak Ben-Zvi is still hanging on the wall."

"Why? Because he's still your guru?"

"You have a good one who's better?"

"You don't need a good guru, just a smart one."

Luria carefully lays his head between her thighs, bares her belly, and kisses her navel, and his hands feel their way slowly to her breasts, and his passion is joined by the memory of her first night of illness, when she staggered into the children's room so he could save her from the flood of tea in her bed. Now that you're better and the bug is gone, he tells her, it's time to get back to normal. Only making love can invigorate a long marriage weakened by fatigue and illness. Little by little, let me get a bit stronger, she says, stroking his hair. Don't worry, the time will come, here I am at home, I'm not going anywhere. I know you're at home, but the question is if I'll still remember where this home is. Just now, for example, I took the wrong road, I went south instead of north, and until I realized it, time went by. But at least you got here, she comforts him, from now on use the GPS even if the place is familiar, and turn on the sound, because the human voice is better than lines and arrows on a map. And don't worry about my desire, it's on the way, I feel I'm well, and I told the clinic I'll return to work tomorrow. And you also have a job to do tomorrow. Your genetic thread is finally severed. Your sister called to say that your relative died and the institution asked the two of you to come and decide what to do with what's left of her.

"To decide what?" Luria springs upright. "What's left? We have to take care of the burial?"

"No burial, don't get excited. She died a few days ago, and the executor, apparently a son or grandson, came in from Paris, and to spare himself any trouble had the body cremated, and you only need to decide what to do with a few belongings, because the Parisian decided to leave something for you as distant relatives."

The next morning he picks up his sister Shlomit from her home and says to her, "Who the hell knows what this Parisian expects us to decide, only two or three months ago I was with her and it didn't look like she would leave any possessions after she died except for her weird flute." "No problem," says his sister, "if they asked us to come, we'll come, if only for Mama, who felt responsible for her and felt guilty because of her illness. But you visited her too?" "I told you, the neurologist was looking for a genetic thread for my atrophy, so I went there, but I didn't tell you anything, because there was nothing to tell."

Shlomit looks at her brother, with worry and indecision. She holds the door handle of the red car, but suggests taking her car. "Why?" asks Zvi suspiciously. "I just told you I was there two or three months ago, and I remember the way." "Fine, then you give me directions, but I'll drive." Now suspicion turns into outright anger. "Tell me the truth, did Dina warn you about my driving?" "Not really," says his sister, "she just said that because you don't rely on a GPS, you could easily get lost, and I have no time for that today." "But I don't need the GPS," says Luria, raising his voice, "I told you I know the way, and I'm insulted that you don't trust me, and so, please, if you don't get in the car now, I'll drive there by myself."

She gives in, but turns on the Waze app on her phone and provides road information in a dramatic tone of voice, as well as a running commentary on her brother's driving, which strikes her as faulty and reckless. "Tell me, are you normal?" she explodes. "You just ran a red light." "No," says Luria, coolly dismissing her outburst, "it wasn't red, it was yellow, which I remember from last time, because it's a very long light."

At the old-age home he confidently leads his sister to the third floor to introduce her to the nurse whose white hair enhanced her elegance and beauty. But he needs a moment to find her, because the white hair has turned black. "Why?" asks Luria with the pained intimacy of old acquaintance. "I said to my wife, after I visited here, that a woman confident of her beauty isn't afraid of white hair. So why did you lose your confidence?"

The head nurse appears to be neither embarrassed nor angered by the crude invasiveness of a stranger. Perhaps, from years of experience, she can spot in his agitation the first signs of what in the end will land him in her ward. She blushes slightly and smiles, and calmly says, You'll have to discuss my hair color not with me, Mr. Luria, but with my husband, and she reaches out to shake his sister's hand, and remarks how she resembles their mother, who loyally visited their relative. And Shlomit, shocked by her brother's behavior, shakes the nurse's hand and asks if the death had been an easy one.

"Not as easy or simple as one might think, in light of her age and prolonged dementia."

"Not easy?" mumbles Luria, disappointed.

"Not at all, I'm sorry to say. With people who have suffered from dementia for many years, and it seems that they've given up on the world and the world has forgotten them too, near the end there's clarity and awakening, *davka* with them, as though the deadening of all those years had been some sort of a pose, or a game, or maybe a defense against people and the world, and as death approaches the masks fall away, and sorrow, mental pain, maybe regret, begin to flow from inside. These patients, who for many years seemed alienated or indifferent to those who took care of them, now hang on to them and are needy for a look or a touch."

Luria freezes. The description terrifies him, and he asks if they might visit their relative's room and look at her bed, if they haven't put in a new patient.

"The bed is empty, we waited for you," says the head nurse.

She leads them to the room familiar to Luria, and as they enter, the old woman in the other bed, still alive, sits up as she did last time, and Luria smiles at her kindly in the hope that she will recognize him. There is a sheet on the dead woman's bed, but the pillow and blanket are gone, and two items lie upon it side by side, the long black flute and a small ceramic jug, sealed with red wax.

"I could swear her neighbor recognizes me," says Luria to the nurse, "look how she's smiling at me. If I'd known she was still alive, I'd have brought the Medjool dates she expects from me. Is there a cafeteria here?"

The nurse chuckles. "No, but if I find a date in the kitchen, I'll give it to her in your name."

Luria is curious about the candidate for the available bed. There are many candidates, says the nurse patiently, but not all are suitable. And Luria tries to come up with other questions to prolong his time with the beautiful nurse who darkened her hair, but his sister interjects: Excuse me, but why exactly did you invite us? Not, it turns out, to sign papers or pay an outstanding bill, but only to take the jug and the black flute, maybe one of their grandchildren will want to play it. My grandchildren, laughs Shlomit, won't want to touch that Arab flute, and surely not to play it. A musical instrument that's not electric is not an instrument to them. Maybe Zvi, who wanders in the desert, will find some Bedouin who would love to have it. But what's this jug?

"Her remains, her ashes," the nurse says.

"All the ashes?" Luria picks up the urn, to estimate its weight.

"I still don't understand," says Shlomit, annoyed, "why the executor who decided to cremate the body didn't take her ashes with him to Paris."

"He said that if she had decided to move to Israel, it wasn't fair to take her away, despite the dementia."

"And to cremate her without asking her opinion is fair? Is it even allowed? Is it Jewish?"

"Don't ask me what's allowed and not allowed for Jews," says the nurse evenly. "Recently they started cremating here and not only burying. Of course, it depends who. Somebody once told me it says in the Bible that the bodies of King Saul and his sons were burned, and if so, why not cremate other Jews?"

"Israelites," Luria corrects her.

"Whatever you say."

Luria puts the urn under his arm and hands the flute to his sister. Okay, we'll take care of it, but are you sure we don't need some authorization, so nobody will say we stole a dead woman's ashes? No, no need for any authorization or signature.

In front of her house, before Shlomit parts ways from her

brother, Luria suggests he look after the flute and she take care of the urn. But his sister's answer is firm and clear-cut: "No, my dear, if we had driven in my car, I might have taken the urn, but because the ashes are in your car, you decide whether to keep them or scatter them in a respectful place. And don't you dare throw them in the garbage or some empty lot. Maybe think about the sea, or the desert. Someplace a little symbolic, she deserves it. But discuss it with Dina, she'll steer you right, as always."

THE TUNNEL PLAN

Dina's answer is clear. When she returns from the clinic, disheartened by changes made in her absence, she decides the urn of ashes will stay in the car, to avoid the risk that little Noam, during Luria's afternoon nap, will try to see what's in it. Who's going to clean up the ashes all over the apartment? On the other hand, the flute can go inside, and if no one can get a decent sound out of it, we'll hang it on the roof patio, and the wind from the sea will play a tune in memory of the deceased.

Meanwhile, there is another matter beyond the urn and the flute. Next week, the committee will meet to discuss the plan for the army road, which needs to be completed this week. As Maimoni summarizes on the phone: "Because the State of Israel has never asked me to plan a tunnel, short nor long, this tunnel will be *your* contribution, dear Zvi, to yet another human predicament arising from two nations living in the same homeland. It's fine with me if you prefer to run the program on your laptop, because friendly computers converse more candidly than people do, so while you're working on the tunnel—depth, length, and height, itemized cost breakdown for materials and equipment—my computer will put it into the overall plan for the road. Therefore, we meet again tomorrow night in our office, and you'll see that in your honor I replaced the cracked glass on the picture of our beloved Ben-Zvi. And one more little thing: please don't argue anymore with the night watchman. He's a former official who was fired for embezzlement, a bitter person, and last night he wrote down your license plate number, and today he filed a complaint with the director general, who learned your identity from the police. When I was asked if I knew anything about your visits to the office at night, I didn't want to say you were involved with planning the secret army road, but I admitted that you came to the office, where we reminisced about my father, your former legal adviser. And because the director general was impressed by a speech you delivered, he said: 'If it's that pensioner wandering here at night, don't bother him, he's not a man who breaks the rules.'"

The next day at dusk, Luria drives to the offices of Israel Roads, and though he's made this drive thousands of times, he keeps his promise to his wife and turns on the GPS, to follow the fluent instructions of a female voice. The office is open and lit, and Maimoni has brought in an extra desk for his unpaid assistant, and he connects his desktop to Luria's laptop, so the two computers can have an intelligent dialogue.

Luria, after carefully studying both the photograph and the diagram image of the hill, draws the opening of its future tunnel, outlining its height and width, then slowly digs it out with the cursor in bright purple, joining it to the army road that appears in minute detail on Maimoni's screen. The pensioner praises the road. Very nice, Asael, exemplary professional work. But the time has come for the previous generation to prove itself, first by planning the supports and anchor bolts, then the interior width and coating of the walls, and the angles of vaults and arches that will prevent internal collapse. And, of course, several mandatory air vents, and the source of light in the tunnel, to be provided not by the Israel Electric Corporation but from solar collectors of the desert sun, which according to Hanadi's camera has a twin in the Ramon Crater.

Maimoni rises from his chair, stands behind Luria, looks with interest at his work, then glances at his watch and says: "I hope, Zvi, that you won't be angry if I leave you now, because the twins are getting back from a school trip to Jerusalem and my wife is abroad, so I have to pick them up."

"How old are your twins? They must be older than the pictures you have here."

"For sure, the world doesn't stop, they're ten now. I really should bring a more recent picture."

"How is it that already at age ten they schlep them to Jerusalem? It's not dangerous there?"

"They don't take them to the Temple Mount, only Mount Herzl and Yad Vashem, and for dessert, the Biblical Zoo. That's the itinerary. God knows who in the Education Ministry plans such trips, but there it is. So I hope you won't mind working here alone, and when you're done, turn off the lights and lock the door. Tomorrow I'll submit the plan to the committee we'll be facing next week."

"*We'll* be facing? You want to drag me there too?"

"Why not? Even if you don't say a word, your presence, as a former division chief, is a strong endorsement of the tunnel."

"Okay, then," says Luria with a smile of satisfaction. "Drive carefully."

Here he is again, working in his office at night, the indispensable pensioner. After he estimates the time needed to dig the tunnel, and decides that the excavator with the rotating cutting head is perfect for this terrain, he goes to the internet to learn more about the Nabateans, the better to protect their heritage. Clearly they offer proof that in antiquity the Negev was not an accursed wilderness. As he jots down a few ideas on Maimoni's notepaper, his old office phone sounds a forgotten ring.

Luria hesitates. Both Dina and Maimoni have the numbers of his two mobiles, so it makes no sense they would call an ancient office phone. It must be the night watchman, who has recognized his car in the parking lot. But the ring is persistent, even desperate, and when he picks up the receiver a soft voice whimpers: "Asael? Are you there?"

"Hanadi?" Luria quickly fixes on the young resident-without-identity. "Hanadi?" he persists, eager to breach the sudden silence on the line. "Is that you? Is it? Maimoni's not here, I'm alone, you remember me? I'm the other engineer, the older one. I'm here alone, Maimoni's gone, you can try his cell, you have that number? Can you hear me? Hanadi? You remember me, Hanadi?"

More silence. But from years of experience with this phone, Luria can tell that the line isn't dead. If he were younger, he could even hear the sounds of her silence. But his compassion for the flustered young woman won't let him hang up, and again he says, "I'm here, I hear you, but if it's urgent, Hanadi, why not catch him on his cell?"

His insistence on calling her, over and over, by the Palestinian name she divulged in a moment of weakness might be what persuades her to break her silence, and reply in a soft, delicate voice: "Yes, Mr. Luria, of course I remember you, and I'm sorry I called the office, Maimoni doesn't like it if I call his cell when he's with the kids, but never mind, it's not urgent, I'll find him. Meanwhile, if I may, Mr. Luria, I would like to ask, how is your wife? Maimoni told me she was very, very ill, and I worried about her, though I had no chance of meeting her."

Now Luria understands how deep the bond has become between the Palestinian woman and the engineer who took her under his wing. He is upset, but responds warmly. "Thank you, Hanadi, thank you for caring, my wife is at home now and went back yesterday to her clinic, because she's a doctor, I suppose Maimoni told you that too, she's a pediatrician, which is how she caught some sort of virulent bacteria from a boy who happened to come from you—I mean the Palestinian Authority."

"Of course, of course," says Hanadi excitedly, "I know she's a doctor, and in my family, we spent so much time with doctors when my mother was ill, we never thought that doctors could be patients, but now I think that if I were a doctor and also a patient, I would be able to understand my illness better and explain this illness better to sick people and other doctors—"

"But how are you, Hanadi?" he interrupts the girl whose beauty he remembers well. "Would you believe I just finished the plans for the tunnel in your hill so your father can keep hiding there."

"It's not a waste of your time, Mr. Luria?" she says with a little laugh, an Arab lilt in her gentle voice. "Abba will finally give himself up, and us too. Hiding on the hill can't be a permanent arrangement."

Luria does not want to hear that his work will go down the drain, so he asks again: "Meanwhile, Hanadi, what's happening with you? Maimoni says you're studying theater at the Kibbutz Seminar, you're doing some actual acting?"

"I'm acting a little all the time," she laughs, "but you, Mr. Luria, insist on calling me Hanadi, and that's a name from the past, which I never should have told you, because now I am always Ayala."

"In any case, what is Hanadi? What does it mean? You told me a purple flower, but Maimoni told me there's another meaning."

"I didn't want to scare you. The meaning is a sword, not a purple flower."

THE POLICEWOMAN

The night watchman waits in the parking lot, not to reprimand Luria but to apologize for not recognizing him and for giving his license number to the police. "Don't apologize," says Luria, "I don't understand my outbursts either. I was a senior employee here for many years, but there's no reason you should recognize me in the dark. I myself, even in daytime, have a hard time recognizing people. You, for example, who are you?" "I am Haimon, Yosef Haimon from the finance department, and I knew your secretary, who brought me your expense accounts for approval." "Haimon?" says Luria. "I don't have the slightest memory of your name, but don't be offended, you are not alone. More important people than you have been forgotten. How did you go from finance department official to night watchman? "They found financial irregularities, but couldn't tell if it was really embezzlement, so they decided not to go to the police but just send me to the parking lot."

A few raindrops end the conversation. Luria knows that after the tunnel plans are done, he'll have no need to come back at night, yet he gives the watchman a hearty handshake. And however ridiculous and humiliating it may be to use the GPS to go home by a route he has taken thousands of times, he is faithful to the promise he gave his wife, and softly, slightly embarrassed, he gives the glowing screen his home address. After a sharp chirp confirming the request, the navigation system suggests a different way home, long and complicated.

Did something go wrong with the satellite hovering in the sky? Or did it discover something new? He finds the original route, and on the lighted map not one but two icons indicate an accident, surrounded by policemen's caps. Clearly a serious accident, with many vehicles crowded on the two-lane road and nowhere to reverse direction.

But even a smart satellite, directing traffic with great finesse, doesn't know what Luria knows from years of experience: that it's possible to bypass the accident site on a half-decent dirt road that crosses an old orchard. Even the dementia, if it tries hard, can remember the scent of the flowering citrus. And the springtime that fills the empty spaces of his mind overrides the GPS and lures Luria to the original route, to the epicenter of the accident, certain that he can evade it via the orchard. Ambulance and police sirens echo up ahead, and flashing reds blend with blues and yellows, and because the column of cars crawls slower and slower, Luria edges to the right, ready to cross the yellow line of the shoulder, on the assumption that the orchard will soon appear.

But some of the drivers crawling bumper-to-bumper are irked by an elderly white-haired driver, in a red car yet, who tries to break the rules from the right. Since they have no way of knowing that this is a veteran road engineer, who doesn't want to cut ahead but merely to escape to a road they don't know exists, they protest with angry honking, and some also get onto the shoulder to follow him or else to block his path. Either way, progress is sluggish, and finally the row of cars grinds to a halt, and from a distance it's clear that a bad accident has indeed occurred. A bulldozer fell off a huge truck and crushed two private cars, and now in the moonlight it waves its toothy shovel at the sky, like the trunk of a yellow elephant turned on its back.

Ambulances and police cars are still screaming as the cranes of two emergency tow trucks feel their way to the depths of the disaster, to the crushed people, wounded or dead. And policemen and policewomen try to impose order on the chaos and find a way to detour the traffic, and a policewoman is dispatched across the yellow line to intercept anyone who at such a terrible moment tries to circumvent the law. And in the spotlights circling the policewoman, who wears neither cap nor helmet, are shadows of the orchard Luria is determined to reach. Is the young woman, waving a big flashlight, hair cascading to her shoulders, a real policewoman with a gun and handcuffs in her belt, or is this just a young cadet, or an actress? As his brain burns with desire for the flowering citrus, Luria pictures her as none other than Hanadi, playing the part of a Hebrew policewoman for a class at the Kibbutz Seminar, and the young Palestinian waves him to hurry to her, to escape and go quickly to his waiting wife, and he eagerly agrees and steps on the gas and can't stop before the car knocks Hanadi down.

Angry cops rush to assist their comrade. They get her back on her feet and order Luria to go to the edge of the ditch bordering the road. And even as he realizes how close he now is to the dirt road that crosses the orchard, they ask that he turn off the engine and remove the ignition key and produce his documents. One of the cops closely examines his identity card, driver's license, auto registration, and insurance, and another officer peppers him with questions. What kind of driving is this? One accident isn't enough for you? Why are you driving like a madman and on the shoulder, and running over a policewoman on duty?

And the policewoman, her shirt torn and bare arm freshly scratched, accepts a water bottle from a police sergeant, and when she is done drinking she scolds the driver who injured her, in a low voice, not angry. "That's how you drive, sir? I motion for you to stop and go back to your lane, and you speed up and try to run me over?" He is shocked by the blame he had not imagined possible. "Why would I run you over? The opposite, I thought you were telling me to hurry to you." "To me? Hurry to me for what?" For what? He is surprised by the question which has such an obvious answer: to get to the orchard that will take him out of the traffic jam. "Let's say that's what happened," she answers patiently, "then why did you accelerate toward me?" "I didn't think you were a policewoman, in the dark you didn't look like a policewoman, you don't have a hat or a helmet, and your hair is down to your shoulders, I thought you were a different woman calling out to me." "A different woman?" "Exactly, a different woman." "What woman would do that in the middle of a terrible accident, and why? What woman were you thinking about?"

What woman was I thinking about? He mumbles, not wishing to hand over Hanadi to the police. Yes, who could it be? Luria puts the question to himself, then starts to explain that it's only the illusion of a woman. And please understand, he says, now trying to wriggle out with a friendly confession, this is the problem, I've been experiencing a dementia of sorts for a while, not serious, but a bit real.

FRONTIER JUSTICE

Upon hearing the word "dementia" from the lips of the offender, a wise police lieutenant takes a moment, amid the maelstrom of a terrible accident, to think about the future, the uphill battle against carnage on the roads, despite the fact that only a shirt was torn, and the scratches on the policewoman's arm will soon heal, and she bears no grudge against the man who knocked her over. Now, while other police officers are working to clear a path for hundreds of cars in the traffic jam, the lieutenant has a chance to turn his vehicle into a makeshift courtroom and revoke the license of the driver who confessed to dementia.

He leads Luria to the police car and offers him water from the same bottle the policewoman drank from. But Luria, irate and bitter, doesn't want water, he only wants to tell his wife not to worry. Hands trembling, he takes the two cell phones from his pockets and speed-dials his home from one of them, but because in his absence Dina has been talking endlessly with her sister, he doesn't wait for the landline to clear, but uses his second phone to dial her mobile and leave a voice message: I had a tiny accident, Dina, I'm fine and the car is fine, but a policewoman was hurt accidentally, no big deal, just a little scratch, she's here with me smiling, she has already forgotten the scratch. But the main thing, which had nothing to do with me, there was a terrible accident on Highway 461, west of the Savion junction, you'll see it on TV, police all around, and emergency teams and ambulances for the wounded, not just wounded but dead, so because of all this tumult, but not in any way connected, they decided to detain me for a little investigation, maybe because this is a real policewoman, not just a civilian or imposter, but the police are nice, and I'm in good hands, so not to worry if I'm late, I'll get there eventually.

His hands are still shaking as he replaces the two phones in his pockets. He watches with mounting anxiety as the officer taps on a computer that produces a page listing all his traffic violations for the past twenty years. To the officer's surprise and delight, the violations are minor and few, and the latest, an involuntary violation, will not entail a fine, or a court hearing, or points against him. The friendly officer returns his ID card, car registration, and insurance certificate, but tucks the driver's license in his pocket and in exchange gives Luria a piece of paper indicating that the license has been confiscated by the police. "I'm sorry, Mr. Zvi Luria," he says, "you're not allowed to drive until our neurologist evaluates your condition, because your dementia, which you candidly reported, might kill not only you but others too. Look, who knows what happened in the brain of the driver when the bulldozer fell from his truck and crushed to death four passengers in two cars."

"Four?"

"So far."

"But maybe the disaster wasn't his fault," says Luria, trying for some reason to defend the driver. "How about the person who loaded the bulldozer and tied it down? Do you need to examine his head too?"

"Need to? Yes, of course," says the officer without hesitation, "we need to examine everybody's head, including the prime minister's, but for now we'll settle for those who freely admit to their dementia."

The officer gets up to indicate to Luria that the court has concluded its job, and Luria bites his lip helplessly: Damn, what did I do to myself, I have to take back what I said, tell them about the one I actually imagined, but how could I tell them about a Palestinian woman who impersonated a traffic cop? "Look, sir," he pleads, voice quivering, "my wife is a senior physician, director of a hospital clinic, you think she'd let me drive if she wasn't sure my head is clear?"

"Your wife is what kind of doctor?"

"A pediatrician."

"But you're not a child anymore."

"True," admits the pensioner.

"But don't be upset, you didn't get a ticket or points, even though you injured a policewoman. The police neurologist will examine you and maybe return your license, and meanwhile the officer you injured—"

"Only scratched."

"Yes, only scratched, she'll be the one taking you safely home in your car."

The area now looks like the set of an opera or action movie. Rescue crews, paramedics, and police are caught in the spotlight beams tracking a smashed car that dangles in the air en route to a waiting flatbed truck.

The red car is where he left it, heading toward the ditch. The policewoman asks him for the keys, and he hands them over sourly. When they're both seated inside, and she requests the ignition code, he holds out his arm so she can read the tattoo in the darkness. Now she fathoms the mental decline of the driver who hit her. She asks about his line of work, and if he has children and grandchildren, and he suggests, as a veteran highway engineer, that she take the dirt road through the old orchard instead of trying to pass the crawling cars. Amazingly, she believes that professional experience trumps dementia, and turns in the darkness onto the dirt road, where they are enveloped in flowering citrus and chirping irrigation, till they zip to civilization across the fields of Kfar Azar.

So committed is she to the suspension of his license that she maneuvers the car herself into his private parking spot. But as she hands him back his keys so he can lock the car, he is still bothered by the question of why she wasn't wearing a helmet or a cap when she motioned him to stop.

"You needed a cap to know who I was?"

"Yes, because the hair down to your shoulders misled me, made me think you were a different woman altogether."

She smiles, but doesn't feel she needs to respond, and goes off without a word toward a Magen David Adom clinic located among the rabbis of the Basel neighborhood.

Dina drinks tea in the kitchen and offers words of consolation, but her husband brushes them off. "This is it," he says hopelessly, "the beginning of the end."

"No." His wife insists on battling his despondency. "This might be the end of driving, but not of the bright road ahead."

A DRIVER'S LICENSE

Anger and humiliation strengthen his conviction that the driver's license seized in a makeshift traffic court will not be returned. And on that bright road his wife promised as consolation, he will not be the driver. If he tries to go to bed now, the darkness will unnerve him, not help him fall asleep. Better to spread out pillows and blankets on the roof patio, where the winds and sky might possibly explain why he blurted out the dementia to justify a momentary delusion that converted a traffic police officer into a lost, delicate young woman controlled more and more by Maimoni.

"If you know you're going to have a bad night, don't sleep on the terrace, double your sleeping pill. Why torture yourself over a driver's license that you'll have to give up sooner or later?"

"I don't know about that," he mutters, "and you, Dina, are an expert in children's diseases, not driver's licenses. So I'm asking you, as a doctor, how can you double my sleeping pill after you had warned me that it could make me more stupid?"

"Stupid?" She's shocked. "I never said that word, and I'll never even think it. You're being cruel. I simply said, as the neurologist also explained, that in your condition, boundaries can be a bit unclear, also blurring of day and night, so it's not good to plunge into deep sleep that lasts till noon, but if tonight you plan to torment yourself, then as the person who is closest to you in the world and also a doctor, I advise you to take two pills and sleep a few good hours, to ease your needless pain."

"Needless?"

"Of course. Because soon enough, all of us, those who love you and truly care about you, would insist that you give up driving."

"Just a minute, who are the ones 'who love you and truly care about you' apart from you and Yoav and maybe Avigail? Now I get it, Shlomit told on me."

"Told on you? Zvi, what's happening to you? She's your only sister, and she has the right to worry about you after you scared her with totally reckless driving on the way to the nursing home."

He glumly turns out the patio light and looks to the sky to see if it might rain on him tonight. Many stars are visible, so he decides to sleep under their protection. His sadness touches his wife, and she hugs and kisses him, and he is dead silent, head and arms hanging, an old, sad dog. Why, dammit, did the dementia slip from his lips? The policeman's quick reaction turned the dementia into a scapegoat for the wrecked bulldozer. Since there was a shortage of people to blame, because most of them were dead or injured, all that was left was to revoke the license of an innocent old man who drove onto the shoulder to save himself on a dirt road.

And yet he, on his own initiative, facing no interrogation or threats, was quick to offer dementia as the reason he suddenly sped toward the policewoman. Did he want to reveal it to the authorities so from now on they would be partners in whatever damage it might do? He can still see the panic that gripped his sister during the wild ride to the institution. His wife is right. With level-headed love she diagnoses his failures much better than he can. He must therefore not only love her but admire her. He should have given up driving on his own, not waited for the wisdom of a police officer. Even if it hurts to leave the driver's seat, admitting the truth can sometimes ease the pain. Again he looks at the sky. Clouds slowly sail from the sea to the State of Israel, but they cannot produce rain, only deepen the darkness, so there's no need for an extra pill to sharpen the borders of the night. The entire universe will comfort him for the loss of his driving. Amid the dull rumble of traffic in the restless city his eyes fall shut and his mind is cut off from its guilt.

The tapping of raindrops, which could be temporary or the start of something big, spurs Dina to the patio to rouse the mind that found serenity, and she strips her husband's blankets and pillows to return him to the bedroom where he can slumber by her side.

It is midnight, and Luria marvels at sleep attained without special effort, merely from spiritual enlightenment, and after he puts on pajamas he makes herbal tea for himself and his wife, as Dina reports on the events of the past few hours. Yoav phoned and reacted to the lost license with pain and empathy, but with approval. This way, he said, I'll be calmer, because I'll know Abba isn't driving.

"Calmer? That's all he expects of me, to make him calm?"

"Yes, because he loves you, and it's natural for him to worry. But he also said something playful about the ignition code you rushed to tattoo."

"What is so playful about that?"

"I will tell you on condition that you not take it as an insult. He said now that you don't need your tattoo for driving, you can add a few digits and have the number of a grandchild's cell phone."

"This dumb joke you see as playful?"

"A little, but don't be offended."

"In any case, this playfulness didn't help you fall asleep."

"I had to make sure the heavens didn't soak you. Then I realized that in your sorrow you forgot your laptop in the car, so I went and got it."

"I forgot the laptop in the car?"

"Apparently you were excited by the policewoman who brought you home. So here it is, alive and well."

"Thank you."

"Just know that from now on, since I am retiring too, I'll be your driver, day and night."

"That's what I imagined, and it only depresses me more. Because ever since you first got your license, you've never corrected errors in your driving. You still don't know what it means to stay in your lane, you forget to put on the turn signal or switch it off, and you're so afraid of passing other cars that you make the drivers behind you crazy. The fact that from now on you will control the wheel just adds to my depression."

"At least I drive carefully."

"Not carefully, slowly. They're not the same thing. I'd rather get a Filipino caregiver to drive me."

"Whatever you want, just don't be so sad."

"Wait a minute. And Maimoni? How could he not call?"

"He called, but I didn't want to wake you up, you were sleeping so soundly. I told him, of course, about your license, and he felt your pain, and also praised the policeman's action. Thanks to him, he said, we can protect our Luria better for the future."

"What future?" Luria growls. "He expects me to work for him for nothing forever?"

"Those were his words, ask him yourself what he meant. In any case, he looked at the tunnel plan you left in the office and says it's excellent. But the Society for the Protection of Nature heard about the army road and they are raising hell. He'll tell you everything tomorrow. The main thing is, the approvals committee meeting was moved forward, to three days from now, and you have to be there, they're expecting you."

"Three days? So soon?"

"That's what they decided."

"And he didn't mention anything else? Like that Hanadi?"

"Hanadi?"

"I already told you, and you saw her, the young woman feeding Maimoni's twins when we visited during the shiva. Bright-eyed girl, Palestinian, cute, didn't I tell you her story?"

"Maybe, but tell me again."

"She's the daughter of a teacher from a village near Jenin, and the Civil Administration and the security forces, who know everything there is to know about the Palestinians in the West Bank, learned that the wife of this schoolteacher was very sick, heart disease, and only the transplant of a new heart might save her. So Shibbolet, you've heard about him, suggested to the schoolteacher to sell Israeli settlers a parcel of Palestinian land, to finance his wife's treatments and transplant. But the woman, who waited in the hospital for a suitable heart, died before one could be found, and then it turned out that the land sale was a fraud, based on forged documents, and the tormented widower decided to stay on with his family in Israel, fearing what the Palestinians would do to him for tricking them out of land to give the Jews. And because he decided not to return the money he got from the settlers, he has to hide from the Jews too, and Shibbolet, who feels responsible for the whole mess, and keeps an apartment in Mitzpe Ramon because his wife has asthma, offered the Palestinian a hiding place in an ancient ruin on a hill in the crater, which is the hill we won't bulldoze but instead build a tunnel."

"And this is because of a Palestinian who got into trouble?"

"Also because of the daughter."

"Why the daughter?"

"I think that Shibbolet, and now also Maimoni, have fantasies."

"Fantasies about what?"

"All these intense efforts for the father might have a hidden agenda—to control the daughter, separately, or maybe together."

"What do you mean by control?"

"To make her into another wife, a second wife."

"A second wife? What are you talking about? Now you're inventing craziness for other people. Enough, Zvi, don't forget you were very agitated this evening, so listen to me, let's stop here, it's late, we're both tired. It won't hurt you to take another pill and lie down like a normal person beside me in bed, because you, in any event, will always have only one wife."

THE CENTRAL BUS STATION

The doctor no longer waits for Luria to drive her to work. The ignition code is engraved in her memory, and she takes the red car and drives to her pediatric clinic. Officially she is still the director, but has wisely begun to transfer authority to the doctor who will succeed her. She has been invited to a meeting to discuss the rights and responsibilities of her upcoming retirement, while Luria, armed with two phones, goes to the supermarket with not only a shopping list, but a black marker to cross off what has landed in his cart, to avoid duplication. This time flowers are not obligatory but optional, affording him the right to pick the kind and color he likes, but because flowers cannot console him for the lost license, he passes them by, and while the grocery delivery wends its way to the correct home address, Luria wanders the streets to choose the tallest and finest bus, and without knowing where the buses come from or where they're going, he gets on one of them and sits in the rear, where the seats are slightly elevated, and during the pleasant ride he sees familiar streets from a new angle, the shop windows and varieties of people which up till now, as a conscientious driver alert to traffic lights and pedestrians, he could not properly appreciate.

At the huge central bus station of Tel Aviv, which was built thirty years ago but he has never been to before, his bus has reached its last stop, and he must disembark. If he can find the right platform, he can get back on and enjoy the ride home, but the bustle of the station tempts him to diversify his route and experience the world comfortably from a new elevated angle. But where should he head? North or south? East or west? It's not just a matter of distance, which must not be too great, but also the quality of the bus he rides in. But as he wanders through the unimaginably confusing and gloomy central station, the two cell phones loudly ring, one after the other.

His wife in his right hand and Maimoni in his left. As an assistant, albeit unpaid, he prefers to speak with the one he works for, and not his wife, though they've been together forty-eight years. He has a bone to pick with her today, for so quickly confiscating the car, as if he had lost not only the license to drive it, but ownership too. Not now, Dina, he says, I've got Maimoni on the other phone, I'm walking around in the central bus station in south Tel Aviv, a totally surreal place, but don't worry, I bought what you wanted, but not flowers, and hangs up.

You're at the bus station? Maimoni is shocked. Why? We have to meet. I heard you got your license revoked, and I can feel your pain and humiliation, but try to get over it, it's more important that you not endanger yourself and especially others. In the meantime, listen, the Greens came back to life and are opposing the project. But this is not for the phone, only face-to-face. If you tell me exactly where you are now, and promise not to move, I'll be there right away.

His wife calls again, and in a tense and angry tone she wonders what he is doing in the central bus station. Nothing, an innocent visit, when he left the supermarket a beautiful bus came by and took him to a crazy place he had never been, though it's only an hour's walk from home. Dinaleh, this is a place to visit at least once in a lifetime, a dark, alien labyrinth, useless but colorful spaces, filled with quiet Africans and their sweet chocolate children. And don't start worrying that I've gone missing, Maimoni is on his way over to rescue me. By the way, I never imagined that new buses could be such a pleasure. Maybe it's worth it after all to give up driving.

But his wife won't let it go. "I understand," she says bitterly, "your license was revoked and you decided to worry me on purpose, but before you make it worse, tell me, please, what am I guilty of?" "You can't be guilty, my darling," declares Luria, "because you don't have the authority to revoke driver's licenses, but on the other hand, you are guilty, because you wanted them to revoke it." "You also wanted it," counters his wife, "which is why you handed the police your dementia without them asking, and soon you'll turn the dementia into your identity card."

"Maybe."

"But why?"

"To protect myself and you."

It takes a long while for Maimoni to arrive, and in the meantime Luria sits calmly in a small cafeteria. Losing the license has freed him from parking worries, also from finding his way back. Thrilled by the many buses that climb to the sixth floor and glide back to the street, he eats a sandwich, the bread is rather dry, the sliced cheese inside flecked with the fragrance of greenish mold.

"Thanks for staying put," says breathless Maimoni, "or I never would have found you. But before I drive you to the office to fix something in your plan, listen to what happened. Would you believe that the Defense Ministry, and they've been fiddling with this crater road for over a year, never thought of informing the nature protection people, who believe the Ramon Crater is the Holy Basinof Jerusalem. And when they finally showed the nature people the route, they were incensed, and ready to sue the army in the Supreme Court. It turns out my suspicion was right all along, this is a project for a friendly foreign country that wants to install listening devices in the exact place you fed the fox. But miraculously enough," Maimoni enthuses, "and it seems Shibbolet is involved, the Society for the Protection of Nature likes our tunnel. Because they sanctify every hill and ruin, the idea of leaving everything in place makes them happy. Even more amazing, the army doesn't rule out the tunnel, which could allow them, if need be, to block the road or make it disappear. The staunch opponent of the tunnel is Israel Roads, our own department, which casually leveled entire hills in Bab el-Wad. They argue that a tunnel would raise the cost significantly and require constant maintenance. This will be the main subject of tomorrow's battle, which will be waged mainly against our department. If you've already paid the bill, let's move on."

But Luria is planted in place.

"Tomorrow? Not the day after?"

"Correct, the day after, so they don't chop down Shibbolet's hill, and Yasour turns himself in, and drags the son and daughter—"

"Wait, the money from the imaginary sale is still with Shibbolet, no?"

"Yes, and believe me, I trust him to guard every shekel faithfully. He can be cruel and lustful, but he's not corrupt."

"Hanadi was looking for you yesterday," Luria recalls, his head starting to swim.

"Yes," Maimoni says darkly, "and found me in the end, but please, Zvi Luria, stop insisting on the name Hanadi, she too was surprised that you cling to her old name and want to know what it means. What's in his head, this friend of yours, she asked me, and I explained that you mean no harm, but you are no longer young, and you sometimes have trouble with first names."

"Ayala . . . Ayala . . ." mumbles Luria, and feels that the crowded central station, with all its twists and turns, is sliding deep into the hollows of his brain. But Maimoni wants to know if Ayala identified herself on the phone, or if Luria decided on his own that it was she.

"On my own, because there's a special music to her speech. She was afraid to say who she was, until I told her I knew who she was and who I was."

"What did you talk about?" demands Maimoni. "She told me you tried to interrogate her."

"Interrogate her? Ha, ha, that's a good one. I could tell she was lonely so I tried to be nice and take an interest. I asked, for example, if she already had a part in a real play at the Kibbutz Seminar, or was she just acting in class."

"For now she's only getting parts playing Arabs," Maimoni says glumly, "because at the Seminar they caught on to her accent. That's why I'm troubled by your fixation on the former name. What do you really want from her? Explain to me why you are drawn to her."

"Why am I drawn?" snarls the pensioner. "Just to give her, this lost girl, a bit of attention, a bit of empathy, a bit of compassion, because I for one, in any event, have only one wife, who from now on will also be my driver."

THE RESEARCH FUND

The one wife returned from her children's clinic troubled by what she was told in the business office at the hospital. A tidy sum had piled up in her research stipend that could be used only prior to her retirement. Had the doctor taken a greater interest in her financial privileges, she would have known all along that at a public hospital, only active doctors are entitled to receive funding to attend medical conferences. Pensioners may go to scientific conferences, but with no help from the State. And therefore, out of appreciation for the senior physician who overlooked her benefits, and might lose her entire fund, the person allocating the money advised her to come up with a little research project and find a conference somewhere in the world willing to include it in one of their sessions. In any case, the moneyman went on with a clownish smile, eighty percent of the research we fund, so they say, is either wrong or superfluous, or a rehash. Is there, Dr. Luria, anyone who can control the tsunami of the scientific world? So why not take your unused vacation days to make up some innocuous research, and treat yourself and your husband to a nice preretirement trip?

"But can I really come up with a research project, or even an idea, within a couple of months," the doctor complains to her husband, "at a time when I'm handing over the directorship, and also need to keep a close eye on you, so you won't get on some random bus and go missing? By nature I'm a clinician and not a researcher. What always interested me was each individual sick child, how to make him or her well, not to sift through data to fit some preconceived theory. I'm sorry, that's not me."

"How much money is left in your fund?"

"Eight thousand dollars."

"Dinaleh, that's a lot! Imagine a conference in a country we've never been to, like Japan, what a wonderful trip we could have for the price of a twenty-minute lecture nobody will listen to anyway."

"A lecture about what?"

"You can't make something up?"

"I don't make things up. I already told you, I treat real children."

"But who will care in Japan if you invent some theory?"

"I won't make a fool of myself."

"So maybe write a lecture about yourself, about your illness, about the bacteria that attacked you, what did they call it?"

"Meningococcus."

"Say it again?"

"Meningococcus."

"That predator."

"Not a predator, merely virulent."

"So why not write something personal about this 'merely virulent' bacteria. What were the early symptoms, how you got dazed and confused, why I had to rush you to the hospital, why they first gave you the wrong antibiotic and which was the right one, and why they insisted on isolating you for a longer period of time than they first thought. And you could also look at the test results in your file and analyze them from the point of view of a doctor who treats her own illness and understands it from within, a doctor who can not only explain the diagnostic errors of other doctors, but her own as well. This could be interesting, or at least not boring. You said this was a common and famous bacteria, so why shouldn't other doctors get to know it from within? And you also have left-over vacation days, which if you don't use, the State will happily reclaim, so sit down and write. And even if what comes out is not the most scientific, at least we can salvage part of the fund to eat and sleep in good hotels and visit major museums."

The doctor regards her husband with wonder, as if discovering something in him that was never there before. But he's not finished, he's just warming up: "I'm not so naïve as to think you can turn personal illness into scientific truth at a conference, but something new is always of interest. Our tunnel is also personal and not public, and we'll get it approved by the committee nevertheless."

Dina takes him by the shoulders. "This idea, Zvi, did you just now make this up, or did you hear it from someone at the clinic?"

"Neither. The idea, you'll be amazed, came from far away, from her of all people . . . from that Hanadi . . ."

"I don't understand." She flushes, bursts out laughing. "You're chatting every day now with this Palestinian girl? This is a dramatic development in the dementia."

"Not every day, only the one time, at the office at night, before the accident. She was looking for Maimoni, who wasn't there, and then she talked with me for a few minutes, and also asked how you were, because Maimoni told her you were hospitalized."

"Hospitalized? Why is Maimoni talking to her about me?"

"I've been trying to tell you, but you don't listen. This man Maimoni is not so simple or innocent. He constantly tightens his grip on her. Instead of finding her a room in the dormitory, he moved her to live alone in his dead father's house, so he could control her more, and he comes to visit, and who knows what else they do, but even if they're just talking, they would naturally talk about the tunnel and mention me, and then talk about you too. A doctor who got sick and was hospitalized is of interest to her because of her mother's heart disease. Even before the crazy deal with Shibbolet, they would go from doctor to doctor, and she realized that neither the Palestinian nor Israeli doctors really understood what was wrong with her beloved mother's heart. It's a shame, she said to me, as a joke or else in despair, that the doctors who confused them didn't get sick themselves, because maybe only through personal illness could they explain illness to others. There, that's the whole story. No mystery. What now? What's your decision, so that we don't just throw away your stipend?"

"I've decided to think."

THE COMMITTEE MEETING

Half a year has gone by since Luria escaped from a grand retirement party and spotted a strip of light licking the doorstep of his old office on the dark seventh floor of Israel Roads. And that's how he met the son of a dying legal adviser, the young engineer Maimoni, to whom Dina ingeniously appended her husband as an unpaid assistant, so that he could, on the advice of the neurologist, fight better, with the help of roads, interchanges, and tunnels, against the atrophy gnawing away at his brain.

Since then, it is true, Luria has visited his former office twice more, only in the evening, when the building was empty, because Maimoni was unwilling to reveal that an obsolete pensioner was his consultant in a supposedly covert army project. But this morning, when the building teems with employees and a committee meets to approve the plans, the time has come to expose the hidden assistant, not as a voting member of the staff but merely a consultant, in case of controversy or confusion, who sits not at the big table but in the corner, against the wall.

Luria is excited by the morning activity on the floor of offices where he worked for many years. True, not all the employees recognize him, but those who remember him—engineers, secretaries, cleaning workers—greet him with affection, not just a handshake but a pat on the back, to confirm that the rumor of his dementia is highly exaggerated.

Participants in the meeting gradually assemble in the conference room. The guest of honor, Maimoni, in a new tie and jacket, boots up his computer. Early arrivals include a civilian representative of the Defense Ministry and an army officer in uniform, and the two introduce themselves by first name only, and quickly spread out maps and documents, ready to deliver precise observations. Then the door is flung wide open and Yoel Drucker, chief accountant of the department, sails into the room in his wheelchair. An engineer by training, wounded in war, he worked for a while under Luria's baton, until his physical torments forced him to give up fieldwork and move to the budget department, where he swiftly converted his engineering know-how into financial acumen capable of exposing flaws and errors in any calculation or balance sheet. When he sees Luria in the corner, he quickly rolls toward him. He got the news only yesterday that Maimoni had recruited the senior pensioner as an adviser and partner, and Drucker announced right away that if Zvi Luria is signing his name on a plan, it can be approved with eyes closed. Hearing such praise from this precious man, a disabled war veteran, Luria cannot resist the urge to stand up and hug the head of his former employee, who never asked for special treatment when he was sent to the hills on surveying trips. My dear friend, says the pensioner, choking up, it's true I never inquired about your war injury, because I could feel that you weren't asking me for pity, and now I don't ask you to pity me, but if you knew that they took away my driver's license, you'd see how far I've declined.

A secretary wheels in a little cart with a coffee pot and cups, bottles of mineral water, and salted pretzels. It's a revolution, Drucker whispers to Luria, no more bourekas or cookies or mini-quiches that dull the mind and attract hungry people to meetings they have no reason to attend. It was decided to offer only modest refreshments, so modest that I recognize a few pretzels that have been to three meetings and no one went near them. And you will soon see that spartan refreshments make for shorter meetings.

Two women—one young, the other older—representatives of the southern branch of the Society for the Protection of Nature, are shown inside and seated at the big table. The concern of the older woman for the younger suggests that the two have more than just a professional relationship. First they pour themselves coffee, to recover from the long trip, and when they realize there is no hope of better food they begin to devour, politely and methodically, the salted pretzels, and when those are nearly gone, they spread out their colorful plastic map of the Ramon Crater, filled with miniature images of people, camels, foxes, and birds, and dotted with vehicles making their way, each according to its abilities, between places on roads marked in various colors.

Last to enter is the new director general, young and enthusiastic, who hurries to Luria to express the thanks of the agency for all his unpaid help, and not least, believe it or not, for that short, unforgettable speech at the African retirement party. For him, the separation between personal and public that Luria spoke of has become a guiding principle in the Sisyphean war against corruption. In addition to the cutback in refreshments, it was decided also to eliminate the excuses of illnesses and family troubles for absences and lateness, along with school events and grandchildren's birthday parties. The new policy is radical, we accept in good faith every absence and lateness, with no need to justify them, but they are recorded in employees' files to facilitate future promotions and firings. And woe betide the secretary who puts flowers or cake on his desk for his birthday. Politely but firmly he turns down invitations to bar mitzvahs, weddings, and circumcisions, and sends others to funerals, to eulogize and console. He is willing only to attend funerals of pensioners like Luria, and only as a silent participant. Israel Roads is a governmental body and not a kibbutz or religious community, and not a theatrical troupe or army reserve unit, which cannot get free of memories from their past. A governmental body does not belong to its employees but to the State, where the personal can easily slide into ethical pollution. And here we are, continues the director general, an institution spending millions, if not billions, dealing with contractors and suppliers for whom bribery is fuel for the soul. And you, Zvi Luria, who taught me total indifference to the personal, even my wife blesses you. Because I totally avoid the personal parties of employees, she is free from being dragged to all sorts of dubious events and can instead read thrillers translated into Hebrew.

And as Luria marvels at the unexpected compliment, the director general introduces himself to participants who are not his employees, and calls upon Maimoni to turn down the lights to screen his material in semi-darkness. A spectacular aerial photograph opens the PowerPoint presentation, and the young woman from the Nature Protection Society stands up in her torn jeans and hiking boots and halts the proceedings. In a clear voice, tense with anger, she addresses the army people, wondering what on earth they were thinking when they commissioned a road in a first-rate nature reserve, a sacred space for hikers and tourists, with not a word to the Society for the Protection of Nature. You in the army are accustomed to thinking that the State is your toy. We were going to ask that you explain who benefits from this sneaky bastard of a road, but since we are not naïve, and know that you can always wave the flag of national security and secrecy, we can keep this short. We came prepared to request only one change, not dramatic but essential, which we will not forgo. And the young woman grabs the ruler from Maimoni's hand and approaches the crater projected on the screen. This—she taps the westernmost corner of the crater—is the Israel Cistern, a favorite spot for hikers, even if there's no water in it, only the promise of water. And it's *davka* here, according to the plan you sent us, that you want to hide your installations, or whatever they may be, so please, turn your annoying road to the southwest, toward the so-called Geological Path—and again she pokes the screen—and then you can hide your thing, whatever it is, in the Nabatean granary, adjacent to the western edge of the cliff. It's a pagan storehouse with no connection to our history, and any military or civilian nonsense can go inside it.

She hands the ruler to Maimoni and returns to her seat, her colleague watching her with admiration.

"And the tunnel?" The voice of the accountant is heard in the dark. "What does the Nature Protection Society think about the tunnel?"

"The tunnel actually appeals to us, and we could certainly put it to good use."

"For example?"

"For example, a sheltered space for the care of wounded animals. Something dreadful is happening lately in the crater, we're finding animals with bullet wounds. Someone is going around with a rifle, shooting wolves, foxes, rabbits, gazelles. This tunnel could be used as a makeshift emergency room, for first aid."

And now the chief accountant wants to know what the army thinks about the tunnel.

"We didn't request it," the officer replies, "and therefore we didn't think about it, we were surprised to find it in the plan you sent us. It is likely to raise the cost of the project. But on the assumption that your planners had a good reason for this tunnel, the army will try to support it."

"For example?"

"If necessary, it would be possible to set up a roadblock at the entrance and oversee who goes in and out, or conceal the entrance and that way hide the road, which in principle is supposed to be secret."

"You are planning a war for us, aren't you?"

"Otherwise, why would we exist?" The officer smiles.

The door opens slowly and a white skull glows in the dark. "Yes, it's here," a voice whispers. And after the man, slipping in like a colorful ghost, head bowed, hair cropped, is gentle Ayala, who of all the empty chairs chooses the one beside Luria.

Maimoni is startled at the sight of his former army commander, who stands erect and self-assured, introducing himself as a volunteer member of the Archaeological Foundation of the Northern Negev. He cites his highest military rank, does not omit to mention his former position in the Civil Administration, and joins the conference table without asking permission or apologizing for his presence.

"What happened to your hair?" Luria whispers to the young woman without identity. "It's a pity, no?"

"It is a pity," she confirms sadly, "but the Seminar gave me the role of an Arab boy, and I wanted it to be easy for both me and the audience to love him."

Despite the darkness, he has no doubt that she has grown more beautiful since he saw her letting down her hair in Maimoni's jeep. The affection and caring, also maybe lust, bestowed on her by two Israeli adults magnify her grace, and Luria is fascinated by her little feet, crisscrossed with leather straps. Can this be a place, the pensioner wonders, where the medical lust prescribed by the neurologist also happens?

"How is your father?" he whispers. "How is Rahman?" "Yeruham," she corrects him, smiling. "Abba has given up. Again he wants to turn himself in. He is sure there's no chance they'll approve the tunnel." "They will, they'll approve it," the senior engineer whispers emotionally, placing an avuncular hand on her shoulder.

Their whispering attracts glances from around the room, where attention is paid to Maimoni, who screens every detail of his road, slide after slide. The director general loses patience, stops the PowerPoint to bid goodbye to all, transferring authority to his chief accountant, who rolls toward the screen to improve his view.

The representatives of the army and the Nature Protection Society are following Maimoni's explanations with an eye to details of their own maps of the Ramon Crater, but Shibbolet has no need of a map. Makhtesh Ramon is embedded deep in his brain, he need only close his eyes and tilt back his head to follow the presentation. Luria is dazzled by Maimoni, so well prepared, armed with a wealth of photos, diagrams, and simulations, till it seems that the tunnel exists in reality.

Finally, the detailed breakdown of costs, and then the show is over, the window blinds are raised, and a friendly sun smiles through the clouds. Is the Palestinian Ayala only devoted to acting at the Kibbutz Seminar, or is she still faithful to her beloved photography? If she is, maybe she can double the sun here in Tel Aviv, not only in the desert.

The time has come to summarize, and Yoel Drucker, with the authority vested in him, rolls back to the head of the table. In general, the plan looks good and accurate to him, and also, as far as possible, does not harm nature too much. The road cannot be a total secret, but to conceal its true purpose in the Nabatean granary, and not the Israel Cistern, as the Nature Protection Society demands, would not require complicated changes. Therefore, approval is granted in principle, with one condition: no tunnel. It should be removed from the plan. It serves no purpose, it raises the cost, and will entail the added expense of continual maintenance. So we should bring the contractor from Kafr Yasif down to the crater, the guy who in Bab el-Wad pulverized entire hills considered eternal in the annals of Zionism. He'll know how to knock down a pesky little hill.

The army people are folding their maps. The women from the Nature Protection Society look toward the door, as if hoping for more pretzels. Drucker is about to fill out the authorization form. But the white-haired former officer raises his hand with the serious look of a well-behaved student, asking permission to speak.

"Why can't your father find a different place to hide?" Luria whispers to the Palestinian woman, who is bent over in despair.

"He just can't," she insists, miserable but determined, "this is the only place for him, and from there it's easy to phone his cousin in Jordan. For this reason he will give back the money and turn himself in, and then they'll kick me out of Israel too, over the Green Line."

THE NABATEANS

An hour ago, when Luria, aglow over an unexpected compliment, hugged the head of the chief accountant, disabled in a distant war, he knew that a man with serious engineering experience and financial know-how would not be quick to approve a tunnel that lacks a natural rationale. Thus he is not surprised that Shibbolet decided not to depend on Maimoni and his unpaid assistant, but showed up at the committee meeting as an uninvited guest, in an attempt to save the idea of the tunnel. To avoid provoking opposition, Shibbolet is on his best behavior. He waits patiently until the accountant, in the midst of signing documents, looks up with wonder at the white-haired former high-ranking officer raising his hand like a schoolboy and waiting for permission to speak.

And when it is granted with a smile, Shibbolet warns, in an even tone of voice, against hiring the contractor who widened Bab el-Wad before giving some thought to what it means to destroy a hill crowned by a Nabatean structure from the third century BCE. True, it's not a unique or distinctive relic of the great Nabatean civilization, but it is still a valuable part of the historic heritage left us by a wise and ancient people, who in the spirit of Ben-Gurion didn't just talk about Negev settlement but did it, and knew how to live their lives in this wilderness, how to discover its treasures of water, and store it in cisterns on the caravan routes of brisk international trade.

"Interesting," mumbles Drucker, trying to dampen the enthusiasm of the former army commander. "Of course these Nabateans deserve our respect, but let's not forget, bottom line, they were idol worshipers."

"First of all, what's wrong with idol worshipers?" replies Shibbolet with mild sarcasm. "Most Israelis today are idol worshipers, if not in their faith, in their behavior. All we need to do is stroll through the big shopping malls, the banks and the restaurants, to find proof of their devotion to the idols of materialism."

"But nonetheless," the army representative interjects, "none of us still prays or bows down to statues or masks."

"Not yet, that's true. But you may be surprised to learn that the Nabateans in the Negev also had a prohibition against rituals of idolatry, and sufficed with plain stone monuments, with no images of angels or people. And monuments and graves, if we're being honest, are a big hit now in Jewish culture too."

Shibbolet bursts into wild, twisted laughter. Maimoni stops packing up his gear and gingerly approaches the officer possessed by the spirit of prophecy. Hanadi turns red and trembles, but Luria is quite sure she's heard this speech before.

"Forgive me," says Drucker respectfully, "could you please repeat your name?"

"Shibbolet."

"Shibbolet what?"

"Shibbolet, just Shibbolet. A united name, personal and family."

"And you've really come on behalf of the Archaeological Foundation of the Northern Negev?"

"Yes. It broke off from the Society for the Protection of Nature, because protecting nature is different from protecting history and archaeology."

"Obviously. And how many members are there in this foundation?"

"Not many. I didn't count."

"In Mitzpe Ramon, say."

"Only two for now, my wife and I."

"And you fight for the memory of an ancient civilization of idols—excuse me, of monuments?"

"Not just idols, in the fifth century the Nabateans converted to Christianity, and when Islam arrived they became Muslims, and if the Jews had not abandoned the land, they would surely have embraced Judaism, because the Nabateans, deep down, are worshipers of the sun."

"The sun?"

"Yes."

"Only the sun?"

"Isn't that enough? The sun transcends religion, the sun is a precondition for religion. You'd be surprised," Shibbolet says, carried away, "surprised to know that the Nabateans in the desert had myriad connections with the Hasmonean kingdom in Jerusalem. And the admirable King Herod, who ruled our nation for almost forty years, and was like the Office for Public Works and Israeli Roads rolled into one, who built fortresses and towers, and paved roads, and dug tunnels, the greatest builder in the history of our people, and most famously, rebuilt the Temple and the whole Temple Mount—this creative and cunning ruler, a fixture in imperial Rome, like our Bibi in the White House, was Nabatean on his mother's side, his mother, Cypros, was a Nabatean princess, and his being Nabatean did not bother the priests who worked for him in the newly restored Temple. Imagine, for example, if we were to discover that flowing in the veins of our prime minister, from either his mother's or his father's side, is Nabatean blood, how would we react? Laugh or cry? Almost certainly this would not disturb us, and we would go about our business without being upset."

The man in the wheelchair, still smiling faintly, is losing patience. "In any event, Mr. Shibbolet, what more can we do in behalf of your Nabateans?" "It's simple," roars the officer, "do not destroy a historic hill in favor of a military road. For you will damage not only the past of the Negev, but also its future. Permit the engineers who planned a tunnel to make it a reality. And if it slightly inflates the budget, at least history will remember you."

Shibbolet sips water as he finishes his sermon, and afternoon sunlight suddenly floods the conference room, and Luria believes that the delicate resident without identity, who now shields her beautiful face with her hand, is the true source of the Nabatean spark that burst here into flame. Is the former West Bank officer fighting for the sake of the father, who could incriminate him, or for the daughter, an occasional guest at his apartment in Mitzpe Ramon when his wife's asthma lets up?

The accountant's wheelchair moves with a quiet sigh. Drucker admits that one can respect a person fighting for the memory of a vanished people and can even identify with his arguments, but unfortunately, at the conclusion of every project of Israel Roads, there arrives an official of the government Comptroller's Office, whose sole desire is to discover needless waste. With all my good will, he concludes, the national budget is not my personal budget.

And here Luria's head spins with a faint memory, and he stands up, to his own surprise, and calls out from his corner: "Wait, Drucker, wait, Yoel, the road to Ein Ziv is coming back to me now, and how and why we ran into trouble there."

AWAD AWAD

The engine of dementia bores into the gray matter, and with mounting lucidity a road emerges from its interstices, a road in the green hills of Galilee, a steep, rocky road from Tarshiha to Ein Ziv. A bumpy dirt road from the days of the British Mandate, which after the State was founded was slightly upgraded as a narrow strip of asphalt. But in the 1980s, following several terrible accidents, there was a need to widen the road, enough to give it shoulders that would slow down, or warn off, wheels drawn to the abyss. Among those who worked on the project was a young engineer who lost a leg in the Lebanon War and was equipped with a wondrous new prosthesis, courtesy of the State that had sent him into needless battle, so he could gallivant over roads and fields with his measuring devices. Yes, yes, says Luria, approaching the conference table, it's not just you, Drucker, rolling into memory, coming into focus, there are others with you, surveyors, drivers, laborers, all still nameless but very human, and among them, here he comes, a big earthworks contractor from Sakhnin, who warned us all, over and over, that if we try to widen this steep and narrow road, it will one day crumble and collapse, and take with it the hill, which will spill over and swallow it. A different, simpler idea is preferable, namely, to stick this problematic road into a tunnel.

But the proposed tunnel, Luria continues bitterly, provoked opposition on your part, Drucker, and on the part of others. Too expensive, too complicated, and most of all, unnecessary, why would a road or a hill collapse? And then, when work began, the road collapsed under the bulldozer, which plunged headlong into the abyss, pulling after it a chunk of the hill. We had to bring a special crane from far away to rescue the bulldozer, and plan a new, roundabout route for the road we lost. You surely remember, Drucker, you were there, running around, showing your prosthesis no mercy, and now I remember the name of the contractor, Awad Awad, Awad Awad, those big trucks and cement mixers with his name on them are still barreling around everyplace, even if he himself is gone, because successful Arab families never disappear.

And the thought that the enchanting Palestinian girl who sat down beside him is praying for his success empowers Luria, who in a strong, unexpected move pulls the wheelchair toward him and shakes it a bit, as if to awaken the memory of the man who sits on it. Can the head accountant relate to the unreliable memory of a pensioner, very senior and much loved, but whose driver's license has been revoked? Is this a true memory, or just a fabricated delusion about a road that collapsed and a bulldozer that crashed and a contractor who warned in advance to dig a tunnel. And though it is only a delusion, a small truth flutters inside it, an absolute truth in the form of a new, wondrously flexible prosthesis, which Luria can remember with compassion, a prosthesis that served its owner for many years, until the stump could bear it no longer and it was traded in for a wheelchair.

"A hill fell down?" ventures Drucker, shocked but sympathetic. "What hill?"

"You don't remember?"

"No, Luria, I really don't."

"And the tunnel, at least you remember that?"

Drucker turns his eyes to Maimoni as if hoping the latter will rescue him from prosecution by his unpaid assistant, but Maimoni is silent, and Shibbolet is silent, and the representatives who have folded their documents are frozen in place.

"But Zvi," says Drucker with an awkward smile, "you're asking me to remember a tunnel that was never built, or even planned, and it was so many years ago."

"Of course you won't remember a tunnel that was rejected," Luria scolds him, "and why remember if today you're rejecting it again—I mean, not actually that one, but the idea of one."

At this point the disabled veteran of a misguided war is overwhelmed with sorrow, and the pain of that lost war is not forgotten even in a comfortable new wheelchair. And he takes in his hands the rejected plan, which lies orphaned beside the plan that was approved, and turns gently to the man who had been both his boss and his mentor, who stands before him pale and tormented, and asks: "So what's the length?"

"As written. A modest, homey tunnel, only one hundred eighty-five meters."

"And the width?"

"As you can see, we kept it to a minimum. Only six meters, one lane in each direction, we saved on digging expenses, there'll be little traffic, and entry and exit can be controlled, or blocked off."

"And the height?"

"Only four meters thirty."

"That's enough?"

"It's not a tunnel for heavy vehicles."

"But still, how will they bring the installations?"

"No problem. These are state-of-the-art installations—in other words, miniaturized and transported in pieces."

"But even a homey tunnel, as you describe it, Zvi, needs light and ventilation. Where will you run the electrical cable?"

"Why cable, Yoel? We just heard a historical sermon about a

people whose god was the sun. All we have to do is put up a big solar collector and it will provide everything we need, and for free."

And the clear, decisive response delights the chief accountant, who is persuaded that despite the revoked driver's license, Luria's professional insight is strong as ever, drawing its power from pure reason, and he looks at the people around him to confirm from their silence that their positions are unchanged, so that he can reject his rejection and include the tunnel in the overall plan just approved.

THE DOCTOR WRITES HER DISEASE

Luria expects some sign of appreciation from the Palestinian girl who saw herself being thrown over the Green Line, but she has vanished. It was for her, not for the widower mourning his wife, that he dug a private, delusional tunnel into his atrophy. The meeting is disintegrating. The two lovers from the Nature Protection Society are still angry at the army, and cheerfully threaten to sue the Defense Ministry, whose representative calmly smiles. Maimoni, who has returned his plans and documents to their hefty binder, quietly helps the chief accountant roll his way out, waving goodbye from his wheelchair. Then the army officer and Shibbolet begin sniffing each other like two hunting dogs, but since they find no battlefields in common or commanders to praise or dislike, they separate, and Shibbolet goes to the window to look at the sun. From behind, his white hair looks tangled and wild, as if he had taken vows of abstinence. Luria joins him to marvel at the sun burning in the heart of the sky. He needs to check out Nabatean sun rituals on the internet. He mumbles: "So we forced his hand in the end." "You did," says Shibbolet, "Maimoni already gave up, and my Nabateans didn't convince him, until you stunned him with the story about his prosthesis, but where did that come from? From memory or imagination? Was there really a steep road in Galilee that crumbled in the 1980s? Is there even a town called Ein Ziv?" "Why wouldn't there be?" The pensioner defends his story. "And even if a village decides to change its name, the road number stays the same." Shibbolet wants to express his doubts, but keeps quiet. "For now, at least," Luria goes on, "that Rahman of yours, that Yasour, will stop threatening to turn himself in." Shibbolet seems troubled by the pensioner who knows too much, and quickly demurs: "I'm not sure the threats will stop, a husband's need to punish himself for his wife's death is not something that disappears." But the money he is planning to return to the would-be buyers is running out. Maimoni squanders too much on the Druze soldier and the actress. "But she suddenly disappeared, where is she?" asks Luria, voice trembling. "She hurried to the Seminar, she always has some rehearsal. I was against bringing her here, she would most likely arouse suspicion, but she insisted on seeing you." "Me?" Luria is shocked. "Why me?" "Because she believed that you, more than the two of us, would get the tunnel approved. She wanted to encourage you, she thinks that your dementia is good dementia."

"Good?" Luria laughs and his face reddens. "What is good dementia? It doesn't stand to reason."

"Ask *her,*" says Shibbolet, ending the conversation. "That's what she thought."

The conference room has emptied. Everything left on the table that could be used at the next meeting has been collected in a large plastic bag. Only now does Luria remember he is without a car and has no idea how to find a bus to take him close to home.

"Where are you off to from here? Back to Mitzpe Ramon?"

"Where do you need to go?"

"Home. Here in Tel Aviv."

"So I'll drive you, you deserve it. What happened to your car?"

"Nothing happened to it, but it happened to me. I told a police officer about my dementia, and he immediately took away my driver's license, unaware that this is good dementia."

"Where do you live?"

But Luria is afraid of again getting his home address wrong. It's fine to drop him off at Rabin's grave.

"You mean the memorial monument?"

"Of course, only for the memory."

And it's good that he got out at Rabin Square, because again he gets lost on his way home, but at least without disgracing himself in front of others. He realizes he has gone the wrong way when he sees the sea before him, and since he assumes no one knows where Emden Street is, he takes Basel Street, and will find his way from there.

At home he is surprised to see that his wife has returned early. She sits at the living room table chewing on a pencil, a new notebook open before her. As he gently nudges her head forward to cover her neck with kisses, she takes an interest in the fate of the tunnel.

"They approved it. Perhaps thanks to me, because the meeting was run by a man named Drucker, who lost a leg in the first Lebanon War and worked for me in the past, and is now the chief accountant."

His wife remembers the engineer who had impressed Luria with his ability to get around in the field with his prosthesis.

"Today he's in a wheelchair, but his spirit is still strong."

"So what now? Where will we find you a new tunnel?"

"Only here, at home, under the floor. I got lost again on my way home. But you, why'd you come back in the middle of the day? I hope it's not your bacteria again. What's its name?"

"Meningococcus."

"What?"

"Meningococcus."

"The predator."

"Not a predator, just virulent."

"And maybe left a few of its babies in your bloodstream."

"Don't worry," she laughs, "its babies are all gone."

"In any case, why are you home early?"

"Because I realized that you're right. To give the corrupt State a gift of my vacation days, plus the research money I didn't use, is not generosity but supercilious stupidity. Therefore today I handed over the management of the clinic to Boaz, and during my remaining time there I'll work as an ordinary soldier. And meanwhile, in keeping with that woman's idea, what's her name?"

"Ayala . . ."

"Ayala, right, I'll try to tease some sliver of research out of my illness, and you, who were my hero in all this, will now also be a hero in writing."

"But why in the notebook and not the computer?"

"Because this is a first draft, and I want the ideas to flow freely, the left pages facing the right ones, since it's not yet clear to me how I get from describing the illness to unraveling its complexity. I have to feel my way carefully, with many question marks, and I can do this only by hand and not on the computer, which makes the written word clear and definitive. When the draft is done, I'll read it aloud and you'll type it, and that way you'll have work to do until we find you a new tunnel."

"Don't try to dictate medical terms and test results, because I'll make mistakes you won't notice later. And in general you overestimate my remaining intelligence. In today's meeting I apparently hallucinated a Galilee road that collapsed, and a tunnel that never existed, and Drucker, maybe out of pity for me, approved the tunnel for Maimoni. Dina, be careful, don't depend on me for anything. I am sinking, I am confused, I don't know what day it is."

The smile that had brightened her face is fading, and her eyelids flutter with compassion for a dear man whose despair is not unfounded. So she gets up and grabs his hips and takes his face in her hands for a long, deep lovers' kiss. And while he wavers between evasion and surrender, she pulls his shirt from his pants, strokes and kisses his chest and arms, and whispers, Does it matter what day it is, if there is love every day? And although it isn't clear if her passion is real or just supportive, he is obliged, as she lies before him, to forgo his depression and get down on his knees to pleasure the one person who can slow his decline.

In the evening they go to the Tel Aviv Museum for a concert of chamber music, arriving early because they also want to see two new exhibitions. And because their midday lovemaking had gone so well, they are still tightly holding hands. The two exhibitions are on the same floor. The first is of a thirty-year-old Israeli painter living in Amsterdam, the other of an older Finnish artist. What the two shows have in common is that the works constitute a series. The Israeli's series is called *Beginning of an Earthquake,* and the Finn's series is *Resurrection of the Dead.* The Israeli's canvases are of medium size, ten paintings of Israeli families from various tribes and social classes eating dinner at home, at the start of an earthquake. The colors of the Finnish artist, who at age seventy is back in vogue, are softer and more muted than the Israeli's, the canvases are smaller, with white spaces of snow or ice that seem infinite. The human figures are tiny, blurry, but numerous and presumably dead, seeking to return to life in order to depart from it again.

"But how can you tell that these are zombies and not just people?" wonders Luria.

"Because they have no eyes," explains his wife. "Look closely, they're blind."

But they lack the time to dig deeply into the mass resurrection of the dead in the far north, because they are rushing to a concert that has two parts. The first turns out to be pure punishment, a very contemporary musical creation, and long, unlike contemporary works that typically quit while they're ahead. But the second half is ample compensation, namely, Brahms's Piano Quintet, which Luria could once hum by heart. Despite the marvelous music, he peeks from time to time at his two mobiles, to see if Maimoni has tried to reach him by phone or text. But there's no trace of Maimoni, as he too has vanished into thin air with his Ayala. "Why don't you call him," says his wife after the concert, aware of his disappointment. "Because," replies Luria, "a woman once warned me to remember that my dignity was hers too, so I've learned to wait patiently."

When they get home, Dina returns immediately to her notebook. It turns out that listening to that first insufferable piece had sparked an inspiration: her research project will seek to clarify why the first antibiotic not only failed to kill the germs, but encouraged them to make matters worse. That will be the question in search of an answer.

The next day, Luria goes back to the Tel Aviv Museum to check if the Finn's resurrected dead are really blind. And indeed, the eyes of the tiny figures are missing, or shut, and perhaps these are members of a different, northern race, whose gaze is directed inward. And since it's too early to go home, Luria decides also to visit the Land of Israel Museum, and the map in his cell phone suggests he go on foot, an hour's walk along the Yarkon riverbank, through the western part of Ganei Yehoshua Park.

And he obeys the phone, because the second phone concurs, and he walks through Hamedina Square to the bank of the river, which is no more than a stream so feeble that there's no telling which way it flows. Here and there, on a bench or in a wheelchair, sit men or women near whom, at a watchful distance, perhaps taking pity, sit foreign caregivers, darker-skinned, male or female, sometimes the same sex as the supervised person, sometimes the opposite—there seems to be no consensus in the kingdom of dementia—and the look of the two is similar, quiet, reflective, rather curious, without pain but also without hope.

And then Luria says to himself, Maybe something happened to Maimoni, maybe the tunnel was ultimately canceled by a higher authority. Here, amid grass and trees, alongside the joy of joggers, the whir of bicycles, the laughter of children playing, his wife's dignity and his own seem less important, so he phones Maimoni, who immediately confesses, Dear Luria, it's my fault, forgive me. By the time I delivered the signed documents to the operations department, it was evening and I didn't want to bother you, you seemed tense and frightened enough in the meeting.

"Frightened? Why?"

"It doesn't matter."

"But this Hanadi who sat next to me also disappeared, and even Shibbolet didn't know where to. Did you take her?"

"No, she disappeared on me too, apparently returned to her rehearsals, but problems are arising there as well, because without an actual Israeli ID she has no chance of acting in a play on the stage."

"What's the connection?"

"The connection is the insurance required by law to cover any accidents during stage performances. By the way, this applies to you too, we were remiss regarding insurance."

"Applies to me? How? I'm a pensioner working on a voluntary basis."

"Voluntary for you, but not for Drucker, who already bawled me out for employing you without insurance, even though you're not paid, and if you fell and got hurt, or worse, went missing in the Ramon Crater, the State would ignore you, but sue us."

"Ignore me? Why? I'm a card-carrying citizen, covered in every conceivable way."

"You are you, but *we* would get sued for employing you without accident insurance, even if we didn't pay you a salary."

"So why not get me insurance?"

"What for?"

"For next time."

"And who will pay for that?"

"I will."

"Your pension from Israel Roads covers your life insurance premiums, but how will you transfer money to Israel Roads for accident insurance for a person not listed as a worker?"

"I'll find a way."

"There is no way. So far as I know, no one will accept that payment. I'm telling you, Drucker warned me, even though he loves you. He didn't remember the road that crumbled in the Galilee or the tunnel that wasn't dug, but he remembered your human kindness to him from thirty years ago, even though you tried to hide it."

Luria says nothing.

"Zvi, are you with me?"

"Yes, when do they start work on our road?"

"Soon, the army is impatient."

"Incidentally, regarding Hanadi, if it doesn't work out at the Seminar, I could hire her as a companion, sort of a foreign worker."

"To do what?"

"You know, when it gets worse. Because it will soon get worse. I can feel it."

"What will get worse?"

"The confusion, the forgetting, which I gather she heard about from you. But she told Shibbolet that my dementia was the good dementia, not the bad."

NEVO

The inspiration sparked during the first half of the museum concert, regarding the strange relationship between the first antibiotic and the virulent bacteria, has blossomed into a fertile research idea that can rescue Dina's funding from the avaricious State. So besides reading articles on Google Scholar, Dina sits in the hospital library and looks at studies that support her hypothesis or challenge it. Meanwhile, the cynical bureaucrat in the personnel department, who on principle disparages research he is asked to fund, tells the pediatrician about a conference in Munich in early summer, at a German institute specializing in bacteria and viruses. Dr. Luria's lecture is written, translated into English and edited, its abstract sent to the conference organizers and approved, and her talk is assigned a time slot in the schedule. The conference coordinator gets in touch with Dina to confirm her acceptance, and also to add a personal word of warning. The organizers expect the participants to be present for the whole three days and not just on the day of their own lecture. Apparently the Germans have had unpleasant experiences with Israeli researchers, who after their lecture go shopping or tour the area.

The question now arises whether Luria ought to make the trip. He won't be able to wander around Munich by himself and will be imprisoned in the hall, listening to lectures in German or English that would bore him even if they were in Hebrew. They decide that the doctor will travel alone and limit her trip to only four days, and with the money left over they will vacation together in Tuscany or the Swiss Alps. This is the logical solution. But Dina imposes a condition that must be met, otherwise she will cancel her trip: on the nights she is not in Israel, Luria must stay with one of their two children. Obviously it would be best to send him north to Yoav, who has a lovely guest suite in his big house, but unfortunately the house is surrounded by fields, and since Yoav and his wife are at work most of the day, and the grandchildren have their after-school activities, Luria would likely be tempted to go walking in the fields, where there's no Rabin Square to anchor his whereabouts. There is thus no alternative but to send him to his daughter Avigail, who lives nearby. And since her apartment is quite small, with no guest room, Grandpa will have to spend the night in the child's room, next to his soundly sleeping grandson, or sleep in the office of his son-in-law, a young psychiatrist who generally prescribes drugs for his patients and only rarely has them lie on the couch.

It's impossible to ignore a simple condition imposed by a wife who wants peace of mind when she is far from her husband. But despite his promise to honor her request, the doctor flies off with a quivering heart, slightly reassured by the presence of two cell phones.

As nine weeks have passed since the committee meeting, it's fair to ask Maimoni whether construction of the army road has begun. Maimoni, who has moved on to a new project, promises to find out, and an hour later reports to Luria that a mole bulldozer has gone down into the crater to start boring through the hill. As the work progresses, he will take his former unpaid assistant, even without accident insurance, to see it.

As promised to her mother, Avigail arrives at five in the afternoon to take her father to her apartment. And Luria, who has already showered and shaved, stuffs pajamas, slippers, and a toothbrush into a plastic bag, tucks both phones in his pockets, and leaves home reluctantly to spend the night in the room of a child. On the car phone, a call from overseas, to allay the worry that has migrated to Munich by confirming that the condition was met. Yes, Imma, says Avigail, Abba is here beside me, and seems relaxed and happy.

But Noam's room contains a small surprise. Nevo, the son of a single parent, is here too, not to stay overnight, only until the harpist picks him up after her rehearsal. Nevo turns pale and mute at the sight of the old man who had promised him that his missing father would not only resurface but come and visit. Luria, too, is rattled by the child vegetarian who hysterically flung his shakshuka plate when Noam announced cruelly that he had no father. This is the boy who for his bar mitzvah will be taken to the summit of Mount Nevo, across the Jordan River, to see whether Israel will suit him for the rest of his life, or if he should find someplace more rational. Luria avoids contact with him and goes to the living room to watch the news, and he wonders how three news programs on three channels decide, with no advance coordination, on exactly the same stories in the same order. But furious Nevo abandons his friend and games, enters the living room, and stares at Luria with such sad longing that Luria invites him to cuddle up on his lap.

Even when his mother Noga arrives, Nevo is unwilling to part from Luria, and like that time at lunch, he throws himself down and pummels the floor with fists and feet. His mother knows why he's gone berserk, but doesn't try to calm him, and though she could easily, with her strong harpist's hands, pluck the boy from the floor and carry him to her car, she stands quietly waiting for his pain and disappointment to subside, hoping to make Luria feel guilty for his foolish, gratuitous words. The bearer of false news does indeed feel terrible about the boy who won't say goodbye, waiting for Luria to keep his promise, so to ease Nevo's pain he suggests they take a drive in his mother's car, to make the separation gradual. To his delight, Noga accepts the offer, and Luria buckles himself into the back seat to keep Nevo company, and takes his little hand in his, and says to the driver, her face reflected in the mirror: Yes, I know I caused this pain, but I wanted to give him hope. It's theoretically possible some father will turn up, maybe not biological, but at least fatherly, why not? But who would believe he'd remember my little promise? But he remembered.

Did Avigail drop a hint to her friend about her father's dementia to justify his blunder, or has Noga, who seems strong and intelligent, figured out the confusion on her own? Either way, this woman is kind to him, and he's chattering from the back seat.

"When you told me about Mount Nevo and that you want him to decide on the mountaintop if this land is right for him, I said to myself, All in all it's good that I gave him hope, to ensure the right decision. Because if some father does turn up, he will come here, not Amsterdam or Munich. But even so, I apologize, I didn't know this would be so important to him."

"It's okay," she says finally. "But do you really believe in this country?"

"Do I have a choice?"

"There's always a choice," she states with the confidence of a harpist plucking a single string. "I'll run you back to Avigail now that the boy is resting."

But Luria doesn't want to spend the night in the child's room, or on the therapist's couch in his son-in-law's office. He says to Noga, if you don't mind, let me off near Rabin Square, because I forgot to bring my sleeping pills. I'll call Avigail from home and try to free myself from her worrying mother. In any case, I have two mobile phones, and I'm always available. More than anything, an old man loves his own bed.

But when he gets to Emden Street he doesn't go up to his apartment, but down to the garage, and gazes with desire at the forbidden red car. He finally summons his courage and informs Avigail that he will sleep at home tonight after all. "Your mother went a bit nuts from all that worrying, maybe feeling guilty for going alone to Germany. Listen, I don't want to toss and turn all night in a child's room, surrounded by strange toys that would confuse me even more. I have two mobile phones, and I'm always available. So let me sleep in my bed, I deserve it." He's not surprised that his daughter approves the change, no doubt he is a burden, a needless nuisance.

"It's fine, Abba," she confirms, "sleep tonight in your bed, and if Imma tries to check if you're with me, I'll tell her you're asleep, but only on condition that you put both your phones under the pillow, for whatever might happen."

"They'll be under the pillow, but no ring, just vibration."

THE SOLDIER

He trades his shoes for hiking boots, and despite the hot weather, he dons a faded leather jacket that served him well as a road engineer. Equipped with his car keys, he locks the front door securely and returns to Ibn Gabirol Street. At a bus stop, he sees a soldier with full gear and a rifle, a big overstuffed duffel bag at his feet. May I ask you a question, he says, are you perhaps going to the central bus station? I am, replies the soldier. And from there you're going south or north? North, says the soldier. North is fine, says Luria, but meanwhile I have to drive to the central bus station to pick up a foreigner from far away, and I lost my driving glasses, which are required on my license, and without them, especially when it's getting dark, I could get lost, and I'm afraid a policeman will catch me. So perhaps you could drive me to the bus station in my car, on condition, of course, that you have a driver's license. Of course I do, confirms the soldier, and Luria continues, The car is insured and the registration is valid, just as I said—

"Where is it?"

"Very near here. A hundred meters at most. It has automatic transmission and is in excellent condition, you'll enjoy driving it."

The soldier hesitates a moment, glances at his watch, and finally smiles and decides to accept the strange invitation. Luria takes him to his house and down to the garage, and the gun, gear, and duffel are tossed in the back seat, and the two get in the car. Before Luria hands the soldier the keys, he asks to see his driver's license, to be sure it is genuine and unexpired. Then he takes a quick glance at his arm and dictates the ignition code, digit by digit, and the car shoots from the lot into the street.

"You know how to get to the central bus station, or should I turn on the GPS?"

"I know the way."

They speak in sentence fragments about the tension in the North, the soldier predicting the worst, but Luria dismisses his forecast. No one will gain from a new war, remember how the last ones ended. In the central bus station the soldier looks for the elevator that goes from the parking garage straight to the bus platforms on the sixth floor, and at first can't find it, and drives round and round in the gloomy, desolate garage until he does, but Luria doesn't complain, just jots down the floor number and zone in his little pad.

On the sixth floor, on the way to the buses, Luria gratefully bids farewell to the soldier in full gear, duffel on his shoulders, automatic rifle in hand, ready for battle. But the soldier needs no thanks. "I thank you, sir," he firmly declares, and goes on his way.

THE COUPLE FROM ASHKELON

Before Luria reaches the buses, one of the phones rings and Yoav asks how he's doing. I went home, the father cheerfully announces, and I'm already in my pajamas and going to bed. Avigail and I agreed that Imma's anxiety is over the top, maybe out of guilt that she traveled without me, but why because of someone else's guilt should I have to sleep for four nights with toys and games all around me to intensify my delusions? Therefore you also should not say a word, and please don't call the landline and wake me up, in case of emergency you can call the cell phones, which will be set on vibrate under my pillow, only vibrate, so the ring won't interrupt a dream that I'm trying to understand.

At this twilight hour the bus station looks even more chaotic. Some of the shops have closed, but kiosks have opened for the evening, and the population has changed ages and colors, with more young people, more soldiers, more Africans, and more police. The platform for Beersheba is empty, and someone explains that the bus left a few minutes ago, and the next one is an hour and a half from now. He must therefore find a different bus to take him to the South. He thinks first of Arad, as a stopover en route to the desert, but according to the road map in his brain, that could be a dead end, so he prefers to head south through Ashkelon, and maybe in his own car after all. He sees a few people waiting for the Ashkelon bus. It's a long trip, and he can't risk a solitary driver who might throw him out in the middle of the journey and make off with the car. He turns to a couple, a man and woman of about sixty, who seem reasonable and just right. The man is stocky and serious, the wife delicate and wrinkled. He retells the story of the lost driving glasses, and sings the praises of the car, reliably Japanese with automatic transmission, smooth and pleasant to drive.

In principle, the man would be glad to help, but alas, his driver's license was revoked four months ago and has not been reinstated. Why was it revoked? Luria is curious. It turns out this man ran over a motorcyclist, who absolutely, positively, ran a red light through the intersection, and since the police couldn't harass the dead man, they decided to give some moral compensation to the bereaved relatives by revoking the license of the man who killed him legally.

And your wife? Luria keeps trying. My wife, the man says sadly, has a license but drives only short distances. For your own good, sir, I wouldn't risk riding with her on intercity highways. What exactly is the problem? says Luria, who likes the smile in the woman's eyes. Like many women, the husband explains on good authority, she doesn't stay in her lane, forgets to switch off the turn signal, and is afraid to pass other cars, making the drivers behind her crazy. That's all right, says Luria, maybe with you sitting next to her, she gets nervous, but if I sit beside her, she'll relax. Come with me, I'll take responsibility. You'll save time and money. If you say so, says the husband, who takes the suitcase, and they go down to the garage, and what Luria wrote down earlier turns out to be correct. The red car stands alone in the desolate lot, which resembles a giant atomic bomb shelter preparing for the worst.

But before the woman sits in the driver's seat, the husband wants to see the car's registration and insurance. As he examines the documents, he asks who Dr. Dina Luria is. My wife, explains Luria, director of a pediatric clinic, lecturing now in Munich, at a conference on predatory bacteria. And why are you going to Ashkelon? the husband continues his investigation. I need to go to my sister, I told her to meet me at the bus station.

The husband is finally reassured, and lays his suitcase in the trunk beside the urn of ashes. The woman gets the ignition code from Luria, next to her, while the husband sits in back. The wife, clearly excited by the trust placed in her, quickly starts the car, steers it deftly from the bowels of the garage, and makes her way to Route 20, hopeful that it leads to Route 4.

She is relaxed behind the wheel. Her husband ventures a remark from the back seat, but Luria silences him. Let me supervise her myself, she's doing very well, trust me, I was a highway engineer for many years at Israel Roads, I have hundreds of kilometers in my soul. For the last twenty kilometers before Ashkelon, the husband allows himself a deep sleep, so untroubled is he by his wife's rapport with the road engineer sitting beside her.

In the parking lot of the Ashkelon bus station, the couple's car awaits to take them to their home by the sea. Do you want us to stay here with you till your sister comes? they inquire gratefully. No, there's no need, I trust her, she'll come. Thanks a million to you for your help.

"You're thanking us?" say the two in unison. "We thank *you.*"

THE MEDICAL STUDENT

It's almost nine o'clock. The red Suzuki stands silently in the near-empty parking lot. There are four platforms in the Ashkelon bus station, but only two buses, both empty. He sees people at a food counter, and walks over and gets himself a large coffee. Then he goes to check on the bus to Beersheba, and learns that although Beersheba is only sixty kilometers away, the trip takes an hour and a half, because the bus stops for passengers at every conceivable kibbutz or moshav. In that case, I'm stuck, Luria chastises himself, I lied and got stuck, and I'll have no choice but to defy the law and drive the car back to Tel Aviv myself, hoping I won't get in an accident or pulled over for a traffic violation. Instead of curling up in bed, I have to take the forbidden car to the place where the tunnel will begin, because only that way can I understand what it symbolizes and where it's leading me. My time is running out, and in a few months, when Maimoni remembers to bring me down to the crater, the dementia will no longer understand what I fought for here.

Passengers to Beersheba assemble little by little. A tall young woman with a backpack and a very old man carrying her shoulder bag join the group that has not yet formed a queue. The pair seem promising to Luria, who approaches them with the same story about the eyeglasses, and for good measure citing his profession, retired road engineer. To his surprise, the old man knows something about Luria from his early days at Israel Roads. He himself had been an independent contractor, and here down south had heard the rumor about the bulldozer that flipped over and tumbled to the bottom of the wadi. Luria is excited. Sometimes there are solid facts after all, not just fantasies. In that case, he warmly says, come, sir, and drive me to Beersheba and we'll reminisce some more on the way. But the old man is not going to Beersheba, just his granddaughter, a student in her fifth year at the medical school of Ben-Gurion University, who hopped over to Ashkelon for a few hours to visit her sick grandma and is now returning to Beersheba for her night shift in the emergency room at Soroka Hospital. What kind of doctor do you want to be? Luria asks the medical student, who studies him with a practiced eye. She still has time to decide, but is inclined to join the fight against cancer. But Luria has another suggestion, and if she will drive him to Beersheba, he will try to persuade her en route to pick neurology and not oncology, because the brain, which cannot be transplanted, will forever be more complicated and challenging than all the mysteries of cancer. The brain is devious. When they try to diagnose its weakness and illness, it sometimes masquerades as healthy.

And with mutual trust, with no examination of licenses or insurance, the student's pack goes into the back seat, and the driver's seat is adjusted to accommodate the long legs of the future doctor, and only then does Luria display his forearm tattooed with the ignition code. And without caring why Luria is headed for Beersheba so late at night, she drives eastward to Route 35, to continue past Kiryat Gat to the southern on-ramp of the Trans-Israel Highway.

THE TRACKER

On the drive to Beersheba he felt the persistent vibration of both cell phones, but declined to answer with the car engine roaring. Now the driver grabs her backpack and runs to her shift, leaving him in the dark parking lot of the hospital, which even at this late hour is far from empty. Luria walks away from his car, parked near the main entrance, and stands in a quiet spot beside a big truck, to return the call that earlier vibrated in vain and tell his wife in a soothing voice, Yes, my love, it's me, what happened? You're not asleep yet?

Where are you? She screams when she hears his voice, why didn't you answer? I'm alive and well under the blanket, I figure Avigail broke down and confessed to you that we agreed I would go back and sleep at home, because at my age and in my condition it's hard for me to sleep in a child's room surrounded by strange and frightening toys. So I'm here in our bedroom, lying in bed, and everything is familiar but sad because your side is empty. So why didn't you answer? I called several times. But I told Avigail I was unplugging the landline and putting the cell phones on vibrate, and apparently your vibration disappeared into a deep dream. Why be mad at me, I'm already sad enough without you. I'm at home, nothing's happening here, and now that you have woken me, talk to me. Tell me, how was your first day? How are the lectures? What's the quality overall?

But Dina will not yet oblige him. Just tell me the truth, what part of the house are you talking from? Why? Because your voice seems far away, as if you're outdoors, with winds blowing. Winds? He laughs. What winds? The ghosts that drift between Germany and Israel? Enough, Dina, it's not fair. Since you're the one who traveled and I stayed behind, please, you talk and I'll listen.

She backs off. Yes, there are new things she didn't know about, real developments in the research, there are devices and drugs that she's hearing about only now. In recent years she has neglected to read new medical literature and didn't participate in conferences. She got carried away in the day-to-day administration of the clinic.

"But nevertheless," he says, quick to lift her spirits, "it's you, and not the articles you didn't read, who healed the sick children."

But her honest soul refuses to be encouraged from afar. "No, Zvi, not all the children, you forget there were also children who died in my clinic."

Yes, she knows that some bad mistakes were made in treatments, mistakes that cannot be corrected, and now she's joining him in retirement. But at least without dementia, her husband consoles her.

And then, a few meters away, a spray of sparks, a discarded ember, and an indistinct figure, who apparently heard the conversation, passes him, and heads toward the hospital. To whom might this man report what he overheard? Luria quickly ends the phone call and follows the figure, hoping to speak with him. "Excuse me?" He dares to tap the young man on the shoulder. "Can you spare a cigarette?"

From within his foggy brain, wearied by the arduous journey, he takes a look at a young Bedouin man in an army work shirt with sergeant's stripes, but civilian trousers, torn jeans in the fashion of high school girls.

"A cigarette, why not?" says the young man, removing a long, thick cigarette from his shirt pocket. "But be careful, this is strong tobacco that I rolled myself."

With much trepidation he is willing to try stronger-than-usual tobacco, and though he hasn't indulged in years, he places the cigarette between his lips and bows his head toward a long flame, and is immediately scorched by acrid smoke that dizzies his senses and dims his vision. He ejects the cigarette from his mouth but feels the dementia catching fire within him, igniting a deep cough that doubles him over. He extends a hand to the young man for support, but before the man can respond, the choking knocks Luria to his knees, and in a panic he clings to the jeans and rips them further.

"I knew it," the young man says coolly to the person kneeling before him, choking and coughing, "this is not a cigarette for you."

As the coughing continues unabated, and seems to be getting worse, the young man suggests he go to the emergency room to be given something to calm it. But a person who enters an emergency room in the middle of the night risks being diagnosed with unimaginable illnesses. No, he will overcome the coughing on his own. He has a long way to go tonight, to Mitzpe Ramon, and he needs someone to drive him there, because unfortunately his driving glasses disappeared. And for the fourth time Luria tells a story about glasses, including the epilogue about his identity as a retired road engineer.

"How much will you give the driver?"

"How much will he ask?"

"Round-trip?"

"One way for now, maybe also return."

"A hundred and fifty shekels each way, not just for the distance but for the time."

"Agreed. But do you have a driver's license?"

"How could I not? You don't see I'm a tracker for the army?"

"We still need trackers?" Luria chuckles, his coughing now soft and polite. "I thought that women soldiers sitting in front of screens see better than all your sniffing after fresh footprints on blurry trails."

"We trackers see things those girls will never see, even in a dream. So we agree. You agree that I take you in your car to Mitzpe Ramon."

"Not the town, the Ramon Crater."

"The crater is included in the price, but give me a minute to see if the birth has begun."

"What birth?"

"My sister, I brought her here in an ambulance, but she insists on not giving birth until her husband arrives from the North."

"He will arrive?"

"We'll soon see."

THE TUNNEL

The tracker disappears into the maternity wing, and Luria, free of his cough, readies himself in sheer exhaustion for the rest of the trip. He takes an old blanket from the trunk, and is startled anew by the urn of ashes. He covers himself up in the back seat, curled like a fetus, unsettled by the thought of how far he has traveled tonight from his home and family for the sake of a mysterious tunnel, with only two cell phones to protect him. And though it's not a long way from Beersheba to the crater, the night is growing short, and the return home will be complicated. Maybe a Bedouin tracker is just the right person to whisk him back to Tel Aviv without a scandal. Must remember to fill the tank at the first gas station.

Time goes by before the Bedouin wakes the napper to take his car keys. What's going on? Has she delivered? Yes, the husband came and my sister agreed to pull the trigger. And you? Luria wants to know. What are you? Married or not? A little married, smiles the young man. What is a little for you? A little is only one wife. She's not enough for you? She is enough for me, but not for herself. She wants us to get another wife, so she can pester her. And what is your name? Hamid, like my father. And what is your name? he asks Luria. A jolt of panic. During the drive from Tel Aviv he sensed the darkness thickening around his first name. My name is Luria. He tries avoidance. Call me Mr. Luria, that will be fine. But the Bedouin insists, No, that isn't enough, I told you my first name, why can't you tell me yours, and we'll travel like friends. But Luria rebuffs him: No, call me Mister Luria. That's enough. I'm older than you.

The tracker seems insulted, he wanted closeness and was met with inexplicable anger. He gets behind the wheel and asks for the ignition code. Luria switches on the overhead light so he can read out the numbers from his arm. So, teases the Bedouin, you also have to remember things from your tattoos? Why also? demands Luria. Because in our tribe there are old people who make tattoos of things they don't remember, if you like we can hop over and visit them on the way back. Now Luria is gripped with terror: I took a lunatic as my driver. And in the gargle of the ignition he hears the murmur of the manufacturer's girl. If so, she hasn't given up on me, luckily the tracker can't hear her.

At the first gas station Luria is too tired to get out of the car, and he hands his wallet to the tracker, who asks for his permission to pay with cash and not a credit card, so he can generously tip the pump attendant, who is his cousin. Where are you all from? asks Luria. From Tlalim Junction, answers Hamid, but we sometimes move from there.

Although the back seat in the red car is comfortable, Luria is uneasy lying supine in his own car while someone else drives. He sits up and watches the desert go by. Here are the big prisons, and after the prisons, Giv'at Hablanim, and a few kilometers later, the forest of Ramat Beka. Negev Junction, announces the driver, now what? Continue on Route 40? Of course, barks Luria, I have no other route.

Kibbutz Mashabei Sadeh is drenched in total darkness, except for its brightly lit security fence. What a fine name this kibbutz chose, thinks Luria, maybe I should join a kibbutz before I am completely demented.

From Tlalim Junction they head toward Halukim Junction, and to the left and right isolated farms are perched in the hills. With the road deserted, the car picks up speed. At Halukim Junction they bear to the west and continue to Hadarim. You still awake? Luria asks his driver. Like a demon who fell into a well, grins the tracker, and steps on the gas.

It's three in the morning, and there are no lights in Sde Boker or the Ben-Gurion School. What is this? Nobody here with insomnia, or reading a book or watching a movie?

"Tell me, do you Bedouins ever visit Ben-Gurion's grave?"

"Why do you ask?"

"Because someone told me that Ben-Gurion thought that you, the Bedouins, are actually Jews who forgot they were Jewish."

"And if we forgot, so what? That's a reason to torment us left and right?"

The road races by, the desert expands left and right, bathed in bluish purity. New stars emerge from deep space, the heavens billowing with glory. A wind rises from the Valley of Tzin, swirling above the wilderness, spinning sand into dervishes, dancing toward a vanishing horizon. The primal sadness of ancient people who passed this way, never to return, pierces the heart of the backseat rider, who gropes with secret terror for his first name, which left not a trace of a syllable behind.

"Soon," announces Hamid, "we will arrive at a luxury hotel called Genesis, like the book *Beresheet* you have in the Bible, and in the lobby at night they have a little corner with coffee and tea for anyone in the hotel who can't sleep. Do you think we should wake ourselves up before we go down into the crater?"

"But that coffee's not for us, only for hotel guests."

"Also for us, because I have a cousin who cleans rooms at night for guests who arrive the next day, and she'll take care of us."

A strange thought flashes in the back seat. Maybe Maimoni is sleeping tonight at the Genesis Hotel, to supervise his tunnel, and Luria can gently wheedle his vanished name from him. So he says to the tracker, Okay, let's stop, but keep it short, because you remember we agreed you would also take me back from the crater to the Center.

"Not to worry."

There is nobody at the reception desk of the Genesis, but near the entrance to the dining room there is indeed a table with pitchers of coffee and tea and milk, as well as two elegant plates of different kinds of dates. The tracker pours coffee for himself and milk for his passenger, and selects some dates and puts them in his pockets.

"I don't see any cousin of yours."

"How could you see her if she is cleaning rooms now in the cabins."

"So call her, because I've been here several times but never seen what the rooms look like. What I really want to see is an unmade room."

The tracker takes out his cell phone and sends his cousin a text message, and a while later a smiling Bedouin woman arrives in a chambermaid's uniform. And Hamid says, This is Mr. Luria, who wants to see an unmade room.

"You also call it an unmade room?" Luria is astounded.

"What else should we call it?"

The chambermaid leads them from the lobby to one of the stone cabins, a small pool sparkling near its front door. She opens the door, and Luria enters a messy room, the blankets bunched up, bath towels thrown in a heap, with dirty glasses and desiccated olive pits on the table, and crumpled newspapers in the trash. The perfect unmade room, with no trace of personal items.

"Making up this room is a lot of work," Luria remarks to the chambermaid.

"It's fine," says the Bedouin, "she's used to it."

And again, Independence Road, and Luria recalls every curve that Maimoni rounded in his American car. Now his private Japanese girl will wind her way down, though someone else is the driver making sure she won't tumble into the abyss. He asks the tracker to stop at the top of the cliff so he can move to the front seat. From there it will be easier to locate the hill that yearns for a tunnel. The moon has retired for the night, leaving the darkness behind, but stars still loyal to the crater will assist navigation. Soon, silhouettes of a truck and a spike-fisted boring machine, with a big tent nearby where workers sleep, and perhaps the contractor too, and at its entrance a long-haired dog, indifferently drowsing. This is the place, Luria tells his tracker. When they get out of the car, the dog wakes up and sluggishly approaches them, wagging its tail, then hunches submissively at the feet of Hamid. Why doesn't this dog bark at us? asks Luria. Why should it bark if it smells that I am Muslim, and you, the Jew, are under my protection? Luria says nothing. On the truck, in big letters: SHAFIK SHAFIK, KFAR YASIF. From inside the tent, complete silence, no one rising to greet them. And with nobody to say hello, Luria walks toward the hill. Even from afar he can make out yellow ribbons in the darkness, waving in the wind, marking the mouth of the tunnel. With the keen eye of a veteran road engineer he confirms that the dimensions sketched on paper are becoming a reality.

LAND OF THE HART

But inspecting the mouth of the tunnel is not the true purpose of his burning journey, and they cannot yet return to the Center. It's half past four. In the darkness, gathering now to forestall the impending dawn, will he be able to find the route of Shibbolet's four-wheeler? He climbs a bit and waits for the sun to send a sign that on this morning it has again not forgotten its job. From higher up he sees the tracker tying a rope to the dog that latched onto him, tying the other end to the tunneling machine. The tracker gets into the red car to have a rest. Good thing I picked a tracker for a driver, thinks Luria, because they have infinite patience for time and space. But it's also good that the ignition code stays with me, so the car will still be here when I get back. He climbs a few more meters in the darkness, but his feet stumble on the stones, so he decides to wait for the first rays of sunlight. And since he is certain that his children and even his wife will not dare call him at this hour, he turns off both his phones, for only this way will he be able to prove that going down to the desert was a dream and not reality. He sits down on a rock and half dozes off, and the first glint of eastern light opens his eyes, and as he waits for the flash above Mahmal Valley to become a ray, another spark appears in the distance, above the Valley of Ardon. Will a plumper sun than usual shine upon the crater this morning, wonders Luria, or maybe two separate suns will shine? Emboldened by the thought, he hazards a steep incline that last time seemed cruel for a man his age, but this morning, despite his exhaustion, it seems suited to his dementia. And then, in the growing light of two possible suns, he can see fresh tire tracks, meaning the former officer Shibbolet visited here not long ago.

The ancient, broken stone steps, remembered well from the visit with Maimoni, announce that the Nabatean ruin is not far away, and he is soon walking between the two humps of the summit.

Here is the village schoolteacher, this Rahman, this Yasour, who has still not turned himself in. Shibbolet has dressed him in a blue shirt with the insignia of the Society for the Protection of Nature, in the hope that nature will provide protection for the Palestinian. The teacher seems not at all surprised to see Luria at his ruin at early dawn, perhaps because he assumes Luria has climbed to the summit not for him but for his daughter Hanadi, and points at her without a word. She lies asleep at the foot of the stone table, under a pile of colorful patchwork blankets, and from its shape he not only senses, but knows, as on the night he hospitalized his wife and lay beside the bed of a strange woman, that the sleeping girl is not alone, for she has a fetus in her belly.

Is this the only way for Maimoni, or Shibbolet, to provide her missing Israeli identity?

"Zvi," the teacher speaks the name of the pensioner who climbed this hill many months ago, "aren't you Zvi?"

"Yes, Zvi," Luria accepts the return of his name with excitement and gratitude, and is filled with fear.

"So, here's another Zvi," says the teacher, and seizes Luria by the shoulders and points him to the south, toward an adjacent hill. And standing tall, as if hovering in midair, is a *zvi,* a male deer, which Maimoni, on their last trip to the crater, thought was only Luria's fantasy, but here he is, not an illusion, a large living hart, and it seems that all the light in the world is condensed between his antlers. And the village schoolteacher goes into the ruin and brings out an ancient rifle, a hybrid of uncertain identity and provenance, and aims it at the deer, who is lost in thought, silently spreading his light. And Luria has no time to cry out before the teacher fires one bullet precisely into the brain of the buck, who refuses to accept his death and tries to escape. But the bullet planted between his radiant antlers topples him, and he slowly drags himself toward a crevice, and disappears.

Givatayim, 2015–2018